The Sword Went Out to Sea

UNIVERSITY PRESS OF FLORIDA

Florida A&M University, Tallahassee
Florida Atlantic University, Boca Raton
Florida Gulf Coast University, Ft. Myers
Florida International University, Miami
Florida State University, Tallahassee
New College of Florida, Sarasota
University of Central Florida, Orlando
University of Florida, Gainesville
University of North Florida, Jacksonville
University of South Florida, Tampa
University of West Florida, Pensacola

The Sword Went Out to Sea

❧

(Synthesis of a Dream), by Delia Alton

H.D.

Edited by Cynthia Hogue and Julie Vandivere

UNIVERSITY PRESS OF FLORIDA
Gainesville · Tallahassee · Tampa · Boca Raton
Pensacola · Orlando · Miami · Jacksonville · Ft. Myers · Sarasota

30 29 28 27 26 25   7 6 5 4 3 2

First cloth printing, 2007
First paperback printing, 2009

Library of Congress Cataloging-in-Publication Data
H. D. (Hilda Doolittle), 1886–1961.
The sword went out to sea: synthesis of a dream, by Delia Alton/H.D.; edited by Cynthia Hogue and Julie Vandivere.
p. cm.
Includes index.
ISBN 978-0-8130-3066-1 (cloth)
ISBN 978-0-8130-3454-6 (pbk)
I. Hogue, Cynthia. II. Vandivere, Julie. III. Title.
PS3507.O726S96   2007
813.'529–dc22   2007001328

The University Press of Florida is the scholarly publishing agency for the State University System of Florida, comprising Florida A&M University, Florida Atlantic University, Florida Gulf Coast University, Florida International University, Florida State University, New College of Florida, University of Central Florida, University of Florida, University of North Florida, University of South Florida, and University of West Florida.

University Press of Florida
2046 NE Waldo Road
Suite 2100
Gainesville, FL 32609
http://upress.ufl.edu

To
Gareth

"It's not lost. This will go on somewhere."

Contents

A Note on the Edition

There are three marked typescript "drafts" of *The Sword Went Out to Sea*, held in the H.D. Papers in the Yale Collection of American Literature at the Beinecke Rare Book and Manuscript Library at Yale University. For this first edition of the novel, we have used the typescript marked "third typed draft" (YCAL MSS 24, Box 26, folders 729–734, and Box 27, folders 735–737). These three drafts are quite similar, especially Drafts II and III, and they are not dated *as* revisions. Indeed, all three drafts bear the dates of composition (1946–1947) rather than the dates of revisions (1948–1950). Thus, we have retained those dates in our edition, as H.D. wished *Sword* to bear, as follows:

Book I, Part I: 6 December 1946
Book I, Part II: 6 May 1947
Book II: 17 July 1947

For the purpose of critical placement of *Sword* in H.D.'s oeuvre, we have dated both the composition and revision of the novel by tracking her references to it in correspondence and both published and unpublished memoirs (see nn. 25–43).

Between Drafts II and III, H.D. made only minor editorial changes. Draft I, which does differ in places from Drafts II and III, is unfortunately partial; although "Summerdream" is extant, both sections of "Wintersleep" are missing. How close the partial Draft I is to the very first version of *Sword* (started at Küsnacht)—or whether it is itself the first typed version completed in 1947—is difficult to confirm because of the absence of dates of revisions on the drafts. Between Drafts I and II, words, lines, and in some very few places whole passages have been excised. The novel's vision does not, however, significantly change from one draft to the next. Thus, while H.D. may have edited quite heavily over the years in which she was trying to prepare *Sword* for publication, trying to make its structure and scope clearer, she may not have extensively revised the original version conceptually or perhaps even technically. From the earliest letter to Richard Aldington before she had sent him the novel, she described it as "well written" (see n. 34).

Following the precedent established by Robert Spoo and Jane Augustine in their superb editions of *Asphodel* and *The Gift*, respectively, we have not changed the wording, spelling, or punctuation, including the use of hyphens which appears, at first glance, to be for some words used at times inconsistently: in some parts of the novel H.D. hyphenates a word ("painted-lady," for example) that she does not hyphenate in another section. We agree with the earlier editors that the variations in spelling, hyphenations, and the occasional, idiosyncratic use of the comma have to do with H.D.'s poetics. Thus, deviations have been left as they occur in the typescript and not regularized. Similarly, we have not changed any idiosyncratic spelling, or regularized H.D.'s occasional shifts from British to American spelling. We have as well left alone the odd word that may or may not have been a neologism (thus, for example, the unusual word "triology" has not been changed to "trilogy"). But where there occurred a clear typographical or grammatical error, following not only Spoo and Augustine, but also Cassandra Laity's edition of *Paint It Today*, we have quietly corrected the error. We have also quietly shifted the punctuation from outside to inside the quotation marks, that is, from British to American usage.

Finally, we have tried to provide in our scholarly introduction an extensive, contextualizing discussion necessary to understanding the vision and concept of H.D.'s novel. We have not, however, provided notes in the body of the novel itself, in order to foster the novel being read *as* a novel, as H.D. had hoped it would be.

Acknowledgments

Many thanks to those near and far are in order, which we wish to extend both individually and together.

For two summer Faculty Research Fellowships, spent at the Beinecke Rare Book and Manuscript Library at Yale University, during which time this project was first contemplated, Cynthia Hogue at last has a chance to thank Bucknell University. Its early support of this project was crucial, as was the later support from the Women's Studies Department at Arizona State University (ASU) for a Women's Studies Summer Research Award, which offered a return in 2004 to the Beinecke Library, when the editing of this edition began in earnest. Julie Vandivere would like to thank Bloomsburg University and Chair Ervene Gulley particularly for a Reassigned Time Award and research support. We thank our research assistants: Matt Perakovich at Bucknell; poets Sarah Vap, Elizabyth Hiscox, and Katie Cappello at ASU; and Melanie Dworsak and Elena Brobyn-Navarro at Bloomsburg University.

At the time that we decided to coedit *Sword*, we did not, perhaps, realize that we were beginning together a challenging quest to decode the novel's rich and intricate and (we came to believe) important symbolism. Once neighbors, as well as colleagues and friends when we both lived in Pennsylvania, we have savored our time at the Beinecke. Without the H.D. Fellowship in American Literature from the Beinecke Library, which made it possible for us to work together on the edition for a month in 2005, completing this project would have been far more difficult. During our month, we benefited from the wise guidance of the curator of the American Literature Collection, Patricia Willis, Una Belau (Fellowship Coordinator), Nancy Kuhl (Assistant Curator of the American Literature Collection), Stephen Jones (Assistant Head of Public Services), and extend our deep thanks to all for their help and cordial welcome over the month of our residency.

We have also benefited from the support and guidance of H.D. scholars and critics of modernism around the country, most especially: Jane Augustine, who made herself generously available to us for extensive e-mail consultations over the better part of a year (!), sharing with us her expertise in H.D.'s very specific esotericism, this particular novel and its relationship to H.D.'s canon, and biographical facts culled from years of researching H.D.'s relationship to Lord Dowding; Eileen Gregory and Donna Hollenberg, who supported this project so crucially over the years, and whose readers' reports provided suggestions essential to the quality of this edition; as well as others for general consultation and timely help, especially Susan McCabe, Cristanne Miller, Cassandra Laity, Tamar Katz, Nancy Bentley, Marilyn Mumford, and Adalaide Morris. We were delighted to coincide for a week at the Beinecke with two H.D. scholars, Annette Debo and Lara Vetter, whom we now have a chance to thank for the lively discussions and our ideas about approaching this work, as well as their help in wending our way through some of the correspondence. We thank the H.D. community of scholars and critics for the scholarship and editions on which we have drawn.

We are deeply grateful to our editor, Amy Gorelick, and the University Press of Florida for steadfast interest in and support of this project over the years it took us to bring this project to fruition. And to the project editor, Jacqueline Kinghorn Brown, we offer our gratitude for guidance through the final stages of publication.

For permission to publish *The Sword Went Out to Sea*, we thank the Schaffner Family Foundation, especially Timothy Schaffner, and the New Directions Publishing Corporation, for its crucial help in negotiating the contract with the Schaffner Family Foundation.

Finally, we thank our families, who have been patient and supportive and loving during times of all-consuming editing work. Julie Vandivere would like to thank her partner, Elise Nicol, for caring for the children, Genie and Gwen, so she was able to spend the month at the Beinecke. For his timely stint as "research assistant," Cynthia Hogue thanks her husband, Sylvain Gallais.

Abbreviations

Bryher Papers, YGC/Beinecke	Bryher Papers, Yale General Collection, Beinecke Rare Book and Manuscript Library, Yale University.
"H.D."	"H.D. by *Delia Alton*," ed. Adalaide Morris, *Iowa Review* 16, no. 3 (1986): 174–221; cited parenthetically in text, followed by the page number.
H.D. Papers, YCAL/Beinecke	H.D. Papers, Yale Collection of American Literature at the Beinecke Rare Book and Manuscript Library.
MR	Ts. *Majic Ring*, H.D. Papers, Yale Collection of American Literature at the Beinecke Rare Book and Manuscript Library.
S	Ts. *The Sword Went Out to Sea*, H.D. Papers, Yale Collection of American Literature at the Beinecke Rare Book and Manuscript Library.
T	H.D., *Trilogy* (New York: New Directions, 1973) (cited parenthetically in text, followed by the page number).
TF	H.D., *Tribute to Freud*, 1956 (rpt. Boston: David R. Godine, 1974).

Introduction

*But my Roland, no word he said
When the sword went out to sea;
But only turn'd away his head,-
A quick shriek came from me:
'Come back, dear lord, to your white maid!'-
The sword went out to sea.*

William Morris, from "Sailing of the Sword"[1]

I

The Sword Went Out to Sea, by modernist poet H.D. (the nom de plume of Hilda Doolittle, 1886–1961), which draws from the 1942–46 spiritualist séances that she conducted during and following World War II, is published here in this first edition, as H.D. had hoped to publish it. *Sword* is an ambitiously structured novel, completed and polished and readied for a publication that never materialized, because the vision was too nonlinear, the prose too insularly encoded. This work has puzzled many who have read it in manuscript. Despite H.D.'s conviction of its significance, it has been viewed as, at best, an artistic dress rehearsal for *Helen in Egypt*, begun in 1952 during the year after *Sword*'s final revision, and at worst, the symptomatic sublimation of H.D.'s 1946 breakdown and institutionalization at the Klinik Brunner at Küsnacht in Switzerland.

Although few novels are as densely or symbolically threaded as *Sword*, we propose that it be approached initially as a testament to and working through of a grief that is generational and gender-specific: the grief sustained, repressed, sublimated by the generation of women who saw two world wars and were called "shrill" or mad or both when they tried to protest that *war* is mad. It is a grief sustained over the all-encompassing devastation of World War II, including the genocide of Jewish and other populations and dropping the atom bomb on Japanese civilians. It is a grief that the generation of the American editors of this first edition have come of late to understand. One might say that it is a mad grief—something that looks like madness but isn't, something that is closer to fury. As the H.D. surrogate in the novel, Delia Alton, remarks, assessing how she might seem to others in an extreme time:

Madness might do; provided I didn't gibber and hurl things at people, I
didn't mind [being] thought ... a little crazy. But I didn't think I was. Later,
I was to reconstruct a world of fantastic terror[.] (*S*, 90)

H.D. does not deny "madness" in this passage but strategically repositions and
redefines it with the goal of explaining particular behavior that may or may not
actually be madness, a revisionary reading of her response to the "fantastic terror"
of the war and the blitz of London.

    The Sword Went Out to Sea not only comprises an incredible effort to rise from
sorrow but also, like her other work at this time, reclaims female agency in order
to alchemize the "hawk" of war into the "dove" of peace. As Susan Edmunds
argues analogously of *Trilogy*, H.D. accepts the "woman's work" of cultural grief
in narratives of loss, neither refusing nor denying grief, but imaginatively redis-
tributes its burden in the scenarios dramatized in her works.[2] Similarly, as H.D.
writes in an earlier spiritualist novel, *Majic Ring* (an unpublished roman à clef
with the same characters), "'blessed are they that mourn' for sometimes peril
and depression sharpen or clarify the inner perceptions and we 'dream true'"
(*MR*, YCAL/Beinecke). The activities *Sword* employs to redistribute grief (me-
diumship, the reading of prophetic signs, acting) are active rather than passive.
The main character doesn't passively receive oracular wisdom, for example, but
actively interprets messages, codes, and signs, which she then attempts to convey
to others. Such activities permitted H.D. in her life, as they permitted an earlier
generation of liberated women, "the exercise of a 'masculine temperament' and
provided an intellectual and spiritual outreach that were difficult to find elsewhere."[3] Although *Sword*'s writing is, finally, less compelling than H.D.'s best
works, we suggest that it can take its place as part of a body of women's literature
written around World War II the collective concerns of which—the destructiv-
ity of nationalism, the need for a "feminized" vision to be heard in the public
sphere, among others—are helping us to reorient and reconfigure modernism.[4]

    Other female modernists were, of course, engaged in investigating how to
think politically in the 1930s and 1940s. Virginia Woolf, Storm Jameson, Nancy
Cunard, and Sylvia Townsend Warner, for example, were all thinking creatively
and compellingly about how to link the political to the aesthetic. *The Sword
Went Out to Sea* does not resemble any of their works, however; instead, H.D. is
interested in exploring the nether regions of the soul of the individual and the
soul of civilization. She is thus continuing a trajectory begun in *Trilogy* and *The
Gift* of moving beyond the political and toward a spiritual solution as a goal in
itself. H.D. confronts the ecstasies and disorders of the mind, which she sees as
the form of the spirit. As Jane Augustine asserts, H.D. shared a belief with the-
osophists and spiritualists that "Thoughts are things," having a materiality that

could be manifested through mediums. For H.D., moreover, "words are things," too, referring to "a pre-existing truth or solid external reality."[5] The contemporary origins of such mystical quests for an Eternal Truth lie in a cultural response to what Alex Owen terms, discussing fin-de-siècle occultism and its roots, "soul sickness."[6] In *Sword*, among her other late works, H.D. reaches for spirituality as a cure—one that will help *form* to heal *soul*.

Subtitled *Synthesis of a Dream, Sword* integrates the insights drawn from the tragedies in her individual life into a larger structure or pattern, associating the "dream" at once with Sigmund Freud's notion of the unconscious, with mystery play (vision of and union with the divine), with personal healing dream, and finally, with the dream (or fantasy) of healing a war-torn world. "*The Sword*," she says, "is reality or truth," the answer to the meaning and pattern of "the heartache of one person," but "given by many to the whole world" ("H.D.," 205). Written under the late-life signature of Delia Alton, author of a number of the later works, *Sword* is a hope-filled novel, looking "into the future, in spite of all the darkness."[7]

A good deal of the passion of *Sword* derives from its near-obsessive focus on the surrogate figure of the spiritualist Lord Howell, with whom the main character of *Sword*, Delia Alton, hoped and failed to join forces. Lord Howell is based on the distinguished World War II hero, Hugh Caswall Tremenheere Lord Dowding, who had been Chief Air Marshal of the Royal Air Force (RAF) in 1940. It was his strategies and foresight that had been crucial to defeating the Luftwaffe in the Battle of Britain in 1940, the first Allied victory to stop the tide of Nazi expansion.[8] H.D.'s complicated relationship with Lord Dowding, the last and greatest of the various men who played for her, imaginatively, the mythic role of the Eternal Lover who betrayed her, is central to the story *Sword* tells and the resolution that she attempts to achieve in the retelling. It was his repudiation of the spiritualist work she was attempting to do in concert with his own (the more optimistic story that *Majic Ring* tells) that seems to have immediately catalyzed her breakdown, although the stress of the war and malnourishment surely contributed.

Contemporary publishers rejected the novel as too strange and incoherent to reach a broad audience, obsessive in its ruminations on personal repudiation. Nor was the subject of spiritualism considered an appropriate topic for serious literature (with some well-known exceptions). Friends and supporters, like H.D.'s former husband, writer Richard Aldington, encouraged her initially, giving her constructive feedback, and at least for a time, tried to help her publish it through one of his own publishers in New York.[9] H.D.'s lifelong friend and companion, the novelist Bryher (Annie Winifred Ellerman), also initially encouraged her, though finally, Bryher cautioned that *Sword* remained too close to actual events, and thus, too revelatory of the people on whom characters were based. Although scholars and critics have found the novel unsuccessful in real-izing its aims, some have importantly placed it in the context of H.D.'s canon, an approach that gives us a more accurate sense of its literary significance. In her groundbreaking study, *Psyche Reborn*, Susan Stanford Friedman discusses *Sword* in terms of H.D.'s relation not only to William Morris, her "spiritual father," but also to her decades-long quest for "la Sagesse."[10] Cassandra Laity extends Fried-man's thinking, offering a nuanced discussion of H.D.'s return after World War II to the Pre-Raphaelites. This move, she argues, formed "the literary, historical, and cultural blueprint" for H.D.'s late-life aesthetic, renewed her faith in the world, and allowed her to find a "new direction" in her poetry.[11] As Rachel Con-nor has recently argued, both *Sword* and *Majic Ring* are essential to understand-ing and assessing H.D.'s late-life oeuvre, because they document the centrality of spiritualism in her writing, which strongly informs her later poetics.[12]

H.D. believed in *Sword*, commenting that it was the "crown of all my effort," the single work that brought her "intellectual and emotional life . . . to its ful-fillment" ("H.D.," 190). It is important to clarify that she meant this statement less as a claim to the work's quality as great literature (although initially she *had* thought it her masterpiece), than to convey a sense of the spiritual as well as psychological truths that she had worked so hard to cull from her experiences. Extending Friedman's analysis of H.D.'s prose as creating "generic hybrids,"[13] Augustine describes *Sword* as a "non-ecclesiastical, post-religious 'spiritual au-tobiography,'" which H.D. has "disguised as the sub-genre of fiction, the *roman à clef*." Augustine suggests that the work be positioned in some sense between aesthetic genres because of H.D.'s intention that *Sword* function both as inspi-rational literature and as a recovery document.[14] Initially writing a fictionalized memoir (a *roman vecu*, as she puts it), H.D. engaged her "gift" to see further than individual circumstances and attempted to create *Sword* as a cultural "autobiog-raphy," speaking not only of individual trauma but working through the trauma of a civilization in critical transition (in some sense from colonial Empire to postcolonial nation-states).

H.D.'s interest in using psychological insights to confront and interpret cul-tural disasters can be traced to her work with Freud in the early 1930s, when she learned to read "the hieroglyph of the unconscious" through free association. As Friedman recounts, H.D. regarded her sessions with Freud in part as train-ing in psychoanalytic methodology "in order to fortify and equip myself to face war when it came, . . . and to help in some subsidiary way . . . with war-shocked and war-shattered people" (*TF*, 93).[15] By the time she was writing her ambi-tious works of the 1940s, H.D. had begun to conceive of herself as poet-analyst, and her language, as Diane Chisholm elegantly puts it, as "healing anodyne," therapeutic "antidote to patriarchy."[16] Like many artists, H.D. hoped in a post-Freudian world to be able to foster a cure through her art for the patriarchy's addiction to violence. As Friedman explains, moreover, H.D. considered her "séances" with Freud as preparation for her spiritualist séances a decade later, in which "the polarities of science and religion could be integrated."[17] While social critics skeptical that the world can be changed by art have criticized artists for their naiveté, we contend that to give ground to such criticism is itself a sterile negation of the power of art and myth historically and spiritually in human culture.

The modes in which *Sword* writes its way out of the individual and collective shattering of two world wars and years of unremitting bombing remain eerily relevant today not only as exemplary representation and resolution of pain, but also as painstaking, philosophical inquiry into emotional survival in a world increasingly defined by recurring regional wars and the terrorizing possibility of global annihilation. Obsessed and vulnerable, stubbornly, intricately symbolic, *Sword* tracks the record of recovery from the deep psychic wound that we abstract as "war's violence," but its epistemological and ontological insights are derived from the lived experience of a woman at the edge of Logos. To put it in H.D.'s terminology, we might say that in *Sword*, the Delphic Sibyl is translated not by the priests this time, but by the Trojan Cassandra, who now attempts to warn the world of atomic destruction.[18] As she wrote Aldington on June 6, 1947, in a letter preceding the manuscript, "the 'message' . . . [of *Sword* is] that the world was, perhaps is and possibly will be 'crashing to extinction,' if these in authority . . . don't stop smashing up things with fly-bombs, V2 and the ubiquitous (possibly) so called 'atom.'"[19] *Sword* represents the specifics of what H.D. describes so hauntingly in *Trilogy*, in language so beautifully controlled that we have only taken in what she means intellectually: "now the heart's alabaster / is broken"; "*oneness lost, madness*" (*T*, 39, 43). *Sword*'s language is less lyrical and beautiful, and thus doesn't mesmerize us, but even so, we cannot avoid confronting the profound psychic consequences of violence in our age. Whether a working through of trauma or the repetition compulsion (or both at once), *Sword* functions like the canary's song in a mine.

The novel is positioned as a fusion of the political (or time-bound) and eternal (or out-of-time), a work that tries to articulate the psychoanalytic cure she sought for the political violence of the twentieth century. Adalaide Morris makes the case for the continuing reemergence of H.D.'s work as a more political reconception of gynocentric modernism. Morris builds on the argument, first posited by Friedman and other important early critics like Rachel Blau DuPlessis, that we need to reassert H.D.'s political relevance.[20] Morris contends that to try to understand H.D.'s works as primarily referential, pointing to something identifiable outside the text's framework, is to miss "*how* they think":

> As forms of cultural meditation and mediation, they [*Trilogy* and *Helen in Egypt*] instantiate, exercise, and advocate a kind of attention that is crucial to the ongoing life of a culture. In this sense, they think *about* thinking and they think *toward* action: they are, that is, philosophical and ethical. They do cultural work.[21]

Morris' analysis of how H.D.'s later poetry is "enactive," thinking toward action, accurately encapsulates our sense of her linguistically exploratory prose and its structures in *Sword*. H.D. creates in this work, we suggest, highly original conceptions of how to think about *being* in a time of cultural crisis.

Sword's critical importance is multifold. It amplifies and tries to complete H.D.'s earlier autobiographical and palimpsestic novels (*Majic Ring*, *Bid Me to Live*, and *Palimpsest*, for example), which focus on the story of heterosexual love and loss in the hopes at last of re-integrating the wounded ego-shards and universalizing the story. It also more fully contextualizes the earlier *Trilogy*. To give a brief example, the "nameless initiates" who are what H.D. calls in "The Walls Do Not Fall" "companions / of the flame," who "pass each other on the pavement," snarling a "brief greeting" (*T*, 20–21), are identified in *Sword* not as poets, but spiritualists. *Sword* also allows us now to appreciate the intertextual framework of *Helen in Egypt*, *Trilogy*, *The Gift*, and *Tribute to Freud*,[22] as well as gives us a fuller sense of the ambitious range of her thinking.

By the time she was writing her works of the 1940s, she was moving beyond the "self-centered," spinning out of the personal to a farther-reaching, mystical and political sphere.[23] She wrote Bryher on July 1, 1947, about *Sword*,

> I am so busy on this new work. I can not tell you how funny it is, a sort of War and Peace cum The Last Days of Pompeii. [. . .] It will be one huge fat Vic[torian] vol[ume], or two or three short or long-short "novels" [. . .] I call them WINTERSLEEP and SUMMERDREAM - sleep and dream and so-called "reality" values contrasted. . . . It is also re-incarnation - but on a rather mosaic or Bulwer L[ytton][24] Pompeii style, scenes with the players at Delphi - worked up from my Stratford experience.[25] . . . I just sit down and automatic-write. I feel I have a gattling-gun in my hands - whatever a gattling-gun is. It is a fight to the finish of war and peace! (Bryher Papers, YGC/Beinecke)

Here, H.D. is using the term "re-incarnation" in the literal sense, the same soul living through many lifetimes of different bodies,[26] just as she is signifying a more literal power in the act of writing than is usually attributed to the pen. Unlike the magic writing instrument in *Trilogy*, the first born "*Word*" (*T*, 17), which is metaphorically greater than the younger Sword, the pen in the passage above is characterized by H.D. *as* a weapon, and as such, potentially as mighty (and lethal) as an actual "gattling-gun - whatever a gattling-gun is." As she formulated her methodology for her friend, consultant, and eventual literary executor, Norman Holmes Pearson, she demurred that the writing of *Sword* was "automatic writing" in the sense of Yeats' automatic writing in *A Vision*.[27] Rather, H.D. is careful to claim to Pearson that she wrote like "a skilled musician": "the technical reward of more than thirty years of actual practice. I mean, practice in the *art* of writing" ("H.D.," 194; H.D.'s emphasis).

2

Sword was harvested from what H.D. called her "vintage-years, 1943–1945" ("H.D.," 212), and comprises an important "hinge" text, contextualizing the remarkable, late outpouring of poems and prose from H.D. during and after World War II, in the second to last decade of her life. From 1941 to 1952, H.D. drafted from journals and notes, polished into working drafts, and in the case of her poetry, wrote and published *Trilogy* (initially published as three separate volumes by Oxford University Press in 1944, 1945, and 1946); *The Gift* (drafted 1940–44); "Advent" (worked up from her journal dating from 1934) and "The Writing on the Wall" that together compose *Tribute to Freud* (drafted in 1944 and published in 1956); *By Avon River* (written in 1945–46 and published in 1949); *Majic Ring* (drafted 1943–44); *The Sword Went Out to Sea* (drafted and revised 1946–50); her Pre-Raphaelite novel *White Rose and the Red* (drafted and revised 1948–49); her Moravian novel *Mystery* (drafted 1949–50); and her epic poem *Helen in Egypt* (drafted 1952–55 and published in 1960). Although uneven, when taken together, these works constitute an astonishing literary output over a decade of world crisis. Not surprisingly, all of these pieces are in dialogue, intertwining imaginatively, intellectually, and poetically.

H.D. began the first book of *Sword* (part 1 of "Wintersleep") during her time at Küsnacht clinic where she resided from March to November of 1946, following her nervous breakdown in London in February 1946. As she recalls in a letter to Norman Holmes Pearson dated April 16, 1951, she completed *Sword* "after my 6 months at Küsnacht," but she began it "well before I left," starting "*Sword*, after finishing *Avon*," which was "five years ago, May 13 [1946]."[28] She is referring in this letter only to part 1 of "Wintersleep," which is dated in all drafts as December 6, 1946. How consistently she was able to work on the section while at the clinic is difficult to say, for her correspondence makes no mention of *Sword* (even by its earliest working title of *Synthesis of a Dream*), mentioning only *By Avon River* and "Writing on the Wall."[29] Why she was silent about a new work dealing in the opening chapters with her solo séances, her obsession with Lord Dowding, and her subsequent breakdown (including some of her hallucinations) is not difficult to understand. Upon her release from Küsnacht in early November 1946, H.D. turned immediately to completing the first part of "Wintersleep," but she continued to remain silent on the subject of her undertaking. As she notes in the novel itself, which often narrates the process of its composition,

> I finished the first section of these notes [to *Sword*], in Lausanne, before Christmas 1946. I did not expect to go on with them. I had parted conclusively with Lord Howell and with the work [that is, the séances]. But I had made my testament, I had been witness to the strange truth of a rare adventure.[30] (*S*, 111)

The remainder of *Sword*, part 2 of "Wintersleep" and all of "Summerdream," was drafted in 1947, possibly with the benefit of notebooks kept in London before her breakdown, which may have contained an early sketch for the novel and most certainly contained lost séance notes.

That she drew on an earlier draft for some portion of the current version of *Sword*, however, is impossible to confirm. Although we can tell from her correspondence that she had kept notes and notebooks during her last year in London before and up to the onset of her breakdown, she did not have access to them while at the clinic in Küsnacht, and in fact did not know that they had survived her breakdown until her release. On November 1, 1946, she writes to Bryher that she is "shocked" that her "London note-books had not been destroyed" as she had requested and asks Bryher not to read them. "I was working on a subconscious fantasy," she writes, "and intended to change all names etc. and turn it into a dream of the *Id* bubbling up into consciousness. It did not seem the time to do it, all too recent so I decided to scrap it, after making excerps [*sic*]" (Bryher Papers, YGC/Beinecke). But "scrap it" she did not have a chance to do before her breakdown; nor had Bryher destroyed the notebooks as H.D. had requested. Some time after H.D. received the notebooks from Bryher in 1947, she destroyed every record of the originating "subconscious fantasy" upon which she had worked over the winter of 1945–46.[31] The lacuna in the evidence for that year speaks volumes, although it remains silent about the role of those papers in *Sword*'s composition.

In the years just previous to 1945, there remains plenty of evidence of H.D.'s work on séances, however, and references to the war that found their way into *Majic Ring* (which has the same characters as *Sword*). In that novel there are extant séance notes from the home-circle's channeled sessions that ran from September 3, 1943, to October 1944,[32] as well as letters to and from Lord Howell (Dowding) for this same period.[33] These letters and séance notes make up a significant portion of the unpublished *Majic Ring*, the novel written during 1943–44 that is similar in theme, historical context, and wordplay to the later, more polished *Sword*. But nothing remains of any séance notes from late 1944 to early 1946 (just before her breakdown), although there are tantalizing references to what has been lost. A letter dated January 3, 1946, from Lord Dowding, for example, thanks her for the séance "notes" that she has typed up and sent him (H.D. Papers, YCAL/Beinecke).

H.D. was not ready until May 1947 to let her circle of friends know of *Sword*'s existence, first alluding to it in a letter dated May 20, 1947, to her former husband, Richard Aldington, as merely "some worm-y writing" that she was very excited for him to read once she had it typed. She described the plot of *Sword* and continued, "It is very well written, the outcome of more than 20 years of not so much experimental as explorational prose. It is a story that I have been at, off and on, since after the last war."[34] For the rest of the year, H.D. discussed the methodology of *Sword* with Aldington at length while he was reading and commenting on it. By June 22, 1947, she mentioned both "Wintersleep" and "Summerdream" (which she described as nearing completion), and her hopes to publish them as two volumes, "one to follow on the heels of the other."[35] By July 26, however, already resisting Aldington's practical counsel to write "straight fiction" for the "Common Reader," H.D. defended her hybrid style and poetic method: "I am thankful to be here in this most startling oasis of mixed genres."[36] Their most intensive correspondence continues throughout 1947 and into 1948, as she completed and began the revisions of the novel.[37]

While busy consulting Aldington, H.D. was silent on the topic of *Sword* in her letters to Bryher, until she had received Aldington's general encouragement. Not until a letter to Bryher dated July 1, 1947, does she indicate that she has been writing a new novel (of some 600 typescript pages!). Her silence, she confesses, was because "I did not want to worry you with the war part" (Bryher Papers, YGC/Beinecke). H.D. was sensitive about her breakdown after the war, and the extremity of the measures to which Bryher had gone to procure the best care for her (indeed, the novel insistently represents delirium as a kind of higher wisdom). She accurately anticipated Bryher's issues with the spiritualism (Bryher repudiated her involvement), and the novel's roman à clef mode. She was therefore understandably cautious about revealing to Bryher that she was involved in an ambitious, "explorational" prose project derived from her solo séances during the war—a work that more passionately engaged the psychic and social costs of war than any writing she completed while recovering in Switzerland that year.

The years 1948–52 were a period when H.D. was trying hard to turn *Sword* into a publishable work (albeit on her own terms), because she believed in its significance, calling it variously, in letters dated August 14, 1948, and July 15, 1951, to Pearson, a "*tour de force*" and her "MAGISTER LUDI."[38] She sought and received feedback, and revised steadily, trying to address conceptual issues raised by Bryher and Aldington without betraying her own vision for the novel. In addition, she wrestled with the problem that in its first half, "Wintersleep," the character of Lord Dowding was readily recognizable, and thus, she attempted to procure his support. At first, she held up what she hoped would be rapid publication in New York while she sent a copy to Lord Dowding. Although he was the first to concede that he had no legal means of preventing her from publishing the novel, he was for years loath to give his approval without her fictionalizing her account more radically. Call the Lord Howell character "Sir Somebody Something," he wrote her in the last letter of their exchange about *Sword* in the spring of 1951, "or plain Mr [*sic*] Whatnot," but in its current form, it was too "near the knuckle" for comfort.[39]

For her part, she variously summarized her exchanges with Dowding in these years to Pearson. In a letter dated August 14, 1948, H.D. defensively trivialized Dowding's spiritualism as merely "sincere," suggesting irritably that his books were published with "third-rate publishers."[40] A few years later, on October 4, 1950, after sending Dowding the final version (edited for the last time), and having tried unsuccessfully to procure his blessing, she wrote Pearson breezily that Dowding was given the nickname in the RAF of "Stuffy," noting, "Well Stuffy is being stuffy, as per usual," about *Sword*.[41] But with or without the blessing of "Stuffy," she could not publish the novel in England—or anywhere else, for that matter.

Pearson and H.D. had been corresponding about *Sword* since late 1947, when she first piqued his interest by writing him about the novel. In 1949 he traveled to Italy, where H.D. summered for years at a hotel in Lugano, for the specific purpose of discussing the revision and possible publication of the novel, on which she worked over the next year. Writing him on July 26, 1950, that she had "cut out some weedy bits" and "re-arranged conversations" into chronological and "clear, dramatic parallels,"[42] H.D. sent him what is probably this current version in December of 1950, marked as the third typed draft held in the H.D. archives in the Beinecke Rare Book and Manuscript Library at Yale University.[43] She hoped that Pearson's influence (along with Aldington's connections with publishers) could help her find a home for the work in the United States, so that she could simply write Lord Dowding that the publication was a fait accompli to which he might yet give a nod. Neither H.D.'s status as a well-respected poet, however, nor Pearson's or Aldington's New York connections, could overcome the publishing world's wariness about so involuted a work on spiritualism (book 1, "Wintersleep") and reincarnation (book 2, "Summerdream"). Thus, although she would refer to the novel wistfully and respectfully at times for the rest of her life, by 1952, she had begun to "synthesize the dream" into her epic poem, *Helen in Egypt*, the work in which the composite figure of Achilles is based on Dowding, Helen on H.D., and Paris likely on one of her Küsnacht analysts, Erich Heydt (with some Aldington and Pound mixed in). As critics generally agree, *Helen* is more successful as literature, better integrating H.D.'s personal themes into the mythic frame, but *Sword* is, we suggest, a more ambitious if messier work, and remains compelling in what it attempts to achieve.

3

The psychic research in which the H.D. surrogate in *Sword*, Delia Alton, participates begins sometime before Christmas 1941 (thus, although unmentioned in the novel, shortly after the attack on Pearl Harbor). But H.D.'s own forays into occultism began much earlier, as readers of Susan Stanford Friedman's *Psyche Reborn* will recall. As Friedman contends, "personal initiation [as an adept] became poetry of prophecy as H.D. transformed her psychic experiences and esoteric research" in the 1920s and 1930s into syncretic, mythmaking poetry.[44] Leonora Woodman argues that details in *Trilogy* confirm that H.D. was conversant with theosophy, esotericism, and spiritualism, and quite specifically employed the popularized image of psychic mediums as human telegraphic "receiving stations."[45] H.D.'s interest in the early 1940s in spiritualism was perhaps intensified by the entry of the United States into the war, as well as by the experience of enduring the blitz.

According to her unpublished Hirslanden notebooks (closely following Delia Alton's story in *Sword*), H.D. joined "one of the psychic-research societies, in Walton Street, not far from Lowndes Square where I lived" (Stanford House in the novel), in order to attend some lectures and classes, as well as to use their library collection of esoteric literature.[46] There, she attended a lecture by a young Eurasian medium, Arthur Bhaduri (Ben Manisi in *Sword*), whom she thought "a 'seer.'" But, as she hastened to reassure her friend Viola Baxter Jordan, "I am not 'mixed up' with him or anyone of the sort,"[47] a statement that will surely surprise readers of both *Majic Ring* and *Sword*. H.D. herself was surprised, however, when she was able to convince the usually skeptical Bryher (Gareth in the novel) to consult Bhaduri about her "dangerous war work."[48] Bryher was impressed with Bhaduri's counsel, and by 1943, H.D., Bryher, Bhaduri, and his mother, May Bhaduri (Ada Manisi in the novel), had formed a home-circle, as individual séance circles were called in the spiritualist movement.[49]

This circle met regularly over 1943–44, almost every other Friday at H.D.'s Lowndes Square apartment, channeling a friendly, Native American "spirit guide" known as "K," and later, one known as "Z," by messages tapped out laboriously in code on a round, tripod table once owned by the Socialist founder of the Arts and Crafts Movement, the Pre-Raphaelite writer and artist, William Morris. H.D. had inherited this table after the death of her friend, Violet Hunt, an expert on the Pre-Raphaelites, author of *Wife of Rossetti*, who significantly influenced H.D.'s views on the Victorian romantics.[50] H.D. describes this table as a "clock":

> We tell time with this clock, but it is not our time.
>
> It is time-out-of-time, recorded by the ticking or the tapping of one of the three hands or rather by one of the three feet of the tripod.
>
> Our left hand is on the table. Our right hand is scribbling in a notebook, a sort of rough shorthand of the messages.
>
> As I have just said, the messages are from air-men, not so very recently lost in the Battle of Britain. ("H.D.," 187)

The first part of *Sword*, "Wintersleep," relates the story of H.D.'s actual relationship to the Morris table, which provides the link of the out-of-time with the historical, the personal with the universal, and the spiritual/spiritualist with the secular world of war. Such activities as H.D.'s table-tapping, although not common, were not unusual either, as the usually skeptical Bryher's involvement indicates. As Augustine recounts, it "was not considered heretical, insane or socially stigmatizing to consult mediums, clairvoyants and clairaudients" under the extreme pressure and crisis conditions of not only the war raging across the Channel, but also of the blitz, where Londoners were dying every night that bombs fell.[51]

Among the most venerable organizations conducting psychic-research was the Society for Psychic Research, founded in 1882 by the intellectual and scientific elite of the previous century who wished to investigate otherworldly phenomena for themselves, hoping to preserve in a post-Darwinian age, as Alex Owen asserts, "some spiritual aspect to the universe or gain new insight into the laws of nature."[52] As Demetres Tryphonopoulos remarks, London was for the better part of half a century teeming with occult activities.[53] H.D.'s exuberant belief in the scientific validity of psychic phenomena was shared by some of her most distinguished contemporaries, and her confident interpretations of the scribbled messages, at least until the apocalyptic closing of the war, were to her for a time the key to her purpose on earth, a crucial spiritualizing of her psychoanalysis a decade earlier.[54]

On October 20, 1943, Bhaduri was traveling outside of London in conjunction with his work as a medium, and gave H.D. his ticket to attend a lecture by Lord Dowding.[55] After the Battle of Britain, he had been forced to retire, most likely because of a political power struggle. Despite claims to the contrary, Dowding was not asked to retire because of his increasing involvement in spiritualism, which was initially a personal response to the loss of so many young RAF pilots under his command (whom he thought of as his "sons").[56] Because of messages from the table about the fatefulness of their meeting, H.D. intensified her psychic engagement with Dowding. But also, her memories of losses sustained in World War I (her first child stillborn, her brother Gilbert killed in battle, and her father dead soon afterwards) were being triggered by the blitz of London, quite understandably. She had read Dowding's articles on spiritualism in newspapers, and his first spiritualist book, *Many Mansions*, and was eager to hear him in person. His lecture was about communicating with the spirits of the RAF pilots whom he had commanded and lost in the Battle of Britain. She was prompted to write him a note after his lecture about her own spiritualist circle, inquiring whether she might join his, too. Dowding responded that his circle was closed, but remarkably, given that she was a complete stranger, he left the door open in case the "spirits" recommended enlarging his circle.

A few days later, on October 29, 1943, the spirit guide of H.D.'s circle, K, brought Z to her home-circle (both channeled by Bhaduri), and told the group that Z was a "good Indian" whose "totem" was the "nénufar," French for water lily ("Notes on Séances," H.D. Papers, YCAL/Beinecke). Z was the spirit guide in both *Majic Ring* and *Sword* for the H.D. surrogate, Delia Alton. Although H.D. would not discover until she read Dowding's second spiritualist book the odd coincidence that his circle channeled a Z (or the Z) as well,[57] she was quick to associate Z's totem with Lord Dowding. As she ruminates in both *Majic Ring* and *Sword*, the "nenu" of "Nénufar" is also Nenu, the Egyptian sky-god, with whom she associates the Air Marshal. Moreover, the "far" of "Nénufar" spelled backwards made not only Ra (the Egyptian and Mithraic sun-god who figures so centrally in "The Walls Do Not Fall"), but also RAF.[58]

According to the séance notes, in sessions on November 4 and 18, 1943, the central figures that H.D. would also come to associate with Lord Dowding in both *Majic Ring* and *Sword* began coming through—the Viking named Hallblithe, his Viking ship with the blue wings painted on its sides, and the Lone Eagle, who was for H.D. both Hal, the Viking sea-king, and Howell, Lord Dowding.[59] As Aldington would remind H.D. when he read *Sword* in 1947, Hallblithe is the main character of William Morris' "Icelandic saga," *The Glittering Plain*, an Avalon-like isle beyond death to which H.D. refers a number of times, in a rather sibylline fashion, in "Summerdream."[60] H.D. was struck by the coincidence of Morris' hero figuring so centrally in her séances, because the little table had been used by William Morris for his paints and brushes ("Notes on Séances," H.D. Papers, YCAL/Beinecke). At Aldington's suggestion, H.D. took her title from a Morris poem, "Sailing of the Sword," relegating the original title, *Synthesis of a Dream*, to the subtitle.

H.D. was drawn to Lord Dowding, perhaps in part because when she first met him, he was a widower. But she consulted Bhaduri before taking more action than writing a note after his lecture. As she recounts in both the séance notes and *Sword*, she brought Bhaduri the note that Dowding had written her in response to her own note after his lecture, not telling Bhaduri who had written the letter. Possibly he was intuiting H.D.'s secret desire, but in any event, while he held the letter, he received a number of messages for Hilda, that she had a "psychic link" with "a gentlemen who has suffered," the figure with whom she directly linked Lord Dowding because of the letter. That gentleman had not "expressed" his "real self" in this life. Hilda was to "rescue" this man as a way toward her own "salvation," the séance notes say on November 4, 1943. She was hesitant, however, and decided that if a particular word came up in further sessions—the word was "wings"—it was a "sign" that Bhaduri's reading was accurate—that she was fated to be linked to this "gentleman." At that point, the Viking ship was revealed to have been painted with two "blue wings," and the figure of the Lone Eagle appeared as well. H.D. felt she had her sign. Two weeks later, her connection to this man became more erotically spiritual in the séances: they were to be linked by the "fire of divine love." (Much of this account is included in *Sword*, but this last note, the possibility in which H.D. so deeply invested for a time, has of course been expunged.)

H.D. was, as the extant séance notes detail, alternately confident and hesitant about a "relationship" with someone with whom she was, after all, occasionally corresponding and annually exchanging Christmas cards, someone whom she was not actually to meet in person until 1945. She was told in a session on December 16, 1943, for example, not to "worry" that he seemed unresponsive to her overtures, to have "patience," because he was "ill" and "overworked." On January 20, 1944, she was told to "keep contact with little notes," which she did, and that later there would be a "full opening." We get a sense from reading these notes and the scenes in *Sword* that reconstruct this period not of H.D. jumping to conclusions, but as impressionable, cautious, vulnerable, hopeful, earnest. She was seeking, as so many did at the time, some comfort from somewhere other than the world at war—and more important, some way to help, however fantasized. Spiritualism was for her a more spiritual and prophetic domain—and, characteristically, not associated with orthodox religion (the source of comfort for the other expatriate American who remained in London during the blitz, T. S. Eliot).

Thus, as Lord Dowding became imaginatively for H.D. the greatest of her "*héros fatals*," "four extravagant and illuminating occasions that ended with a shut door," as she remarks (*S*, 61), she contemplated this life-pattern as completing a four-square design of fate:

> *The Sword* gives us . . . four squares[,] four friendships: Peter van Eck [the surrogate for Peter Rodeck] of the condensed Greek adventure, a young American poet of Delia's Philadelphia school-days [Ezra Pound], her husband Geoffrey Alton [Richard Aldington], and a certain young scholar who was actually an analysand or student [J. J. van der Leeuw] of the Professor [Sigmund Freud, the archeologist Frederik von Alten in the novel] during my first sessions in Vienna [in the novel, Dresden]. The names are altered. . . . But the ingredients or the "contents of the test-tube" or the crucible are the same. ("H.D.," 192)

To analyze or characterize this dynamic pattern in her life, H.D. adopts a trope that literalizes sexual and erotic chemistry. Her life is a "test-tube" that has the same ingredients at any point in time. Thus, when Delia meets Lord Howell, he becomes the catalyst, the "alien substance" added to the test tube that "crystallized out Geoffrey and the others," as H.D. describes the process of discerning the pattern in *Sword* (*S*, 61, 155). The other men who make up this all-important pattern remain in elemental ways the "base substances" that H.D. would alchemically alter into the "gold" of poetic mythologizing, the "LEGEND" of her life.[61]

The first *héro*, Ezra Pound (Allen Flint in the novel), broke off their 1907 engagement for another woman, according to Barbara Guest.[62] H.D.'s husband, the writer Richard Aldington, was the second. During the few years of cohabitation in their marriage (1913-1918), interrupted by World War I, he often had affairs, but stayed attached to H.D. Once Dorothy "Arabella" Yorke (Miranda in *Sword*) became his "mistress" in 1918, however, a relationship too serious to call "an affair," H.D. felt wounded and rejected. She and Aldington remained for a time very attached to each other, as Guest recounts, but by 1919, Aldington had left H.D. in order to live with Arabella for the better part of the next decade, and H.D. had given birth to her daughter Perdita, fathered by a man she did not love, the composer Cecil Gray.[63] H.D. ruminated for decades in her works on this sexual "betrayal," by both Aldington and Pound, the mythic pattern of her life, the painful chapters of which she would try repeatedly to process and integrate through narrative.

Aldington was actually the basis for two characters in *Sword*: Delia's young husband, Geoffrey Alton, who has an affair with Miranda, accusing Delia of not loving him, before dying in World War I; and the older journalist friend, Randolph Spencer. H.D. is two characters as well. She is the writer-surrogate and spiritualist, Delia Alton; and the sixteen year old Delia, a girl in Philadelphia, some of whose past lives are touched upon scenically in "Summerdream," where the Delia analogs are also paired as young girls and aging wisewomen. As Carolyn Zilboorg argues insightfully, H.D.'s complex "layering process involves multiple doubling" throughout *Sword*.[64] In a section recalling "Geoffrey" and contemplating "the traces of direction" in her life, for example, Delia associates Geoffrey with "the Tristram story" and the table with the Round Table of King Arthur. In response to Geoffrey's accusation that Delia doesn't love him, she says, "There were two Iseults, Iseult Blanchmain and Iseult Blanchfleur. I was both Iseults" (*S*, 82). Although "Iseult Blanchmain loved well enough," Iseult Blanchfleur was a "*belle fantôme*" who "did not know" her feelings or her mind. The one was "the statue that the poet prayed to," the feminine ideal; the other, "a ghost, a spectre" herself (*S*, 83), in the doubled, phantasmic identity that Helen in *Helen in Egypt* occupies as well. Iseult Blanchfleur has implicitly stepped outside the definitions imposed on women by society. She is associated in "Summerdream" with the older, wisewoman Rose Beauvais of Normandy, who signifies herself (like Helen) as "a witch, a fury" (*S*, 266)

The third of these men was, like the later figure of Lord Dowding, a more fantasized than real person in terms of the significance brought to bear on their characters in H.D.'s work, although there was a solid basis in the actual. When H.D. was traveling with Bryher to Greece in 1920, she met an older British man named Peter Rodeck. She had a shipboard flirtation with him, and he asked her to continue traveling with him, which she refused to do. In a number of her prose works, however, H.D. makes much of this dalliance and its meaning, and Rodeck's surrogate, the character of Peter Van Eck, is described in *Sword* as a "Prince Lointain." His younger version, the character of Jan Verstigen, based on the analysand who saw Freud the hour before her own, was an eminent Dutch scholar and theosophist who died in a plane crash, J. J. Van der Leeuw, the fourth of these *héros fatals* who preceded Lord Dowding. Dowding became the greatest of these, the lost "companion" or "twin" whom H.D. sought and found throughout her life, only to lose each time to circumstances beyond her control. As Friedman explains, the importance of this pattern for H.D. was that each reoccurrence constituted a further "initiation" as an adept of esoteric knowledge.[65] She believed that her spiritualist activities were the final "initiation" into the mystery, preparing her to meet her soul's mate (and in terms of her belief in the cycles of reincarnation, completing her soul's journey toward illumination).

At least through the writing of *Sword*, H.D. maintained a belief that her contemplation of this pattern could provide the answer to Why?—both why she felt that Lord Dowding's unexpected interest in her was divinely ordained, rather than fantasized on her part, and also, why the "betrayal" happened *again*. In late 1944, H.D.'s home-circle disbanded, when Bhaduri announced his plans to marry. Bryher stopped such activity altogether, but H.D. daringly began to conduct séances alone (against both Bryher's and Lord Dowding's counsel), filled with a sense of purpose because she was receiving messages from the RAF pilots *for* Lord Dowding:

> When I think of it now - I mean, the little tripod-table - things seem even less complicated than they did when I took the RAF messages for Lord Howell, in London. I said we had our shorthand technique and I said it was the winged word that they wanted. Z had given me the first clue or code.[66] They said that I would "hear" this but that he would understand it. They wanted Lord Howell and myself to work together. (*S*, 139)

H.D. invited him to tea occasionally, from February of 1945 to 1946, in order to convey messages from the "star-cluster" or "Cloud of Witnesses," as she sometimes called them, which she believed to be "air-men" lost in the Battle of Britain, trying to warn the world of the dangers of the atomic bomb ("H.D.," 186, 193). Although impossible to date precisely over the course of that year because of the gap in the records, the import of those messages suggests that they were received around or following August 1945, when the bomb was dropped on a Japanese civilian population. There is every indication in the first section of *Sword* that this action deeply upset H.D., and that in her later delirium, she ruminated on this fateful step.

Occasionally over the course of the year before H.D.'s breakdown, Lord Dowding had accepted her invitations to tea, and they seem cordially, probably intensively, to have discussed their shared spiritualist interests. But after the last of these occasions in February 1946, Lord Dowding rejected the validity of the messages that H.D. had been receiving "for him," firmly if gently, in the note written to H.D. Perhaps he was more blunt at the tea itself.[67] Certainly her versions in both *Sword* and later in *Helen in Egypt* of this final meeting are filled with the effects of a violent repudiation, at least in her perception, which is literalized (and fantastically eroticized between Helen and Achilles) in *Helen*. Dowding's full rejection of her work swept away the fragile world she had constructed as psychic protection from the horrors of wartime. As Augustine argues, this repudiation destroyed "her self-identity as a 'gifted' writer—a complete fragmentation and disunion."[68] It destroyed her sense of herself as psychically gifted, albeit Cassandra-like (in that no one believed her). H.D. would not attempt to give Lord Dowding any more messages, or in fact, ever again to channel messages on the little table, which was left with her other things in England at the time of her breakdown.

4

Giles and Miles and Gervaise there,
Ladies' Gard must meet the war;
Whatsoever Knights these are,
Man the walls withouten fear!

Axes to the apple-trees,
Axes to the aspens tall!
Barriers without the wall
May be lightly made of these.
William Morris, from "Golden Wings"[69]

The two books of *The Sword Went Out to Sea*, "Wintersleep" and "Summer-dream," both have to do with the past and present lives (including past lives in other incarnations) of the author-surrogate, Delia Alton, mostly at her contemporary age at the end of World War II (nearing sixty), but occasionally at that of her youth in Philadelphia (a girl of sixteen). *Sword*'s various subplots are structurally similar, but as characters shift among the narratives—often without forewarning—the novel comes to seem bewilderingly complex. We try in this last section to give detailed enough summaries of the main characters, events, and symbolism for all readers to approach H.D.'s "Synthesis of a Dream" to be oriented to its unfamiliar world, to appreciate its at-times startling beauty. The rich and intricate symbolism will be readily familiar to all who know *Trilogy*, *The Gift*, and *Helen in Egypt*, among H.D.'s other major late-life works.

Sword opens in postwar London, and moves among Delia's memories of past loves and visions of past lives, in H.D.'s most sustained attempt in prose to relate them in an overarching design of parallel stories through time. Adopting an architectural metaphor that also has esoteric resonance (if one thinks of the mathematical symbolism of medieval cathedrals, or even of the "chapter houses" of the visionary Christianity of H.D.'s Moravian heritage), she terms her chapters "chapels" and the work as a whole a "Cathedral" in its design conception. H.D. speaks of her writing from 1926 to 1948 as "Chapter-houses" that adjoin "some vast Cathedral": "The Cathedral is the Dream, the *Synthesis of a Dream*" ("H.D.," 204). The "Dream" is the Eternal, the out-of-time overlaying the historical time, the territory that her greatest poetic epics, *Trilogy* and *Helen in Egypt*, explore as well. The characters in *Sword* function precisely as dream-figures, in Freud's sense of dream-composites.

As challenging as *Sword* is to follow from a narrative standpoint, H.D. worked hard over 1949–50 to make it structurally clear, as well as to offer frequent meta-narrative clues to reading the novel. The key to the design of the novel is found in three images that H.D. uses to explain her conceptualization of the work: a spiral shell, folds or pleats of time, and the spatial "bee-lines." In the repeating story of love and loss through time, only the structure is repeated:

> They say we make the pattern or spiral of our life, as a shell-fish does. We go round and round. . . . Life advances in a spiral, we all know. (*S*, 40–41)

Like the shell of a shellfish, the spiral movement circles upward, creating a pattern that is progressing toward an apex by moving vertically. Thus, while the characters' souls remain the same, they are going through a necessary process of both repetition and ascension.

Somewhat differently, H.D. perceives chronology in the novel as structural folds of a paper, much like the folding paper that children make as a game, or alternatively, like accordion "pleats." The pleats fold together so different time periods touch, or unfold to reveal a different historical time within the folds, relying for continuity on a repeated action, which takes on different names and locations as the paper opens or closes. History, she explains, "is the same story. The years had come like the lenses of the opera-glass. . . . It was one of those folds or pleats in time, but if you understand one fold or pleat, one superimposition, you understand another" (*S*, 91). *Sword*'s repetitions should in this sense also be understood as part of such relative patterns. Like the circularity of the shell, the narrative repeats the pattern, coming on the same events as it moves up and around, or opens and closes like an accordion—the same structure but not the same place or time. Indeed, when the pleats fold, characters from different historical time periods can touch (are superimposed, palimpsestically, on each other).

In "Summerdream," H.D. describes her narrative's symbolic method as itself composite, in the chapter entitled "*Belle Dame*":

> We followed the Z or the bee-line in its zig-zag track or path across time. Time was conveniently pleated and the pleats lay flat under the chart or map that took us from London to Lausanne, to Lugano, to Knossos, to Athens, to Delphi . . . back to London, to Venice. . . . There are to-and-fro journeys and return flights, but this briefly is our path or our zig-zag in space. Time is another matter. But this bee-line or Z-line has this advantage over time, time is neatly folded; the pleats are disproportionate, it is true, but under the Z-map, no-one will notice. (*S*, 214; H.D.'s ellipses)

Sword's characters follow spirals, and its chronology is structured as accordion-like pleating patterns. But spatially, its parallel stories "zig-zag in space," charting "bee-line or Z-line" movements. Time opens and folds. Different characters touch different times and events, all with the same pattern. The "folds" function

figuratively like tailored pleats: the novel compresses and expands with movement, history's fabric connected by H.D.'s careful zig-zag stitch in time.

The first part of book 1 of *Sword*, "Wintersleep," is made up of three chapters.
The first chapter is obsessively concerned with Delia's attempts to associate with
Lord Howell and details the creation of a spiritualist community consisting of
Gareth, Delia, Ada Manisi, and directed by the medium, Ben Manisi. The group
receives spiritualist communications, some of which focus on Delia's fascina-
tion with contacting Lord Howell, and for the first time, the medium Manisi
sees images of a Viking ship and its warriors going to sea. Delia seems to be the
rune-reader and seer on board. The chapter ends as the group disintegrates and
Delia continues the séance sessions alone. The second chapter includes recol-
lections of Geoffrey's rejection of Delia for Miranda, and recounts Delia's solo
communications at the round table and the messages she begins to receive from
dead RAF pilots, with whom she associates the Knights of the Round Table.
These pilots speak of the impending danger of the annihilation of society from
the atom bomb and ask that H.D. communicate their messages to Lord Howell,
who rejects them.

Chapter 3 recounts hallucinatory visions, highly selective accounts of what
were actual hallucinations that H.D. experienced during her 1946 breakdown,
which include the story of the destruction of London around Saint Paul's Cathedral by a small atom bomb. Delia writes, "I was quite alone; in my isolation,
I re-lived the first war, the second war and pre-visioned a third war" (*S*, 67).
The chapter then folds back to include details of Delia's early relationship with
Allen Flint in Philadelphia. Importantly, this chapter is not simply a catalogue
of Delia's hallucinations, but also a revisionary reading of them. H.D. employs
the hallucinations to introduce a pacifist theme that moves across temporal and
geographical boundaries in order to work through the horrendous destruction
of war: "There was love and hate. Love was eternal, hate was ephemeral. That is
what I learned during my illness. Fear was another word for hate, or hate was another word for fear" (*S*, 49). The probing analysis of hate in this passage, which
is actually fear, is noteworthy.

H.D. puts specific faces on her insight in this passage. To give an example,
we turn to a representative hallucination among several throughout the novel
that mourns the devastation rained on children during the war. In this chapter
there appears to Delia a tawny boy, from Lapland it seems to her at first, part of
a "horde" of Barbarians (of which she is one as well) moving across a desolate
land. The Barbarian passage precedes Delia's vision of a small atom bomb falling
on London and forcing the population to tunnel under the city in an effort to
survive. Then, Delia suddenly recalls Hiroshima, and the reason behind her sense

that she was one of a population of "Barbarians" becomes tellingly clear: The boy in Delia's hallucination is not a Laplander, but most likely a Japanese child. H.D. writes,

> I had felt the scar. The earth was furrowed with the irrational assaults that man had made upon her. . . . I can also see the slant eyes and ashen face of a small boy. The face is ash-coloured, though originally, it may have been fawn-brown. (*S*, 54)

There is a tenderness in these details that is marked by mourning, even as the narrative jumps about mercurially: Barbarians of the past, London of the future, and trenchantly, "Barbarians" in the present who have dropped a bomb on civilians. The small boy moves in a spiral, and with each turn, his appearance shifts: the fawn-brown face of the Laplander becoming the ashen face of a Japanese child among thousands of children displaced or killed during the war.

Part 2 of book 1 consists of six chapters of intricate, interlocking symbolism. The opening chapters announce that the "*Synthesis of a Dream* manifests," as sixteen-year-old Delia sits on a porch in Philadelphia with sixty-three-year-old Lord Howell, who is speaking of reincarnation and transfiguration. The scene is the Philadelphia of H.D.'s youth, during preparations for a production of *Iphigenia in Tauris* at the Academy of Music just before the class of 1903 is to graduate. There is a tea, an Ivy Ball, and the performance. The Pound-surrogate, Allen Flint, who is portrayed as attached to the H.D.-surrogate, Delia, is characterized as disruptively flamboyant, more attention-seeking than attractive.[70] And it is to an avatar of the Prince Lointain, a classmate of Allen's who plays Phydias in *Iphigenia*, who asks to meet the beautiful young Delia, and later to dance with her at the Ivy Ball, that Delia is attracted. He is, however, as she soon finds out, already engaged.

The chapters are narrated as memoir, but in fact are a dream that gives Delia the clue to how to relate the different men in her life, and the time-palimpsests in the novel, as parallel points on the spiral of her life. As in this section, wherein the H.D.-surrogates are doubled (the mature and young "Delia"), so the various men in her life are both composite and doubled figures. The pleats of time in "Wintersleep" fold over events and important characters: the war, the séances, the repudiation by Lord Howell in February 1946, and Delia's earliest encounter with her first Prince Lointain.

As in the familiar Shakespearean trope (and Woolf's posthumously published *Between the Acts*), H.D. plays with the way events and persons seem staged. But suddenly, eerily, when Delia acknowledges that the war has been a historic tragedy, she loses a sense of the separation between theatre and life. This recognition is accompanied by a loss of self. On the day commemorating the Battle of Britain, Delia attends a memorial at Westminster with her friend Philip Manning (the novel surrogate for Robert Herring, editor of *Life and Letters Today*):

> I was watching the tragedy, but when I stood beside Philip Manning and heard the roll of drums, I was in the tragedy. I was no longer outside things, watching. I was inside. I was one of the few main actors, though ... *I* no longer mattered. (*S*, 85; emphasis added)

The breakdown and loss of self that Delia suffers is associated with, and redeemed by, connecting "madness to its source, the source of all western poetry, the source of philosophy and mythology, the Greek drama" (*S*, 101). Thus, the approach H.D. adopts to work through her experience, representing it as healing dream for a broken land, is to turn the "theatre of war" into the culturally originary ritual of the drama festival (that is, to *poetry*), as potential, curative performance: quite literally, acting/writing (out) *as* cure.

As such, Delia affirms the strength of her vision, associating her narrative method not only with the male-dominated lineage of theatrical arts, but also with women's art, the hidden method of connecting the threads that enables H.D.—Philomela-like—to tell her tale at all: "I worked on the wrong side of the tapestry; the threads reached from Philadelphia to Tauris, from London to Paris, from London to Athens ... (and for the last time, on the reverse or underside), to Lausanne" (*S*, 104).[71] By turns, H.D.'s narrative takes on the rich embellishments of poetic description as she focuses meditatively on the sensory objects (especially the scent of lilacs triggering memory) that surround her in the hotel at Lugano, which take her back to the Pennsylvania of her youth. Other chapters stand as witness to the shifting boundaries of time and nation-states that are a part of the postwar world. In making an argument for her spiritualist activities, H.D. draws an analogy common to that movement between such technological advances as the telephone and telegraph, for example, and the science of telepathic communication, which she argues can be advanced in a modern world.[72]

"Summerdream," the second book of *Sword*, comprises fourteen chapters. In recounting the reaction of the older Aldington-surrogate, journalist Randolph Spencer, to "Wintersleep" in the opening of "Summerdream," H.D. sets up the second book's structure—as performative enactment, as well as palimpsestic overlay of transcendent experience through time—in relation to the first book. "Summerdream" is a more fanciful and complex section, establishing historical parallels to the London threatened and finally saved in "Wintersleep." H.D. conceived of "Summerdream" as a series of "fairy-tales," which hold the key to unlocking their meaning: the *sun* in various figurative and symbolic manifestations (thus, among other possible interpretations, rebirth). This single volume retells the story of Delia's falling out with Lord Howell in 1946 in several earlier time periods. Tracking the sun through those periods in relation to the various female characters in essence follows the trajectory of Delia's return to psychic and physical health (and therefore, by implication, to the restoration of hope for humanity). The first chapters of the second book are transitional, set in contemporary London after Lord Howell's repudiation of Delia, and in Lugano, Italy, where Delia is spending the summer after her release from the clinic in Küsnacht. The ensuing major chapters are then set in Athens at the time of Pericles (fifth century BCE), Rome at the time of Julius Caesar (first century BCE), and finally, in a reversal of World War II's D-day, Normandy on the eve of the 1066 Norman invasion of Britain, in which Dowding-Normandy will reunite the old Britain of Arthur and Rome with the lost land of Lyoness (in legend, Brittany-Normandy).

In the opening passages, H.D. plays onomatopoetically with nature's "language"—for example, the sonorous effect of the zzzzs of bees (resignifying vibrationally the disembodied Z of the séances, as well as resounding her biographical and narrative zig-zag "traces of direction"). She observes in a later chapter that the narrative creates a kind of "spiritual map" of "various layers of experience, different lives, if you will or manifestations of the same life" (*S*, 215). Like "Wintersleep," these chapters include here and there the stories of children, but whereas the children in "Wintersleep" were uniformly exposed and vulnerable, the children in "Summerdream" have reached a turning point: there are memories of lost children, but there are also child-survivors. H.D. called the chapters of "Summerdream" märchen, hoping to create a place of resounding revision of dominant cultural narratives of war. The Z-map, she remarks, "is very easy to understand . . . if you like fairy-tales or Märchen." But, she continues, "If you do not like fairy-tales, it is not easy to understand. Once upon a time . . . " (*S*, 214).

From there we move into the psychic landscape of the "glittering plain," the land of "living men" beyond death to which William Morris' hero, Hallblithe, journeys to find his lost lover. H.D. revises the dynamic of *The Glittering Plain*, for her female characters are not the quest's object, but are themselves seeking a return to self, a self-reclamation.[73] With each character, H.D. represents the restoration of the lost strength of the feminine in order to balance the world skewed by the dominance of a warrior ethos. As the first, unnamed female character, "the painted-lady," puts it, "it was still dark outside, but the sun was rising in my heart" (*S*, 170). This symbolic healing crosses the boundaries of time, space, and individual ego in order to signify universally, and in some sense, eternally.

In the several chapters that focus on ancient Greece, H.D. uses the female figure to move imaginatively between two major historic periods, Athens between 432 and 429 BCE and Crete at about 1400 BCE, with fleeting allusions to the Persian wars of 490 to 479 BCE and the Trojan War of about 1200 BCE—all times of great cultural shifts and conflict in ancient Greece. The narrative H.D. creates out of these stories interweaves the lives of the heroic male leader (Howell-Pericles-Theseus) and his consort (Delia-the "painted-lady"-Ariadne), a wisewoman, who has been in each case abandoned by the hero. She has been ill, and is at last healed with the help of a friend, Pheidias, nicknamed the "Bear" in H.D.'s version, the great sculptor of Athens.[74] The lovers zig-zag imaginatively across ancient, historical eras. Such narrative charts suggest the importance of bringing the two characters together again and again to aid a civilization through crises and threats (both from man and nature) to its very survival. The female character's designation as the painted-lady not only indicates her sacred consort status (as suggested by the fact that she lives in a "golden house"), but also constitutes a complex illustration of the dense, associational wordplay and intricate symbolism in this novel as a whole. The painted-lady is at once the butterfly of that name (in French, *La Belle Dame*), Psyche (the awakened Soul of *Trilogy*), and a symbol of restorative, classic values (Beauty and Truth).

The Greek scenes between the painted-lady, Pericles' abandoned consort, and her friend, Pheidias, take place as Athens is devastated by war and plague. The time is late in Pericles' reign (circa 432 BCE), at the beginning of the first Peloponnesian War, when the Delian League was dissolving. Athens, which had been dominant, was being attacked by "vandals" (historically, the rebellious Spartans). The Attican peninsular population surrounding Athens took shelter behind the walls of the fortified city. The historical Pericles had reasoned that Athens' inferior army could never win by land, but if he forced the Spartan army to fight at sea, where Athens dominated, he would be able to defeat them. The plan was feasible, but it neglected what would happen were a plague (probably cholera) to break out in the crowded city.

As this section opens in H.D.'s novel, Pheidias and the painted-lady contemplate the city in near-ruin, beleaguered, its social structures having been devastated by the plague or the siege (or both). She regards the wooden figurines from an ancient temple site that Pheidias has uncovered while building the Parthenon—figures of shells, dolphins, sea horses, brightly painted octopuses—symbols from the earlier goddess culture of Crete (Minoan), a sensual, less warrior-dominated culture that the Greeks had conquered long ago. Pheidias has asked her to burn these icons. She goes into a trance, a "delirium," staring into the flame like a "witch-woman, or like the drugged Pythia" (*S*, 167). As she laments, in a passage that will be reconfigured in *Helen in Egypt*,

We have sacrificed Beauty - and to what? You will tell me to the spear-shaft of the goddess. You will tell me that the past will live after us, or this present. But these inviolate images belonged to the Eternal. (*S*, 169)

She does not wish to burn any more of them. Her sensibility of inviolate and timeless values is opposed to Pheidias' time-bound pragmatism. He cautions that unless they keep the fire going, which signals to those fighting at sea that Athens' walls have held, "they will think the enemy has scaled the walls, has retaken the Acropolis" (*S*, 169). She counters, must there always be desecration? But in the end, she burns the remaining icons.

The painted-lady realizes during an illness' delirium following the burning of the ancient figurines that she and Pheidias share past-life memories of Minoan Crete. H.D. links Athens to Crete by describing a procession of young girls, a ceremony important to both Athenian and Minoan cultures. The procession underscores one of H.D.'s Freudian emphases in *Sword*—that humanity finds its best hope for cultural recovery in marrying the ideals of art to the individual's psychic health. This intersection can be facilitated by embodied participation in artistic ritual: the ancient, ceremonial processions that H.D. portrays in this section, as well as the Elizabethan and Venetian court plays in an earlier chapter, and in H.D.'s own lifetime, the Academy of Music's performance of a Greek tragedy around the festivities of graduation.[75] Her delirium is a visionary memory of another, older way of life in which masculine and feminine elements were balanced, and the sacred feminine, of which the figurines were symbols, was still honored (whereas Athena was honored as a goddess of war as well as wisdom).

That vision or cultural memory is preserved in art, which offers us access to this knowledge through time. Thus, as the now time-traveling narrator recalls, the Cretan goddess' dress is "like" Primavera's dress in Botticelli's painting some three thousand years later: implicitly, not only Mary but also the ancient Mother goddess (*S*, 171). The painted-lady travels back in memory, via an allusion to Achilles, suggesting that it was he who actually had sacked Knossos, using "a new war-weapon and a new technique, and attacked a defenceless people without warning" (*S*, 171). Later, to cover their ruthlessness, the Greeks said that it was Troy he sacked. But in remembering Knossos, the narrator recalls Greece's originating ties to Crete: "Athens like Troy, Mycenae and Delphi was a Cretan colony" (*S*, 173). Through her vision, now of Athens, now of a past-life memory of Crete, the painted-lady links fifth century BCE "masculine" Athens with its originary ties to "feminine" Minoan culture a thousand years earlier, in order to restore a balance that had been lost.

Like the Athenians during the Peloponnesian War of the fifth century BCE, the fifteenth century BCE Minoans were a civilization caught in a time of transition. The warlike, seafaring Mycenaeans (Greeks) began to overrun the Minoans just as a series of earthquakes and volcanoes destroyed its great temples and artistic artifacts around 1400 BCE. The unnamed characters in the Minoan passages bear a resemblance to the historical and mythical figures, Theseus and Ariadne. In all versions of the myth, Ariadne helps the Athenian Theseus to save other Athenians from the Minotaur by giving Theseus a ball of yarn from her weaving and the plans to the labyrinth. She then escapes with him (or is kidnapped) and sails away from Crete. In most of the different versions of the myth she eventually has several sons by him; in H.D.'s version, she has five (the RAF pilots), who grow up to become seafarers and warriors like their father.[76]

The Theseus-figure (called simply "I-command") parallels Pericles, and the Ariadne-figure, who gives Theseus the key to the secret way of her people in and out of the labyrinth, parallels the later painted-lady. The central motif, too, remains consistent: a male hero and his consort have somehow separated and should reunite. As the narrator tells us,

> I don't know how many times he came back, nor how many times she came back. The point was, to get them both together at the turn of the tide - I mean, the turn-about or turn-over of one civilization or one era to another. He [Pheidias] was right when he said, it doesn't matter what you are or what you have been. All that mattered, was to get them both together. (*S*, 174)

As this passage indicates, the narrative comprises a tale of two soul mates, poised to reunite as one civilization turns over into another, a rite of passage that will complete their souls' journeys. But, as in the fantasized reality that H.D. is working through via narrative, they find only to lose each other. Thus, for the H.D.-surrogate, there is no other way to complete the journey except imaginatively, through the "old words," through story and song (*S*, 180).

In some versions of the inherited myth, Ariadne dies, perhaps symbolizing the death of the more artistic and sensuous Minoan culture and the rise of the more militaristic Mycenaean one. In H.D.'s revisionary telling, the Minoan culture had at the time of its destruction expanded its influence throughout the Aegean, but it was specifically through its wisdom rites, the Minoan outposts including the oracles at Delphi. Although the later Greeks expanded their influence by military and political means, the heritage of Crete was still accessible to fifth century BCE Athenians through their drama, the High Festival of the Sacred College at Delphi, which contained vestiges of the older rites of the "serpent" goddess (just as the Acropolis in H.D.'s version housed and preserved icons of that same goddess, forgotten, but still potent).

H.D.'s border-crossing, liminal Ariadne-figure is one version of the reincarnated female characters whose lives parallel each other throughout *Sword*: a wisewoman abandoned by the military leader she loves and aids, the psychic wound from which she at last heals. In the last chapters of the Greek section ("The Road to Daphne," "And Five Others," and "Athens"), the painted-lady's past-life memories of Crete overlay the Ariadne-figure's journey with Theseus to Athens. She remembers participating as a girl in the Eleusian Mysteries of the Labyrinth on Mt. Ida in Crete, memories that Pheidias (as Scrag, the Master of Ceremonies at the Sacred College at Delphi) shares. She remembers the "fire-balls" that helped to destroy Crete on the day she met and saved Theseus by betraying her own people, forfeiting her place among them by showing the stranger the key to the labyrinth. Her past-life memories intertwine with those of the younger fifth century BCE Ariadne-double, who is preparing for the High Festival in Athens. This character's name is Day-Star, a "temple-child" trained in the dramatic arts of the Sacred College. Recovering on Pheidias' estate at Daphne from illness, the painted-lady interweaves in her fevered dreams the imaginary doubling of Day-Star and Ariadne, whose parallel lives touch in the pleated folds of time and place (Athens-Crete).

Upon her return to Athens, Day-Star finds that she has no speaking role, or has "a speaking part at last, but it was in the wrong play" (*S*, 197). When she finally accedes to a speaking role in the right play, she discovers that not only must she leave the "golden house," but also Pericles' Athens (London) altogether. The reason for Pericles' displeasure with her is not her failure to play her part well. Indeed, the prophetic "Voice" had spoken through her authentically, but like Cassandra, she was not believed, perhaps because she is "only" Day-Star. Her name nevertheless functions as an indicator of her power, for "day-star," of course, is the *sun*. The narrative pleats in the Greek section are dense: the character of the painted-lady moving from the Golden Palace of Crete to the "golden house" of Athens to the Ca d'oro of Venice (where on her honeymoon with Geoffrey, Delia remembers seeing the painted-lady's portrait). Then she moves to Queen Elizabeth's Golden Age London with Elizabethan court players (where Scrag-Pheidias is again the stage manager). In this way, we might say, she moves out of history into art, which is to say, out of time into the timeless.

The character's next major märchen is set in Rome in 44 BCE, on the eve of Caesar's assassination. Like the Greek chapters, the Rome section takes place in a time of critical transition. On the eve of the Ides of March by the old calendar (although by the new calendar that Caesar had decreed, they are past), his former consort, Stella, has summoned him. Like the painted-lady in Athens, Stella is a wisewoman. She asks Caesar to stay at her villa for three days (incidentally, until the Ides by the old calendar are past). But Caesar, a military leader parallel to both Pericles and Theseus, ignores Stella and returns to Rome and his fate.

He and Stella had fallen out long ago, apparently because of the fate of her sons. Ver and Verus (who may have been her sons by Caesar, although they know him only as Uncle Julius)[77] followed him to the wars in his various campaigns, where they died. Stella has been ill all the last winter and is still weak, though recovering. Their reunion is promising, but despite her pleas, Caesar leaves for Rome when she falls into a deep sleep after their meal. But he sends her a message the next day that he has tired of politics and will secretly leave for "*ultimus Brittanus.*" There he plans first to build a wall across the north, to protect Britain from the "Nordics," then to send for her and together create an Avalon-like "garden."

The chapter closes on a hopeful (if ambiguous) note. Over the three months that Caesar has been gone, Stella is happier than she has been in a long time—too isolated perhaps from news of events in the capital to have heard of Caesar's death, or possibly, as she claims, she knows a greater truth. Three months after Caesar's departure (that is, nearing the summer solstice honored in Druidic Britain), she is envisioning the fruitfulness of a green Britain, while at the same time planting her own lush garden of heliotropes (literally, sun-turners). She understands "everything," having (like the honeybee queen) "stored up enough happiness to live on for the rest of my life - to live on and perhaps, to help others to live on" (*S*, 241). Stella seems here to be turning from her own illness to a restored vision of plenitude and peace, to which the vision of Caesar's actual or symbolic journey to King Arthur's blessed isle has opened her.

The Normandy chapters, the final portion of the book, attempt to pull together the threads in "one palimpsestic overlay all the Prince Lointain stories with the composite" figure of the Duke of Normandy.[78] These chapters take their setting from William Morris' "Golden Wings" (from which all the names are also taken), set in Ladies' Gard, the castle that did not know war. The setting is a Normandy that recasts and reverses the conquest of Britain by Guillaume Duke of Normandy in September 1066 by signifying a composite of the Battle of Britain (September 1940) and D-day (June 1944), both of which "saved civilization." Images of invasion, defense, and siege permeate *Sword*, constellating a civilian-survivor's contemplation of why war happens. Because this final narrative is also a composite of the Norman invasion of Britain and Pre-Raphaelite/Arthurian legend, however, H.D. brings into the configurative history of the creation and defense of nation-states in Europe the frame-symbolism of the Round Table (the mystical Knights Templar), the Grail (the Church of Love [*S*, 91–92, 242–67]), and a visionary Avalon-Britain (a restoration of the Isles of the Blest).[79]

The H.D. figure is the still-beautiful, widowed aristocrat, Rose Beauvais, and like Ariadne-Stella before her and Helen in Egypt after her, Rose is a wisewoman, "a witch" (*S*, 266), and as such, an unwelcome guest of the Duke of Normandy. Like Ariadne and Stella, Rose has been ill, and like them, is recovering her strength in order to protect the female domain of Ladies' Gard if war comes. She tells her story to her younger double, Blanchfleur, who has been promised to the young cousin of the Duke of Normandy, Geffray. Rose warns Blanchfleur that such marital alliances between territories result in unforeseen claims, and the justification to go to war, much as her marriage to a cousin of the Duke of Brittany had resulted in a war for territory that claimed her husband's life. She counsels Blanchfleur to believe that "a woman may have, may one day have a complete life of her own" (*S*, 250).

Rose had believed that the Duke of Normandy was, like her, secretly a part of the "religion" encoded in "the Story of the Round Table" (to abbreviate a complex theology, the Church of Love), in part because the Duke carries with him two eagles, Fleet and Goldwings, which connect him to the ancient military mystery sects. H.D. associates eagles in this section with "the few" who helped to save Britain, thus signifying not only the military "wings" of the RAF, but also the older imperial Roman mysteries of Mithra, a Sun god.[80] Rose thought that she had received a sign from the Duke, but as she tells Blanchfleur, "when the trial came or when I thought the trial was over and that he was one of us, he turned and flared out at me" (*S*, 256). After having been rejected by Normandy, she falls ill, and is healed by the ministrations of the Duke of Brittany.[81] As she recovers, however, Rose realizes that Normandy had to test her so that all her "weakness [was] uncovered," for it was imperative that she be strong enough to help when "*Ladies' Gard must meet the war*" (*S*, 257). As Normandy readies to set sail, the signs and portents of change (recurring images throughout "Summerdream" of bee-swarms and star-clouds) coalesce when Normandy hears the bells of the lost land of Lyoness, portending "a new manifestation or a new circle of life" (*S*, 262). This new circle will synthesize "the dream," which is also, in the theatrical metaphor to which H.D. has returned throughout *Sword*, "the play": that is, the eternal mystery play.

The novel ends with a brief chapter entitled *Goldwings*, alluding both to "the few" (the RAF boys) and the poem by William Morris, "Golden Wings," about a land that knew "[l]ittle war," which in the end must go to war. Interestingly, in the letter to Norman Holmes Pearson dated August 14, 1948, that includes the "key" to *Sword* (on which we have based the expanded key that follows below), H.D. appends to the list a note in caps, "THE FEW GOLDWINGS." Although it is difficult to tell how exactly she intends her characterization to be understood, we observe that these "goldwings" are not simply her spiritualist home-circle, but also her intimate, social circle through the years.[82]

Sword's closing thus makes clear the parallels between play, myth, or legend and how an individual life's zig-zag "traces of direction" connect past life with present life, historical time with eternal time. "We went on with the play," H.D. writes. "We followed it to Elizabethan England and we went back to London." H.D. concludes "Summerdream" by pulling in one of the folds or pleats from "Wintersleep," returning not simply to England but to an earlier, artistic (and specifically female-dominated) ideal of culture and civilization that Dowding along with "'the few,'" whose names are inscribed in vellum at Westminster Abbey, had helped to preserve.

NOTES

1. From William Morris, *The Defence of Guenevere, and Other Poems.* The poem is about war, "the sword" that goes to sea a metonym for a "knight," and betrayal in love, one of the knights returning not to the beloved he had left behind but with a new love. Thus the poem neatly encapsulates the overarching plot structure of H.D.'s *Sword*, as well as *Sword*'s roots in Pre-Raphaelite balladic retelling of folklore.

2. Susan Edmunds, *Out of Line: Psychoanalysis and Montage in H.D. Long Poems,* 70.

3. See Alex Owen, *The Place of Enchantment: British Occultism and the Culture of the Modern,* 90–91. Ann Braude makes a similar point about the earlier spiritualist rage in the United States, in *Radical Spirits: Spiritualism and Women's Rights in Nineteenth-Century America* (Boston, Mass.: Beacon Press, 1989).

4. On the "feminization" of male modernism, see Cassandra Laity, *H.D. and the Victorian Fin de Siècle: Gender, Modernism, Decadence.* For an analysis of how postcolonial feminism remaps modernism, see Susan Stanford Friedman, *Mappings: Feminism and the Cultural Geographies of Encounter.* On H.D. and nationalism, see Annette Debo, "America in H.D.'s Palimpsest: Place, Race, and Gender in Her Early Poetry and Prose" (Ph.D. diss., University of Maryland, 1998).

5. See Jane Augustine, "Preliminary Comments on the Meaning of H.D.'s *The Sword Went Out to Sea,*" 130. For a discussion of theosophy and early abstract works, including Kandinsky's *Concerning the Spiritual in Art* (1911) and surrealism, see Owen, *The Place of Enchantment,* 230–31.

6. Owen, 221.

7. Letter dated October 19, 1948, H.D. to her friend and literary executor, Norman Holmes Pearson. This letter is summarized and quoted in Donna Hollenberg, *Between History and Poetry: The Letters of H.D. and Norman Holmes Pearson,* 81.

8. England's victory in the Battle of Britain, when Lord Dowding was Chief Air Marshal, was due in part to Dowding's innovative introduction of the wireless in planes, to communicate between the air and the ground, whereby a pilot could transmit mile by mile via stations set up along the coast for "air to ground radio-telephony." For a discussion of this strategic innovation, see Basil Collier, *Leader of the Few: The Authorised Biography of Air Chief Marshal, the Lord Dowding of Bentley Priory,* 101–2. See also John Ray, *The Battle of Britain: New Perspectives Behind the Scenes of the Great Air War.* H.D.

refers in *Sword*, in highly encoded passages, to such radio-like stations. See also Barbara Guest, *Herself Defined: The Poet H.D. and Her World,* 260–61; and Jane Augustine's forthcoming biographical account of H.D.'s relationship with Lord Dowding, *The Poet and the Airman* (University Press of Florida).

9. There is a rich exchange between H.D. and Richard Aldington, most intensively in 1947–48 as H.D. was revising *Sword.* She sent the manuscript to him on June 6, 1947. By June 10, 1947, he was writing a note to say that it was "a remarkable piece of work." His response the next day and throughout their correspondence while she completed and revised the novel was more mixed, but Aldington tried with constructive concern to give H.D. practical advice to make the work commercially viable. See Caroline Zilboorg, *Richard Aldington and H.D.: The Later Years in Letters,* 90–110 passim. Zilboorg's edition of some of the most important letters in their exchanges over that year, her astute insights into H.D.'s process of composition, and her summaries of some of their other exchanges are extremely useful to an understanding of how *Sword* came into being. And as Hollenberg remarks, H.D. "was very grateful to [Aldington] for his receptive reading of that manuscript" (102).

10. Although Guest characterizes H.D.'s belief in *Sword* "a delusion" (285), and Friedman herself ultimately considers it "unsuccessful" (*Penelope's Web,* 357), in the earlier monograph, she usefully places *Sword* in the context of H.D.'s serious and engaged spiritualist quest for "initiation" and "wisdom." See *Psyche Reborn: The Emergence of H.D.,* 186–87, 199–200.

11. See Laity, 117–18, 157; and Eileen Gregory, *H.D. and Hellenism: Classic Lines,* whose chapter on H.D. and Walter Pater builds on Laity's thinking (75–107). In a vital sense, as both Gregory and Laity demonstrate, *Sword* is saturated with H.D.'s love for the Victorian fin-de-siècle poets of her youth.

12. See Rachel Connor, *H.D. and the Image,* 115.

13. Friedman, *Penelope's Web,* 72.

14. Augustine, "Preliminary Comments," 130–32.

15. H.D., *Tribute to Freud*; quoted and discussed in Friedman, *Psyche Reborn,* 21–22.

16. For an analysis that extends Friedman's thinking on H.D. and Freud, see the specific discussion of H.D.'s recovery of the reserves of language in the unconscious via poetry, in Diane Chisholm, *H.D.'s Freudian Poetics: Psychoanalysis in Translation,* 179, 177.

17. Friedman, *Psyche Reborn,* 188.

18. As Friedman notes, the RAF pilots whom H.D. channeled in her solo sessions had selected her to be their "Cassandra of atomic doom, but neither Dowding nor the materialist world was willing to hear her message of future wars" (Ibid., 187).

19. Zilboorg, 92.

20. See, for example, Rachel Blau DuPlessis, *H.D.: The Career of That Struggle* (Brighton, Eng.: Harvester, 1986); and Friedman and DuPlessis, editors, *Signets: Reading H.D.*

21. See Adalaide Morris, *How to Live/What to Do: H.D.'s Cultural Poetics*, 2; Morris' emphasis.

22. We extend a point made by Augustine, that now that the full-length edition of *The Gift* has been published, *Trilogy* can be understood as "intertextual." See Augustine's introduction to *The Gift by H.D.*, 2. Augustine is discussing a point that Friedman first made in *Penelope's Web*. Friedman comments that H.D. rejects in her fiction modernism's model of "impersonality," writing prose that is "personal and relational, . . . re-creating her own experience set within history, overriding genre boundaries, and conspicuously gendered," in the manner and method of Gertrude Stein, Virginia Woolf, and Dorothy Richardson (3).

23. For a discussion of this aspect of H.D.'s prose during the 1940s and 1950s, see Friedman, ibid., 26–28.

24. The prolific Victorian novelist and politician, Sir Edward Bulwer-Lytton, is best known today for his historical novel, *The Last Days of Pompeii* (1834), but he was also part of a group of mid-century occultists who influenced the development of British ritual magic later in the century. According to Owen, Bulwer-Lytton "was involved with Rosicrucian Freemasonry and in 1871 became Grand Patron of the Societas Rosicruciana in Anglia," a secret Masonic order whose membership "was involved in the formation of the Hermetic Order of the Golden Dawn," in which the other modernist poet who was "a serious student of the esoteric, W. B. Yeats, was an active member." See Owen, 44, 267n84, 267n89.

25. In addition to the London players' scenes in *Sword*, H.D. was revising her "Elizabethan" poems, "The Good Friend" series, and an essay-memoir, "The Guest," begun after visiting Stratford on Shakespeare's birthday in 1945, which she published as *By Avon River* (1949).

26. In the correspondence with Lord Dowding and in *Majic Ring*, H.D. is clearly debating reincarnation: "You are interested but past-lives are not important, the personality has left them behind. They are old coats and the links with the past are . . . chains binding one to the darkness of earth condition" (*MR*, 16). H.D. Papers, YCAL/Beinecke.

27. Automatic writing was commonly used in spiritualism, termed also "spirit writing," a means of accessing spirits beyond the visible plane of existence. On the interest in the occult that H.D. shared with Yeats, albeit distantly, see Helen Sword, *Ghostwriting Modernism*: "H.D., like Yeats, was a credulous, committed spiritualist whose experiences with mediumistic communication colored her modernist poetics and whose modernist aesthetics likewise influenced her spiritualism" (118). See also Timothy Materer, *Modernist Alchemy: Poetry and the Occult* (Ithaca, N.Y.: Cornell University Press, 1995).

28. Hollenberg, 102.

29. References to writing *By Avon River* occur in H.D.'s letters to Bryher dated October 12 and 27, and November 2, 1946 (Bryher Papers, YGC/Beinecke). References to "Writing on the Wall" occur in H.D.'s letter to her cousin, Francis Wolle, a professor at

the University of Colorado, June 22, 1946 (originals owned by the University of Colorado Chinook Library Special Collections; photocopies available in the H.D. Papers, YCAL/Beinecke).

30. H.D. is putting her text subtly into dialogue with Ezra Pound. In 1948, a year in which she worked hard on *Sword*'s revision, H.D. read *The Pisan Cantos*, which Pound had sent to her from Saint Elizabeth's Hospital, where he was incarcerated in lieu of being tried for treason (which could have resulted in execution). With its direct textual allusions to François Villon's *Le Testament*, Pound wrote *The Pisan Cantos* in anticipation of his possible death (see especially Canto 74.178). See Pound, *The Pisan Cantos,* edited with introduction and annotations by Richard Sieburth (New York: New Directions, 2003), xxiv. H.D. suggests here that *Sword* is her own "testament," an account documenting the war through the eyes of an aging woman and civilian-survivor.

31. Two postwar sources, a memoir, *Compassionate Friendship* (1955), and a roman à clef, *Magic Mirror* (1956) also suggest that there were notebooks of draft writing and séance notes, possibly containing raw material she drew on for *Sword*. In *Magic Mirror*, H.D. writes of her discomfort with "these note-books, about seven" of them, which she had asked "Garry" (Gareth-Bryher) to destroy, but which Garry had returned to her, full of "not exactly automatic-writing." In *Compassionate Friendship* she recalls that after finishing *By Avon River* (thus, sometime during the spring of 1947), she "destroyed a mass of preliminary notes and plunged anew into The Sword." Both works are unpublished, held in the H.D. Papers, YCAL/Beinecke.

32. Folder marked: "Source materials: notes on séances, 1924–45," H.D. Papers, YCAL/Beinecke.

33. In an e-mail note to the editors written on May 18, 2005, Augustine confirms that the letters are "actual"—that she has been able to match Lord Dowding's extant replies to H.D.'s fictionalized letters in *Majic Ring* (there are to date no extant originals). Augustine's documentation will be included in *The Poet and the Airman*.

34. "Worm-y" writing could be shorthand for prose at the gestational stage, but it might also refer to transformational work, of the sort that characterizes *Trilogy*, and that H.D. will be doing for the rest of her life. The originals of her letters to Aldington are held at Southern Illinois University Morris Library in the Richard Aldington Papers (photocopies available in the H.D. Papers, YCAL/Beinecke).

35. See Zilboorg, 89–93, for H.D.'s letters to Aldington dated May 25, and June 1 and 6, 1947. Zilboorg does not reproduce H.D.'s letter to Aldington dated May 20; she quotes the salient section of the letter dated June 22, 1947 (98). H.D.'s letters to Aldington throughout the year in which she wrote and revised the novel offer fascinating insight into her complex conceptualization of *Sword*. See Zilboorg, 102–10 passim.

36. Richard Aldington Papers (photocopy in the H.D. Papers, YCAL/Beinecke).

37. See H.D.'s letters to Aldington in the fall of 1947, especially September 3, 1947, and October 10, 1947 (which contains *Sword*'s original table of contents), in Zilboorg, 102–10. It is clear from this earliest table of contents, in which all the current chapters are represented (with the exception that the chapter entitled "Ariadne" is by the third

draft entitled "Belle Dame"), that H.D. arrived at the novel's present form quite early in its drafting process—at least, as far as we can tell in relation to the extant copies.

38. See Hollenberg, 79; and H.D. to Norman Holmes Pearson, uncatalogued correspondence, Za Pearson Archives, YCAL/Beinecke.

39. Lord Dowding's letters to H.D. from 1949 to 1951 follow a fascinating trajectory, from gracious disinterest to strenuous protest. In a letter dated July 31, 1949, he writes, "You are correct in supposing that I should strongly deprecate the publication of this book as it stands." Two years later, when she sends the latest version, he writes in a letter dated May 21, 1951, "Of course I haven't the slightest *right* to object to your publishing the Sword in England or anywhere else, and if you would alter Lord Howell into Sir Somebody Something or the Duke of Sark . . . , I shouldn't mind its publication in the least" (H.D. Papers, YCAL/ Beinecke).

40. See Hollenberg, 104, 79.

41. Za Pearson, uncatalogued correspondence, YCAL/Beinecke.

42. Hollenberg, 95.

43. *The Sword Went Out to Sea: Synthesis of a Dream*, H.D. Papers, YCAL/Beinecke. The second and third drafts at the Beinecke are not markedly different and most likely comprise the penultimate and final drafts that H.D. sent to Pearson during that time, in hopes of his finding a publisher. As she writes him on August 16, 1949, "I have the copy III [of *Sword*] and D[owding] has the carbon of it. I will carefully indicated [*sic*] in II, what corrections I want made, so that you can either have it typed, or else later, when/if D. wants any drastic alternations [*sic*] we can have fresh and final copy made. I do not want to change anything" (Za Pearson, uncatalogued correspondence, YCAL/Beinecke).

44. Friedman, *Psyche Reborn*, 207.

45. In *Majic Ring*, H.D. describes the channeled sessions around the Morris table as her group having "set up a little private wireless station" (11), for example (H.D. Papers, YCAL/Beinecke). For a discussion that relates the esotericism in *Notes on Thought and Vision* to *Trilogy*, see Leonora Woodman, "H.D. and the Poetics of Initiation," 139–41. See also Friedman, *Psyche Reborn,* 157–296 passim. For a study that explores modernism's debt to occultism, see Leon Surette, *The Birth of Modernism: Ezra Pound, T. S. Eliot, W. B. Yeats, and the Occult* (Montreal: McGill-Queen's University Press, 1993).

46. Hirslanden notebook, 3: 4–5 (H.D. Papers, YCAL/Beinecke).

47. H.D. to Viola Baxter Jordan, July 28, 1942 (Viola Baxter Jordan Papers, YCAL/Beinecke).

48. Up to the start of World War II, Bryher had stayed in Switzerland, helping Jewish refugees to leave Europe (Freud was a notable success; Walter Benjamin a tragic failure to reach in time). During the war she worked for the British government, where she met Norman Holmes Pearson, who was at the time a liaison with British intelligence for the Office of Strategic Services (OSS) in London (code name "Puritan"). For a fascinating discussion of Pearson's work, which includes his relationship to a number of modernist poets, see Robin W. Winks, *Cloak and Gown: Scholars in The Secret War, 1939-1961,*

247–321. H.D. refers in *Sword* in highly encoded versions to the charade that she was not to know of Bryher's, her daughter Perdita's, or Pearson's confidential war work. As early as January 3, 1940, however, H.D. knew that Bryher was being approached to do intelligence work, writing quite breezily to her in Switzerland that a friend of André Gide's inquired, months before the fall of France, whether Bryher might "Do some hush-hush work (unpaid) for the frogs. I didn't know whether you would jump at it or not, anyhow, I simply gave the information. It might be funny but there may be a catch, and I know how particular you are about your comings and goings to England. However—it sounds very funny" (Bryher Papers, YGC/Beinecke). We thank Annette Debo for alerting us to this letter.

49. See Friedman, *Psyche Reborn*, 172–74. We thank Jane Augustine, who notes in an e-mail to the editors dated May 18, 2005, that the SPR and Stanford House are not one and the same, sending us back to the Hirslanden Notebooks to confirm that fact. The society that H.D. joined was the International Institute for Psychic Investigation on Walton Street near Lowndes Square, according to Augustine (e-mail to the editors dated May 27, 2005).

50. Laity suggests that it was a novel by Violet Hunt, *The Wife of Rossetti, Her Life and Death* (New York: E.P. Dutton, 1932), "which very probably first alerted H.D. to the feminist possibilities of the grotesque femme fatale" of the fin-de-siècle Victorians (161).

51. Augustine, "Preliminary Comments," 123.

52. See Owen, who recounts members of the intellectual elite on both sides of the Atlantic and all over Europe were numbered among the society's members. For example, William James was the society's president from 1893 to 1894, and other members included Charles Dodgson (Lewis Carroll), Alfred Lord Tennyson, philosopher Henri Bergson, and as a corresponding member by 1911, Sigmund Freud (21–22, 33–35, 17–50 passim, and 284n15).

53. See Tryphonopoulos' introduction to *Literary Modernism and the Occult Tradition*.

54. See Augustine, "Preliminary Comments," 122, 130–31.

55. See Guest, 260–66 passim, who writes briefly of H.D.'s relationship with Lord Dowding and H.D.'s "table-tipping"; and Augustine, "Preliminary Comments," esp. 125–26.

56. Why Dowding retired following the Battle of Britain, whether it had to do with personal loss or his "conversion" to spiritualism, has been the subject of some debate. Zilboorg remarks that it was Dowding's spiritualism that caused his superiors to force his retirement (93). Guest notes that Dowding lost his pilot son in "combat" (260), the source of which is H.D.'s own letter to Pearson on August 14, 1948 (see Hollenberg, 80). Hollenberg cites a corrective, an article by D. Bruce Ogilvie, a former RAF pilot, who wrote that Dowding's son was not killed in World War II, but estranged (113n50). In an e-mail to Hogue dated June 5, 2005, Augustine writes a corrective based on her ongo-

ing research for *The Poet and the Airman*: "Dowding did not lose a son in WW2 (his brother did). . . . [and] Dowding's spiritualism did not cause him to lose his command in fall 1940" (it was a power struggle that he lost).

57. In a letter dated January 3, 1946, Dowding wrote H.D.: "I have read them [her séance notes] all through twice very carefully, but I am afraid I can't make very much out of them. You see, we are in touch with Z in our own circle, and so it is only natural that we should devote our principal attention to what he tells us there" (H.D. Papers, YCAL/Beinecke). H.D. would, of course, already have known this from his published accounts.

58. For a discussion of H.D.'s thinking about the symbols emerging from the channeled sessions in her home-circle in 1943, see Helen Sword, "H.D.'s *Majic Ring*," 359. Additionally, in *Majic Ring*, H.D.-Delia looks at a hieroglyph dictionary—E. A. Wallis Budge, *A Hieroglyph Vocabulary to the Theban Recension of the Book of the Dead*, vol. 31, 2nd. ed. (London: Kegan Paul, Trench, Trübner, 1911)—and notes that the hieroglyph for the sky-god, *Nu*, is the "same symbol as the Astrological and Astronomical sign Aquarius," which she associates with the Viking ship "sailing into [the Age of] Aquarius, the House of Friends, out of the House of Enemies" (37). The copy of the Budge at the Beinecke is H.D.'s own (H.D. Papers, YCAL/Beinecke).

59. In a letter to Lord Dowding dated June 2, 1945, the only extant letter of H.D.'s to Dowding in the H.D. Papers, H.D. discusses the "Viking motif" from her séance notes, giving us clear insight into how she constructs characters as composites in *Sword* as well as other works. Remarking that Dowding both is and is not the Viking in Bhaduri's visions, she comments that what she finds important is the "wider application," in Freud's sense of the relationship of the individual psyche to the collective. The first stage of artistic, integrative work, H.D. writes, is "to remember our own personal past," and then to open up "a very, very wide field . . . built up on the dream content or the subconscious material. . . . [M]y own father or my half-brother Eric, also an astronomer, might have 'projected' something of the Viking material, though I did not . . . connect them with the sequence." Then she notes that she associates Dowding with the Viking: "The sea - the sky. You - the sky!" But she adds, "Each man in his life plays many parts if I have got the tag correctly," suggesting that Dowding will come to figure in multiple manifestations in *Sword*, as in his own life (H.D. Papers, YCAL/Beinecke).

60. William Morris, *The Story of the Glittering Plain which has been also called the Land of the Living Men or the Acre of the Undying* (Hammersmith, Eng.: Kelmscott Press, 1894). Aldington supplied the Pre-Raphaelite sources for "Wintersleep," reminding H.D. that her image of wings came from William Morris' poem, "Golden Wings," and that Hallblithe was the hero of Morris' *The Glittering Plain*. See Zilboorg, 93.

61. As she wrote Pearson on June 17, 1951, "Yes - the *Sword* is important. But simply again, as a record and a record I could not have done, if I had not persisted, even at Küsnacht, on REMEMBERING. For me, it was so important, my own LEGEND. Yes, my own L E G E N D. Then, to get well and re-create it." See Hollenberg, 104–5.

62. Guest, 6.

63. Ibid., 92.

64. See Zilboorg's brief but useful discussion of H.D.'s modernist method, 108.

65. See Friedman, *Psyche Reborn*, 186–87.

66. For a discussion of "wingéd words," the same term used by H.D. in her acceptance speech written for the American Academy of Arts and Letters' Award of Merit in 1960, to refer to "the swift-flying, time-based, performative medium of orators, bards, rhapsodes, and other masters of the sounded word" (20), most obviously as used in *Sword*, spiritualists, see Adalaide Morris' chapter, entitled "Wingéd Words," in *How to Live*, 19–55.

67. In a letter dated February 24, 1946, Lord Dowding wrote to say that he did not intend "to join you in the reception of this sort of message," because he had his own circle, and didn't recognize the RAF pilots: "I don't know who Charles is, or Roland, or John, or anyone, but the whole tone is trivial and uninspiring." Then he advised her, quite kindly, "I know it is none of my business, but I hope you are not now communicating by yourself, and that you are availing yourself of the balancing presence of your friend Bryher. Solitary communication is liable to be very dangerous except upon the highest wave lengths" (H.D. Papers, YCAL/Beinecke).

68. Augustine, "Preliminary Comments," 130.

69. In his letter dated June 10, 1947, Aldington included a typed copy of "Golden Wings" that he had made for H.D., and as Zilboorg remarks, this poem is about "a woman [who] beckons her knight to come to her from 'across the sea' and vividly describes the autumn wildlife (a swan, a moorhen, a stoat, a bat, a wasp) and nature (the wind, wheat, grass, apples) in a foreboding atmosphere of moonlit romance" (93–94).

70. Though horrified by Pound's politics, H.D. was saddened by his fate and thought of him kindly in these years (see Guest, 290). Though honest, she softened her portrait of him in the third draft of *Sword*. To give a brief example, from the original line, "Poor Allen, the American traitor, read William Morris to me," H.D. has crossed out "the American traitor."

71. In the June 2, 1945, letter to Dowding, H.D. includes the following insight about her narrative technique in her prose pieces, including *Sword*, that the "weaving of threads from one pattern to another, from one state of being or perception to another, is in a sense my personal concern" (H.D. papers, YCAL/Beinecke).

72. Our thanks to Lara Vetter for discussions that informed this insight. See her "*Sparks and Scattered Light*": *The Discourse of Science, Religion, and Sexuality in Modern American Literature* (in progress).

73. Morris' *The Glittering Plain* tells the story of the Viking Hallblithe who went in search of his beloved, Hostage, who had been kidnapped by marauders. Hallblithe is tricked into traveling to a land of eternal youth, the land of Ransom, also called the Glittering Plain, where the king's daughter had fallen in love with an image of him in a book and summoned all her resources to bring him to her. Hallblithe rejects her advances and continues his search for Hostage, striving all the while to leave Ransom. Hallblithe and Hostage are reunited and able to return home. The theme of Morris' Dorian Gray-like

tale is that eternal youth, the glittering plain, is a trap that undermines life's greatest complexities and joys. H.D.'s use of Morris' tale as trope for her novel is thus revisionary, focusing on a woman's finding place and agency though the world's gone to hell.

74. "Bear" is the nickname for the character, Pheidias, who is a composite of Walter Schmideberg, the psychoanalyst and friend to whom H.D. and Bryher gave this nickname, and Richard Aldington. The historic Pheidias (circa 493–430 BCE) was the preeminent sculptor of fifth-century Greece. After Persia sacked Athens in 480 BCE, he was responsible for rebuilding the city. He supervised the reconstructions and created the sculptures of Athena in the Parthenon on the Acropolis, dedicated in 438 in a ceremony to which "Summerdream" loosely refers.

75. The Greek procession in the Athenian section perhaps alludes to the procession of virgins during the Greater Panathenaia, the celebration that occurred every fourth year on Athena's birthday. During the festivities, virgins would lead a parade of worshippers bringing sacrifices to Athena. The mention of Mount Ida, however, signals another procession, connected with the Minoan rituals depicted on the walls at Knossos. For a discussion of the various processions with which H.D. would have been familiar through study and travel, see Gregory, 240. For our revised discussion in this section and the following, we thank Eileen Gregory, whose expertise in classical Greek and Roman history and literature, and H.D.'s knowledge of both, helped us accurately to date the intricately layered composites in this narrative.

76. The fathers of the sons and the number of sons vary from version to version in the Ariadne myth. In some versions, Ariadne has two sons with Theseus. In other versions, she has them with Dionysus. In most versions, she is abandoned by Theseus, or dies in childbirth.

77. There were two "Veruses" important to the development of the Roman Empire prior to Caesar. One was the great Roman emperor, Marcus Aurelius Antoninus Augustus (Marcus Annius Verus upon marriage), who like Pericles, ruled over his empire at a time when it was attacked both by external forces and by a devastating plague. He co-ruled for eight years with his adopted brother, Lucius Verus. H.D. keeps the main action in the Roman section within the time frame of Caesar's reign, but she uses the sons' names to create palimpsestic links among the great transitional leaders in the Roman Empire: Julius Caesar, Marcus Aurelius "Verus," and his co-ruler, Lucius "Ver."

78. Augustine, e-mail correspondence to Hogue, January 22, 2005. For this section of our discussion, we are indebted to Jane Augustine, who helped us to unravel the narrative. As Augustine remarks, in addition to Lord Dowding, Aldington and Pound are a part of the heroic and healing composite figures throughout *Sword,* because H.D. "wants to show them co-existing together in an eternal Dream."

79. In addition to William Morris' Arthurian poems, H.D. was conversant with a number of literary and anthropological sources. Jessie L. Weston's *From Ritual to Romance* traces back the Arthurian legends to their Gallic-Celtic and Indo-European

origins. Denis de Rougemont's *Love in the Western World* traces the influence of the expunged Albigensians on the Moravians, which H.D. cites in a letter to Francis Wolle dated April 10, 1945 (Francis Wolle Papers, University of Colorado Chinook Library Special Collections). On the influence of anthropologist Jane Harrison on H.D., see Gregory, 108–28. Reading *Sword* with such contemporary sources of the meaning of encoded symbols, an early handbook of comparative myth—for example, Harold Bayley's *The Lost Language of Symbolism* (2 vols. 1912)—one finds the symbolic patterns sewn into H.D.'s prose as intricately as tapestry. To give a brief example, the root of "Avalon" (the RAF boys' code word) is Welsh for *summer*, "hav," and is related to words that readers of *Trilogy* will know: *haven* and *heaven* (with the implication of *rest* and *safety*). Interestingly, "haven" is the word Lord Dowding uses in a letter dated August 5, 1944, to H.D., who was summering in Cornwall, about damage from bombs in London: "I am glad you found a haven. There is no point in subjecting oneself to unnecessary nervous strain" (H.D. Papers, YCAL/Beinecke). We thank Susan Howe for her discussion of Avalon's symbolic significance, in conjunction with a reading of Bryher's *Visa for Avalon* (1965; rpt. Northampton, Mass.: Paris Press, 2003), held at the Beinecke Library, May 4, 2005; and personal communication to the editors, May 7, 2005.

80. Eagles figure in hermetic tradition, and in *Majic Ring* and *Sword* connect to the Church of Love through the Templars (*MR*, 18; H.D. Papers, YCAL/Beinecke). As G.R.S. Mead tells us in a book that H.D. knew well, "The highest degree of the Mithriaca [purified suppliant] was that of the Fathers or Eagles, sometimes also called the Hawks," and that through the blessing of Mithra, the suppliant declares himself in possession of "eagle-power" (164). See Mead, *Quests Old and New* (London: G. Bell and Sons, 1913). For the connection of the cult of Mithra to Arthurian legend, see Weston, *From Ritual to Romance*, 155–64.

81. According to Augustine, "Normandy is LD [Lord Dowding] the military leader and public figure who has to repudiate [Rose] to test her 'gifts' and make her stronger so that she can 'meet the war.' Brittany is LD the spiritual leader, the true lover; ultimately Brittany blends with the healing doctor." There is as well a complex doubled triangle— Rose and the Duke and Duchess of Brittany; and the two mythic Iseults (Blanchmain and Blanchfleur) and Tristran (*tristesse*)—"dream" versions of the H.D.-Aldington-Arabella triangle from World War I. The mythic significance of this personal triangle is crystallized in the Arthurian overlay, with its allusion to an idealized Britain (Britain-Brittany) that Dowding-Normandy will re-unite "with the help of 'the few'"—that is, the RAF "boys" (Augustine, e-mail correspondence to Hogue, January 22, 2005).

82. See Hollenberg, 79. We suggest that H.D. has in mind something like a circle of spiritual "guardians" of "Albion." For a speculative discussion of Albion's guardians and H.D. and Lord Dowding, see Ogilvie, "H.D. and Hugh Dowding."

Key to the Characters

Richard Aldington:
Writer, H.D.'s husband during World War I, and, in later years, her critic-friend. In *Sword*, he is a doubled figure like H.D. In "Wintersleep," he is Delia Alton's young husband, killed in the war, *Geoffrey Alton,* and the older journalist, *Randolph Spencer*. His surrogates in "Summerdream" are composites: in the main, the *Duke of Brittany*, who befriends and helps to heal Rose Beauvais; *Geffray*, Normandy's young cousin, who is engaged to Blanchfleur; and in the Sacred College (Delphi and Athens) and Elizabethan scenes, probably the stage manager, *Scrag* (a composite figure in which there are elements of Ezra Pound as well).

Arthur Bhaduri:
Spiritualist medium who led H.D.'s home-circle during World War II, whom she met at the International Institute for Psychic Investigation at Walton House (Stanford House in *Sword*). He is *Ben Manisi* in "Wintersleep." His mother, May Bhaduri, is *Ada Manisi*.

Bryher (Annie Winifred Ellerman):
Writer and publisher; H.D.'s lifelong intimate; adoptive mother of H.D.'s daughter, Perdita. She is *Gareth (Garry)*, in "Wintersleep," and a composite figure, probably the boy *Florian* in the Normandy sequence in "Summerdream." Because of Bryher's instrumental support of H.D. during and following her breakdown, it is possible that Bryher is part of the *Pheidias-Caesar-Britanny* composite as well.

H.D.:
Delia Alton, both the nom de plume that H.D. used in a number of her late-life works, and the character in the novel, *Delia Alton*, a spiritualist. Other paired author-surrogates are *Iseult Blanchfleur/Iseult Blanchmain*, *Ariadne* (the painted-

lady)/*Day-Star*, and *Rose Beauvais/Blanchfleur*. She is also the *Queen Elizabeth* figure paired with the actor *Stella* in the brief theatre scene set in Elizabethan London.

Lord Hugh Dowding:
Air Chief Marshal and commander of air battles over London during the Battle of Britain (1940). He is *Lord John Howell* in "Wintersleep" and the early parts of "Summerdream." In the later sections of "Summerdream," he appears as part of the composite figures of military leaders: *Pericles* (Athens), *Julius Caesar* (Rome), and *Guillaume Duke of Normandy*.

Sigmund Freud:
A composite figure (with esoteric anthropologist Leo Frobenius) named *Frederik von Alten*, a distinguished archeologist who lives (and dies) in *Dresden* (Vienna-London).

Norman Holmes Pearson:
OSS officer during World War II, and connected to the CIA after the war. A professor of English at Yale University. Pearson employed Perdita during World War II, and became a close friend of both Bryher and H.D., acting eventually as literary editor-agent of H.D.'s late-life work. Instrumental in augmenting the holdings of the Yale Collection of American Literature, a premier archive of American modernism. He is the character *Howard Wilton Dean*.

Ezra Pound:
Impresario of the Imagist and Vorticist movements, briefly engaged to H.D. in Philadelphia (H.D.'s first *héro fatal*), accused of treason for broadcasting Fascist propaganda to American troops after the fall of Italy. He is *Allen Flint*. He is also a composite (with Lord Dowding) of the Viking *Hal Brith*; and the "traitor" who loved Queen Elizabeth, *Robert Devereaux, Earl of Essex*.

Walter Schmideberg (nicknamed "Bear"):
Friend of both Bryher and H.D., H.D.'s psychoanalyst for a time. Was in London at the time of her breakdown and instrumental in helping Bryher to arrange for H.D.'s treatment in Switzerland. He is *Pheidias* (also nicknamed Bear).

Dorothy Yorke (Arabella):
Aldington's lover for whom he separated from H.D. She is *Miranda*.

ALPHABETICAL KEY TO THE MINOR CHARACTERS

Mrs. Ash: H.D.'s housekeeper. *Beata*; *Mrs. Moss*; *Nina.*

Mrs. Clark: Wife to drama director at University of Pennsylvania in 1906. *Mrs. Atherton.*

John Cournos: Companion of Dorothy Arabella Yorke. *Boris.*

Gilbert Doolittle: H.D.'s brother, killed in World War I. *Miles*; *Verus-Ver.*

Howard Doolittle: H.D.'s brother. *Robert.*

Dorothy Cole Henderson: Novelist and friend of H.D. *Madge Burton.*

Robert Herring: Friend of H.D. and Bryher, editor of *Life and Letters Today. Philip Manning.*

Violet Hunt: Friend of H.D., from whom she inherited the William Morris table. Daughter of Pre-Raphaelite artists, and author of *Wife of Rossetti. Dorothy Maitland.*

Viola Baxter Jordan: Friend of Pound's who remained in touch with him. *Susan.*

Peter Rodeck: One of H.D.'s *héros fatals.* She met him during a boat trip to Greece in 1920. *Peter van Eck.*

Walter Rummel: Musician friend whom H.D. met through Pound. *Arthur Lovatt.*

Dorothy Shakespear: Friend of H.D. Pound's wife. *Marjory Radcliffe.*

Margaret and Ethelwyn Snively: Childhood friends of H.D. *Bessie and Virginia Childs*; *Myra.*

J.J. Van der Leeuw: Analysand and theosophist whose appointment with Freud fell the hour before H.D.'s. appointment. He is a younger double of the *héro fatal*, Peter Rodeck. *Jan Verstigen.*

The Sword Went Out to Sea

⅍

(Synthesis of a Dream), by Delia Alton

H.D.

Wintersleep

For in that sleep of death, what dreams may come.

I

Viking Ship

I had no claim on him, whatever. None at all. He came to see me after we had been corresponding a year and a half. I had heard him lecture. He was taller than Gareth had led me to imagine. That is, he looked tall and gaunt when I saw him, but Gareth had been nearer at the Cathedral. When she came back, she said, "I saw Howell." I didn't say anything. I had shown her his letter. She pretended to be unimpressed. I had told him that I didn't expect him to answer my first letter. But he did answer. He need not have answered it. What he said was that he was very busy. Well, I knew that. "Then, why does he answer a second time?" I said to Gareth. I had the second letter in my hand. I went to my desk and got out the first. It was not the same letter. He said the same thing but he said it differently. But he could not have expected an answer to his first letter. I said, "Why does he do this, Gareth?"

It was then that she shrugged him off. "Well - if you *will* write to people like that - " But when she came back from the Cathedral, she qualified the shrug. "I saw your Lord Howell - he's not much taller than I am. He has the eyes of a fanatic. I don't think he's English."

"He looks English enough," I said.

She said, "His eyes aren't English. I think he must be Welsh."

I sent him three Christmas cards, so I must have known him for some time. I mean, we had been writing as I have said for a year and a half, at any rate. He came to see me early in February, 1945. That was after the second Christmas card. That is how it was. If I send him a card this Christmas, that will make four Christmas cards. But I only knew him for one Christmas card, the one I sent last. It was a scene in the snow, a barn with mountains. The first was an old card from America. I had kept it for some years. I cut off the margin and sent the picture, dark blue sky, dark blue sea and the prow of a sailing-ship, just moving into the left-hand corner. It was just the mast and the wooden beams and one star in the dark sky. It was an old card, but then, that was 1943 and it was London.

I am already wondering, shall I send him a card this Christmas? I forgot him for over six months. It didn't make any difference. Then, I remembered him. His last letter had or had not precipitated my illness. It wasn't only that he was Air Chief Marshall Lord Howell. He had made himself accessible by his lectures. He must have had hundreds of letters from women. What was one, more or less? It's true, most of these women must have had sons, must have lost sons. I had no son. Still, I had been in London. I had been there when he broke the Steel Wall, as Goering called the *Luftwaffe*. That meant, September fifteenth, 1940, civilization had been saved, as the press described it. Then he disappeared. When he came back they said, "Poor Howell, no wonder, after what he's been through." What happened was that Lord Howell appeared at public meetings. He wanted to tell people that their sons were not dead.

Lord Howell and myself belong to the last war. I don't know when he first began this "work," as we came to call it. I had always been afraid of getting involved in psychic-research work, so for better or worse, I had let the whole subject alone. However, before Christmas 1941, I thought I might safely embark. I enrolled as a member of Stanford House. I had heard that they had an excellent library and a research scholarship. Even so, I felt a little shy and self-conscious and asked Gareth's advice. She said, "By all means - they're eminently respectable." I thought her recommendation a little chilling but I found my way, all the same, to Stanford House. My first class or lecture was held by a young Eurasian.

. . . . .

The second card I sent Lord Howell was a ship, too. It was not what I wanted for him. It was a British Museum card from an illuminated manuscript *Roman de la Rose*. I thought it hardly suitable, but Christmas cards were hard to find that year; 1944, it must have been. I had hesitated between the ship and a white hawk, a Chinese painting, but I finally sent the ship. It was drawn up against flower-strewn grass, in what seemed to be a river. It bulked large in the picture and three kings stood beside it. I called them kings, one of them at any rate, wore a crown. Lord Howell wrote and thanked me, but said the boat was out of drawing. He may have meant to be whimsical, as he added, "I am like the central figure. I wear my crown over my hat."

Stanford House started the whole thing. It was the young Eurasian. Before Christmas 1941, he suggested that, as a new member of his class, I might like to have an extra session. I went one chill afternoon. I explained that I had done no previous work of this sort. He drew the faded-rose curtains across the London fog. He felt around for a clue. To save time, I told him frankly that there was really no-one in my life that I wanted to discuss. I knew where I was or thought I did. Still, the past was there.

"Yes," I explained, "five years ago or ten years ago, I might have come for help about some person. In fact, it is because I have given up the thought of that person or people, in a personal sense, that I felt free to come at all. It is my writing that matters." I did not want to talk about my writing, but I felt frustrated when I looked back and recalled the number of times I had re-written that novel of myself and Peter van Eck, after the last war.

Having said that I didn't want advice about anyone here or communications from anyone there, Mr. Manisi went off at a tangent.

"Wait a minute - here is a stretch of desert; sand; it's so warm. Here is a wall, no, not a wall, yes - I mean - did you ever do any excavating?" I said no, trying not to think of Peter van Eck. "Here is a long track in the sand. It goes on. There are foot-prints. Now the foot-prints branch off. There are two tracks. This gentleman is no longer in your life." But I had not mentioned a gentleman and had been careful to imply that I didn't want to. "Look - he's running his hand over a box. It must be a coffin. Why, look - this is very interesting. There's blue here, but very blue - "

"Lapis-lazuli," I suggested.

"Well, something stone - and the pictures are set in the lid, not painted. He is measuring the - the - "

"Tomb," I said, remembering Mr. van Eck's descriptions of his work in Asia Minor and in Egypt.

"Well, or temple. It's small." Mr. Manisi went on describing museum objects, but that was easy, even if he had never been to Egypt. I interrupted him:

"Do you know Egypt?"

No, he had never been out of England. But he went on,

"Now, if this were a little earlier, it would be - "

"The Shepherd Kings."

"No - no - it's - "

I began to feel uneasy. I particularly wanted to get away from that time. I had lived too much with the memory of Karnak. I had tried to write about it, but the writing wouldn't come true. I again prompted him,

"It's not the person, it's the story. The person went out of my life years ago. I hate to leave things unfinished. I wrote a sort of - a sort of novel. I wrote it over and over. I can't finish it and I can't destroy it. What shall I do?"

Mr. Manisi's thin hands emerged from the winter twilight. They were as golden as the sand he spoke of. I thought how beautiful his hands are. He said, "Throw it away." He lifted *it*, as if *it* were surplus cargo on a boat, and flung *it*, as it were, over the deck-rail.

I don't know how long we had been talking, but I knew he was very busy so I fastened up my coat and began looking for my gloves.

"Wait a minute - " said Mr. Manisi. "There's a lady here. I thought it was your mother, but she says, 'Tell Sister and Garry that I never forget their Christmas.'"

At first, I think I was just shocked. Delightful as Mr. Manisi's travel pictures had been, he might easily have asked Mrs. Sinclair about any new member of Stanford House. I had, I remember, told Mrs. Sinclair that I felt cooped-up in London as, before the war, I usually spent the winters out of England. Mr. Manisi might possibly have heard that I was not born in England. But except for the purely formal talk I had had, on making my application, and a social reference or so, Mrs. Sinclair knew nothing at all about me.

I say, I was just shocked, shocked because this last remark, in its simplicity, meant so much more to me than the minute details Mr. Manisi gave me of things that Peter van Eck had described to me, on that boat. Certainly, Manisi had got hold of something. But this third winter of the war, after the dreadful nights and the growing squalor of the days, I was somehow too near reality to care any more for the dream that had kept me alive for so many years.

"I thought this lady was your mother, but she calls you sister." She had always called me sister - no, not always - but it was my mother speaking.

. . . . .

Like most things in my life, I went too far with it. In the end, February 1946, I received none too uncertain words from Lord Howell to that effect. The impact of his letter left me cold, as the impact of the high explosives and the bombs had done. I handed the letter to Gareth. She said, "It's not lost. This will go on somewhere." She had a way of saying simply things of the most profound significance. Well, that letter did not require an answer. I put it with the others and with a sense of finality, searched the pigeon-holes in my desk for an elastic-band or a bit of string to tie round the bundle. There must have been about twenty letters in all, counting a news-cutting he had sent me and several that I had cut out of the papers. There was a post-card, too. In about five words, he told me that I had been mistaken about the publication and publicity of his last book - or rather, it was then his last book. There was another one afterwards.

I tied up the letters and flung them in the bottom drawer of my desk.

. . . . .

It must have been soon after Christmas 1941 that Garry came into it. She had come back to England. She had been offered a job, some sort of complicated, confidential work. It was difficult to talk to her at that time, as I was not supposed to know that the work was confidential. I did know, however, that it would be fatal for her to go to Iceland, that winter. The idea was preposterous. Apparently she was to go on to Sweden and be marooned there, or worse, sent to Russia. Naturally, she didn't or couldn't listen to my arguments. Then, I had a bright idea. I suggested Manisi. I was surprised, however, when she agreed to see him. I did not really think for one minute that she would.

"I'll get him at once," I said, thinking she might change her mind.

. . . . .

Not only did Gareth not change her mind, but after seeing Ben Manisi, she became even more enthusiastic than I was. This complicated things too, as she said they - whoever "they" were - would give her a very black mark indeed if she were known to have confided her troubles, re confidential work, to an outsider and especially to anyone in his world. There had been trouble, at this time, about various clairvoyants, fines, imprisonments and an unsuccessful effort to repeal the old Witchcraft Act which was still functioning in England. I had met Mr. Manisi at Stanford House. That came under a different heading. But Manisi confided to us later that he himself walked in daily terror of his life. He was a frail little being, so except for some rather strenuous fire-watching, he was exempt from military service.

He could see and did see Gareth privately, in his own house. Then he and Ada Manisi, his mother, came to our apartment, off and on. By 1943, however, we met regularly every other week.

. . . . .

We had a little round table, which had belonged to William Morris. It was an ordinary tripod-table, as I believe they are called, of dull oak. William Morris had used it for his paints and brushes. Manisi was interested and said, "I wonder if anyone will come to this table." I admit the table rather suggested old-fashioned table-tipping, as I believe it is called. In fact, the friend who had given it to me said, "It belongs here." She made some joke about it, "Don't let it keep you awake nights," or something of that sort. "What do you mean?" I asked her. "Well - it's just asking for it," she said. "Oh - then - take it back, or better still, come along and see what you make of it." This had happened only a few months ago. Madge Burton was only joking, I know, but there was an under-current of tender finality about our jokes in those days. Actually, later, her own house was struck by a flying-bomb and most of her belongings were lost.

"If anyone will come?" I asked Manisi. I knew perfectly well what he meant. He had talked to us, given us advice and "messages," as he called them, but in a rather set, you might say stylized and professional manner. Actually, by this time, I had begun to wonder if Gareth had made a mistake, and if it wouldn't have been better to have kept our domestic life and the "work" separate. An occasional hour at Stanford House was enough for me, besides that, it got me away from the house and the constant obsessions we all had, menial duties, the telephone and relays of worried people dropping in, morning, afternoon and evening. I did not like to seem inhospitable or selfish but Ada Manisi seemed, most of the time, just another harassed, worried woman, and poor Ben Manisi had become restricted and restless under new threat of conscription and the more recent attacks on various people in the "movement," as he called it.

I had had three letters from Lord Howell, by the time we embarked with the table. Manisi hardly had to tell us what to do. Poor Ada - I think she was rather bored with the whole thing, but she had few friends of her own and depended on her son's clients for whatever social life she saw fit to accept. People liked her but she made it difficult for them, as she always came back to the story about her family in England and his family in India. Her family would not forgive her, which one rather took for granted. But she had to explain that his family was even worse. Ada just couldn't forget. One wanted to forget for her, but she wouldn't let one, and then she was more than a little deaf. This, combined with the people likely to drop in and the air-raids, made our sessions more than a little erratic; they were either commonplace and pedestrian or else overstimulating. When Manisi said, "I wonder if anyone will come to this table," he turned in his chair and placed his hands flat on it. Gareth automatically followed, and when Ada Manisi resignedly laid her hands on the table opposite Gareth, I followed suit.

. . . . .

I seemed, for the most part, to be pulled sideways. I hardly know how to describe it. I seemed to feel weights and tensions that they did not. I was too interested, I think. To Ada, this was routine work, you might say. Gareth surprised me by her own understanding and yet she seemed to be in water-tight compartments. While the work was going on, she seemed to give and get, in a way, the lion's share. I felt she was physically as well as psychically so much stronger. And yet I knew that I was more sensitive. Sometimes, the sessions lasted twenty minutes, sometimes an hour and a half. I felt there should be more balance about it. The Manisis and Gareth alike, went straight into another world when we left the table. I felt there should be some margin in between, in which to re-adjust and to recover.

. . . . .

As I say, there had been three letters from Lord Howell, if you count the first one which he had written twice. Manisi made a ceremony of the table and offered up a little invocation, after we turned out the light. I suppose, sitting in the dark, helped too. I tried to concentrate on his prayer for help or "guidance" as he called it. Well, I thought, yes, it is time I decide whether or not to answer that last letter. Was it just politeness on Howell's part that made him answer my letters at all? Evidently he had no secretary. He must be, like the rest of us, harassed and busy. If I just don't answer this last friendly but politely formal letter, that will at least spare him further trouble about me. So, sitting there with my hands clasped under the table, I sent out my own invocation. "If," I said to myself, "Manisi gives me a message that has any - that has any - " I tried to think of something suitable " - *wings* in it, then I will answer this last letter." I was somehow not surprised, a moment after Manisi finished his prayer, when he said,

"If the others don't mind, before we begin, I have a picture for Delia."

The others didn't mind. There was a stretch of water. There were circles on circles. Each circle touched another and then went on, until the whole ocean was covered with circles.

"But there is a boat, Delia."

I should have expected a ship in a picture of this sort, but Manisi seemed to think this an astonishing thing, he really was excited. "It's not an ordinary boat, Delia. Now, I must tell you. I don't know where this boat comes from." I said,

"Well, I'll tell you. I was a little worried about - something. I said to myself while we were sitting here, now *if* I am to go on with this - this - then you or the table will give me some indication as to whether or not - what I am worried about is important or whether I shall just let it go."

"Oh, but - yes - it's important. This boat just came along. Oh, I tell you, Delia, it's wonderful. I can't say exactly where this boat comes from. It's not my world. Why, they are shouting and laughing. There's one here in the front. His name is - why, yes, they shout it - it sounds like Hill, but it's not Hill. I think it's his name they shout."

"It's Hal," said Gareth.

"They go on shouting," said Manisi. "There's such a lot of them. Oh, they are eager, vital people. They are so *well*. Why, they have such vitality. They go on shouting his name - yes - it is Hal, but they say it differently, and Britt, I think is the second part of his name. Halbritt - his name is Halbritt, I think."

"His name is Hal Brith," said Gareth.

. . . . .

The ship or boat, as Ben Manisi called it, was evidently for Gareth as well as for myself. Manisi had said it wasn't his world. He was more at home in ancient Egypt. (I never liked to ask Ada exactly what her husband had been but they were evidently people of importance, as Manisi *père* had already been, so to speak, excommunicated when he came to England on some idealistic mission, having to do with the usual Indian troubles.)

Manisi went on, "There's a sort of edge to the boat, here from the top end to the other end." Even then, I was surprised to see how oddly he evaded any ordinary ship-terms.

"The edge of the boat?" I remember I repeated it. It sounded so odd.

"Yes," he said, as if he had never seen a boat in his life. "This is a sort of - sort of decoration. It comes along the side in a curve, then the other side. It's blue. Then the men with the oars are in the middle. There are oars both sides." I began to think he was translating, his phrases were so odd, as if, as I say, he had not only never seen a boat but that he had not even heard of one. This was all right, but had it anything to do with my question, regarding Lord Howell's letter? "We are going somewhere," said Ben Manisi.

We were certainly going somewhere. But where? There is no use going into that now - rocking houses and furrowed pavements and the over-familiar wail of the sirens, fire-bells, fire-engines or even more disturbing, now and again, a space of absolute, uncanny quiet. These things happened every day. They happened during our sessions at the table. This over-emphasized our predicament. We were going somewhere - but where? I don't think we ever let any of the noises-off interrupt us. Nor am I going to punctuate this narrative with continued cross-references to what was going on outside. Let me say only that to me - and I think to Gareth - at that time the pictures Manisi conjured up in my rooms, off Hyde Park, were more real, have proved more enduring than all the high explosives and the sirens.

But to return to the ship. There it was. The sea was quiet. Not around it nor actually of it, but afterwards there were dolphins. That, I think and then thought, was a return to our first talk or "sitting" as Manisi called it, at Stanford House. We continued our table-session with the usual "messages." Gareth was to embark on some land scheme - well, she knew that. I had to be prepared to appear at a public meeting. I must do this. I would try to get out of it, but it was important, there were important people who would help me. Well, that was in the air, too. One felt sometimes that Manisi was simply reading one's thoughts, not that that made what he said any the less effective, from the psychic or psychological angle, but why sit in the dark and be told things accurately and in nice detail, that one already knows. I did not know about the ship, though Gareth had lately been reading a rather profound study on Norse religions. Maybe the name, Hal Brith, had been in that book, but I didn't ask her.

What I wanted to know was, whether or not to answer Lord Howell's letter.

. . . . .

The Manisis, as I say, came every other week, at that time. I could not wait two weeks. I had not seen Ben Manisi alone since my session at Stanford House. Time that went so slowly was speeded up. I don't know how it happened. Now, looking back, the six - or seven years, as I count them - are accordion-pleated. Events overlapped and time was nonexistent. It is only little things that stand out, like the Christmas-cards I speak of. But Christmas 1941 is clear enough because of the confusion and conflict caused by Gareth's uncertainty about her future plans. It was after that Christmas that she went to the Manisis' apartment on the ground-floor of an elegant but derelict dwelling, off Regents Park. We both went there to tea one day, and, not very long after, invited Mrs. Manisi to the house. We met occasionally during 1942 but by 1943, I believe we attained the status of what the "movement" calls a "home-circle."

Well, there was Christmas 1941, actually the third Christmas of the war. The first two hardly counted. The tide-wave had been hovering in some volcanic region for almost a year before it finally broke, September 1940. The wave was broken - as far as civilization was concerned, its dead-weight did not fall and submerge England, but it branched off into rapids, currents and whirlpools of night and day attack, chiefly on the town we lived in.

As I say, Christmas 1941 stands out clearly. After that, everything seemed different. I began to write again, and early in the new year, 1942, Gareth was allowed to help in a city office, instead of being sent to Sweden. Manisi had put her off Sweden, I am thankful to say. He told her that she had the choice of an uneventful war-career in London or a chance of some unprecedented experience in some foreign country, the north, (he did not specify), and then a sudden, unpredictable move which would land her, he thought, in Russia. He got Russia all right. From Russia, he informed her, she would probably not return. Gareth decided to stay in England. This was not the first nor the last time that I blessed Ben Manisi.

Well, that was early 1942, and the following Christmas, the Manisis came in and I lighted the circle of candles for them, under the tree. The little tree was on the corner-table in the hall. That was just a year after our first meeting at Stanford House. And it was in 1943, about October, that I heard Lord Howell lecture.

It was Manisi, early in the year, who first drew my attention to the fact that a certain retired Air Marshal was lecturing. He brought me an article from one of the Sunday papers, but I was not particularly interested and the matter dropped there. However, later, Manisi wanted me to hear Lord Howell lecture; he was going to Scotland, would I have his ticket?

I went to the lecture. The hall was crowded. I sat in the last row of the gallery. Lord Howell made an appeal to the audience, would they let him know if they could not hear him. He said one outstanding thing. At this time of conflict and confusion, Beings of a higher order could and would enter regions (which otherwise they avoided) because of and for the sake of certain individuals. Later, he said, these higher Beings would probably no longer communicate with the lower circles. He ended with a message. It was to this effect. Now was the time, if ever, to strive to attain some sort of attitude that would make possible the work and effort of the higher spheres. He ended with these words, "Strike and strike quickly."

Perhaps I took this message too literally. Certainly, if I did not strike quickly, I would not strike at all. I made my excuse for writing the fact that he had asked his audience if they could hear him. I assured him that he need have no anxiety on that account. It might gratify him to know that I was seated in the gallery, in the very last row. I concluded tentatively that I would be glad if he could tell me of any work he was doing, in the way of research or investigation. If he directed any small group, I wondered if I could join it.

He answered promptly. He thanked me for my letter. His "circle," as he called it, was doing a special sort of work. In other words, he had his own people and neither he nor they needed nor wanted outsiders. That was clear enough. I wouldn't worry him again. Either he was busy and confused, or my letter was so unimportant that it escaped his notice, for he answered it a second time. He said the same thing, with slight modifications. It seemed that unconsciously, he wanted to forget me, or he didn't want to forget me. I didn't know which.

I answered the second letter. In order to hide my disappointment that he had definitely closed the door on any personal work we might have done together, I said that I too had a small group of my own - I may even have said a "circle." This either interested him or put his mind at rest, for he answered in a rather more religious tone, on the necessity for serious workers along these lines. The letter was cordial but depressing, somehow. We couldn't go on this way. Was there any reason for going on, at all? It was then, with my hands clasped under the table, that I asked the question.

I had a part answer, indeed, I had the whole answer when Manisi said, "I have a picture for Delia." But I wanted to know more about the picture and I wanted to know if there were any reason to connect the picture with my key-word, *wings*.

. . . . .

I would see Manisi alone, if possible. By this time, our room seemed more conducive to the "work" than the semi-publicity of Stanford House, so I asked him if we could have a private talk or "sitting" as he called it, as soon as possible. He came a few days later, one afternoon about a month after I had heard Lord Howell lecture. I had thanked Manisi for the ticket and told him that the lecture had been interesting, but that was all. I did not tell him that I had written Howell and I carefully avoided any further reference to him. We put out the light as usual, and after a few preliminaries, I handed Manisi Lord Howell's last letter.

I said casually, "This is not really important, there's just a little snag here." Manisi seemed to be feeling round the edge of the envelope. He did not take out the letter. I could see the outline of his thin fingers as my eyes became accustomed to the darkness. I waited for him to take the letter from the envelope, but he did not. He said,

"Yes, this is important to you."

I said, "Well, no, it's not important really."

Manisi answered, "Yes, but it is important, it's about writing." I remembered that my first session with him had brought in the fact that I wanted to finish or discard an old novel. He probably thought that this had something to do with that. It seemed odd, when I came to think of it, that I had not seen Manisi alone oftener. This was only the second time.

"It has to do with writing, Delia. This gentleman is a writer but there is something else that is more important. There is something looming up, I can tell you. There are mountains. You get to the mountains, but it's going to be a lot in the way. It's your writing but it's not your writing. What is accomplished will be in the writing, but the writing does not matter. Oh, you would be surprised to know what it is, after you get through." All this seemed a little vague and I felt I was losing the clue or the key-word in this generalization.

"Tell me," I said, "it doesn't really matter - yes, you are right, there is writing in a sort of way - but do you think this letter is worth answering?"

He did not take out the letter but he still held the envelope. "Oh, here is something funny. Do you remember last time, I had a picture for you?" I said,

"Yes, I remember."

He said, "Oh, but now there is life - there is much life. Has this gentleman ever been to India?"

I said I didn't know.

"Well, I'll tell you. He has been to India. Has this gentleman ever been to America?"

"I must tell you, Manisi, this is a more or less formal letter from a person I have only just - only just seen. I don't know very much about him."

"Well, he has been to America," said Manisi. "Look," he continued, "have you and this gentleman been discussing some writing or some work together?"

"I can't say that we have - well, yes - "

"Well, there *is* work, there is important work. There is writing but that is not the work. I don't think you will do any good with this gentleman in England, Delia."

He went on about America. But I did not see myself there, nor did I see Lord Howell there. Least of all could I imagine us both there together. Yes, we might possibly work together here in London. But "There is work, there is America," said Manisi, and then something, as it were, clicked in my consciousness, like a key turning in a lock. I had thought of a word, I called it a key-word, *wings*. I remembered that ship, obviously they were Norsemen. Gareth knew all about it. He had told Gareth she would have a successful war-career, as he called it, in the north. Garry had been reading that rather obtuse volume on Religion and Philosophy, she got from the London Library. America apparently had nothing to do with any of this, but suddenly I remembered Eric Ericson and tales of skulls and helmets being dug up in Rhode Island - I think it was - and that word *vineland*.

"Now, wait a minute," said Manisi.

I waited a minute. I waited several minutes.

"Yes, it's the same ship. It's come back. Now, I will tell you. You are standing on a cliff. You are saying good-bye to them. They are going off. They are going after treasure. I don't understand this. Do you remember what I told you?" He did not wait for an answer. "You remember I told you that you and Gareth were on the boat. You were on the boat. I don't really see this. You could not have been on the boat. It was warriors. You are a woman on this cliff. Gareth might have been on the boat. Oh - wait a minute - now - this. You are two people here. I can't say I understand it. You were on the boat - maybe - yes. Didn't they have a sort of - sort of musician? Not that, exactly. Someone who gave the signals - no, not signals, *signs*," said Manisi, "that's nearer. Someone told them when a bird flew - " he stopped. I remembered my own key-word, *wings*. But it wasn't just birds that I meant. I was thinking of Lord Howell and that photograph in the newspaper that Manisi had brought me. Howell was in uniform. I meant something special by *wings*. I must stop Manisi now, quickly. But he was quicker than I was. "I think you were a sort of *seer*," said Ben Manisi.

"That's it," he went on, "but I still don't understand it. You were with them, at first. Now, you are a woman on this cliff, waving good-bye."

Well, they were going off and they had left me. Who they were, I didn't quite know. "They're here again - Oh, such vitality - they're shouting." But what they were shouting, he had no need to tell me. It wasn't that I heard their shouting or their voices. He said they had left me, but they hadn't left me. How that was, I couldn't say. I didn't even care to know. It was not myself that I was thinking of. I wanted an answer to my question, the question that had started the whole thing, *do you think this letter is worth answering*?

"There's just one thing," I said. "I didn't tell you the other evening that I qualified my question. You remember, I told you that I had asked a question about something. Well, the question was about that letter you are holding. I said to myself that you or the table would give me an answer, if the letter were important. The minute you finished your prayer, you said you had a picture for me. Well, I wanted to be sure, if I had an answer, that it would be something to do with this letter, so I tried to think of a - a key-word. The key-word was wings, but I didn't mean it in a vague, general way. Now, you have just spoken of birds flying. But I didn't mean just that."

"But I told you - " said Manisi.

"Yes, I know - that's just what I said. You told me about birds flying, and they did, I think, have certain auguries - you know what I mean - about the flight of birds - and there's that *seer* - though I don't think it's me - "

"I mean, the sides of the boat," he interrupted. I remembered how odd I had found it, when he first spoke of the sides of the boat, the top of the boat, the end of the boat and so on, as if he had never heard of, or only just seen a ship. "Yes, but I told you," he continued, "the sides of the boat were blue and they curved over from the top of the boat and folded round it. They were very blue."

"What were very blue?" I said, although I knew perfectly well what he meant.

"I have just told you," he said, "they curved over, they weren't decoration exactly. I mean, they were part of the boat."

"What were part of the boat?" I went on, still wondering if he had never heard those familiar monosyllables, prow, stern, bow, deck or even the word ship. "What were part of the boat?" I asked him again, knowing perfectly well what he meant.

"The blue wings," he said. "And anyhow, I told you in the beginning that one of them had a sort of small eagle, perched on his wrist."

Well, I had my key-word, more than one - or rather the same word was presented in three different ways. But Manisi had not mentioned the hawk at all, or the small eagle as he called it, the other evening when he told us about the picture. Nor had he exactly specified who was on the boat. Gareth and I were part of it, but as Garry explained, after they had gone, she didn't think she was a warrior. She seemed very clear about what she was not and also about what she might have been.

"I wasn't the harper, either," she said, "though I may have helped with the runes." It was like her to find a part for herself. No, I don't think I was a warrior either, and though, in some way, the seer or his seer-ship possibly depended on me, I don't think I was the seer either.

One might conclude that Lord Howell, who just a little over two years ago had, as they said, saved civilization, was the vibrant Hal Brith. But I don't think he was.

It was devastating how time went. I have just said it was two years since Lord Howell "saved civilization." But it was three. Manisi seemed sure that there was something important indicated by the picture. I didn't know what. Certainly, the fact that there was a picture, in answer to my direct but unspoken question, was significant. I would write Lord Howell.

I am afraid I was rather carried away with my own enthusiasm. I wrote him at some length. He answered at once, and cordially. He even suggested that if "there were any more of the story" he would like to hear it.

. . . . .

I myself now found the "work" more interesting and a few weeks later I asked Manisi if he would come in again. I had not told him who the letter was from. We went on from where we had left off, there were more details. There was a "lone eagle" hovering. This "lone eagle" had, it appeared, a "nest" somewhere. I had told Howell about the hawk in the picture and he had written that he himself claimed an heraldic hawk on one of his bearings. It seemed understood between us that he was one of the warriors, probably the one with the hawk perched on his wrist.

I wrote him freely because it seemed understood that he was a very busy person with endless claims on his time and energy, and that having his own "circle" as he put it, there was no reason for our meeting. I don't know why, but it came as a shock when toward the end of a three-page letter he suggested that he would like to join our circle, or would I prefer coming to his? This upset me. I could not visualize Lord Howell in the room, with the tea-things on the table and the general domestic bustle that went on before we put out the light and settled down around the little table. I told Gareth about this suggestion of Lord Howell's, but she made no comment, one way or another. Well, there was nothing to do but ask the table. This time I waited for my "message" and then said,

"Do you think the table will let me ask a question?" The table, or Ben Manisi's "guide," as he called him, seemed affable about it, so I said, "Ask K if he thinks it might be a good thing now to have a new member in our circle?" We used one tap for *yes*, two taps for *no*. The table or K tapped a somewhat over-emphatic *no*.

As Lord Howell, in his book, had described various means of communication, I explained this and wrote frankly that I was very sorry. (I had also suggested to the table that I might expand my own knowledge by working with other people, but the table or the "guide" had been equally emphatic with *no-no*.) I wrote that I was sorry that I could not meet him, as the "table" had indicated that it was not yet time.

. . . . .

It was actually some time after, that I met Lord Howell. It was, as I have said, February 1945. Gareth didn't want to meet him or was shy about it, but I dragged her in finally, for a cup of tea. I really did want Gareth to see him, but apart from that, I felt a bit shattered, as he had made a somewhat occult little speech the minute he dropped his overcoat in the hall. It was difficult enough to keep alive those days, to keep *in* one's body, so it did not really help me when Lord Howell, with none of the usual preliminaries, said, "Reincarnation is not a thing that really matters." We had, I think, taken for granted that this was by no means our first "life" on earth. But a "life" it was and a difficult life, however you care to look at it. Besides that, it was not yet quite over. Yes, I had written to him, perhaps impulsively, and I had certainly written *ex cathedra*, as you might say, about my general philosophy and certain, to me, fascinating findings. I dare say he did sum me up pretty thoroughly. I did not challenge his statement about reincarnation.

"You yourself," he went on, "for instance, do not matter." Well, maybe that was all right, but I confess I wanted to be given credit for having kept that "you yourself" intact through these war years. "It doesn't matter what you are or what you have been - an Egyptian dancing-girl or a North American puritan."

. . . . .

Garry was shy with him and crouched on the other side of the table and would say nothing. I hadn't expected him to stay to tea, though I was glad that he did. We had only two buns and I cut them in half, that somehow offended me. I tried to cover the cake-plate with the remains of a stale raisin-cake. I don't know what it was, that was its name anyway, but it had no raisins in it. The room seemed too small. I was horrified to think that he had contemplated joining our "circle." I wondered what he thought of us now. Garry tried to slide off the couch and get back to her room but I shoved my chair over so she couldn't get out. We had cigarettes, but I had a sudden qualm - would he approve of ladies smoking? I wanted a cigarette, it would have made all the difference, but I refrained from reaching for the box on the table. Lord Howell pushed back his chair and stood before the fireplace.

. . . . .

We wrote again, once or twice. Then I let the cat out of the bag and told Manisi that the letter he had "read" for me in the dark was from Lord Howell. That was perhaps a mistake because now any advice he gave me about our "work" together would necessarily be tinged with his own conception of Howell, his lectures and what the "movement" said and thought about him. However, that did not really matter, as I had had two very rewarding "sittings" alone with Manisi and had taken rough notes in the dark then, and as well Gareth and I had kept an account of our general meetings and she typed out some of the more interesting material for me. Yes, I think on the whole it was just as well that I stopped there. It was all right as far as we went.

As Manisi had brought the news-cutting in the first place and had given me the ticket for the lecture, I felt too, that it was only courteous to tell him about Lord Howell. Of course, now he wanted to meet him. He produced his pocket-diary in a business-like way. "Oh, there is Scotland again - " leafing over the pages, "and when I come back, I have Tunbridge Wells and Paignton." It was astonishing how he got about. But we arranged two tentative dates, a full month ahead, and I wrote Lord Howell.

He chose the latter of these dates. He was travelling about the country, lecturing too, but he and Manisi had not, so far, met.

. . . . .

That was the second time Lord Howell came to the house. Spring was coming on, for I remember I had a cluster of early iris on the table. I slid out to get tea. There was a slight awkwardness about it somehow, as Ben Manisi had taken the big chair and left Howell the only other armchair in the room, a small, low chair that wasn't very comfortable.

"You sit at the other end of the table, Manisi," I said, "and I think Lord Howell, you better take the big chair."

Well, there was the usual stage-business of tea, sugar, milk and passing the buns. Fortunately there were enough, this time. Manisi was rather on his professional behaviour, I thought, and asked,

"Lord Howell, what are you doing about getting the movement out of the lower astral?" Manisi and Lord Howell did almost all the talking. Gareth said she'd rather have tea at the office, that day.

It must have been some months later that I saw Lord Howell again. It was a hot July day. I asked Lord Howell in, as Manisi wanted to see him again. We had tea as usual, but the occasion was marred for me, as Manisi had come a full half hour earlier, in order to tell me great news. I am afraid I really was upset. Gareth was on her summer holiday, so Manisi broke it to me alone. He was getting married. Well, that might have been all right, but he had confided to us both, separately and together, his doubts and difficulties.

"It would be all wrong," he had insisted, not three months ago. "She is a lovely little companion, but we don't either of us believe in marriage." Gareth had run across Doris at their house. It was all rather difficult, as the brother, an "eminently respectable" (to use Gareth's phrase) Indian Office official, was sharing the place with them. Gareth and I were devoted to Manisi and Gareth especially wanted him to be happy. She had even made provisional inquiries about a booking out to India.

I couldn't really listen to what they were saying. I had enough to do to pull myself together and recover from the blow. For blow it was. Obviously, under the circumstances, our work would have to be modified, as Doris would now expect to be part of our lives. In fact, it meant as far as I was concerned, that the work would stop altogether.

About Doris, I knew nothing. "If you would only see her," Manisi kept insisting, before Lord Howell came in. I couldn't tell him how Gareth felt, though Gareth admitted that the girl was pretty and, moreover, very clever. She might do very well as a wife for Manisi, but she wasn't in the picture, as far as we were concerned. She just wasn't. And then, too, I felt that Manisi ought to get out to India and see his father's people before he made up his mind. It always astonished and immensely saddened me to feel that this child of a Brahman had never been out of England.

. . . . .

We had known him for almost four years, and those four years were admittedly the most devastating and dangerous years any of us had ever experienced. If only we could have a little time to think it over. Indeed, I had argued that with Manisi, before the others came in, for later a young journalist rang the bell. He had brought back some books of Gareth's. It seemed that he might help me through the afternoon.

"One minute," I said, "you remember meeting our Indian friend, Manisi, here one day? Well, he dropped in for tea." This was not a hint to Philip Manning to be off, in fact, the contrary.

"I'll just drop the books," he said, "in Gareth's room, and go."

I followed him into Garry's room. "No - but just wait." I had closed the door of the front room. I opened it, shut it again and wondered what I would say. "Lord Howell, a friend has just dropped in to return some books. He helps edit a magazine I write for. He's really a charming person. Would you mind if I asked him to join us for a glass of sherry?" Howell was actually smoking a pipe. He looked rather like Sherlock Holmes, stretched out in the big chair.

He said, "Why - no," and then I had to tell Philip, who was there. It seemed that I was doing a good deal of whispering and stage-business for so small an occasion. But it could hardly be called a small occasion when Lord Howell came to tea. Philip, in his usual diplomatic manner, filled in the gap, without asking any questions.

. . . . .

Well, that was the third occasion. I didn't want to let it drop there, but how was I to go on? We had, as a matter of fact, gradually reduced our sessions. Manisi, for the past six months, had been rushing about and one felt, when he did come in, he was tired and one should be as ordinary as possible and as practical. Where are you going next? Who do you see? How is the work going? He had a fund of anecdotes about various mediums, meetings and people connected with the "movement." He could be really very funny. I had tried tactfully to find out more about Lord Howell, but except for accounts of public meetings, Manisi seemed to know even less than I did. Now I felt that I must be very careful about what I said. Manisi used to drop in once or twice a week, on his way to or from Stanford House. But Stanford House was closed for the summer. Gareth was away. There seemed no longer any possible excuse for writing to Lord Howell.

I said we had "reduced" our sessions, rather as if the work were a drug, and perhaps it was. I felt completely lost without it. Even although Manisi and I had only chatted together for some months about the "movement," there was always in his gay mockery a feeling that he really belonged somehow. I mean, a feeling that he was seeing through and into things, in a way I had never met before. He made mistakes, it is true, and his mind worked unevenly, but it was working in two dimensions, there was no doubt about that. I was now terrified lest the lure of comfort and stability should lead him into some of the subterfuges and half-truths about which he was so amusing and astute, when it came to other mediums.

One Sunday, I took a day off. In other words, as Gareth was away, I refused to answer the telephone. Perhaps this was a mistake. It left a curious vacuum in the room. Why, I was alone. I was sitting over a tea-tray and the usually cluttered table was empty. I would finish my cigarette and write Gareth. I really couldn't answer the telephone, as poor Ada was on the horizon and I could do nothing now to help her. I didn't want to seem to take sides, although I had already done that. That is, when Manisi said, "But what will you and Gareth do if I marry Doris?"

I had answered, "I don't know what Gareth will do, but I won't see you any more." He didn't understand, and I became perhaps over-effusive and motherly. "You see, Manisi, we are both so terribly fond of you. Gareth can do what she wants. I have loved our work together and I can't mix it up with - with other things."

"But you yourself used to say that you did think mother difficult and I should lead my own life."

"Yes - I meant that - " Now I could not say that his decision seemed too sudden to be reliable. Something had happened. "Wait a bit - that's all I mean. Go out to India. Ada always said, after your father's death, that his people were heartbroken to realise that they might have helped you and your brother - only she was too proud to ask them. Why, Manisi, they must be interesting people."

"You mean, you want to get me away from Doris?"

"I only want you to wait. I only want you to see your father's country, your own country." He was desperate like the rest of us. He thought this sudden decision would settle something. Well, maybe it would.

For me, temporarily at least, it settled something. I had other friends I wanted to see in London, but there wasn't one, with the possible exception of Philip Manning, that I could talk to about Manisi. Gareth had insisted - and she was right there - that we keep the fact of our "circle" strictly to ourselves. That had meant intrigue and awkwardness from the beginning. I couldn't ring up Madge Burton, as I usually did in an emergency, and tell her the whole story. Madge Burton? "Don't let it keep you awake nights," she had said when she left the table. I put out my cigarette. I turned my chair, the straight-backed one I sat in, at our meetings. I did not have to get up. I reached forward and drew the table toward me.

II

Round Table

I laid my hands flat on it. I closed my eyes and said,

"Well, I have come back. If there is anything I can do, I want to do it. Is there anything I can do?"

The table said, "Yes."

Was it possible that the table would talk to me alone? Was it the table that had answered? I had read criticisms of this sort of thing. One's unconscious mind, I think Camille Flammarion said, was entirely responsible for certain muscular reactions, but he wasn't apparently, entirely convinced himself - all this was in a book, I forget its name, I got from Stanford House - for as I remember, he followed his ouija-board and table-tapping analysis with a long account of some French officers who had contacted a brother officer; I think it was in Africa. One had to see for oneself. I would just sit quietly. The telephone rang again. I didn't answer it. I tried to think of nothing in particular.

The table spelt, "John."

There are plenty of Johns in this world. There was the Dutch Jan, sometimes they called him Johann, whom I first met in Dresden in the early thirties, at the von Altens. He had done some work in India and was going back there. He was killed at the outbreak of the war, in some mysterious manner. There was my husband - but oddly enough, there had never been any intimation, at the time of his death or after, that he was or had been anxious to keep in touch with me. In any case, people never called him John; his name was John Geoffrey. Was it Geoffrey come back?

"Wait a minute," I said to myself in the best Manisi manner. This was too much. If I were doing this "spelling" myself, then it rather knocked the whole thing on the head. You may say that four people - our circle - couldn't all simultaneously think of the same letter and spell the same word, but I always felt that pull and strain I spoke of. One person or one person's unconscious mind might be stronger than another's or the others. Or one person might be physically more robust, simply stronger. Gareth at one time, as I have said, got the lion's share of messages. I was deeply touched when Manisi gave me that first message about my mother, but it seemed that there was no-one, no one person there or here (for the matter of all that) who meant supremely everything. Oh, there was old von Alten to be sure, but one would not think of conversing casually with him, this or the other side of the grave. There was my disappointment too, with his brilliant pupil, Jan Verstigen, but I think that was because I associated Verstigen with Peter van Eck. Peter van Eck was English-born, it is true, but he had that Dutch name and he and Verstigen were both working along the same lines. I didn't think it was John or Jan Verstigen.

. . . . .

Sometimes, I was terribly cold when we were all together. I had read in one of the Stanford House books that this sometimes happened. Maybe, it was Flammarion again. It was such a bad translation. I wondered if I could find the original. Geoffrey and I had been so happy in Paris. He used to buy me bunches of *oeillets*. The boy with the barrow shouted, *trois sous le boite* or something that sounded like it. But it wasn't *boite*. My French like everything else, had gone. That was the first real raid, after the fall of France. The fall of France? Everything had fallen. But it couldn't be Geoffrey. They said at the time, that I was very brave about it. I wasn't brave. I was just frozen. I just didn't care. Now, I was so cold. It would have been all right if we hadn't quarreled. No, of course, I didn't kill him. It was something else that killed him. He said, "I love you but I desire *l'autre*." I loved him too, but I didn't want him or anybody any more. The baby only lived three days. Geoffrey said I didn't care about the baby, either. How could I? I was so ill. Geoffrey couldn't know. No man could ever know. He was born in the spring. I went out and sat under a flowering tree. It was full of bees. Geoffrey was going back to France. He would stay if I needed him. He had already out-stayed the precious *permission* as he would call it, but the baby was late. There was a sort of air-raid. Not what we call an air-raid, but the matron said, "We have the stretcher ready. We will take you to the cellar." I don't know if it was the air-raid. I wrote Geoffrey. He wrote back, "God, God - don't you really care, Astraea?" He called me Astraea, from a poem of Robert Herrick. He used to read poetry to me. There was Anthea too, he used to sing it:

Bid me to live and I will live
Thy Protestant to be,
Or bid me die and I will dare
E'en death to die for thee.

. . . . .

That is how the thing started. As I say, fortunately or unfortunately, I was alone in the flat. I realized that I had hardly been alone at all, during the whole war. I went about and did a little shopping, but I didn't see anybody. I wrote Gareth every day. I told her I had decided after all, to accept the job they had offered me in America. I found suddenly that I wanted to read all the things I had so terribly loved before and during the last war. I got out my books again and began making lists of things I wanted to remember. I had in one way and another, met a good many people. I began writing them and telling them about the lectures. Would they help me? Howard Wilton Dean had got me the job. He was at the American Embassy during the war, the American part of the war, I mean. He said, "You understand both sides, it's not political but you can tell the girls (along with Christina Rossetti and those things you told me, the Burtons told you, about the Brownings), something that will make them feel better about England." I was too far away from things to know that the old anglo-phobia was taking hold of people again. I would do what I could. I was so happy to do it. We had been too busy just keeping alive to realize that people didn't like us.

By "us," I include Howard and people like him. A minority, I confess. I was flattered by his interest and his overwhelming kindness had helped keep us alive, books, magazines and oddments like side-combs and pudding-powders that Mary Ann Dean sent us. "But what do you really want?" Howard would say, before one of his extraordinary trips. "I'm going to Lisbon." "Bring me back a castle-in-Spain," I said and when he demurred at this, "or a branch of orange-blossom." He came back without the orange-blossom but with a huge melon, instead. "They held the plane an extra minute for your orange-tree. I *was* mad. You would have liked it. It was a tiny tree like you see in Italian paintings, and they said the buds would come out, and there were three orange oranges and half-a-dozen green ones, and the leaves were perfect."

I didn't believe a word of it but it was the sort of thing he might have done.

"I don't believe a word of it."

"All right - I have the receipt somewhere." He searched in the imposing port-folio he always carried.

"Don't look for it," I said, "I wouldn't believe you anyway. But this is luxury." I looked at the melon. It wasn't quite ripe. There was a stout stalk and a string. "What is the string for, Howard?" I asked.

"Why, you hang it in the window, for the sun to ripen."

"Show us the sun, Howard," I said.

It was like that, and now I remembered things in this war as if they had happened twenty-five years ago, and I remembered things in the last war as if they had happened yesterday.

. . . . .

I went on with the table. I didn't want to know who John was. It was enough that the name had somehow opened up the past - or perhaps it was the sudden shock of Manisi veering round that way, that did it. I mean, it was like that with Geoffrey. I didn't dislike Miranda. Oh - why did she have that name? It wasn't really her name and I wished he would call her Elizabeth - but that didn't matter. It wasn't even as if he were the only one who called Elizabeth Chester, Miranda. I suppose I wanted to be the only one with a secret name or names - Astraea and Anthea. He was careful to call me Delia in public. He was nice about things like that. But Miranda was her professional name - and that sounds horrid. I mean, she and her sister had worked with a dress-designer in Paris, before he was called to the front. The sister went to South America and Miranda came to London. She dressed beautifully, of course. Now, I am being horrid again.

I knew when Manisi said, "You want to get me away from Doris," that he had said that before. I mean, I felt though at the time I did not realize it, that it had been said before. The lunge of the words - do I mean that? - the way my chest seemed stuck to my backbone was a sensation I had had before. It wasn't just the V-2 that fell in Hyde Park, that Sunday morning. Anyway, that was back of me behind the book-case, the other side of the wall. When Manisi said, "You want to get me away from Doris," the blow went straight through my heart.

Geoffrey said, "Why did you ask her then, if you didn't like her?"

I said, "I did like her."

He said, "You flung us together, Astraea. It was all your fault."

I said, "You told me in the beginning, that you thought she was amusing but a bit of a handful, and you were glad she finally got engaged to Boris."

"Well, Boris went to Russia and she was very lonely - "

"Well, lots of women are lonely," I said.

Miranda said, "You're letting yourself go." I didn't like her coming in, when I was half-dressed. "You should take more interest in yourself, a handsome woman like you." I didn't like the word handsome. Geoffrey had spoiled me. He was always looking for what they then called the *mot juste*.

"Handsome is not the word, Miranda," I said. She didn't know what I meant. She thought it was mock-modesty, I suppose. It wasn't. I just didn't like her coming in, when Geoffrey was in France. What did she want, anyway? She wouldn't ask me if I had heard from Geoffrey, of course. Nor would I ask her. *Chère belle fantôme*, Geoffrey had called me. Now, there was if you will, the *mot juste*. I knew I looked a sight.

His words went round and round in my head.

Miranda said, "What is the matter?"

I said, "I've got a cold or something, I'm dizzy. I can't hear." I sat down in the arm-chair by the fire-place. The fire had gone out. Geoffrey had stood there. I had on the long, grey-silver skirt and the black velvet bodice. He said, "You are the most beautiful woman in the world, Astraea." I wondered what he wanted. I didn't believe anything, any more. There was only one thing left. I hadn't played my cards very well. I had never spoken of - of John, as I called him.

"It was because I was so ill," I said.

"No," he said, "it was because you didn't love me."

We had said all this before, but I had never spoken of the baby.

"You see, it's different with Miranda," he said. "She wants to have my child."

I didn't know what he meant.

I had heard of people having shell-shock. It was a new word. I wondered if he knew what he was saying.

I looked at Miranda. No, I was looking at myself in the long mirror, after he left.

"I love you, I love you," he had said the last time we were together. "I love you so, Miranda."

I went back to the table. It gave me what Manisi had taken away. I didn't want to know who John was. He kept coming back or maybe, I made him up, contracting my arm and wrist muscles as Flammarion said one did. Or I just drew him back - or drew or spelt or *spelled* the name, John.

. . . . .

When I was with the other three at the table, there was always a feeling of pull and strain. I had heard with this sort of thing, that it was bad to work alone - in fact, impossible. Gareth and I had discussed it. She said she had heard of two people working but even that was difficult. When Manisi went away on one of his lecture-trips, Gareth and I tried the table. We agreed that we wouldn't tell Manisi. We waited a long time for the table to talk. Then, there were brief messages that weren't really important. It really wasn't very satisfactory. I wasn't tired as I so often was with the four of us, but Gareth and I seemed in some way, to negate each other. When I was alone, the table came to life immediately. It's true we started with a lot of questions on my part, and with yes and no from the table. I didn't know who was answering but that didn't make any difference. I kept more or less, to the surface of things. Was it a good thing to go to America? Would I be happy there? Should I go by sea? Should I go by air? And so on. I may have jogged the yes and the no-no from the table each time, by contracting or expanding those arm and wrist muscles, at the prompting of the unconscious mind - or I may not have. The point was, I was happy.

I was reading, working up the notes and sorting out books, papers and clothes in a wholesale post-war spring-cleaning, so I didn't spend much time working at the table, if "work" is the word to be used in this connection. I hadn't written to Lord Howell, either. After my first bewilderment about Manisi, it is true, I did write him. I told him how puzzled and unhappy I was, fearing Manisi might make a mistake and his rare gift be lost. Lord Howell answered the letter in a curt, non-committal manner. Well, after all, why should he care, although good mediums were difficult to find and I had had a feeling that later, he and Manisi might have done some work together.

Yes, I was very happy with the table. I looked forward to the time when I could tell Gareth about it. She would be back soon. I felt selfish and a bit subversive when I didn't answer the telephone, or else explained jauntily that I had a job and had to work up my notes for lecturing in America.

"When are you going? Where are you going? Why are you going?"

Well, I was due just after Christmas, I would explain, or I might be able to put it off till spring.

"But Christmas is a long way off."

"You wouldn't think so if you were doing a complete resumé of English litera-ture from Beowulf to Auden."

"Who's Auden?"

"Don't be silly. He's a gifted young man and I'm trying to catch up to him."

Yes, I felt different about that generation now. They were no longer young. Why, the crowd that followed Geoffrey must be well over forty. I had to laugh now. They were older than Geoffrey. They were no longer rivals of Geoffrey and the others. They were to be tolerated and patronized. I was more than ready to find their brilliance exhilarating. I had found them dull and sterile before. It was my own fault.

I was so happy with the table. I was tempted to make out a list of the words we had used, but I thought better of it. There would be time enough for that. R-A spelt the table. Well, that was no doubt, *rare*. We had had the word often enough. "All right, rare," I said. "Go on." The table tapped R, again. It was like that. The table didn't like being interrupted. It had taken me some time to convince it that it need not, inevitably, spell a familiar word to the end. It came back to A and stopped. I repeated, "I said, *rare*," but that didn't satisfy it. A-B-C-D-E-F, the table tapped and stopped. "Oh, I see, this isn't rare, then?" The table said "Yes," but that didn't mean anything. "I don't understand, go on." It went on, R-A-F, it started all over again. "R-A-F what? Go *on*," I said impatiently. R-A-F, the table repeated stubbornly.

"R-A-F doesn't mean anything." *R-A-F doesn't mean anything.*

Well, there it was. It was as if they had been waiting for a new telephone-girl to learn the technique of the switchboard, before they manifested or announced themselves. I say "they" for eventually, in fact almost at once, there were a num-ber of them. But why for me? I didn't know any of them. They seemed to want me to work for them. I was deeply touched. It was Ralph who made me cry most. You see, I had not cried, except for occasional neurotic or purely physi-cal outbursts (when I had an abscess, for instance) since Geoffrey - Well, that was the worst of it. I hadn't accepted the fact of his death, nor of John's. *John's?* There was a slow, deliberate voice speaking. "Re-incarnation is not a thing that really matters." No, no, it didn't matter. I was crying because Ralph said - what was it Ralph said? I had said, "Are you RAF boys who were lost in the Battle of Britain?" Ralph said, "Lost we are found."

I say, how can you accept reincarnation? Because any of these boys might have been John come back - or even Geoffrey.

That is how I felt about them. There was Lad, there was Larry. There was John, but whether this was the original John or another, I didn't know. Someone was in the background. I had called him John, at first, but finally I decided he must be Z. (Of Z, more later). Z would say, "Wait" and I would wait. Then he would announce Lad or Larry or Ralph or John. When he first announced or introduced John, I decided that John must be one of them, after all. John said, "Are you ready?" "Of course, I'm ready," I said and suddenly realized that that was how the wing-commander ordered the squadron to be off. It wasn't a command, really. It was an indication only that he himself was waiting. Well, it was like that. John spelt, J-O-H-N.

I said, "Yes, I know. Z" - for they called him Z, too - "has told me it's you, John."

He spelt J-O-H-N again.

"What is it? Is this another John?"

"Yes."

"Well, all right, what can I do about it?"

"J-O-H-N T-A-B-L-E," he spelt.

"Yes, I know, John. The table is for you. I was so happy when you all came." It seemed that we were stuck, somehow. I had said all this before. I waited, wondering. He waited too. "Is there anything I can do about it? I mean, anything special."

"Yes," he said, and waited again. (This is a most subtle and intriguing form of communication. I suppose it's a sort of thought transference. He wanted me to find out what he wanted, what they wanted.)

"Will you help me, John? Will you give me some clue, some word?"

"D-O-O-R O-P-E-N-S," spelt John.

I knew that a door had opened. "I know, John," I said. It was like speaking to a child. No doubt, they too, felt they were speaking to a child. I could feel their burning intensity, but I did not want them to feel my own frustration, my impatience. "May I wait a minute?" "Yes." They did not stay very long at first and I was afraid they might go away. It seemed to be a sort of tradition or convention to use first names only. But I felt they wanted another John. If they wanted me to help them, they must break what apparently, was their rule.

"Well, I'm afraid you'll have to tell me John's other name," I said.

"H-O-W-E-L-L," spelt John.

It is true that Lord Howell had not always been Lord Howell. He had signed his name, as is customary, Howell only. I remembered then a reference in the news cutting that Manisi had brought me, to the brilliant career of Sir John Howell, in the last war.

"I'll do everything I can," I promised them. "I'm afraid I can't do much." Now I knew why they had come. They hadn't come for me at all. They had come for Lord Howell.

"Table will very well do," spelt John. This was a little later.

Now I confess, I began to overdo things. I mean, the books, the papers, the lecture notes, the trip to America even, seemed unimportant beside this burning fact, this fact that I was needed.

"Roses red," spelt Larry one day, and "roses white," came later from Lad.

"I'll do my best," I kept assuring them. "You know he's a little difficult."

"*Yes,*" said Lad emphatically. It seemed they had an idea. I knew nothing of the technical or scientific side of flying or of flight mechanics. But it wasn't flying in that sense, it was the old Homeric *winged word*, that they were after. It could be done. It wouldn't be difficult. They would explain it to Lord Howell. Apparently they couldn't explain it to me, but if Howell would come, they could indicate through me, a new means of communication. They didn't want anyone else, and they didn't want me to tell anyone of this.

They gave me numbers and letters which they said Howell would understand, but they needed help. They asked me to tell Lord Howell of this, not to write him.

Later, they would indicate others. I would be able to help in the beginning. Afterwards, the others would not need me. It would need a perceptive ear and to a point, a person trained in rhythm, metre and musical notation to take the first tests. They seemed to think that I would be able to do this. I was mad enough or glad enough to believe it myself.

. . . . .

Now I thought of Geoffrey. I hadn't thought of him for a long time. I hadn't thought of him at all. I remembered the *oeillets* and the word *boîte* that was wrong. I must have been thinking of those funny little places we went to, *éstaminets* he called them afterwards, when he was in France. "We crowded into an *éstaminet*," he wrote. "You should never have sent me that card." It seemed the card I sent him, had gone the length of the trench before he got it. It was a Corregio in the Louvre. "They will never forget it. They ask, has your girl sent you another post-card?" I could hear the clatter and I looked through the cigarette smoke for Geoffrey. He was standing by the door. The door opened and shut and opened and shut, and then someone shouted, *Shut that damned door*. The shout was the last thing I heard. Now I knew how they sounded. I hadn't really heard that sort of whizz-bang (as he called them) in the last war. Now I knew what they were like. It wasn't only the V-2, that Sunday morning.

. . . . .

I managed to jot down numbers and letters and a few names and short messages with my right hand, while I held on to the table or to *them* with my left. They stayed as long as I could keep concentrated and didn't give way under the strain. It was the excitement of the thing I think, that tired me and the almost unbearable poignancy of their simple messages. "Write," they said, "write Howell." It was no good my explaining that we had come to a sort of blind-alley. As to my own feelings in the matter - well, I didn't know what I felt. I began to think that I couldn't bear this alone, and in any case the messages were for Howell, and once I gave them to him and made the connection, my work with them would be moderated and in the end, I supposed, would stop altogether. I didn't want to lose them, to lose touch with them, but I felt like a battery, negative or positive, whichever you will, that had to be completed by another battery. Or I felt like a wire, across which a voice was speaking and if the message were not received at the other end, in some way or other, the wire would break. Yes, I would write. I wrote immediately. He said he would come in on the third of September.

I did not realize that that was the anniversary of the war.

. . . . .

I asked him when tea was over, if he would mind my reading a few notes to him that I had taken at the table. I had to explain that in Garry's absence, I had felt cut off from the work (I hadn't seen Ben Manisi) and that I had been working alone. I hadn't anyone to talk to and I said that the table anyway, didn't want me to talk, and in any case, the messages were for him. I had the note-book with me. It was lying on the couch where Gareth had been sitting that day. I explained that they were RAF messages. I asked him if he would mind, if I read them to him. He said "Why - no," and I reached over for the note-book. He held out his hand to take it.

"I'm afraid I'll have to read them," I said, "it was difficult holding on to the note-book with one hand and the table with the other. They're very badly written." I pushed back my chair and took the one beside him. I started to read the notes. The first was from Ralph. I didn't fill in the sort of telegraphic gaps. I thought I would explain them afterwards.

"The first word is *Advallon*," I said. "I think they mean *Avallon*. Anyway, I suppose that's where they are." He turned and looked at me. I said, "You know - King Arthur - "

He said, "Of course."

"Well, this one is Ralph. He says *love all*. I suppose he means *all send love*. I haven't worked over these notes."

Howell was still looking at me. He said "Thank you." He looked very white and thin suddenly, sitting upright in that chair.

I went on. "It's chiefly that they want to get in touch with you in a more or less natural - in a sort of ordinary, normal way. They want to talk to you as naturally as if they were using a telephone. At least, that is what I gather. They want you to help them - I have letters and numbers here that I don't understand - to set up a sort of inter-communicating radio."

I did not know Lord Howell. At that moment, I felt that I knew him very well. He looked so young sitting there, bolt upright like a school-boy. Was it someone else sitting there? Was it Sir John Howell of the last war? I had on the blue silk dress. I had given up or modified my frenzy of packing and unpacking and going over old books and papers, since the messages became more exciting, and no doubt, I was beginning to feel the general reaction to the five war years in London. Everything was all right. I settled down to outline the rough jottings, preparatory to discussing the details with him. But there was no settling down, that afternoon.

I would never catch up to Auden. I had attempted the impossible. I had leapt beyond him. Andrew Lang was my spring-board - or Manisi was or Geoffrey was, or *they* were. If this was a fairy-tale, it was very real to me. It was true. I never for a moment, doubted the integrity of Lad and Larry, of Ralph, of John, of Howell or of myself. That is, I never doubted his sincerity nor my own. That is why I was so shocked when Lord Howell jumped from the arm-chair. He wasn't the person who had sat there a moment ago, whose voice, familiar, sympathetic, had said "Thank you." That was all. But it had settled my own doubt. I had been nervous and apprehensive about his possible refusal to listen to me at all. But if he had said in the beginning, firmly but politely, that he was not in the mood for receiving messages, or if he had said as he said at the end, that he only took messages from his own people or his own "circle," I would not have let go my own defences. I was undefended when he struck me.

What he said was, "This thing is utterly impossible."

The big chair was empty. It was very empty indeed. Sir John Howell had gone away. A complete stranger was pacing up and down the length of my carpet, from the couch to the window and back again. He went on talking. He talked about the danger of these things. He talked of the danger of beings of a lower order getting hold of notions of that sort and how their control of some such problematical communicating system, could upset the balance of the world. I didn't say anything. To begin with, if beings of a lower order could get hold of some sort of inter-communicating system, they would have done so long ago. I objected to his intimation that Lad and Larry, Ralph, John and the rest of them were beings of a lower order. I didn't say a word. I didn't have a chance to, anyway. He must have sensed my apprehension for he stopped suddenly. I put the note-book back on the couch, where Garry had been sitting that first time he came in. This was the fourth time I saw Lord Howell. It was the first time I had seen him alone. Lord Howell said,

"I don't mean that *you* are a being of a lower order."

This made matters worse, as far as I was concerned. It only seemed to under-line the fact that *they* might be. What would happen next? He went on with some utterly unrelated objection that gangsters in New York, for instance, would in any case, be likely to tap wires or wireless messages of that sort and turn any knowledge they might acquire, to destructive purposes. I did not ask him if his own private telephone could be tapped by gangsters in New York, or in Lon-don for that matter. It was so irrelevant. It was so illiterate, or that is how I felt about it. Then, I had an inspiration. Was he himself working for just this thing? If he were, he would naturally be very secretive about it. He had, I knew, been responsible for some of the new radio inventions. It might even be possible that the British Government was at work, along with the other governments, in this terrible race for more scientific knowledge, having to do with the stratosphere. The full details of the atom-bomb had just been announced.

In which case, his discourtesy, if discourtesy it were, must be discounted.

. . . . .

I could have retrieved the occasion by a suave, feminine show of tact. But somehow or other, I felt that it wasn't my occasion to retrieve. The occasion be-longed to Ralph, to Lad, Larry and John. There were the rest too, "others - many," as one of them had said.

I could have suggested a glass of sherry. I did. He said, "No, thank you," but now was the moment for me to sweep briskly from the room and return with de-canter and glasses. I should have done that, in fact, I would have, but I couldn't. I was helpless. The shock of his *volte face* had left me, not so much frozen as in-animate and lost. I simply wasn't there, any more. I had gone away with Lad and Larry and the rest. I didn't care what happened. Somebody must do something. He said, "And in any case, if there were messages of any importance, they would come to me from my own circle."

So not only did he repudiate the messages themselves and me, as the bearer of the messages, but he repudiated the fact of the messages and their whole content, as not being "of any importance."

. . . . .

Fortunately, Gareth returned a few days later. I told her in a somewhat casual way, that I had put in a little time with the table. I told her it was odd, there were quite new things happening. I tried to be rather off-hand and added that it really didn't matter.

"What sort of things?" said Gareth.

I said, "Oh, words and numbers and names of places - all very simple - it seems to be a group of RAF pilots."

Gareth took this seriously, I am glad to say.

"There seem to be a great many of them," I went on.

She said rather surprisingly, "There was something like that, I remember, in the Boer War. One of my aunts told me that messages came to a woman she knew. There were a great many. This friend of hers didn't know any of the soldiers, it might be something like that. But if you want to go on with it, you had better do a very little at a time, once or twice a week I should say, at the outside."

I didn't tell her that I had seen Lord Howell again, and that the messages were for him.

. . . . .

I said I wasn't frozen, but I was. I was like a tree that bends over in an ice-storm. My top seemed about to touch the ground, but it didn't snap off - some connecting wire or *a* connecting wire - the ice might melt. I didn't know what to do. Automatically, I went back to the table. "Wait," they said.

Perhaps I should have stopped the work there. After all, who was I to think I could do anything to stop or stem the dreadful thing that loomed heavy in all our minds? They had come, in a sense, with the coming of the atom-bomb. I had felt that they had come to stop that.

Psychologically, any-one can work this out. Garry and I were not afraid of the atom-bomb for ourselves. Having sat up all night through so many raids, we agreed that the bomb would be quick, anyway. That was the short view or the selfish view to take of it. What of other people? What of the rest of the world? One was afraid of the end of the world. It was the end of this world, anyway. There must be another world, but where was it? It was there, somewhere. I had never doubted that. But I had made no real emotional connection with it, as my work with Manisi had been for the most part, either impersonal or literary. Lord Howell had stood out for some sort of extension of consciousness. I wanted anyhow to feel things in that way, in a rational way. Perhaps that was what was wrong. Perhaps I was too rational. He had written somewhat extravagantly at times, of luminous scenes and summer-land felicity. Yes, I could accept that too, but I felt there was a qualification about summer-land. It might be winter-land, without being Hell or without containing "beings of a lower order."

If we felt that way about the atom-bomb, what must *they* feel?

. . . . .

I had come to the parting of the ways. Either Lord Howell was himself, as I say, already working in secret on some "psychic radio" - I believe he mentioned some such thing in one of his articles - and didn't think I was to be trusted, or else he felt my antagonism. I didn't actually think it out clearly, but the first war had taken my child and my husband from me. We had known for so long, that another war was coming. The only thing that had reconciled me to both wars, was the thought that these young, vital beings might be able to work rationally. If this was the case, then their premature loss was a gain to the whole world. But my picture of them was the very antithesis of Lord Howell's. They would go on and "finish their education," he had said or written somewhere. It wasn't their education that needed to be finished. It was ours.

But Lord Howell was out of it now. I must go on alone.

Perhaps the "roses red," the "roses white" was an intimation that we were still fighting. If that were the case, I had met a formidable antagonist. Perhaps he had, too. There was no summer-land about this. I don't pretend that I saw them but I imagined them in the mountains somewhere. I may have made the whole thing up, I was working feverishly again, but in a cold fever. They were all together. All they wanted was someone who would understand the numbers and the letters. I didn't know anyone in the Air Force, but Lord Howell and anyway, they wanted him to do this. It all seemed so easy, so simple. "You help," they kept insisting. No, they weren't flying any more, not with machines. I seemed to sense my lungs expanding in that clear air. Did one fly with one's lungs, I wondered? It was in the back of my head and my own lungs now. It was radium and snow.

. . . . .

No-one could go on like this, not alone. I deliberately set to work on my American lecture notes. I may even have done without the table for as much as three days. When I went back, I explained, "I will do anything, anything but I must make up my mind whether to stay in England or not." I said, "Shall I go to America?" "Yes." "But I may lose touch with you, there." "No." "Is there any other way of talking - I mean, I can't take the table with me. Can we talk together without the table?" "Yes." I felt I must be practical. I must continue to prepare for the trip. It was impossible to get off after Christmas. The end of February or early March was the earliest sailing. Then Gareth said I couldn't possibly go by sea and began pulling wires. The air was even more difficult but I had a Government permit. Howard, his end, had seen to all that. I was told, I was lucky to have a chance to get away in February. Well, February was a long way off.

The Steel Wall had been broken five years ago. I was reminded of that by Gareth.

"I went last year to the celebration at Saint Paul's - it's your turn."

I didn't want to go to Westminster Abbey. She said I must. She said, "Take Philip with you, he'd love it and he can't get a ticket."

So Philip Manning and I went to Westminster Abbey together on September 16, 1945.

"There are mountains," Manisi had said, "and there are great difficulties. Oh, Delia, it isn't the writing. The writing comes in but it's something beyond the writing. It's an immense work. I don't know what it is. But it's wonderful. You don't know what you will do. But you will get to the mountains." I heard Manisi saying all that. If only I could talk to him now. I said to the table, "Is this the work I was told of?" They said, "Yes." I said, "I was helped so, by my Indian. Shall I ask him to come back?" They said, "No."

I couldn't see Manisi and I wouldn't see Howell again. Then I saw him at the Abbey. He was standing apart from the crowd. He wasn't in uniform. I was so shocked. I tried to brush past him but I couldn't. He was standing back of the choir-rail. I was on that side. I was face to face with him, before I knew who he was. I was looking straight into a white face and staring, grey eyes. I was frightened and embarrassed. Philip said afterwards, he looked haunted. He looked like a ghost, anyway.

"It's so nice to see you, Lord Howell," I said. I had to say something. That was the fifth time I saw Lord Howell.

The sixth time was before Christmas. He didn't stay long. I had the little tree but it wasn't trimmed yet. There had seemed no reason for asking him, but after the Abbey, I felt I had to see him again. I wrote him that I wasn't staying in England, that I was going to America, that I wanted to see him before I went. He seemed friendly and interested and we kept it on that level. He even asked me if I knew anything about the "work" over there. I told him I had taken a good deal of trouble, trying to find out. I had written various friends in a rather guarded way, as I knew how most of them felt about psychic-research work. I explained that, about a year ago, I had been trying to find out if there was any chance of Manisi getting a job over there. In fact, I had written to almost everyone I knew, but I had had no satisfaction at all. Most of my friends, I said, were horrified to learn that I was interested in a medium, although I explained Manisi's background and his Indian father. I told Lord Howell that I dropped the matter after that, but would do what I could to find out if there were an opening for lecture-work along those lines. I felt that he himself might be thinking of going over later. He asked me about Manisi. I said I hadn't seen him. When Lord Howell left, he said, "But I hope to see you again, before you leave."

I said, "Of course." I saw him once more. I expect I was ill then. Certainly, he didn't look very well. I had told the table that I couldn't do anything, any more. This was the end of January. I had met Lord Howell, early February, just a year ago. The table said - well, what they said or "gave" repeatedly was a single word. They said, if I repeated this code-word twice, without a break in the sentence or conversationally in several sentences, Lord Howell would no longer have any doubt as to the authenticity of the messages nor the senders of them. The word was not difficult to bring in and I managed, I think, rather well. But when I first said the word, Lord Howell raised his voice and began to talk rapidly of ancient Aztec ruins - he was trying to stop me, I felt. I mustn't stop. I just went on. I got the word in a second time, without a break, and then it didn't matter what he said. He went on about the various layers of Aztec or Inca civilizations to be found in Mexico. His trying to interrupt me that way, may or may not have been an accident. Anyhow, I had done what they asked. He left very soon after. This was the seventh time I saw Lord Howell.

Still, they were not satisfied. They said "Write." I wrote him again. He wrote back, "No, I cannot be expected to receive messages of this sort. They are both frivolous and uninspiring." Lord Howell added, "Of course, it is none of my business but it would be better if you gave up this work."

. . . . .

I gave up the work and I gave up a great deal with it.

The war had happened. I could no longer say that there was any reason for it. It had been a crass blunder and anyone who had forwarded these new inventions was part of the evil that had overwhelmed us. There was no use going on. Gareth was already making arrangements to leave. The house was bedlam and the telephone rang all day. Miss Wardour who was arranging Gareth's ticket, was found in the street. She had fainted or lost her memory. Fortunately, she was identified and taken to a hospital. Gareth went in to see her and was down the next day, with a bad cold and temperature. The girl at the office said Miss Wardour had meningitis. I don't suppose Garry had it. She got off, anyway. I don't know how long I had been ill. My one desire was to get Garry off and after I said good-bye, I had nothing else to live for. Mrs. Moss who spasmodically "did" for us, found me very happy but a little dazed because of the V-2 that had broken the bath-room window. She said, "Madame, the war is over," and she went into the bath-room. "The window's all right, Madame," she said.

I said, "Well, it might have been downstairs. I think it was all the windows."

Mrs. Moss said, "I'll ask Janet." She went into our kitchen and out of the back door. She seemed to stay a long time, talking to Mrs. Stevenson's Janet, in the next flat. When she came back she brought Janet with her. I think she must have telephoned from Mrs. Stevenson's, because before Janet left, our doctor had come in.

. . . . .

I think I had been ill a long time, longer than I knew.

I ran up the stairs, the window at the top wasn't broken but the inside shutter sagged and the iron-bar that clamped it shut was bent almost double. It seemed strange that the iron bar should be bent like that and the window-panes not even cracked. The three long French windows in the drawing-room, that looked out on the balcony, seemed all right, but I didn't dare put on the light. I sat half-dressed before the fire-place. The fire had gone out. I told Miranda, I couldn't hear what she was saying. I don't think I wanted to. She had no business coming in, while Geoffrey was in France. She had no business coming in, anyway. I heard the whizz-bang but I heard the voice too, though the whizz-bang and the voice came together. The door opened and shut, the door opened and shut and I looked for Geoffrey through the cigarette smoke. I saw Geoffrey. He was standing by the door. *Shut that damned door, Alton,* someone shouted. But that was my name. I looked at Geoffrey, standing before the fire-place. "You see, it's different with Miranda," he said, "she wants to have my child." I had heard of people having shell-shock. It was a new word. "Where are you going," said Miranda.

I said, "I'm going to shut the door."

Miranda said, "The door is shut."

I sat down again. I said, "Someone's got to sweep up the glass."

Miranda said, "But they've put in the new windows."

I suppose Geoffrey must have told her. I was afraid to put on the light. The curtains hadn't been drawn. They were long, blue curtains and there were the candlesticks on the mantelpiece and the pottery bowl. There were the cups and saucers that we got along the Arno, before the war, in Florence. There was the table. Everything was the same. It was colder. I waited for her to go. What did she want, anyway? She wouldn't ask me if I had had a letter. I didn't need to ask her. She didn't know that Geoffrey was dead.

. . . . .

Now, it all seemed very simple. You went backward to go forward. Geoffrey said, "Who wants to understand this fellow, Einstein? But I wish I knew a little mathematics."

I said, "Then, you do want to understand him."

He said, "What happens is, you bang your head on an obstacle, it whizzes you backward, you turn a double somersault and when you land on your feet, you are going forward."

I said, "Is that all?"

He said, "It's a sort of hurdle-race but you have to have the hurdles or it isn't a race."

I said, "That's rather silly, Geoffrey."

"Oh, no," he said, "it's an obstacle race, the obstacle is or are the mathematics, and I haven't any."

I said, "Well, give me the book."

He said, "No. It's this horrible idea of eternity, and if two plus two doesn't make four, what does?"

I think I had found out. I think I had found out even then, but I didn't know it. I think I struck an obstacle when I heard the whizz-bang and the voice shouting, *Shut that damned door, Alton* and knew that Geoffrey was dead.

If I had gone backward then, conceivably, I would have gone forward. I was afraid to go backward. I don't think I went forward. I didn't exactly stand still, but I was side-tracked somehow. Then I went forward, but perhaps the going forward was right off the rails. It saved me at the time, anyway. Ben Manisi and Lord Howell saved me later. But Manisi had made things impossible.

It is true that the sessions toward the end, exhausted me more than ever, and the constant threat of outside interruption became worse. The sessions would soon have come to an end, in any case, but things would have been more gradual and there would have been no break with the Manisis. The repercussions of Ben Manisi's ultimatum, simply set up vibrations that recalled the other. But even after that, it took some months for me to remember Geoffrey.

. . . . .

What I said to Ben Manisi, I should have said to Geoffrey. I should have said to Geoffrey "It's all or nothing," as Miranda did.

Geoffrey said, "I will go mad. I love you. Don't you see? Women are so stupid." I didn't see. What was there to see? Geoffrey said, "It's my last leave." He didn't say *permission*, that time. It was Miranda who brought the word over, I think. Geoffrey knew more French than most of them because he said, "They don't know any." Maybe they did say *permission*, I don't know. It was one of those things, I might have asked him. I began to worry about things like that, and even though he said it was his last leave, I felt better because he didn't say *permission*. "I will go mad. I love you and I desire *l'autre*." Well, he had said that before, but I really thought he meant it. I didn't know that a woman who loves her husband, doesn't under any circumstances (even if he is going mad or may be killed), connive or contrive to let him love another woman. Maybe, I was too nice to Miranda.

Now, all that happened more than twenty-five years ago, but it didn't make any difference. I had gone forward, even if I was, as Lord Howell implied, off the rails. Now, I was going backward. But the going backward and the going forward were going on together. That is how I found out the answer to Geoffrey's question, "If two plus two doesn't make four, what does?"

I think it was the irony of the thing that was the obstacle. "She can come here," I said. It may have been that Geoffrey was right when he said he loved me. Anyhow, it seemed to be understood between them, that I wanted to be alone.

Naturally, the next step was, I wanted to be alone because I wanted to get rid of them. From there, it was easy to go on to "Delia wants to be with someone else."

"But I didn't know you were here," said Miranda as I jumped up from the armchair. I had on that silver-grey skirt with the black bodice that Geoffrey liked so. I had been out in the dark to post a letter, and my old evening cloak was flung over a chair.

"You've been out?" said Geoffrey. It wasn't very late. It was the way he said it. I looked at Miranda.

I said, "No. But I'm just going."

I don't know where I slept that night. I think it was in Madge Burton's studio.

. . . . .

But somehow, I got stuck there. Not that I went on and on thinking about it, after I heard the whizz-bang and the voice telling me - I mean telling Geoffrey - to *shut that damned door*. A door shut, certainly. They had said at the table, *door opens*. But they didn't mean that door. Or did they? Did other people of my generation have the same door? *Door opens*. It was John who said it. For a long time - I mean about two weeks - we were concerned with the fact that they were worried because Howell didn't want them. This seemed impossible. He had recorded details of the after-life of a number of RAF pilots and men of other services. But for some reason, it seemed, this special set or group couldn't reach him. Or they could reach him only through other people, with whom, perhaps, they were not in sympathy or who were not in sympathy with them.

It's true, I asked a lot of questions and asked them in such a way, that yes or no would give the answer. There is quite an art in doing this and it took me some time to work out a satisfactory short-cut or short-hand technique. I said, "Have you tried to get to him" "Yes." "What is the matter?" "Door shut." "I see. But what do you mean by that? Doesn't he want to see you?" "No." "But this can't be true. He can't *not* want to see you." "Wave work." "You mean, he is busy with some work having to do with this vibration, or something allied to it?" "Yes." "You mean, he is working on this thing already, and you want to help him?" "Yes." "But surely, you can do that?" "No. Door shut."

Then, just as I was about to give up, John said, "Door opens." It was then that I promised to give the word, to repeat twice the not unusual but distinctive word, they gave me. Door opens. It only needed this to prove it. The door may have opened, I can't say, but as far as I was concerned, it was slammed shut immediately.

They say we make the pattern or spiral of our life, as a shell-fish does. We go round and round. Yes, I do think I was getting somewhere, all those years, but it may have been rather a large shell for the fish inside it. I may have put too much of myself into making a shell that would permit me to spiral ahead, without coming back to the exact point I started from, when the door shut. Life advances in a spiral, we all know. Maybe, in going on, I did once in so often - once in seven years, some say - come to the point in the new circle that was just above the one in that "life" or spiral, when a door in a crowded room in a Flanders inn slammed shut. I would always get so far with everything, then simply leave it and leap over an obstacle and begin again. I don't know how many times I had done this. It's more than twenty-five years now, since I did or didn't sleep at Madge Burton's studio that night. I don't suppose the four sevens are evenly spaced, but we might call it four times seven, in order to make a sort of equation to go with Geoffrey's "if two plus two doesn't make four, what does?"

. . . . .

That was the answer to it. There were four people. I can't say they were spaced in seven-year periods, but I can say there were four. There were four extravagant and illuminating occasions that ended with a shut door. There was Peter van Eck, of course, whom I met on a small passenger liner going to Egypt. He was going inland. He was due to get off at Smyrna, but he managed somehow to persuade the authorities that he must see someone of importance in Cairo, before he went to Haifa. As a young man, he had worked with Sir Arthur Evans in Crete. He was still a young man, from my present point of view, but forty-four seemed fairly middle-aged to me then. He was a linguist of some standing and had been with Allenby at Jerusalem. He was technically a staff-interpreter, but one wondered sometimes, what else he "interpreted" besides Levantine dialects, Arabic and Persian.

He stayed more than a day at Cairo and he it was who took me out to Karnak.

. . . . .

There was Jan Verstigen who was really a younger edition of Peter van Eck. By this time, I was much older and Verstigen was some years younger. I was caught up in Dresden because of my devotion to von Alten. Verstigen, when I first met him, was under the impression that I was some relation of von Alten's. I thought Delia von Alten such a wonderful name, but I broke it to him gently.

"I can't claim the *von*," I said one day, but by that time, I had been promoted to the somewhat equivocal position of Frau Delia. There was something very charming to me, *gemütlich*, in this familiar and endearing, yet somehow formal title. I can't say I ever felt like a *frau*, but it put me almost in the position of a daughter of the house.

Things were very bad, by that time. But Dorothea von Alten, frail and delicate as she was, still insisted on the traditional Sunday afternoons for his students and their friends. The tradition went back years before the last war, as far as I could gather. There were things I had forgotten that made me important to them, that made me - by that time, somewhat lost and bewildered - important to myself.

Verstigen would present me proudly to new-comers.

"Frau Delia met the wife of your great Schliemann in Athens."

That opened door upon door. It wasn't only Jan Verstigen and all those people. It took me back to Athens and that feverish two days on shore, and Peter van Eck rushing me around, and at the last, saying, "We must put in a minute at the British School, half a minute at the American, and two minutes with her most august excellency, Madame Schliemann of Troy."

There were Greeks and Trojans. There had been and there always would be, I suppose. At Karnak or to be more exact, in Cairo on the return trip, when I said good-bye with a certain astute finality, to Peter van Eck, I was a Greek, certainly. My mind directed me. It was somehow too much of a risk to throw in my fate with a stranger, I had met on a boat. I think I loved him. But the very fact that I loved him, made me repudiate him. I did not think of Geoffrey. If I had worked that out in 1917, I would have gone off with Peter van Eck. I was Greek, certainly.

My heart was involved with the Maestro, as they inevitably called him. I loved Frederik von Alten, and so did Verstigen. This drew us together. We both felt, too, the unworldly beauty of the old lady for whose sake the young archaeologist had given up his life ambition, the work that Schliemann offered him. He had applied his extensive knowledge to the classification and cataloguing of the antiquities of the whole world. This brought the world to his door.

"But just once," said Jan Verstigen, in his excellent English, "I should like to take the Maestro and set him down in - in - "

"Mycenae?" I asked him, remembering Agamemnon and the bee-hive tombs.

"I don't know," he said. "I don't know."

I realized that he had broken off his sentence, because of a lowering of voices in the group of young officers, across the table.

Greeks and Trojans - we didn't speak of these things. It was understood that we didn't. But the next time I saw Verstigen, he deferentially asked me what I thought we had better do about the Maestro. Apparently, he like myself, had thought of nothing else for years.

"I don't know," I said, "and anyway, he won't leave Dresden."

If I think of Dresden, I think of a set of tea-cups; "not one broken," Frau von Alten triumphantly exclaimed, when I lifted the cup to appraise the tiny coronal of blue, rose and yellow flowers. It was a wedding-gift from his mother. I murmured, I hope, something suitable. I didn't cry in those days.

I came to depend more and more on Verstigen or Jan, as I now called him. If or when there was war, Jan would be there to help me.

There should have been grand-children. No, he couldn't leave her. Dorothea von Alten had always been delicate, one gathered. She looked as frail as the cups that had not broken. She had not broken. Young von Alten, their only child, was killed in the last war.

. . . . .

Jan became more and more determined to get them away. I knew it was impossible. Frederik von Alten's catalogue had grown to immense proportions in the last thirty years, and his least word on folk lore and primitive native taboos and customs was still authoritative. He believed that he was helping the world more by evading what he called "ephemeral political contentions" and staying where he was. I discussed this with him. I was frankly frightened by this time.

"But you," he said, "you say you are going back to England."

I said "I suppose so. Frankly, I am torn between anglo-philia and anglo-phobia."

He said, "You express my sentiments exactly. But would your Golden Bough leave Cambridge, if he thought the bombs were coming?" He always referred to Sir James Frazier as the Golden Bough.

I said, "He isn't exactly my Frazier. But no, I don't think he would."

"Our Max Müller and Willamowitz Müllendorff were both highly thought of, at Oxford," he said. "Have things so changed?"

I didn't explain to him that things had changed vastly, since the eighteen-eighties. He like myself, seemed to have forgotten the last war.

. . . . .

The time came, when I had to go back to London. They offered me the lecture-work in America, but I said no, I would stay in England. I said good-bye to Jan in Dresden. He left before I did. Up to the last, he went on working to get the von Altens away. He had even gone to the extent of arranging the trip out. He had a brother in the Dutch East Indies who came regularly to the Hague by air. He told me of this. He could guarantee the von Altens protection. Possibly India would be better. His brother apparently, had interests in India, as well. He even suggested that we might all go together.

"Is this *Lost Horizon*?" I asked him. Frederik von Alten loved *Lost Horizon*.

Well, it was *Lost Horizon*. I got the thin air-mail letter from Calcutta, and then one from Java. Jan said he was going back to India. There was censorship at the time, and he wrote guardedly. My last letter was not answered. Gareth said innocently, "Is this the Dutchman you met in Dresden?" She evidently didn't realize what Jan meant to me. It was a short notice in the *Guardian*.

When I read it, a door shut. I suppose it was the same door that shut in 1917.

I suppose it was the same door that shut in Shepherd's Hotel, Cairo, when Peter van Eck said with a certain suave mastery, "Well, then it's settled. You *will* come to Haifa with me." I don't know if he did or didn't have the tickets. There were anemones growing in the fields and tulips, he said. He knew all about primitive plant-motives, on pillars and columns, and would trace patterns in pencil, on the back of old envelopes, of what he called the "egg and spoon," right through Aztec and American Indian to the Egyptian lotus-bud, over to Crete and the butterfly patterns of the palace of Knossos. The archaic circles on the signet ring he wore, he said, represented the original cocoon, from which the later butterfly pattern had evolved.

We were standing at the head of the stairs, leading down to the hall and the terrace, where in February, people were sitting in the sun. I took a step down and waited. We had had our tea, on the upper landing. He waited and did not follow.

"Can you find the way down?" I said. I don't know why I said it. Peter van Eck stood on the step below me.

"*That's* easy enough," he said. He bowed stiffly and swung down the stairs. He did not pause and he did not look back. I watched till he reached the door. A small darkie in native costume, handed him his stick and hat. There was yet time for me to run after him. The door opened and the door shut.

. . . . .

The door that shut on Jan, shut on the von Altens. That was early in 1940. By September there were other things to think about. Sometimes when the bombs fell, I was as happy as I have ever been in my life. I don't understand this at all. It was about then, that I went back and tried to make a final version of the *roman vecu*, Karnak and Peter van Eck. It would have been better, I suppose, if I had gone straight back to Geoffrey and our honeymoon in Italy, and the temple at Poseidonia.

There were anemones there too, and tiny striped tulips, under the cypress-trees at Fiesole. We went there to see the Mina da Fiesole. There was a girl lying on a slab of marble, or was it bas-relief, set in the brick of the church wall? We read Walter Pater; many of these things came in. I know that pine-cones always looked different, after we had seen the Lucca della Robia plaques, and the Florentine fruit-vendors, it seemed to me, had learnt how to arrange lemons and oranges, with the green leaves under or around them, from the della Robia porcelains. Or else, in the beginning, the della Robias had learned these things from them. We read about Pico della Mirandola and went to the Villa d'Este above Rome. There was a dust of snow on the mountains but the almonds were in blossom. We stood on the Spanish steps, outside Keats's window and we laid white and rose camellias alternately, in a circle around Shelley's name and *Nothing of him that doth fade*, carved on the stone beneath it.

There was an umbrella-pine that I will never forget, because Geoffrey read me Andrew Lang's *Theocritus* under it. There actually were cicadas, chirping in the noon-day sun. I asked Geoffrey what "wattled" meant. He said a sort of weave of rushes, like the hutch where the boat-man was waiting to take us to the Grotto. Yes, that was Capri. The pear-trees were in blossom. Monte Solaro was stony and we bought rope-shoes. There was a boy playing a pipe. It was too ridiculous. We stopped to listen.

"But," I said, "this is too ridiculous, or am I making it up?"

Geoffrey said I was. There were freezias in earthen boxes the length of a wall. There were jars, through a gateway, filled with calla-lilies. There was a cypress avenue leading to a villa. We stopped and looked in. There was a bank of stock, along a wall. I wouldn't leave, but Geoffrey said, "We don't live here. Come along. I prefer beans." That was new, too, the fragrance of bean-fields in blossom.

Perhaps I was clairvoyant all the time, and didn't know it. I know it now. I saw everything, I wanted to see. It was clear and meticulously lighted - I mean, there were shadows where shadows should be and I remembered or saw that it must have been hot in Capri, because the stock was drenched, although it wasn't raining and it was too late for dew. It was only in the shade that they had watered the flowers.

There was an enormous jar of white daisies on the next wall. The daisies made the wall look dusty. I thought of saying that to Geoffrey, but I asked him instead, if he didn't think the pink wash on the next house might have been made from powdered coral. He said, "*Of his bones*, do you mean?" I didn't know what he meant, and I only remembered when we started to slide down the ravine, the short cut to the light-house. But I was holding on to a clump of genista, and by the time I got my foot-hold, he had found some orchids, bee-orchids, he called them. I had never seen them before. I was flattered that he didn't offer to help me. I went down the ravine mostly with my elbows. When we got to the bottom, he said,

"But we left Theocritus under the umbrella."

"The what?" I said.

"The spreading shade of the dark umbrella-pine was a fit cloak for the lovers."

"You're thinking of the Greek Anthology," I said, "it was -it was - " I didn't know much Greek but I knew enough to know what he said next, wasn't Theocritus. He was quoting Hippolytus' prayer to Artemis. "That's Euripides," I said, "I'm getting to know all your tags."

"They knew it was Shelley, because he had a book in his pocket." He slapped his empty pocket.

"But Shelley was drowned," I said. "That's what I mean," he said. "I must always carry a book in my pocket."

. . . . .

It did not need a clairvoyant, but a humble statistician to know what would happen to me, if anyone came into my life. My instinct had been right in the beginning, but if the table's first advice, as to whether or not, it was advisable to add a new member to our group, was due to my own unconscious fear and the muscular strain and pull that I myself put into the eight hands laid down upon its surface, is a question that I can not answer. Nor can I say positively, that Lad and Larry, Ralph, John and the rest were disembodied spirits, or whether I made them up, as I seemed to have made up the shepherd-boy, playing his pipe on the slopes below Monte Solaro, the day we slid down the ravine, the short-cut to the light-house. All that may have been a dream, too. I think that Lord Howell was acting with admirable caution, when he wrote me, "Of course, it is none of my business but it would be better if you gave up this work." I have said that his last letter precipitated my illness. But that is doubtful. I was bound to break, anyway, whether Garry brought back the meningitis from her visits to Miss Wardour in the hospital, or not. Lord Howell must have had an acute sense of nerves and possible collapses, from his observation of young pilots. We may imagine too, that he was Greek enough to have known himself, as far as know thyself is possible in this world. He also consciously, or unconsciously, was probably aware of the fact that, in some way or other of which I myself was not fully conscious, I, for all my former reserve and repudiation, was no longer a Greek.

I do not mean that as a man of the world, he feared hysteria or hero-worship from me. He had dealt with that sort of thing all his life. It was the thing beyond hero-worship, the impersonal or the fear of de-personalization that he dreaded. Although he himself had said at our first meeting, "Reincarnation is not a thing that matters," I think he was, as they say, whistling in the dark. He himself was a wisp of steel - a sword of the Spirit, if you will, and a sword that had worked God's will, as we all know. It had happened before. *Troy town's down.*

I admit that as a barbarian, I had mingled with the Greeks sufficiently to know that when one of the great tragedians wrote two plays, dealing more or less with the same subject and the same people, he was bound to write another. The three, as we know, make a triology. I had sat in the upper tier of benches and I had watched two harrowing tragedies. The third was bound to come, but I was no longer interested. In my delirium, I lived through the horrors of inevitable plague, slavery of women and children, imprisonment and torture, the imprecations of the damned. I watched in my imagination, migrations of hordes of starving people, driven like cattle in search of pasture. It was only food that mattered. A barbarian like myself, with slant eyes, looked at the swaying, faint and weary people. He asked me what grass was. I told him. I tried to tell him.

"It's what - what cows eat."

He said, "What are cows?"

I did not know the answer. There were streamers and a procession with paper-lanterns. But he did not see the lanterns. You can not see what you do not remember. He had heard of an earthquake. He had seen fire but he had never seen a paper-lantern.

"You hang them on trees in the garden," I said, "you put a candle inside."

"There are no trees," he said.

I was obsessed with paper houses, dwarf umbrella-pines, huge marguerites above white walls. They made the walls look dingy. I found a pencil and made a picture. It was something like the cocoon on Mr. van Eck's signet ring. It would hatch into a butterfly. But the circles and arcs were carved on a sea-shell. There were flying-fish and dolphins and the octopus vase. Tulips grew on the wall, under the marble plaque at Fiesole. There were blue, rose and yellow flowers around the tea-cup. When they said - what they said on the radio, I didn't listen. I couldn't listen any more. They were very old people and young von Alten looked at me from the wall. He looked very young, and then I remembered that we were the same age. I couldn't go with Jan to Shangri-la, because I had to come back to London. I told him I would do what I could, but they stopped writing.

He must have felt it when he looked at me. The table said "Wait." I told him about it, the last time. He said,

"But how can you wait?"

I explained that I could postpone the trip till later. He said,

"But you can not evade responsibility."

I couldn't go into all that, then Garry left and I was so ill. They were right to tell me to wait. Perhaps they were right about everything.

Now I knew how ill I was and how happy I was.

. . . . .

They wanted to stop the bombs altogether. That is what they were after. We had no time for long descriptions of summer-land, no promise of felicity. There was no-one that I knew. If I had made it up, I would have made up Jan and Frederik von Alten and Andrew Lang. I wouldn't have made up Geoffrey to begin with, but I would have made him up later. I would have made up John Geoffrey, as I called him. No-one came that I knew and when they did come, they came for someone else. How could we be working on a lower vibration, as he had seemed to imply? But perhaps we were.

I had told them what had happened. I don't remember what they said, at the end.

"It's not your writing that matters," Ben Manisi had said, "but there's writing in it. You will get to the mountains," he had said. There was some great work to be done but I wasn't going to do it. I was free now.

I was free for the rest of my life. It might end to-morrow, it might end in ten years. But I had made a picture of it, and I could spend the rest of my time putting in the avenue of cypresses, the calla-lilies in the Greek jars and the Anthology flowers around a cup of Dresden china.

III

Closed Circle

There was love and hate. Love was eternal, hate was ephemeral. That is what I learned during my illness. Fear was another word for hate, or hate was another word for fear. I was terribly afraid. I thought that I had broken some law. I thought that I was damned. I was damned. I didn't eat anything. I remembered our discussions about the Witchcraft Act. I wondered what had become of Ben Manisi. No-one came to see me. The telephone stopped ringing.

I thought I had the plague, I had dreamed about, when the other barbarian asked me what grass was. The other barbarian wore clothes like a Lapp. I asked him about the reindeer. He was squinting up into my face. He must have been ten years old, by that time. I had seen a herd of tiny deer rush down a hill, across a clearing from the trees. Each tree stood separate. It seemed the forest had been carefully cleared but there was no path. They were small trees but they looked very old. At the gate, a keeper or a forester was waiting. He opened the gate and the tiny, speckled does and fawns pushed through it, like a flock of sheep. The forester was small, too. The forester turned and faced the camera. At least, that is what I felt. Was I the camera or had I seen this on a film? There was a stone-lantern on the gate-post. The other gate-post was empty. The keeper turned and dragged forward a great basket. He scattered some sort of corn or fodder. The small boy was looking at me.

I think I must have seen it on a film, but I was there now. It was so cold. The forester beat his hands together and blew on them but his breath didn't turn to a frosty cloud as I expected it to. Yes, someone must have been in, for there was a branch of apple-blossom on the table-stand that fitted across the foot of my bed. When the doctor gave me the injection - morphia, I suppose it was - I was lying with my pillows banked up, that end of the bed. Now, I was the other way round, with my head against the wall.

I couldn't do anything about the other barbarian, except try to make him remember the things he had never known.

. . . . .

It was very cold and the grass was brown. It was burnt brown or frozen rather, by the cold. The trees sloped up-hill. It was a small hill. I stood at the gate. The keeper and the deer had gone. The gate stood wide open. We could go through the gate, across the frozen grass to the forest. Well, here was grass, anyway. But it wasn't the sort of grass I meant, and that reminded me of another film I had seen. I think it was called *Grass*. The story was about shepherds. If I told the other barbarian that this was grass, there would be two snags; first, it wasn't the sort of grass I meant, and second, the deer hadn't eaten it, and if they had, they weren't cows. I would have to go into all that.

You couldn't tell people about things if they had never seen them. Maybe, he was from Lapland, then the cows would be reindeer and that would be the reason he didn't know the word, and they wouldn't eat grass, anyway. They would eat moss and lichens. We could go up to the woods, and I could find some moss on the north side of a stone. We went up to the woods. The needles were brown like the grass but there were no stones. I walked round, looking for moss or lichen. The tree-trunks looked the same all round. I couldn't find the north, from the moss on the tree-trunks, and I couldn't find the sun. The air was wonderful. I wondered if he were hungry. I wondered if he would run away. It was so clear in the forest. There were no pine-cones on the ground. I wondered if the forester or the forester's children had gathered them for fire-wood. There were no gleanings of twigs, either. It looked as if the ground had been swept with a broom and the needles had been spread on afterwards, like a carpet.

If it hadn't been so cold, I would have lain down and gone to sleep. But I couldn't go to sleep. That was what was the matter with me. I remembered that I was lying in bed. I remembered how ill I was and I was very happy.

They had said when I had asked them about America, that they could come without the table. Is this what they meant? Is this where they were? Just here? I did not see them. I only saw the forest and the deer. Did the other barbarian see the forest?

"Did you see the reindeer?" I asked him.

But he had not seen the deer, so obviously, he had not seen the forest. I wondered what he did see. I wanted to ask him if he saw the trees, but he had just said there were no trees. We were standing by the gate with the stone-lantern, so we must have come back. The stone-lantern had, no doubt, reminded me of paper-lanterns, but he had never seen paper-lanterns, so I concluded that he would not see the stone one on the gate-post. He could only remember what he had seen. Was I only remembering what I had seen? But I had never seen him before, or had I? Certainly, I had seen many like him, chiefly in newspaper photographs. He might have been hiding with the brigands in the Albanian mountains, or he might have come out of a rat-alley shelter in the island of Malta. He had no shoes but his feet were wrapped round with old puttees, the sort they wore in the last war. His cap was a bit of fur. Is that why I thought he was from Lapland? I had been looking for the north, but there was no moss on the trees. Had the deer eaten it? I bent back my head to see if there were a trace of moss, nearer the top branches, where the deer couldn't reach it. There was none. Then I thought of Hokusai.

This saddened me. I wondered what had happened to the hundred views of Fujiyama in the book that Geoffrey had once given me.

. . . . .

This was a composite of drug, delirium and dream, though the doctor said afterwards it wasn't morphia. When I got well and wrote him, he said: "First, there was the sulpha group. Those had to be given to combat the toxic condition, and in large doses, they are physically depressing. That was bad enough, but the worst feature was your psychic state. You were full of the wildest and most impossible fancies; among others, that the war was still going on."

He was right about that, but which war? It was partly the last war, or the first war and it was this war, or the second war. The V-2 that fell in the park was superimposed on the whizz-bang that I heard when Miranda said, "You should take more interest in yourself, a handsome woman like you." I suppose most people, with or without the sulpha group, whatever that is, would have heard, at the most, in fantasy or delirium, one bomb or one bomb at a time. The two together, I think, pre-visioned a third, or a third war.

I was afraid they would come in and get me, so I staggered out of bed, once in so often, to see if the door was locked. It is true I locked out the sister, and the doctor couldn't get in either. I locked out Mrs. Moss, too. She evidently told Janet, as Janet kept knocking at the kitchen door. In the end, I thought the whole of London had been evacuated because of the plague.

In this war, they had tunneled under the pavements; refugees from France used the channel tunnel. They came out on the river-front and whenever a new rescue party was needed, the sirens went off. I did hear the sirens. There was fighting in the streets too, but the fighting was chiefly in the tunnels. Secret tunnels had been mined right across Europe.

I thought, "I'm glad it's happened now, this is the third war and now it will soon be over."

There were avenues of scaffolds - whole populations were condemned to death. I don't know who the enemy was. It was a sort of world-revolution.

I thought that all my friends had been caught up in this war and that Garry was dead. There was, it is true, a rescue-force still in London, to clear out and disinfect the ruined city. A small - but very small atom bomb had been dropped on Saint Paul's and the rescue workers had moved, for the most part, toward my district and along the river to Richmond. I imagined that certain places in Europe, having foreseen the calamity, had constructed "mercy" tunnels. I imagined that the Saint Bernard hostel, for instance, had prepared an enormous series of tunnels and underground fortresses, and before the war - the third war? - had driven down the cattle and stored great quantities of grain. The dogs had been bred with lions and were of an enormous size. They were used to track down offenders and rescue individuals and parties of "displaced persons" who were dangerously wandering at large. The dogs had been so highly trained and were of such heroic disposition, that they knew even better than the Saint Bernard monks, who was and who was not worth saving.

I remembered when I was staying with Garry, summer 1939, how our Swiss doctor said to me, "But you can not go back to England." I had said good-bye to the von Altens some months before, and Garry had suggested that I stay there with her. I was going back to England anyway, but I went sooner than I expected.

I did not believe the London doctor when he said he had been back and forth to Switzerland with patients. He said he had had such a wonderful melon last time. I remembered Howard and his trip to Lisbon and how I said I wanted a castle-in-Spain. The doctor said, "I can make arrangements to take you out there." I thought he had overheard me talking about the "mercy" tunnels and the Saint Bernard dogs and was only saying this to calm me.

I thought the almost extinct American buffalo was not extinct. I saw thousands of beautiful animals, driven across plains and into the opening of a secret cave. There were other caves, as well. I don't know how these caves could have been secret, but they were. The Indians and a few white men had had a formal conference and decided to save the buffaloes. They left a few at large, to deceive the avaricious fur-traders and the degenerate Indians. The whole race of buffaloes had been saved. I watched them going into the tunnel. A small boy - a Pueblo Indian - was seated at the right of the entrance. He was sitting cross-legged with a drum between his knees. I heard what he played. He was the colour of terracotta. The air was dusty but quite clear. I could see everything.

It seemed the whole centre of the earth was hollowed out, and the happy-hunting-ground was below the earth. It was not in heaven.

. . . . .

The war was going on in the tunnels. Some had been constructed fairly recently. It seems however, that nobody realized that these latter-day tunnels were built over a series or layer of extinct or "dead" tunnels. But under the "dead" tunnels, there were still others. Accidentally, in the fighting, soldiers struggling through the walls, had discovered the second series. They were rescued by the guard. It appears, there were entrances from the extinct or "dead" tunnels, that led down to the bee-hive, as I called it. Here, were packed or stored all the treasures of the world. This may have been a sort of throw-back to von Alten and Shangri-la. But I did not visualize Frederik von Alten there, nor Jan nor anyone I knew. There was a printing-press and a store of "lost" books. The press was used for re-printing and distributing manuscripts. There was a clerk, seated at the press or at a table. I do not know who he was. He wore a black habit, but I do not think he was a monk. Further down, in the third series of tunnels, they were all Indians.

The clerk was really in a sort of half-way house. The Indians were there to safeguard the passes. There were only a few of them. The world above was crashing to extinction, and they had volunteered to come out and help. This had not happened in the history of mankind. But it was decreed that the Indians were not to be sacrificed to the white man. Some of them, however, managed to patrol the "dead" tunnels where the clerk was. I don't know how he got there.

I don't know how I got down to the bee-hive. Maybe, I thought of the bee-hive because of that talk with Jan, when he wanted to take the von Altens to India. And perhaps, I thought of Indians too, because of that, but these were American Indians. The bee-hive was at the very centre of the earth. I only saw one room, or one cell, the one where I was lying. It was as big as Brunelesci's dome, opposite the Baptistery in Florence. The light in the room was given out by the stones. All the stones were radium. There were blocks and squares of solid radium, but by that time, one was conditioned to this. I was supposed to stay there till I got well.

All this is easy to explain. The phrase "the underground" and "underground activities," heard repeatedly on the radio, alone could account for it. Then there was the expected yet none the less shattering blow of the news of Frederik von Alten's death. There was also his archaeological work to consider, as well as my early infatuation with Peter van Eck, who was an archaeologist. There was Jan, too. I had not time to realize his death. Added to this, there was the underground "shelter" life in London, at our door or under our very feet, during those devastating five years.

I hadn't visited the beehive tomb at Mycanae, but I always felt that I had been there. The Indians could be accounted for, by my early work with Ben Manisi, as well as by the research volumes on native, tribal customs that Jan and I used to discuss at the von Altens. There was Frederik von Alten's personal contribution to the subject, as well. I rationalized what, after all, is very easy to understand. I suppose if we delved deep enough, we could rationalize the table, the messages and the whole of the psychic phenomena that Lord Howell and I came to blows about, or it may be, fundamentally, understood together.

I didn't stay long in the bee-hive. I got well there.

. . . . .

Hokusai, the most familiar of the Japanese masters, no doubt, by some magic of association, negated Hiroshima. I had felt the scar. The earth was furrowed with the irrational assaults that man had made upon her. She was always mother-earth. I felt that man was actually assaulting woman. I happened to be a woman. But here, our emotions are of necessity, complex. No doubt, as has since been irrefutably demonstrated, it was a race between two forces, good and evil. I can see that. I can also see the slant eyes and the ashen face of a small boy. The face is ash-coloured, though originally, it may have been fawn-brown.

I have left the young men, the heroes who stemmed the tide, who broke the Steel Wall. They belong to the world of beauty. But I lived to see beauty die. I have accepted that fact. There is still something left, but it lives under the ground. It does not live in heaven. If we want to contact spiritual entities, we must drag them up from the earth. I remember the walls and the pale ghost, called Helen. *Troy town's down* but the beauty they recaptured, is no longer living.

But though the squirrel-like face of the child was staring up at me, and I would have exchanged Troy and Thermopylae for a basket of apples, I couldn't do it.

I wanted to take him with me. I wanted to enter the sewers and release the stranglehold of famine and filth, but I couldn't do it.

I found myself staring at a crystal cross. There was nothing else on the altar. It was not underground.

The cathedral was planted four-square on earth. It was very light, a white or silver reflecting surface gave out the light. There were no images. I had seen a weathered Katherine in the South Kensington Museum, not long ago, and I thought of her, but she had melted in the cool furnace of this illumination. There were other saints, quaint figures. They had been removed from the grimy, inner aisles of Westminster Abbey, before the heavy bombing took place. In the Abbey, they had been shrouded with tattered banners and placed in odd, equivocal niches, where no-one ever saw them. There were saints with contemporary pre-Tudor garments and with attributes, a palm, a cup, a dragon, a book open, a stone book closed. They had been bathed and scraped of the infection of years of casual or ineffectual worship. Some of them were gnawed and weathered like wood. Katherine herself looked as if the sea-wind had left its salt on her crown.

I saw how she was Niké on a ship-prow, and if I had had the will and energy, I could have discerned in each one of them, an attribute of the old Greek Legend. There was the boyish John with the cup like the wine-god, and the dragon that crawled out of it was the old Erechtheus whose temple on the Acropolis, is less weathered and buffeted by time, than these stones.

Although I did not see these quaint endearing images, they were all there. The furnace of the illumination had melted them, had made them its own.

. . . . .

I wrote a story, sitting up in bed, after I locked out the sister. Scotland had disinfected its tunnels. But this was long ago. The Druids from the north were working their way down, to what we now call England. The tunnels had been used for lepers, and the Druids, after collecting them from all the remote plague-pits of the north, segregated and cared for them. They would close the tunnels after cleansing them with hyssop branches and bundles of mistletoe. I could see them sweeping the floors of great underground rooms that led on through corridors, to England. The Druids chanted or recited what I suppose, Garry would call runes. When they got to what is now known as the border, they found that the English - or I suppose the Romans - had blocked off the tunnel with great boulders. The Druids could not get through. Leprosy or the plague went on flourishing in England.

I tore up the story and began another.

If only Gareth had been with me. I suppose the writing took it out of me. I should have stopped writing. Geoffrey didn't really come in, not consciously. I associated him with Ben Manisi. Geoffrey had strange intuitions, sometimes.

I remembered in Paris how upset he was about Dorothy Maitland's death. We were to go there to tea. The maid opened the door. I hesitated on the landing, as Dorothy had so particularly wanted to see us that day. We did not know she was unhappy. The maid hissed in an over-done, theatrical French way, "*Elle est morte - suicide.*" I suppose Geoffrey was trying to help me. He took my arm before I could ask any questions and steered me down the stairs. Dorothy had an apartment at the top of an old house, looking out over the chestnut-trees in the Bois. Geoffrey appeared to take it very calmly, but afterwards, on the Pont Neuf coming home from dinner, he went to pieces.

We were watching the boats. He said, "My God, Astraea, she's here." I thought he was referring to a barge that had got entangled in some river-craft. It had suddenly veered round and was about to nose under the bridge. We were looking down on a sort of gypsy family, preparing their dinner on a brazier.

I said, "Yes," but he clutched my elbow.

"Don't leave me," he said.

I said, "But why should I leave you?"

"Like that poor girl," he said, and I knew then, that he was thinking of Dorothy. He had been thinking of her all the time. He said, "She's been here since that boat turned."

I had no idea that he was, what they call "psychic." It appears that the girl, as he called her, had made only one mistake. She had left money for her maid, with directions to take a fiacre to her lawyer and an intimate friend. She had arranged minute details as to her financial affairs, social engagements and so on.

Geoffrey said, "Tell her it doesn't matter. She says she feels so dreadfully be-cause you had that shock this afternoon, on the stairs."

. . . . .

Dorothy was a friend of Allen Flint. I had known Allen as a schoolgirl. He had taken us to see Dorothy. Allen was a poet of some distinction who was put-ting in time and earning a meager living as a journalist. His news-column was erratic but picturesque, or piccaresque, to use his own word. I had forgotten that I had been in love with Allen. Perhaps Geoffrey was right in London, perhaps Miranda was right. Perhaps I was, unconsciously, looking for someone else, try-ing to go back to childhood. I was only sixteen when Allen returned from his first trip to Europe. We read *L'Aiglon* and *La Princess Lointaine* together. He brought me a fairy-tale illustrated edition of *The Tempest*. I suppose I was too young. Certainly, he was. We took long walks together. All that was long ago. My father found us, curled up in one of the big arm-chairs. He told Allen he would not forbid him the house, but he must not come so often. There was nothing to be done about it. I thought I had forgotten Allen, but he was my first love. For several weeks of the year, we were both seventeen. He said we were twins. I had always wanted a twin-brother. This was the apple-blossom in the apple. Have you ever cut an apple in half the wrong way round? You will find the five-petalled pattern of the blossom in it.

He was very clever. He was a misfit in his world. I fitted in well enough, in a vague sort of way. But after that, everything went wrong. I finished school and had a short time at college. Allen by that time was engaged to a girl from Wilm-ington. Then, that went wrong. He hadn't any money and was always losing his job. However, he had quite a good job for a time, as instructor in romance lan-guages at a small western university. They offered him a travelling fellowship, and he came back. Would I go with him? By that time I had begun to see reason and said, no. He went off to Seville and settled finally, in Venice. He sent me some filagree silver beads from Venice, but I never thanked him. He was twenty-two by that time. I was twenty-one. I couldn't go on with the college work now. I began to do a little writing myself, and was able to place short stories and an occasional article. A friend and her mother were planning a trip to Europe. My parents said that I could go with them.

Allen was very fascinating. Dorothy had an oil-painting of him, in her dining-room. She was a musician and it was rather understood that she was infatuated with Arthur Lovatt, who was a friend of Debussy, and himself a composer. Allen told us about this. But Lovatt said it was a pity that Allen went there so often, now that he was going to be married. I had met Allen's fiancée in London, a tall English girl whose mother had been associated with the pre-Raphaelites. It was Allen who first read the *Blessed Damozel* to me. Marjory Radcliffe looked like

Rossetti's *Beatrice*. She was about my age. I was already married. I was sorry about Dorothy and wondered if my own happiness combined with the announcement of Allen's coming marriage, had precipitated the tragedy. I didn't think Lovatt was responsible.

. . . . .

All this was a long time ago. Allen corresponded erratically. He didn't like my friends. After the last war, he urged me to cut my cables, England was done. The men were effete. He and Marjory had decided never to go back. He did come back once, after Mrs. Radcliffe's death, to help settle up her affairs. I saw him then, and I think, twice in Paris. They had settled in Paris after the war, but Paris like London, was going to the dogs. We wanted a new sort of life, Allen said - where were we to find it? His old obsession with lost beauty, led him back to Italy. They settled in Venice, this time for good. That was all right and a proper setting for the lovely Marjory. But lost beauty must be reasserted. I agreed with him. But I must say, it came as a shock when he began to be known as a follower of Mussolini. I don't think he went in originally, from any sordid motive but they had to live somehow.

I finally stopped writing, as he seemed to go out of his way to abuse non-Aryan races - Jews were his pet aversion. All this was very tiresome. But at the outbreak of the second war, I heard from America that he broadcast regularly.

I can not say that I had time to think much about him. I "forgot" him as I "forgot" Geoffrey.

. . . . .

Why did they come back? How did they come back? A barrier had been broken. The debris that cluttered the streets of London, sometimes left a half-house open, like a doll-house or a stage-set. One looked into rooms in another dimension. So I think this externalization of peoples' private lives, somehow in the end, sliced open one's own house. One looked into one's own interior private life, a life shut off until now, even to oneself. I don't know if this happened to other people. Perhaps I was not alone in this. But perhaps the mind or the soul, or whatever it is that builds this house or this shell around us, was infinitely wise and subtle. It looked superficially, as if I had side-tracked my energy and as I have said, turned it to no good account, or at best neutralized my mind and my emotions. But I wonder. I did love Allen and he did come back.

For in my search for the impossible, *Le Prince Lointain*, shall we say, the old fairy-tale ideal, I somehow never turned back. I went on round the labyrinth, but each turn of the spiral brought me a new personification of the lost companion, the twin. There was Geoffrey, of course. Then Peter van Eck, dynamic and somewhat elder. I suppose Frederik von Alten is really out of this, on the other hand, perhaps the attractive young officer looking down from the wall, reminded me of Geoffrey, and von Alten himself was the beneficent father. It was my own father who had inflicted the first blow, given what I believe is known as the "psychic wound."

I do not blame him for that. Actually, this "psychic wound" saved me from I do not know what vicissitudes. Eventually, Allen Flint was taken prisoner, trying to escape to Switzerland. He was found half-starved on a mountain-trail. He was challenged by the sentry and wounded. I have heard various versions of this tale. One written me from my friend in Delaware, is that Allen was returned to Italy, chained to African deserters and sent to Rome.

. . . . .

The road to Rome was not the road to Venice. Where was Marjory? I began to worry about her. Myself, I might have been Marjory. But for a wound that in retrospect, seemed to have blighted or at least, misdirected or neutralized my life-energy, I might have been huddled over a radio in a cold marble bed-room. I know they had their last apartment near the Riccardi palace. Geoffrey and I had dreamed of settling down in Venice but in the end, we sensibly tried to imagine rain sweeping across the lagoons and the canals rising in the winter storms. We saw no rain. Wisteria climbed over a wall and the bridges were like the moon-bridges, we said, of our beloved Hokusai. He had found me the loosely-bound prints along the quay in Paris.

I had not thought of Marjory for many years. Did she try to escape with Allen? Was she in prison? We had only recently faced the full revelation of the starvation camps. Her beautiful face looked at me, like a reflection seen in water. It was gnawed and furrowed with fear and mal-nutrition. Maybe, she was happy - as happy as could be - with friends. I thought of her as friendless. I began to imagine myself in that cold place. One day, I began packing my clothes. Then, I gave up the idea of taking a suit-case. I did up a few things in a scarf. Janet found me, creeping down the back stairs. I got out of the kitchen door, after the sister had left me "sleeping."

Then, I began to hear guns, police-dogs barking and the intermittent wail of sirens.

Perhaps remembering Marjory, brought back the other girl. There was Dorothy Maitland in Paris. Poor Dorothy! A friend of hers found one of our books in Dorothy's apartment. She asked us to come and get it. Meticulous in everything else, Dorothy Maitland didn't seem to have remembered Geoffrey and myself. The friend - I can't remember her name - pointed this out.

"Dorothy put the library books and some of mine and the Debussy manuscripts that Lovatt sent her, all together on the dining-room table, with a little note." She had the note in her hand. I took it from her.

"Louise dear - will you be so good as to return the library books, one I think, is

overdue, and Lovatt's music. I think there may be one more of your books somewhere, but I can't find it, the second volume of the Landor. Love, Dorothy."

I handed back the note.

"It doesn't matter," I said.

"Yes, Dorothy would have felt so badly to think she had forgotten. I found
this with your name in it." It was Walter Pater's *Imaginary Portraits*. "I don't
know why Dorothy forgot this," she said.

I don't know why, either. Perhaps a psychologist could tell us. Her forgetting
us seemed in some way to stress the fact that she thought of us - or tried *not* to
think of us - in some special way. Now after all these years, I felt responsible again
for Dorothy Maitland.

Now, when the sister came with the usual injection - one of the "sulpha group,"
I suppose - I refused to have it. She thought I was demented. Perhaps I was.

"Louise," I said, although I had just met her, "it doesn't matter at all about the
Imaginary Portraits."

I heard again from my friend in Delaware. She, by the way, was the girl who
was sandwiched in between me and Marjory. She had married before I did and
was as thankful as I, I should imagine, to have escaped the fate of Marjory Radcliffe Flint. We had corresponded for many years. It was she who had written
about Allen. I think she was even more concerned than I. Allen had been an
engaging creature, for all his eccentricity. Perhaps this eccentricity was what was
saving him now. He had quite a little histrionic talent. I did not think him insane,
nor do I think, did Susan. She wrote again:

"Do you remember his Polonius?"

Allen had acted in a college *Hamlet*, but he made Polonius another Shake-
speare fool, which in a way, he was. Poor Polonius! *A rat in the arras*. So was
Allen. Perhaps it was the Nüremburg Trials which had unnerved me, or it was
Allen, but it was then that I began to visualize the streets of gibbets.

Allen, Susan wrote me, was cut off from everyone. She wondered if I could get
in touch with Marjory. Did Marjory want anything? How did I know? I could
tell Susan nothing. She had her three grown children to think of, and it appeared
that anyone who even mentioned Allen Flint was suspect. After all we had been
through in London, this struck me as curiously ironical. It was irony, as I said before, that in the beginning, had sent me spinning backwards. It was ironical that
just before I heard the news of Allen, the messages came to me from the RAF. If
only I could have talked to Lord Howell about this. He was an older man but I
suddenly realized, when he became Sir John Howell, that day - the anniversary of
the second war - that he and I were the same age. Was he another manifestation
of the lost companion, the twin? Before I met him, Ben Manisi had brought me
a psychic journal with an account of Lord Howell's "conversion," as they called

it, to "spiritualism." Although the article defended him, it quoted from various subversive papers. They all intimated indirectly that Lord Howell, after the strain of the first year of the war, had "broken down," in fact was "not himself," in other words, was no longer responsible for his thoughts and actions. This of course, was libellous and the paper was not one in general circulation. It dealt mainly with mediums and various psychic meetings and activities. Now suddenly, Lord Howell of all people, was superimposed on my early memories of Allen.

Here they are my fifty men and women. How Geoffrey loved Browning! I remembered *Fortu* and the yellow melon-flower and thought of our scramble to the light-house, through the tangle of sea-lavender, cistus and flowering gorse. Down, down we went. It was there that Geoffrey found the bee-orchids. So I had been unfaithful to Geoffrey all along, and never knew it. Had Lord Howell ever been unfaithful? His last book dealt chiefly with communications from his *Princesse Lointaine*. This was the lady he had married and lost, soon after the first war. I can not say that I was entirely convinced of the authenticity of all these communications, but I did feel that he had faithfully cherished the memory of his wife. I had not even remembered Geoffrey. I felt when the memories began to seep back, completely unscrupulous and outside the pale. I don't know why I felt this. When finally the crust was broken and my house of life crumbled, I saw why. I had super-imposed Geoffrey - a hero in a small way - on Allen Flint, a traitor. That is why I suddenly veered round. *Troy town's down*. That is why I said I was no longer a Greek.

There was also old Frederik von Alten. It did not matter that he stood outside the circle of war-mongers. He was still a German.

. . . . .

Here they are my fifty men and women. There are more than fifty. I have not chosen this small proportion. I opened a door, or a door was opened by a V-2 that fell in Hyde Park, back of my book-case, behind my wall one Sunday morning, and they just came in. The less than fifty men and women, I have mentioned in this narrative, were not chosen by me. They came into the story with the V-2. They walked through the wall. They hid in the books in the book-case, while I faced the fireplace where Lord Howell stood, on the occasion of our first meeting. Even then, although he had come through the door, left his stick and overcoat, hat and gloves in the hall, he was part of the ruined world that had made it possible for such doors to open. He had come through a door, it is true, on the other hand, he had walked through a wall. So had Geoffrey, Peter van Eck, Jan Verstigen and Allen Flint.

I have said that Geoffrey was unnerved by the problem of eternity. That was a long time ago. I suppose it was settled for him by the whizz-bang that shattered the *éstaminet* - as he called it - in a little cobbled village near the salient. I heard the whizz-bang but I called it imagination. That was winter, 1917. Later, I heard it again but I did not call it imagination. That was winter, 1945. Or maybe, it was spring. Spring and winter merged under the stifling fog and the suffocating trail, left by the high explosives. There was almost thirty years between the two whizz-bangs but - what was it Geoffrey had said? "If two plus two doesn't make four, what does?"

To answer this question, we need a sort of psychic logarithmic table. I never got that far in mathematics, neither did Geoffrey. Or perhaps it is a question of chemistry. I say, I was unfaithful, but was I? I found in each of these four, some quality - however distantly related - of the others. But you can not take Geoffrey, Peter van Eck, Jan Verstigen and Allen Flint and shake them up in a test-tube. However, something happened to this "solution" when Lord Howell laid his coat and stick down in the hall. Maybe, it happened when he said, "It doesn't matter what you are or what you have been - an Egyptian dancing-girl or a North American Puritan."

There wasn't anything for me to say when he said that. So I just sat there, waiting for Gareth to come in. Garry wouldn't come in, so I made an effort, dragged out some words, "I want you to meet my friend, she's in the other room, I'll get her." Garry wouldn't actually come in, till I got tea ready. Perhaps if Garry had come, when I first went for her, the "solution" would have remained forever unresolved. As it was, although I did not recognize the emotional process at work and though I felt impartial and detached, a grain of some alien substance had been added to the test-tube. The "solution" did not begin to simmer and hiss immediately. It took almost a year for the acid to take effect. When it did, it crystallized the emotional content of the test-tube, and after my so-called breakdown, projected clearly these four. So that is the answer to poor Geoffrey's unanswered question, "If two plus two doesn't make four, what does?"

Lord Howell was right to put me outside his special work. I saw it all now. He must have known or felt the alien element in me. He must have felt me watching, appraising, criticising. I had faced two wars in England but that didn't make any difference. I had wanted to stay because of the Steel Wall and the young pilots who with Lord Howell, had "saved civilization." Lord Howell himself stated in his first book that he had no psychic gift and that he depended on others for his messages and communications.

"Strike and strike quickly," he had said, the first time I heard him lecture.

Well, I struck quickly. He waited almost three years, and struck back. It was not stale-mate. I was vanquished.

Perhaps this blow went back to childhood. I was only seventeen when I was separated from Allen. My father was right. That did not mitigate the force of the blow. I lost Allen. I also lost my father. It is true that Lord Howell is not much older than I, but his position, his reputation made him - at least in my relation to his young pilots - a sort of father-symbol. I had taken my stand with the younger generation, perhaps because of Geoffrey. There was young von Alten too, whose smiling eyes always followed me about that pleasant drawing-room, and there was my dear Jan who was the son of the house, a substitute for their beloved, there in Dresden. There was a young poet whom I had "forgotten." We are or we become what we love. Hence I was in my sympathy, only part English, though Geoffrey had given me the right to stay and suffer with them.

The other part was alien. Peter van Eck though born in England, was partly of Dutch extraction. Jan was Dutch. I have already said that he was a younger edition of Peter van Eck, or a substitute son of Frederik von Alten's. The von Alten's were wholly Saxon and Geoffrey was Anglo-Saxon. As to Allen Flint, being an "American" of some seven or eight generations standing, he might have been anything. I do know that his mother was Scotch and that his paternal great-grandfather was a famous New England divine of the usual Puritan antecedents. The Scotch was Highland, one imagines - Allen loved music though he sang badly. It is true at the end, I saw only the Puritan in Lord Howell - the Puritan he sensed in me, at our first meeting. But nobody, even in England, is wholly English. Was Gareth right in the beginning, when she said he was Welsh?

I said, when I commenced this narrative, that there was no-one, no one person there or here, for the matter of all that, who meant supremely, everything. I was right. There was no one person, there were four people.

. . . . .

There were more than four people. There were more than fifty people. There was a swarm of people. They lived every where. They were like a swarm of bees, without a King or a Queen to gather them together. They gathered beauty where they found it. But they had no bee-hive in which to store it. They were buffeted by every wind but they refused to adhere to any yet known collective conscience. They were defenceless. In order to live at all, most of them succumbed to the rigour of whatever régime was in power, in their own country. They had no country. But they didn't know it. Probably they will never know it. They will cling to the land of their birth or of their adoption, because without some outward sign of nationality, they are at the mercy of prison warders or hospital attendants. They may express themselves up to a point, but beyond a certain recognized boundary, they can not go. The demarcations of this boundary threaten us everywhere. It is *sauve qui peut*, even for the best of us. The rest must follow. If you are adroit and have something to offer your followers, you can lead them anywhere. But if you refuse material comfort, you will have no followers. How can you? They will die.

If there is comfort, it is solitary. If you have consolation, do not try to share it.

. . . . .

I confess I was annoyed with Ben Manisi when he insisted, "Delia, your father is here." My father died at the end of the last war. It was my mother that I wanted. My father only gave one message. It was curt and to the point, like the postcard that Lord Howell sent me. Lord Howell condensed what might have been quite a dissertation on publishers and book-sellers into about five words. My father condensed what might have been volumes, into three. This was winter 1943. The usual bombing was at its height though the unusual, the flying bomb and the V-2, were yet to come. My father said, "*Stop this war.*"

That was all he said. Although Ben Manisi told me, before I had arranged my lectures, that my father wanted me to go to America, he didn't give the message direct. It was only afterwards, when I remembered those three words that I regained faith in Ben Manisi.

He was alone like the rest of us, only in a sense, he was more alone.

Back of him for some thousand years before Saxon England had become Norman, his father's people had belonged to a priestly caste. His father was a Brahman and I believe, Brahman means priest. Cutting across the Indian, were his mother's people, partly of Quaker origin. Fire and ice do not mix. His conflicts must have been intolerable. Out of them, he managed to create a new dimension. He lived there, for a time. But mal-nutrition and constant fear of the law, in connection with a recrudescence of intolerance that found legal support in the obsolete Witchcraft Act, proved too much. He took the easy way, or perhaps it was the hard way. I don't know, for by this time, I have completely lost touch with him.

In my delirium last spring, I lived a whole life. I could never face such an ordeal again. I do not mean to imply that Ben Manisi's pictures and messages were caused altogether by his neurotic condition, but contacting entities from outside must take it out of one. Provided there are entities from outside. We know so little, nothing at all really, about these things. He brought comfort to us. Possibly, we made his life a little easier, for the time being. We met in a whirlwind. We parted when the storm had passed. Out of the whirlwind, this strange, sensitive creature brought his pictures, his messages and his naive, oriental fantasies.

He revealed a sunken city. There were great jars. I do not know whether or not, they had decorative motives or pictures drawn or painted on them. It did not sound Greek somehow but "they are under the water," he said. There was a volcanic mountain. I thought of Fujiyama, but it was not Japan. I knew it was not Japan. I remembered the famous octopus vase and the sea-weed pattern, the sea-horses, curled shells, flying-fish and dolphins that Peter van Eck had helped Sir Arthur Evans restore in Crete. I knew it was Crete before Ben Manisi said, "It's Greek but it doesn't seem to be in Greece, somehow." Was Ben Manisi turning over the pages of my own submerged or sub-conscious memories - the talks Peter van Eck and I had had together, the pictures he drew, my own visits to museums, my long day-dreams, after Peter van Eck walked out of the door of Shepherd's Hotel in Cairo? Or was Ben Manisi reading a more abstract, official document? Was he reading or deciphering an allegory? Was it his own submerged self that was speaking?

"You are here - you were here," said Ben Manisi. But even my child-memories of Hans Andersen's *Little Mermaid* could explain this submerged city. Childhood memories and day-dreams could account for the whole thing.

I saw all this in subdued grey-green and dull silver. But I saw him seeing it in fiery colour, vermilion sea-weed seemed to paint the columns. He said,

"This is funny. Now I am here, Delia. Do you know, now I am a fish. I am a diamond-fish, that is, I am square-shaped. I am a sort of goblin-fish. I am swimming along and I swim right across. I swim to a bump-out of land. It is not South America, no, there are islands like small moons, pointed. I get there. I don't know why it is not South America. It should be. It might be Mexico."

"It's Yucatan," I said, "it's central America."

I think this was the last "sitting" I had with Ben Manisi. I said "It's Yucatan" because the table had spelt out a sort of incantation or rune, as Gareth would have called it. I saw it written in two lines:

Yucatan,
A part in plan.

I had looked up Yucatan in our old Atlas. It did bump-out, just as Ben Manisi had said. But was he reading my own thoughts, even to the extent of my own doubts, as to where Yucatan actually was? Why should he say "It's not South America. It should be. It might be Mexico."

The veil, I think is the word for it, was very thin. One saw right through it. Or, like a curtain before a play, the veil was drawn aside from time to time, and one looked on scenes of the near or far past or even of the future. Ruins were all around us. So maybe, this obsession with past civilizations was simply a matter of our own imminent danger and constant preoccupation with death and with dead cities. Rotterdam, Warsaw, London - it was all one. Geographic boundaries were bombed away, so perhaps were the boundaries of time. Past, present and future became one. The distant past and the near past merged. I do not wish to disregard the "findings" and the research work of other people, but on the whole, I think them *parti pris*; they are centered, for the most part, on one country, one group of people, one creed or one philosophy. The romantic and imaginative disregard the scientific, the scientific are apt to frown upon the flights of imagination taken by the perceptive and over-sensitive. Psychology must be taken into account, as well as physical obsessions and the material welfare of the "worker." Yucatan was foreign to me. I did not like the idea of it. But *Yucatan* and *plan* were on more than one occasion, "given" to me by Ben Manisi, his guide K, or the table. Yucatan, it seemed to me, was diametrically opposed to the first vivid messages about the ship, the warriors and Hal Brith.

I did not visualize this ship in the Caribbean. But possibly, it might have been there. They were going off on a voyage of discovery. I had thought of Eric Ericson. They got to Rhode Island, *vineland*. They might have gone on.

Ben Manisi said the ship was at the turn of the era; there were circles on circles on the sea. The circles did not merge but touched one another. Well, the Vikings made one circle or one link in a long chain of historical, psychological and emotional associations. Yucatan was another circle, Crete was in between.

I do not know whether Yucatan came first or the Vikings. There must obviously be many other circles joining these three. The Vikings may have gone from the far north to America, Central America and across to Crete, then back again. Or they may have sailed south, as the Verangian guard did in the great days of Byzantium, and from Crete, set out to America, and then home. In any case, however fantastic the association of Yucatan and Vikings, there is possibly some logic in it. I have said that Ben Manisi's background was fire and ice. The same, in a lesser degree, might be said of my own.

K's whole name as he gave it, might have been Egyptian. Actually, Ben Manisi said he had seen the syllables written out, in a British Museum catalogue, with the translation of the hieroglyphs on a coffin. He actually found the coffin with the help of the catalogue, and was able to decipher the inscription. One of the syllables of K's name was related to Ra, the Egyptian sun-god. But Manisi insisted that K was a North American Indian. You might say that K was really Ben Manisi's father, another Indian.

In the same way, though less obviously, you might say that Z, who came to me, was a father substitute. Z was from Yucatan. It was after I heard Lord Howell lecture that Z came to me.

Lord Howell had spoken of Beings of a higher order coming down to lower or more familiar regions. Z made this clear. He spelt his whole name. But Manisi, usually so ready to welcome new-comers, said the unfamiliar letters made no sense. I insisted on the authenticity of this Z, and Ada said, "Ask K then, Ben, if you aren't sure."

Manisi said, "K, there is some trouble here."

K said, "No."

"Well, these letters don't mean anything."

K carefully spelt out, "Yucatan" again, then, "Z - good Indian."

Z came back. He spelt "Nénufar."

Manisi said, "You see - it's nonsense." It seemed odd that Manisi did not recognize the word *nénufar* or nenuphar, the water-lily.

"It's not nonsense," I said. Then Z spelt, "Water-lis" and I explained that the nenuphar was the water-lily. It was quite clear that Z wanted to indicate that he was from another or "foreign" country and that the message that Manisi would have disregarded, was for me. I also felt that Z had used great subtlety in indicating two countries or two planes, by his quaint insistence on the *nénufar* or nenuphar being water-lis, not water-lily. The use of the word nenuphar was also striking.

I think nenuphar is originally a Persian word. If so, we approach India. Manisi had said in his first "reading" of the letter, that Lord Howell had been in India. He also said he had been in America. I found some time afterwards, another article in which it spoke of Lord Howell's work in America after the Battle of Britain. It also stated that he had been stationed in India, as a young officer before the first war. Perhaps Manisi already knew this, but he did not know who was the writer of the letter he then held in his hand. India however, suggests Indians, whether they are the original Hindus or the natives of the Americans. All this might have been conclusive but I considered these "findings" as a sort of dream. I tried to rationalize the whole content of the table and our private talks together. But I couldn't altogether rationalize Z. The name was most unusual. Had I seen it somewhere? I couldn't imagine where. Certainly, Manisi did not encourage me about Z. I wrote Lord Howell, however, in some detail. He answered in his early, rather distant manner. Well, that did not change my feelings about Z.

A red Indian, whether of South, North or Central America, is associated in our earliest fantasies with war, the war-path, arrows. K was benignity itself, and so was Z. I was certainly surprised when I found out, from a review of Lord Howell's second book, that the guiding spirit of his circle was known as Z. I had written him about Z but he had given me no indication that this was the same entity. Only later when I quoted messages, sent by the RAF and sponsored by Z, did he write me, "We also have Z in our circle." But Lord Howell, though admitting this strange coincidence, seemed to imply that if messages came through Z, it was a matter of small importance. The same Z could and perhaps did give the messages to him, direct.

Again, it was a closed circle. By that time, it no longer mattered. I was going to America, even though the table said "Wait." However, I did not go to America, though I did wait.

. . . . .

I have said that there were more than four people, more than fifty people in my life; there is a swarm of people. Their only hope is to maintain separately, an intense individuality. The more individual they become, the more they will grow to resemble one another. This sounds a paradox but it is how I finally solve the problem of integration.

I have said if you have consolation, do not try to share it, but eventually, if you are consoled or integrated, you help console and integrate the scattered remnant. I don't think society can be reconstructed from outside. I have said if there is comfort, it is solitary. When the ego or centre of our amorphous, scattered personality crystallizes out, then and then only, are we of use to ourselves and to other people. I have said it is *sauve qui peut*, even for the best of us. In saving oneself, one creates a shell, not the isolated, highly individual spiral-shell I spoke of, but a minute coral-shell, one of a million, or a single wax-cell of the honeycomb.

If we think of policies or politics, we are forced to think in vague generalities. As the outer world has expanded, so has the inner. Probably, it was the struggle to comprehend the incomprehensible actions that were taking place outside, that forced me by a law of compensation, to try to grapple with the forces inside myself, or outside the material world.

This, I conclude was wholly logical and reasonable. But in the end, I was working entirely alone. Gareth realized my predicament and had tried to modify my enthusiasm, although she had not suggested that I give up the work. Ben Manisi had, to all intents and purposes, as far as we were concerned, himself admitted that the work was too much for him. Gareth had new work and interests out of England. There was only Lord Howell left. Then, Lord Howell wrote that my messages from the RAF, were trivial and uninspiring. There was no-one left.

I was quite alone; in my isolation, I re-lived the first war, the second war and pre-visioned a third war. But friends returned out of the rubble, Geoffrey from an *éstaminet* in Flanders, Peter van Eck from the ruins of the palace of Knossos in Crete, old Frederik von Alten from Troy and the devastation of Dresden, Allen Flint from a sunken, marble city and my own childhood. Their appearance was as startling and as unexpected as manifestations at a séance. But though I have implicit confidence in the messages of Ben Manisi, none of these people made their appearance or manifested in any way whatever. May we conclude - as far, at least, as I personally am concerned - that the medium drew upon the contents of my own mind, my conscious mind. Lord Howell was in my mind, at the time of our talks together. But the others were not. Thoughts about them would have been unbearable, so I suppressed them. If I could go on from here, it would be interesting to see if "messages" concerning the fate of Allen Flint would be given me or a solution as to the disappearance of the enigmatic Mr. van Eck. These two may or may not be alive. The other two - Geoffrey and Jan Verstigen - are dead.

We may also note that the "messages" came to me at a time of great danger. Would they have come otherwise? If the messages were received by unstable agents, do we conclude that the messages themselves were unreliable? It might be argued that they were. Given ideal conditions, comfort, security, peace of mind would the messages have come at all, or would we ourselves have wanted them? The messages filled a vacuum. But if I with sincerity and conviction, later continue the "work," would my very peace of mind and comparative good health, in a sense, block the communications?

Biologically, I can accept the fact of some inter-relation between dead and living. But I think the whole content of psychic communication can be related, as I said before, to the dream-life of the individual.

We know comparatively little about that dream-life. But we do know that it is only possible to approach the dream-world subjectively. The same might be said of the world of psychic phenomena.

There are, there must be exceptions to this rule. But I do not think that any but the strongest mentalities are fitted to make pronouncements on these matters. Lord Howell seemed peculiarly fitted to judge and assess the findings of psychic-research workers. I had thought myself above the usual type of sensational or hysterical seeker. I still think so. But my valiant - if I may say so - effort to make a bridge between the conscious or scientific mind and the unconscious or dream-mind, met with but scant recognition. Thrown back on myself, myself becomes the arbiter.

I was unhappy. What thinking person was not in those Apocryphal years? But my personal sense of loss and frustration was submerged. If I had accepted the fact of Geoffrey or even of Allen Flint in the first place, the whole pattern of my life would have been different. I would perhaps have been happy in a purely personal or relative sense, but I would not have found the arbiter. Who is this arbiter?

I have just said that biologically, I feel we may continue our relationship with certain people after death. We are and we remain physically, part of our mother and our father. My own mother did seem a living presence, on the occasion of my first talk alone with Ben Manisi. But she did not come back nor manifest again, as I had hoped she would do. You may say that the mother represents the emotional, creative or dream-self, while the father represents the intellectual, critical or constructive self. As I have said, my father - if it was my father - made only one pronouncement, *Stop this war.*

My mother spoke to me or spoke to Manisi, just before Christmas, 1941. My father made his terse pronouncement, two years later. It is now nearing Christmas, 1946.

. . . . .

I have said that I did not go to America, but perhaps I did. The bombs that shattered my house of life revealed another house beneath it. In my first interview with Manisi, he had asked me if I had done any excavating. I had thought of Peter van Eck, trying not to think about him. But I did not think of the buried cities of Crete and Egypt, in terms of the submerged, unconscious mind.

"Here is a long track in the sand," Manisi had said.

It was a long track, certainly. He went on to say,

"There are two tracks." Well, I had gone on, as he had predicted. When I came to journey's end, I had no choice really, as to which track I should take. "There are footprints. Now they branch off," he had said.

The foot-prints branched off, certainly. It was February, 1946, just a year after I had met Lord Howell, that I received my last letter from him. Manisi had recalled Peter van Eck to me when he said, "This gentleman is no longer in your life." Was it a sort of prophecy? I had tried to keep Peter van Eck out of it, though the story that I had especially wanted to know about, was concerned with our meeting after the first war and our few weeks together in Athens and in Egypt. I had asked Manisi about the story, not about any "gentleman," but the story and the "gentleman" were, taken all in all, the same thing. When I asked Manisi what I should do about the story, as I couldn't finish it and didn't feel that I should destroy it, he said "Throw it away." It was surplus emotional cargo, he seemed to imply and I would do no good with it. But I had lived with the story too long. Although I threw away the story, it came back. It is the same story.

6th December, 1946.

Wintersleep

PART II

I

Iphigenia

To-morrow is Palm Sunday. Last night or early this morning, the *Synthesis of a Dream* manifests. We are in America. There is a wooden bench. This is the front-porch of a friend of my mother's. Her husband has lately directed a production of *Iphigenia*, given by his students. Therefore, the dream-year must be 1903. The month must be June. I am therefore, sixteen. But my companion is sixty-three. There is no disparity in our ages, however. We are the same age.

My mind has satisfied itself. I have written or projected the story of my war years in London. I have grieved for my friends there, but a benign Providence has decreed that I am to be spared further suffering. It would be blasphemous to turn back, to reverse this decree of fate.

A friend and her daughter who lost their home in the bombing, are in my London flat. So, seated on Mrs. Atherton's front-porch (Philadelphia, 1903), overlooking a small town-garden, I explain to Lord Howell, "that is the worst of being philanthropic. I can't ask you to come and talk in my flat." I open my handbag. I offer him a cigarette. He accepts it.

"Now," I continue the conversation, "when I get over there, I want to be cremated. Do they cremate people over there?"

Lord Howell, true to type, replies, "But we need not worry about what happens to our bodies when we are dead."

"But these things are important," I say. "You wrote somewhere of someone sloughing off, not one but many bodies. He was running across the sand, throwing off his bodies like old clothes. You can't leave the desert cluttered up with old bodies."

"But," Lord Howell said, "we won't have many bodies, you and I, to throw away. We will step out into nothingness."

In my dream, this did not alarm me. However, a body is a useful appurtenance. Why throw it away?

"But soon," said Lord Howell, "I will see myself looking at myself, in your eyes. You will see yourself looking at yourself, in my eyes."

. . . . .

But at this moment, I am looking at myself with my own eyes. Mrs. Atherton had just given a reception to her husband's students, that is to the chosen few who have lately taken part in Euripides' *Iphigenia*. There were two performances at the Academy of Music. I went to both.

When Pylades stepped forward, toward the end of the play, in the role of epilogue or messenger, to deliver his long speech, I knew that I had seen him before. I saw him again, only a half-hour ago. He suggested that we walk around the garden. I was immensely flattered. On introducing us, Mrs. Atherton had said, "Delia, this is Mr. Moore, Professor Atherton's favorite pupil."

Mr. Moore refused the ice I offered him. I had seen Mr. Moore somewhere. I had seen his name written in my Palgrave's *Golden Treasury*. Was it *The Burial of Sir John Moore*? Or was it,

> *My love is like a red, red rose*
> *That's newly sprung in June?*

There was an Irish poet, called Thomas Moore. But perhaps it was Robert Burns who wrote that. Or I may be confusing the poet with someone in my English History.

"I think I have seen you somewhere," I say.

"Did you by any chance, see our *Iphigenia*?"

"Do you mean, among the Taurians?" I asked, for I felt well up in these things. There was another Iphigenia - in Aulis, Professor Atherton had explained to my mother. Both plays were by Euripides. Euripides was a Greek dramatist. That was all I knew about him. Perhaps Mr. Moore thought me remarkably intelligent, or perhaps the noise and the clatter of tea-cups was getting on his nerves. It was a warm early-summer day. As I turned to continue my arduous duties as "aid" at Mrs. Atherton's at-home, Mr. Moore said,

"I will tell you about Aulis."

Perhaps he thought me singularly receptive. I don't know. He talked in a low-pitched, even voice. I had heard the voice somewhere. We were standing on a grassy platform above a little terrace. It occurred to me that it was my turn to say something. I wondered if Mr. Moore would come to see me, but I was too shy to ask him. Maybe, he would ask me if he could come to see me. It did not occur to me that Mr. Moore was putting in time, that it would not do for Professor Atherton's favourite pupil to bolt half-way through a reception, given in honour of the Greek players. Of course, that is where I had seen him. Standing on the platform of grass, he was speaking his lines. I was sitting in one of the balcony-boxes at the Academy of Music. There was a name on the programme. The name was Thomas Moore. The name, Thomas Moore, was on the right side of the folder. On the left, were the Greek names. Mr. Thomas Moore's Greek name was Pylades.

There was Orestes, too. No doubt, I had just handed Orestes a cup of tea. I might even have encountered Iphigenia, in the long, cool but overcrowded drawing-room. But he (she) was negligible. I did not consciously visualize myself in the role of Iphigenia, but perhaps from the moment the slight, graceful figure stepped from behind the archaic pillars of the temple, anyone who in the end, was to claim Pylades, was abhorrent to me. I thought the boy in the long priestess' robe and the hieratic head-dress, dowdy. Orestes, the brother, was passable and an actor, in a small way. Pylades, however, had stepped out of a Greek frieze. Orestes had the more important part. But toward the end, Pylades stepped forward with his long speech. I knew no Greek, whatever. But I did know that Orestes and Iphigenia were acting in a Greek play, but that Pylades was Greek.

My love is like a red, red rose. But the slim, athletic figure was in white. His short kilt was pleated. His arms were bare. I turned and looked at Mr. Thomas Moore. It was the same head. Orestes had worn a head-band of dull gold. Pylades' head was unbound. As I say, it was the same head. The eyes were blue. He was not looking at me. He was not saying anything. I thought again, he will ask me where I live. I will tell him. He will say, "But this has been delightful. I must see you again."

He said, "Are you going to the Ivy Ball?"

I said that I had been invited. It was Allen Flint who had invited me. I had avoided Allen in the drawing-room. He was one of the Chorus of Maidens.

"You will be there?" I asked. He said he would. Well, he would look for me and he would dance with me. This was his way of saying that he wanted to see me again. I would see him again. They were talking on the porch and some of them were going. I hoped that Allen would keep out of the way.

"Oh, there you are," called Bessie Childs from the porch-steps. She was calling to me. By the time I got rid of Bessie, Mr. Thomas Moore had gone.

When I went back to the drawing-room, Mrs. Atherton said,

"Delia has made a conquest." I looked at Mrs. Atherton. "When Mr. Moore came in, he said 'Will you present me to the girl with the green hair.'"

I put up my hand instinctively, to smooth out the flat ribbon-bow.

That evening, I carefully put away the green ribbon. My mother said,

"I hear you are admired for your green hair." I pretended not to know what she meant. "Mrs. Atherton told me that one of the students wanted to meet the girl with the green hair."

"Oh," I said. "Who - *green hair*?"

"Yes," my mother said, "he really meant hair-ribbon."

I knew that I was the only "aid" with a green hair-ribbon. Nonchalantly, I remarked,

"Did she mean me?"

"Yes - one of the older students. He graduates this year."

I pulled off the ribbon. "It goes nicely with this dress."

The dress was a flowered chiffon. I put the ribbon between the pages of the programme and laid both carefully away, under the heap of linen in my second bureau-drawer. My mother had reminded me that, as well as the Ivy Ball, there were at least two more occasions when I might meet Mr. Moore. There was the graduation of the class of 1903, preceded by the more informal Class Day.

. . . . .

It was very hot and crowded. There were funny speeches which didn't mean anything, except to the groups of students crowding the front benches of Franklin Hall. There was another programme and a long list of names, in small print. Honours' List was short and the print was larger. Martin, Meyer, Moore -Thomas. I had gone with Bessie and Virginia Childs. Their cousin was graduating. They were going to the Ivy Ball, too. We waited in the trophy-room, when the first part of the programme was over. The wide double-door was open and I wanted them to come out and walk around the garden. But Bessie said it wouldn't do. We were three girls alone. But Lee Childs was pushing through the students.

"I think that's your cousin, Bessie," I said.

Lee Childs came across to us.

"We might take a turn in the garden," he said.

Lee walked with Virginia, talking and laughing and introducing Virginia to his friends. He included Bessie and me. He was very polite. He was too polite. The hot sun glared from the paving-stones. It was almost as crowded in the sunken-garden as it was in the trophy-room. My eyes ached, trying to distinguish one student from another. They all looked alike. I told Bessie I felt dizzy. It was easy to lose the others. The trophy-room was almost empty. There were silver cups on shelves and oars with dates, and framed photographs of football teams. I said it would be cooler in the billiard-room but Bessie said we couldn't go there. Then Mrs. Rowe saw us through the glass door and came in. She said,

"What are you two pretty girls doing in here alone - come over at once and do your duty."

Professor Rowe introduced us to some of his graduate students.

I didn't even see Mr. Moore, though I suppose he was there.

I opened my bureau-drawer. I laid the second folder with the *Iphigenia* programme and the green hair-ribbon, under the heap of linen.

. . . . .

I wished Allen wouldn't take so many dances, but he had invited me to the Ivy Ball, so I couldn't say anything. Virginia said,

"Remember, you promised Lee two dances."

That was two more gone. There was a two-step, a waltz, a two-step, a waltz and three or four schottiches and lancers. I tried to save the waltzes. I was looking so hard for Mr. Moore that I didn't even see him when he stood beside me. Maybe, he didn't want to dance; maybe, he didn't even see me.

I said, "Mr. Flint has my dance-card."

Allen was scratching A, with the little pencil on the white cord. There was a gold embossed ivy-leaf on the dance-card and the numbers, 1903. Allen handed me the dance-card.

"Full up," he said, "except for the second schottiche."

I scratched off the A opposite two waltzes and handed the card to Mr. Moore.

Allen said, "Come on, we missed the first waltz."

I waited for Mr. Moore to hand me back my dance-card. It looked as if his own were full. Well, so was mine.

"I don't like the schottiche," I said.

His partner would be waiting for him, but he still held the dance-card.

"I'm afraid - " he said.

"It's all right," I said. I reached for the card. Mr. Moore scratched off a name on his card. He handed me back my own. Allen had swirled me away before I had time to look at it. While we were having refreshments during the interval, I looked for Mr. Moore's name. There was T M, scratched above the second A I had crossed out.

It seemed that I had wasted the whole evening with Allen Flint, Lee Childs and all those others. It wasn't that he danced better than the others, but he danced differently. Everything was different. I suppose I was tired, by that time. I was somewhere else. When they stopped to applaud for the encore, I couldn't think whether it would be better to go on dancing or to get out into the garden. We were near the door. There were other people in the garden, so it would be all right to go out.

"It's hot," I said, though really I was shivering. The waltz was going on, inside. The light from the door showed me the Greek head in profile. He was looking at the lilies. Most of them were closed but there was one at the edge of the square of water, that was wide open. Across the square of water, the stone steps reminded me of the temple in the Greek play.

I put away the dance-card with the gold embossed ivy-leaf and the numbers, 1903, with the *Iphigenia* folder, the Class Day programme and the green hair-ribbon.

. . . . .

Mr. Moore was even further away on Commencement Day than he was on Class Day. We were in the Academy again, but the Greek columns and the steps were replaced by rows of chairs. The faculty in cap and gown, took up the first rows. The class of 1903 was seated in slightly elevated tiers, behind them. I wouldn't have recognized Mr. Moore, even if I had known where he was sitting. A famous Shakespeare scholar gave the opening address. He wore a velvet hat like someone in a play. Mrs. MacMaster who was with us, said he looked like Holbein (whoever that was) and that his red hood was from Oxford, England. He said, swirling around from the audience to face the students, "a little learning is *not* a dangerous thing." I looked for his name on the programme. It was Howard Horace Furness. The programme had about twenty pages. There was the usual list of names and a separate photograph of each one of the graduates, with a quotation. I found Thomas Moore. The quotation was, "His face was like a benediction."

I cut out the photograph when I got home. It just fitted into my silver locket. I would wear the locket under my dress, so that no-one would see it. I would sleep with it under my pillow. I had two initials scribbled with a blunt pencil. I had the very pencil. I had the gold ivy-leaf. I had four numbers, 1, 9, 0, 3, if 0 can be called a number. I had the Class Day folder with his name in small print and his name in large print. I had his name in still larger print, with the list of players. I had his Greek name, Pylades.

He had said, "Did you by any chance, see our *Iphigenia*?" He had said, "I will tell you about Aulis." He had said, "Are you going to the Ivy Ball?" He had said, "I'm afraid - " but he still held the dance-card, then he scribbled in the letters. I don't know what he said when we were dancing. I don't think he said anything. He looked at the lily in the square of water. I don't think he said anything.

He said (Mrs. Atherton said), "Will you present me to the girl with the green hair."

He said a great many other things but I didn't understand them. He was looking straight at the balcony-box where I was sitting. His legs were bound almost to the knees, with narrow strips of leather. He did not walk about like Orestes, but stood on the side of the stage while Orestes did the talking. He did say a few words to Orestes. He listened to Iphigenia. When Pallas Athené appeared on the temple roof or gable, in a helmet with a silver spear, he turned his back to the audience and listened to her. He had only one long speech, it was very long and he stood right in front of the stage. He seemed to be explaining everything to me. I would never see him again and anyway, he had already told me all about it. He had told me about it before it happened, but I did not understand Greek. That is why he did not come to see me. That is why he looked at the water-lily and didn't say anything. There was really nothing to say. He need not have asked to meet me. Then, I would never have known. But he wanted me to know. Even so, he must have wondered if he should speak to me. He didn't say he wanted to meet the girl with the green hair-ribbon. He must have been startled and confused when he saw me at Mrs. Atherton's reception. He said he wanted to be presented to the girl with the green hair. He did not have to be presented. People just came up for tea and ices. But he wanted to be presented. We had been introduced formally, like people in a play. He didn't really have to dance with me. He took the last waltz. He had to scratch out a name on his own dance-card. He had to explain why, to someone else afterwards. He didn't have to explain anything to me. I would never see him again.

. . . . .

I managed after Commencement, to get away from the others, but I had to pretend to be looking for Bessie Childs on the stairs, in the hall, on the parquet floor, even in the stage boxes. The boxes were empty now. I sat for a little while, behind a heavy velvet curtain. Then, I rushed out to the entrance and back again, up the stairs to the balcony. The Academy was almost empty by this time, but there was still a group of students in the main hall. They were going on, I supposed, to some sort of class banquet. I waited out of sight by the coat-hangers, but it was summer and there were no coats. There were men's hats and a few canes and umbrellas. I pretended that I had lost a parasol. I was afraid that someone would come in, that I knew. There were two boys at the other end of the counter.

"It's that small case," one said.

"Has Zeus Atherton gone yet?" asked the other.

"He's getting the Iphi crowd together."

Iphi? "No," I said to the girl with the ruffled apron, "it's a plain silk parasol - green silk - not dark green - leaf-green. I don't know where I left it."

"Go on out, Nick, and say I'm coming." The boy was looking in his pockets, for the check for the small case. The other boy came back.

"I saw Zeus. I saw Tom, too."

"Tom? Tom Street?"

"No - Street didn't even make the chorus of the Iphi. I mean Tom Moore. Zeus has got the main crowd together, but Tom's not coming."

I heard what they were saying. I asked the girl with the ruffled apron to write my name and address in the Lost and Found book that was lying on the counter. I didn't have to do that. I had heard everything.

"No, it isn't dark green," I insisted, "it's leaf-green." The girl looked at me. "Water-lily leaf-green," I said.

The girl said, "Miss, I'll get you a glass of water."

She took me behind the desk, through a little door and I sat in a chair in a tiny room with photographs of opera-singers, tacked up on the wall. I said I was all right, but could I wait five minutes till the crowd left. I told her it was Professor Atherton's crowd and he was giving a lunch, I thought, to his students or to some of them, who were in a play - perhaps she saw it - called *Iphigenia among the Taurians*. There were two plays, I explained carefully. The other was *Iphigenia in Aulis*. I didn't know where Aulis was but I said that I had met some of the Greek players. No, I didn't know any Greek.

He didn't have to explain anything. No one would ever know about it. Mr. Moore wasn't going to Professor Atherton's lunch, after the Commencement exercises, because his fiancée and her mother had come especially from Albany for the graduate celebration, and were taking the late afternoon train home.

———————————

II

Lost and Found

He didn't have to explain anything. But he said,

"Soon, I will see myself, looking at myself, in your eyes."

There was nothing to explain really. It was the Saturday before Palm Sunday, early in the morning. Next Sunday will be Easter. Mr. Moore had said good-bye to Mrs. Atherton. Lord Howell was sixty-three and I was sixteen. I did not know that I was sixteen, until I found myself sitting on Mrs. Atherton's front-porch. The windows of the drawing-room were open but the drawing-room was empty. Everyone had gone but Lord Howell and myself. He said, "We won't have many bodies, you and I, to throw away."

I don't know about Lord Howell but running across the desert of the war-years, like the bomber he wrote about, I had thrown away at least four bodies. I felt stripped and bare and rather cold. The bodies were not cluttering up the desert. I had collected them and labelled them carefully and laid them away. I did not lay them in white linen but between the pages of a book. There was the Allen Flint body, the Geoffrey Alton body, the Peter van Eck and the Jan Verstigen.

I had said that Lord Howell had added a grain of alien substance to a solution in a test-tube and that he had projected these four bodies. But there was a fifth body that I had not recognized - my own. I still had a body. We do not have to wait till we are dead, to cast off our various bodies like old clothes.

Allen returns as one of a circle of tall Maidens in the set ring-dances of a Greek play. He always was eccentric. Bessie said afterwards,

"You could trust Allen to think up something at the last minute, to make himself important."

The Maidens were the same height and in their long robes and head-dress-es, they were indistinguishable from one another. But Allen had said to Bessie, "You'll know which I am." The chorus formed a circle facing the audience, and revolved like a group of statues on a pedestal. Their pleated robes hung even, to their ankles. Their feet were bound with silver sandals. Their scarves were white-silver. They held their scarves, to form a silver circle. Bessie said that Professor

Atherton said, it had something to do with the moon-circle. There was a white band around their knees and there was music, harps and flutes and a drum sometimes. The drum began to beat very softly, like the sound of feet walking, then running and they went round faster. They looked like one person or one statue but there were twelve, I think. Bessie knew all about it. She said they were the twelve months. But when they stood still, while the priest said something at the altar, you could see which was Allen. Bessie whispered, "You see he's spoiled it." One of the twelve Maidens, still motionless with the others, had crumpled up her silver scarf, so that the moon circle as it faced the audience, was broken.

. . . . .

The moon-circle was broken. It was a hot summer. We took long walks and lay under the trees. Allen read William Morris to me. *Two red roses across the moon.* There were two red roses but the ice-flower had not melted. I do not know at what exact moment, I pasted the programme, the graduation folders and the dance-card in my Memory Book. I do not know what became of the green hair-ribbon. I do not remember taking Mr. Moore's picture out of the silver locket. I had only seen him two times. I had seen Pylades two times. I had seen Allen in a long robe and a priestess' head-dress. There was music of strings and pipes. Allen acted in a Greek play, but he was not Greek. He was like one of the pages that I saw afterwards, with Geoffrey in Florence. The Gozzoli pages formed a procession round the wall, in a small golden chapel.

Allen was tawny like a young lion. There was all of the sun in him. He brought me a *de luxe* edition of the Tristram story. There were two Iseults, Iseult Blanch-main and Iseult Blanchfleur. I was both Iseults, but the white ice-flower was floating in a square of dark water and a waltz was playing. There was a face half-turned, in profile. I never had another green dress. I did not know why I disliked the lovely colour. *Come with bow bent*, Allen read to me, *Maiden of months.* I can not remember Swinburne's lines now. I had pledged myself to the Maiden of months in the temple - was it Tauris, Aulis, Ephesis? The pledge was ratified, signed and sealed. We had been formally presented. Mr. Moore wanted to be presented. He could have come over to the table and asked for ice-cream, like everyone else did, but he asked to be presented. Orestes wore a crown and was a king's son. His friend Pylades had princely manners. Allen was rough and acted like an overgrown school-boy. He was an overgrown school-boy. He did not melt the ice-flower but he broke the moon-circle.

There was the rat-ta-ta-tat of the drum beating. The Maidens revolved in their circle, as if they were carved of marble. There was always a reason for waiting, for sitting quietly under the lamp with my bag of bright wool. I would watch my hand when the crash came, and it did not tremble. There were people to live for, each of us was an example to the others, but it was like being in a huge theatre that has caught fire. The fire might be put out, but if one of us screamed, it would start a panic. We would all be trampled to death. I was one of a million others but I had my place, my seat in the theatre. I was sitting in a balcony-box, facing the stage. Professor Atherton had saved it for my mother. I took Bessie Childs the first time. Rat-ta-ta-tat. They were revolving slowly, slowly, then faster, faster in their circle. Bessie said, "You could trust Allen to think up something to make himself important." He had thought up something. He wasn't dead, I had heard recently from Susan. He was still locked up, she asked me to try to get some books for him in Switzerland. She began her letter, "The person to whom I sent your letter, after carefully removing all traces of direction, writes me...." And she gave me the list of the books.

I don't know what she meant by "traces of direction." I wondered what I had written in the letter. I had told her that I was going to Lugano. I asked her if there had been any news of "poor A." She evidently sent my letter to him, after "removing all traces of direction."

. . . . .

But I have found the traces of direction. I could at the eleventh hour, remember Allen but I could not remember further than that. I had seen a ghost, a spectre; *chère belle fantôme*, Geoffrey had once called me, and he was right to say I didn't love him. Iseult Blanchmain loved well enough and I protested. But Geoffrey knew enough to know there was another. He knew there was another, but I didn't know it. He sensed in me the *belle fantôme* but he could not know what I did not know. He "shouted," as he called it, Hippolytus and that was a play by a Greek poet, called Euripides. He "shouted" it in Greek and I stood frozen while I listened. I was the statue that the poet prayed to. He wore a short pleated kilt, his arms were bare and there were narrow bands of leather, crossed over each other, almost to his knees. I saw Hippolytus.

My mind was luminous and I saw tiny pictures of Greek temples. They were white, though I had read by this time, that the columns were painted sea-blue and vermilion. I had read that the paint had weathered or worn off, but I did not believe it. The temple was set above a flight of steps. It is true, I had seen the temple at Posedonia with Geoffrey, and later, I climbed the Parthenon steps with Peter van Eck. I saw the Parthenon frieze and I filled in the empty gaps, with a slim, athletic figure in a short kilt. His head was unbound. I could see Orestes pursued by the Furies. He found sanctuary by the altar of the goddess. I would stand by the altar. We were pursued by the Furies. Rat-ta-ta-tat - the years were revolving on their pedestal. They went slowly at first, then faster, faster as the drum beat louder. Rat-ta-ta-tat - they went faster, faster. I sent him a card. There was a boat, a sort of Ark, drawn up in a green meadow. The dress was leaf-green with little sprays of flowers. The Maidens wove the goddess a flowered garment. But they kept it in the temple. She had put on her helmet. Orestes found sanctuary in the temple. He said, "I am like the centre figure. I wear my crown over my hat." He may have meant to be whimsical for he had just said that the boat was out of drawing. It was all out of drawing though I saw it all - or thought I saw it all - so clearly. But when Bessie handed me the opera-glasses, I saw it differently.

I did not want the opera-glasses but it seemed more polite to take them. I held them the wrong way round and turned the screw to get the stage in focus. It was far away and small and very clear in the crystal lens. I heard the harps and saw the carved group, turning to the music. Then the drum beat, the harps stopped and they went faster. They seemed nearer, though they were so far away. They were in my head now. They kept turning in my head, as I took the glass of water from the girl with the ruffled apron. I saw Orestes reflected in the tumbler, with the dull gold round his forehead. I did not see Pylades. At the Abbey, Philip Manning said that Lord Howell looked like a ghost. We were ghosts together. We were out of the same play.

Philip Manning said that Lord Howell looked haunted. I was haunted, obsessed by a slim athletic figure in a short kilt. After Peter van Eck bowed stiffly and walked down the stairs of Shepherd's Hotel in Cairo, I began in my daydreams to live a story, the novel that wouldn't come true. It wouldn't come true for I was building my temple on a false foundation. Now, I knew the temple was placed four-square at the top of some steps. Or there might have been only one step, like the famous foundation of the Parthenon at Athens. Mr. van Eck explained what I already knew, that Ictinus, in order to make the foundation look straight, had curved it slightly. The temple was empty but the Abbey was crowded and people stood, four deep on the pavements and on the roofs of the houses. The slim athletic figure waited behind the choir-stalls. He looked older than when I had last seen him at my flat, on September 3, 1945, the anniversary of the second war. I didn't know it was Lord Howell until I looked into the wide-staring grey eyes.

"It's so nice to see you, Lord Howell," I said. I had to say something.

Now I had another programme. I did not think of it at the time, but now I know why I treasured the pages of the Abbey folder, with the Albatross and the motto on the cover. It belonged with the *Iphigenia* and the dance-card with the embossed ivy-leaf and the numbers, 1903. These numbers were 1945. There was, as they called it, a fanfare before the service. There were silver trumpets and drums. I did not think of Lord Howell when I heard the trumpets. I did not think of him when I stood frozen at the roll of drums. I knew that I had ended my search, my pilgrimage was over. I had put down my name and address in the Lost and Found book, lying at my elbow on the counter below the hat-racks, at the Academy of Music, Philadelphia, June 1903. This was September 16, 1945. I had had a birthday a few days before. This was my birthday.

I had put my name down in the Lost and Found, when I heard the students talking. I had been lost for a long time. I was found when I stood beside Philip Manning. I was frozen stiff as a marble statue. I was marble. Indeed, I did not know what was happening to me. I had said that I wouldn't see Lord Howell again, after his *volte face* and his repudiation of the messages. The odd thing was, I meant it. I didn't want to see him. Now frozen, I was found. I recognized the fact that something had happened to me. It had happened here in London. It could have happened nowhere else, for some odd reason. This was the reason that I had stayed in London. This was the reason that I sat under the lamp and when the crash came, looked at my hand and the needle with the length of bright wool. I watched carefully but I think I am right in saying that I never saw the hand tremble, when the crash came. This was Iseult Blanchmain. But now my knees trembled and I clutched convulsively at the back of the chair before me. I was afraid I would fall. But the drums held me steady. I stopped trembling. I was frozen this time, for good. I was Iseult Blanchfleur.

. . . . .

It was only last Saturday, three days ago, that I remembered Mr. Moore. I did not see Mr. Moore in my dream, and I wondered why I and Lord Howell were sitting on Mrs. Atherton's front porch. Then I remembered Professor Atherton and the Greek play. In London, I had sat out the tragedy of the second World War, but I had been watching it with millions of other people. It is true, I had a good seat in the theatre. I even had an opera-glass, though I turned it the wrong way round. I saw from my bed-room window, flares and search-lights. The drums I confess, were overpowering; the great anti-aircraft guns from Hyde Park seemed pounding my head to pieces. But at the worst sometimes, I saw reflected in a mirror, on the polished surface of a door-knob, even in the bowl of a silver tea-spoon, a tiny scene projected. The scenes were always the same, there were miniature ranges of snow-mountains, there were tiny bays and harbours, there was a rock-precipice and a temple. There was economy of colour, blue, ice-crystal, snow-colour; actually, now I think of it, there was only blue and white and silver. I would get to the mountains, Ben Manisi had said. I had got to the mountains.

I was watching the tragedy, but when I stood beside Philip Manning and heard the roll of drums, I was in the tragedy. I was no longer outside things, watching. I was inside. I was one of the few main actors, though the Abbey was crowded; the door was open and I saw the people to the right of the altar, outside on the pavement. I no longer mattered. What I did and thought was not important. It did not matter that Lord Howell had turned away. He was an important person.

I had known him less than a year. Although I felt that I was one of the few main actors, I had merged my personality in the great drama. I had lost myself. Myself, to all intents and purposes, was Blanchmain. I did not then know there was another Iseult. I did not know her name was Blanchfleur.

Blanchfleur returned in a dream.

. . . . .

I don't know what made Lord Howell angry. It was our fourth meeting, September 3, 1945. I did not argue with him when he repudiated the simple touching messages of love and friendship from the RAF. I let him go on talking. I should have thought that he would have let the matter drop there. But as he stood in the door, about to retrieve his hat and stick in the hall, he let fly another barbed shaft.

"And that *Hal* - " he said. He waited an almost imperceptible moment for me to answer, to explain or to defend the earlier messages, the "story" as he had called it, and of which he had said he would like to hear more; "if there is any more of the story, I would like to hear it," he had written. He may have wanted to renew the conversation, to return to the earlier mood, or he may even, humanely have wanted to deliver the *coup de grâce*. It was, as I say, an almost imperceptible moment that he paused and waited. Did he think I would flare out in anger? It was Hal, Hal Brith, who had started the whole thing.

I had my own private opinion about Hal Brith. I may possibly have conveyed it, in a round-about way, to Gareth. I did not mention it to Lord Howell. He may have suspected that I had something up my sleeve. He may have been suspicious of my silence, my blank acceptance of his statement that gangsters in New York might get hold of any radio communication from his own RAF. Yes, now I think that he may have wondered how it happened that he had so easily, so signally and so completely vanquished me. An experienced hunter knows that some animals "play dead." Perhaps I wasn't dead after all.

If he had shown any emotion that afternoon, it was in the very beginning, when I said, "the first word is Advallon, I think they mean Avallon."

I had turned in my chair, facing him in the door-way. It was the same chair I had sat in that Sunday afternoon when I drew the table toward me. Lord Howell had said, if there were messages of any importance, they would come to him from his own circle. His own circle was the dull oak table with the tripod feet that Ben Manisi had wondered about.

"I wonder if anyone will come to this table," he had said.

No outstanding messages had come until I sent out my request, with the key-word *wings*.

"His name is Hal Brith," said Gareth. His name was William Morris. It was clear, from the beginning. It seemed unnecessary even to tell Gareth, that I knew this. I would not now enter into any discussion about Hal Brith. It was very obvious. Ralph, John, Lad, Larry and the rest had not floated off into a no-man's-land of vague felicity. They were real people. They were more real than the bomber in the desert who had thrown away his bodies. They had not thrown away their bodies and neither had William Morris.

Ah, once again, ah, once again,
The black prow plunges through the sea,

he had written,

Nor yet shall all your dreams be vain,
Nor you forgot, O Minyae.

Their dreams were not in vain, nor they forgot while I was alive to remember them.

————————

III

Crashing Rocks

My second Christmas-card was the boat that was out of drawing. It was in point of time, medieval, an illumination from the *Roman de la Rose*. It was this same Argo or Ark of the William Morris *Life and Death of Jason*. The ship that Ben Manisi had so graphically described, was another Ark or Argo. We called it the Viking ship, but it might have been archaic Greek. Manisi had given us the name Hill or Hal, then Britt. Hal Brith was obviously a Norse name. William Morris had travelled in Iceland and had translated or reconstructed many of the old saga. I never thought that Hal Brith was Lord Howell.

William Morris had followed his own "traces of direction," with his poems and stories. The Jason myth would have preceded the Viking by some thousands of years. The Viking was historically and geographically, nearer to England. Manisi had said that he himself had nothing to do with this boat. He didn't understand it. Gareth understood it but she didn't see it. I saw it and understood it but with my imagination - or perhaps I saw it in different settings, in different periods of time, with my imagination plus my opera-glasses. I had actually adjusted my opera-glasses the wrong way round, to the Greek scene. But with a little manipulation, I could at least imagine, if I did not actually see this same Viking ship in different settings. The hawk or falcon for instance, perched on the wrist of one of the warriors, suggested to me from the beginning, not so much Norsemen as Normans. The Normans derived their name, as we all know, from the Norsemen. The warrior with the hawk perched on his wrist, belonged to the clumsy boat drawn up in the flower-strewn grasses of the *Roman de la Rose* card, I had sent Lord Howell.

My demand or request for an answer to my key-word *wings*, had come from Hal Brith. But it had come to me, as a poem or a myth, something that had to be translated. As I faced Lord Howell standing in the door-way, I was myself on that earlier Viking ship, the Greek Argo. Scylla and Carybdis lay before us. I had

had my key-word *wings*, and I still had it. It was not a hawk but a dove that I held in my hands.

The rock Scylla faced me in Lord Howell's repudiation of my messages, "and anyway, if there were messages of any importance, they would come to me from my own circle." That was not enough and Carybdis followed it up with, "and that *Hal* - "

It was I who held the dove in my hands. The ship Argo, the Viking ship, the Norman ship, the English ship was blocked by the crashing-rocks, Scylla and Carybdis. They would part, those rocks, for an imperceptible moment, but could we get through? Our whole quest, our mission, our pilgrimage would be in vain, we would have failed if we stopped now. If a bird could dart through the portal of the crashing-rocks, a ship could follow. The crashing-rocks had parted for a moment at the word *Avallon*.

Manisi had said that I was the seer on that boat. I had denied this. But maybe, I was the seer now. I did not answer Lord Howell. I did not defend the messages or the table. I did not ask him to come again. I opened my hand and the dove winged through the rock-door. The ship could wait until the rocks parted again, and it would follow.

. . . . .

A little more, a little more,
You carriers of the Golden Fleece,
A little labour of the oar,
Before we reach the land of Greece.

They had reached the land of Greece. It was outside somewhere. But it was inside my head too. They had spelt o-a-r, on more than one occasion. They had spelt c-o-r-n.

"Table will very well do," they had insisted.

It was a round table, maybe for all I knew, it was the Round Table, or a lineal descendant of it. There was the circle of dancers at the Greek play. Bessie said there were twelve of them. Tradition had it that the Round Table had descended from the old sun-cycle, the twelve months of the year, the twelve hours of the day. She said their silver circle had something to do with the moon, but the sun and the moon were twins. The moon was contemplative, ruler of dream; the sun was active, ruler of life. The Argonauts were in search of the Golden Fleece; Aries or the Ram is a sun-symbol; he is Ares or Mars, ruler of war and battle. But the moon stood equal with her brother; his arrows brought quick death, but hers brought madness.

"And that *Hal* - "

His barbed shaft had not killed me; perhaps, he feared that mine might drive him mad.

Madness might do; provided I didn't gibber and hurl things at people, I didn't mind if he thought me a little crazy. But I didn't think I was. Later, I was to reconstruct a world of fantastic terror; I heard sirens and guns, after the war was over. I thought my friends were dead and the city struck down with plague. I saw a child from Malta or Whitechapel; I wondered if he were hungry. I had said that I would exchange Troy and Thermopylae for a basket of apples, but I couldn't do it. I had imagined a street of gibbets, but that was before I knew that Allen Flint was alive. I had said that my friendship or my love for Allen was like the five-petalled pattern in the apple. If you cut an apple the wrong way round, I had said, you will see the shape of the apple-blossom in it. I had seen the shape of the apple-blossom in the ripe fruit. I had not seen the blossom. Some say that *Avallon* means valley-of-the-apple-trees. The apple is related to the rose, they tell us. They had spelt out on the table, "roses red"; they had followed it later with "roses white." Perhaps this was an intimation, I had suggested, that the war was not yet over. The war was not yet over.

We were to have pooled our resources. I had visualized famine and floods. They had spelt out, again and again, c-o-r-n, as if that were all that mattered. They had spelt g-a-l-e. If I, in my fever, had a pre-vision of disaster, it may be presumed that they, with their heightened perceptions, had an ever more acute sense of coming events. C-o-r-n, g-a-l-e, o-a-r. I read these words in the news-cutting a friend sends me from London. I did not pretend to predict the future; it was the present that concerned us. I don't know what they wanted to tell Lord Howell. I don't know what Lord Howell could have done about it.

. . . . .

Poor Allen read William Morris to me, under the apple-trees, *Ah, quelle est belle la Marguerite* and *la belle jaune giroflé*. Geoffrey told me that the *giroflé* was clove-pink; he called them sops-in-wine, too. There was the *de luxe* edition of the Tristram legend that Allen brought me. That was part of the same story. There was a quest too, in that story, and a ship and a cup of poison. Lord Howell looked like Tristram, when I saw him at the Abbey. I was only Blanchmain, when I laid my left hand on the table and painfully took down their messages with my right. But "Table will very well do," they kept repeating, and "Wait," they said.

I have been spared lecturing on poetry in America. Whatever I said, would have been too old-fashioned. I had met and mingled with the older generation. I had heard personal reminiscences and anecdotes about Swinburne, Browning, Rossetti and William Morris. William Morris designed medieval tapestry. I had worked on a panel of fruit-trees - it seemed useless work - for three years. Now, it seems the only thing that matters. It is true, it was only Blanchmain who threaded the needle with rose, deep-green, blue-green. They had asked me to wait and I had waited. There were two Iseults, perhaps there were two Tristrams. When I said, *Avallon* and *love all*, (their message to him), he said, "Thank you." That was one Tristram. The other said, "And that *Hal* - " It was as if the other Tristram, the one standing in the door-way waiting to retrieve his stick and hat in the hall, had offered me the poison. Perhaps I drank the poison. I don't know. In any case, his doubt and suspicion eventually came between us. But if he killed Blanchmain and the "work" that we were to have done together, he did not break the faith of Blanchfleur.

. . . . .

The Maidens were turning in their circle. They were the years, the months that had passed between the June day when I saw my first Greek play, in 1903 in Philadelphia, and the September day, 1945, when I heard the roll of drums from the same great tragedy. June and September, two of the twelve months, the twelve Maidens, were superimposed on one another, and 1903 and 1945, two of the twelve thousand years were superimposed on one another. This was one of those mathematical folds or pleats in time, that Geoffrey had worried about. It was all quite easy to work out, when you knew the answer. I mean, after you had the answer, you saw how it all happened.

There were other months and other years, but these particular months and years had acted like the two separate lenses of the opera-glass that make one picture. It was the same picture. It was a temple, an altar, a High Priest and the celebration of a sacrifice. Iphigenia was to have been sacrificed in the first instance, but at the intervention of the goddess, she was saved. It was *they* who were the sacrifice, but through the mediation of the little table, they were not dead. They spoke, they laughed, they crowded around the table. But what they said or what they would have said, could now no more concern us. There was the roll of drums. There was the moon-circle that was broken. It was all a dream, a fantasy, a delusion. The arrows of the Moon bring madness. It had never happened, really. It was far too beautiful to have happened, even in a dream. They were dead and I was a middle-aged, tired woman.

. . . . .

There was the Grail, the very communion-cup upon the altar to my right as I stood there with Philip Manning, that September Sunday. I do not remember many of the names in Malory's *Morte d'Arthur*. There was Lancelot, Parsival, Gawain and the others. There was Lord Howell, Ralph, Lad, Larry and the others. It was the same story. The years had come together like the lenses of the opera-glass. King Arthur was perhaps, the year five hundred in Britain, and the Battle of Britain was nineteen-forty. It was one of those folds or pleats in time, but if you understand one fold or pleat, one superimposition, you understand another.

"Strike and strike quickly," he had said. I let fly an arrow, a winged word. He let fly another. But the Battle of Britain had happened five years ago. It was 1945 when I heard the roll of drums at the Abbey. I should have let them go then, but I didn't. I knew that he didn't want to hear from me, but I went on writing. It was all an anticlimax. It was asking for a second *coup de grâce*, though I was dead already. "They are frivolous and uninspiring," he had said of the last messages. C-o-r-n, g-a-l-e, o-a-r. It may have seemed nonsense to him then. It may have seemed frivolous and uninspiring when I sent him my last letter in February, 1946, just a year after our first meeting. I don't know anyone who knows Lord Howell and I have heard nothing of him. But if he thinks of me at all, or remembers those last messages, I wonder if he still finds them uninspiring. In the light of later events, he could hardly find them frivolous.

. . . . .

To-day is Good Friday. I think of the Parsival music which I heard as a schoolgirl, at that same Academy of Music. I had not then associated the Grail legend with the Greek drama, yet now that I think of it, the slim athletic Pylades was not so unlike the opera-singer who I now remember, stood for some time on that same stage. Parsival stood before a grey-walled chapel, blocked in, in the then more modern manner. This might have been the wall of any legendary city. He, like Pylades, wore a belted, white garment. Like Pylades, his head was unbound. Like Pylades, his arms and legs were bare and he wore strapped-over sandals. This professional opera-singer had not the quality of the young intellectual, but Parsival in that scene might have stepped out of a Greek play.

I can not remember a note of the Good Friday music. I can not identify any single word that Pylades spoke in that play. The Greek words that I did not understand, were music. The Grail legend was Greek. The Round Table was the symbol of the sun, the twelve months of the year, as we learned so long ago in this same opera-house, though Bessie said it was the moon-circle.

The Argonauts were on a sun-quest. The Golden Fleece was a sun symbol. They brought back the sun, returning after the perils of winter, the crashing-rocks.

The Knights of King Arthur were on the same quest, though their symbol was the cup or chalice. The Golden Fleece represents activity, valour. The Grail represents religious contemplation and dream. There is no question as to the activity and valour of Ralph, Lad, Larry and the rest of them. It is all written somewhere, but they wanted something else written; they called it the "true tale." It was Lord Howell that they wanted - "John table true tale." It was something that he hadn't yet told. They wanted him to tell the story; q-u-e-s-t, they had said. It was something that hadn't been said but he could say it.

IV

Revenant

Putting aside any hypothetical problem of psychic radio-communication, we still have the little oak-table of the Icelandic scholar, the designer of tapestries, the teller of tales of Knights and Ladies. "Table will very well do." They had been gathered together on this Ark or Argo. They wanted to correlate their spiritual entities with certain individuals who on earth, would repeat the pattern of their brotherhood. There was Gareth, though I did not tell her of this. It was enough to know that they were waiting for us. We had only to wait for them. There was Lord Howell. There was myself. Later, they had said, they would tell him the names of others. I don't know what they wanted us to do but it doesn't matter. If Lord Howell wouldn't or couldn't tell the true tale, then I would have to do it.

If they could tap out the messages on the table, it is very obvious that they could do other things. They could for instance, no doubt, easily manipulate a magnetic needle.

Though we spelt very quickly at the end, there is yet a considerable waste of time and energy, running through the alphabet. It is true, we had reduced the spelling to a sort of shorthand. I knew nothing of codes and signals but I did know that a single letter or a group of letters or numbers, or numbers interspersed with letters, pauses or dots and dashes could express what it would take pages of paper or telegraph forms to say.

They wanted to convey something. It may have been advice of a purely practical nature. Something of this sort: *atmospheric conditions due to atomic disturbance possibly about to cause unexpected cloud-bursts and erosions - fen country in particular susceptible to inundation - see to dykes dams river-banks - tides unpredictable - unprecedented cold-wave imminent and floating icebergs - danger to Thames estuary district - irreparable loss fertile land and pasture - cattle and sheep should be removed to highlands.*

They might have said something of this sort and given names of departments and agricultural experts who would take the matter in hand. No doubt, Lord Howell had access to some of these people and could have entered his statement or his plea, in his own name or in that of those officers of the RAF, who had charge of the air-patrols. Maybe, nothing would have come of it, but certainly the weather-bureau must have had some intimation of the coming disaster. I had no contact with any of these officials. I had told Ralph, Lad and Larry that I would do what I could. I had then, no logical reason for connecting their c-o-r-n, g-a-l-e, o-a-r with the present crisis.

It is conceivable of course, given precise directions, accurately verified by the statistics of the weather-bureau and formally drawn up from maps and charts, as observed from the air by these same RAF patrols, that the officials in high office, even though entirely unaware of the original source of the information, might casually have shelved the matter. Putting aside the question of the manner of the delivery of these warnings, the matter itself might have been pigeon-holed or at best, forwarded to another department or another part of the country for consideration. Lord Howell, if he had received the messages, might have refused to court humiliation by talking over the matter with even the most enlightened of his associates.

But if these associates had fabricated a concise scientific statement, purporting to prove conclusively that atomic energy had caused a change in say, the temperature of the Gulf Stream, or had caused certain subterranean or submarine activities, which were bound to bring disaster of one sort and another, would such a report have been taken seriously by any-one in a position to send immediate labour-battalions to reconstruct and strengthen the dykes and dams and to deepen the river-channels?

In the general confusion and disintegration that set in, soon after the announcement of a world at peace, I don't think even a most arid, statistical report of this kind would have been taken seriously. Perhaps it is just as well that we confined our famine report to those few words, so dear and so precious to me, c-o-r-n, g-a-l-e, o-a-r.

. . . . .

I read in another news-cutting that has been sent me, that it is estimated that there is a £20,000,000 loss of grain, cattle and foodstuffs already reported in a country suffering from years of malnutrition. Perhaps we were too practical, too logical altogether. Perhaps I still am. I did not want vague generalities, I do not want them now. I did not even want to write about the messages. I did not want to remember Allen Flint and Geoffrey and the others. I had got away from England. I was free now. But with the return of Lord Howell in a dream, I was bound by an old pledge. I had told them I would do what I could. But I did not then see the actual sequence of the story, nor its real foundation. I only saw it when I remembered the opera-house in Philadelphia. The true tale was founded on a rock, it was the tale of redemption and regeneration, the tale of sacrifice. I had really sacrificed so little. I had been humiliated and brow-beaten by Lord Howell, but perhaps Lord Howell too, had been humiliated. Perhaps the young pilots who died in September 1940, had been humiliated.

. . . . .

Lord Howell had said when I told him that I was planning to go to America but they wanted me to wait, "but you can not evade responsibility." I was evading responsibility, not so much to the RAF and the messages, but to the story that wouldn't come true. I couldn't write it, as it was built, not so much on a false foundation, as on a wrong one. The foundation was really the stone of the Parthenon that Ictinus had curved slightly, so as to make it look straight. I had (until I dreamed a week ago, of Lord Howell on Mrs. Atherton's front-porch in Philadelphia), thought I had laid my foundation-stone symmetrically. But in fifth-century Athens, the actual straight line was curved, in the foundation of the most famous temple of antiquity and of all time. I had taken the direct, dynamic, detached (I thought) intellectual attitude to Lord Howell, the RAF, the messages and to Lord Howell's final repudiation of them.

I had drained the last drop of poison; my mind had been poisoned by his tirade that September day, when he elaborated his objections to my findings. I had thought that I was watching, shocked but intelligently weighing the evidence as to "beings of a lower order." It is true that he had added, "not that *you* are a being of a lower order," but that made things worse. I had thought his intimations of the danger of these messages and his reference to gangsters in New York, merely illiterate. But though I sat there, numb with fatigue and a sort of emotional apathy, I see now how this doubt and repudiation had dripped its slow poison into my brain.

I had no fear of psychic entities, of beings of a lower order. I had not thought about them. It was only after his last letter, dismissing my communications as "frivolous and uninspiring," that the poison took effect. It was then that I felt myself plague-stricken. It was then that I visualized the streets of gibbets. It was then that I walked with eyes wide open, into Hell.

. . . . .

But that was a long time ago; it was last spring. I carefully outlined the first part of this true tale, before Christmas 1946. The straight line of the narrative satisfied my mind. I had recorded the details of a most interesting experience or experiment. As far as my mind was concerned, I had found the answer. I was satisfied. But it was the satisfaction of the philosopher or the psychologist. It was the same satisfaction that I had had on September 16, 1945, when I heard the roll of drums and knew that they were dead and that I was a middle-aged, tired woman.

But the true foundation-stone curves slightly. I had made no allowance for that. When Lord Howell said in a dream "Soon, I will see myself looking at my-self, in your eyes," I had the satisfaction of the artist and of the child.

. . . . .

Painfully, I had gone over every word, every gesture of Lord Howell's, as far as I could recall them. I had left his letters just as they were, when (February 1946) I tied them with a bit of string and flung them in the drawer of my desk. I had also left my first note-books, though I had destroyed the later rough jottings of messages that I had scribbled down awkwardly, while my left hand rested on the William Morris table. I had read Lord Howell's books but I had left them, too, in London. The phrases from his letters, I remember. His words, I remember, his gestures, the occasion of his six visits and the intermediate occasion of my seeing him at Westminster Abbey. Then, he didn't say anything. It was our fifth time of meeting. I said, "It's nice to see you, Lord Howell." I had to say something. It was hardly "nice" to see him, it was like meeting a *revenant*. It was meeting a *revenant*.

A character from a Greek play stood in the choir-stalls at Westminster Abbey. He was older than when I had first seen him. He did not wear his princely gar-ments, his winged sandals. He was not the sacrifice, he was not the High Priest at the altar. He was not even the king's son who later, was to be pursued by Furies. He was, in some indescribable manner, standing alone. So, Pylades had stood on the stage and delivered the long speech that had explained everything. I had thought that Lord Howell would explain everything. I had thought, when I gave him the messages, that he would say "Thank you," but that he would follow his acknowledgment with some simple confirmation of my findings. I had not asked them if the names that they had given me, were those they were known by in the RAF. Many of them, as we all know, adopted or had conferred on them, quaint and unusual RAF names, so that the names themselves didn't prove or disprove anything. I did not discuss this matter with Lord Howell. It was he himself, I now remember, who said, after stating that if there were any messages of importance, they would come to him from his own circle, "in any case, you might give me a hundred names of pilots, and I wouldn't know one of them."

He had said this just two weeks ago; I had not expected to see him again. I did not think of Pylades when I saw him behind the choir-stalls, nor did I remember him afterwards. It was only lately in a dream, that Lord Howell seemed to explain everything. "Soon, I will see myself looking at myself, in your eyes." But what he meant by that, I don't know.

. . . . .

His eyes were grey-glass, staring like someone in a trance. He said he had no psychic gifts but I remembered how Gareth had said, "He has the eyes of a fa-natic." They were not the observant, slightly cynical eyes that I had looked into when I turned in my chair and faced him in the door-way. They were not the eyes that went with the mockery of those last words, "and that *Hal -*"

He had told me a singularly boring story of a group of Canadians who had been led astray by messages from lying spirits. He had followed up his repudiation of the idea of any sort of radio-communication (although he himself mentioned some such thing in one of his books), with a still more lurid denunciation, this time of amateurs who are led astray by messages. These Canadians, he explained, had been told to get rid of their property, form a community, guided by these "beings of a lower order," and come to England, where a great opportunity awaited them. The moral of the tale was that they squandered all their money, were left high and dry, and never even got to England. As he swung across the room, that short space from the tea-table to the window, like an officer on the quarter-deck, I only had strength to ask myself why he thought it necessary to tell me all this.

In the end, he explained that it was later discovered that this particular group of entities, were from Hollywood. They were film actors, banded together to trick the unwary and to trap amateur dabblers.

Did I look like the sort of person who would be taken in by "beings of a lower order," this or the other side of the grave?

Maybe I did: I am for the moment, trying to see myself with his eyes. But I am immediately aware of another pair of eyes, the grey-glass eyes that stared out of the white face, just thirteen days later, at the Abbey. Perhaps those eyes saw too much. Perhaps Lord Howell was trying to spare me the Hell into which I walked, in my fever and delirium, last spring.

. . . . .

The scales weighed heavily against me or against *them*. I shifted the evidence from one side of the balance to the other, deliriously in my fever. When the fever left me, the fear left me and they left me. I said, for six months I forgot Lord Howell. When I remembered him, he was far away; I saw him in perspective, through the wrong end of the opera-glass. It was all quite clear; I had been very ill. I had been shaken by the bombing. I had been in London, with the exception of a short break each summer, for six years. There had been, beside the ceaseless trail of flying-bombs, a V-2 near us in Hyde Park. I was depleted by nerve-strain and malnutrition. It was all over. I had come back to life. I was well again.

I saw Lord Howell through the right end of the opera-glasses, just over a week ago. His words did not fall on deaf ears and I was no longer shifting the evidence for and against the messages. I had done that in the first half of this narrative. But now there is fresh evidence. I had concluded that psychic phenomena must be regarded subjectively, as dream. But I had not actually believed that further material, regarding Lord Howell and the messages would come to me. In the dream, we talked calmly. We discussed his findings. They had said that I would go to America. I had gone to America and Lord Howell had gone with me.

. . . . .

When Ben Manisi said there were circles on circles, not merging but touching one another, I had imagined the sea traced with a pattern, rather like chain-mail. I could imagine this, even though I could not think of the sea around the Viking ship as level. The ship was riding the waves, there must have been storm and ground-swells. It could not have been a level surface. Yet I could imagine these "circles on circles on the sea, touching but not merging with one another." Then, they seemed to me the same size. Now, I see them differently. The ship itself was like the proverbial stone, thrown on the surface of a pond. The circles went out from the ship, toward the horizon. The table was the ship. The circles went out, wider and wider.

I would have enlarged our group. Indeed, *they* had suggested that I do this. The further circle or circles were to apply the inner message, in some way. Naturally, I felt the sooner we could assemble or form another group, the sooner my own over-taxed perceptions would be modified. Lord Howell had implied that it was not good to work alone. But I could not give over the work to any one but those designated by the ship or by the table. Gareth was one of them. Ben Manisi was no longer with us. Lord Howell, or rather my request for a hint as to whether I was to answer his letter, had projected the whole thing.

But having taken counsel from the table, having had an answer to my key-word *wings*, I could not expect help from anyone but the ship. They did not want anyone but Lord Howell to collect or to direct a second or a third circumference. The ship itself was the centre of the circle. I must, by some unwritten law, implicit in our brotherhood, take orders only from the Viking ship. I had, against my so-called better judgment, carried out those orders. I had written when they said *write*, I had waited when they said *wait*.

Lord Howell was not Hal Brith.

. . . . .

He was a middle-aged man with a strong sense of duty and we may imagine, an iron will. His respect for established religion was made clear in his first book, but he was careful to affirm that he was no ritualist. He said, he did not care for music, but I doubt this. He said, his more than thirty years in the service had given him little time for reading. He was pleasant and informal with Philip Manning and Ben Manisi, the day we were all together. He seemed to confuse Gareth, that first day, when he stared at her across the table. Gareth said when he left, "He has a blind spot; he is blinded for a purpose."

The purpose may or may not have been the directing of a battle, known as the Battle of Britain. Lord Howell has been compared to Nelson, the Battle has been classed among the world's great decisive victories. It was a defensive battle. Lord Howell had retired, before the actual destruction of the ancient cathedrals, on the Continent. The senders of the messages had "retired" before he did.

Lord Howell in his first book, tells us about certain of these pilots; some of them were collected and sent to country-houses by the sea. To Lord Howell, the scene of their home-coming seems to suggest a peculiarly rural, not to say parochial England. To him, these young men belonged exclusively to England. They belong to the world. Moreover, admit that they belong to England, there is the England of the poets to consider. Lord Howell said he had read little, in the last thirty years. I have read a great deal.

I have read far too much. But my constant preoccupation with writing and with writers has been recognized. The table itself had spurred me on to further effort, when they said that the rather onerous task of assembling the notes for the lecture-tour, was indicated. I was working on the lectures, during the time when the messages were most compelling. There was one as yet, unexploited line of approach to the transcendental. I could have scrapped the lectures and sought refuge, comfort and even an explanation of the why and wherefore of the messages, from one of the mediums at Stanford House. I could even have capitulated, argued with the table, told them that I respected their wishes but that, under the circumstances, I must talk to someone, and recalled Manisi. I might conceivably have received help and comfort from him. It is, I agree with Lord Howell, not good to work alone. Gareth was about to leave. At this moment, fortunately or unfortunately, the matter was taken out of my hands. But I know that my natural instinct to discuss this unique experience, would have led to compromise.

We had not compromised. The messages might stop at any moment. I might die at any moment. I might have reached Lord Howell on the telephone. He had given me his number but I had never used it. I have no doubt, if I had told him how ill I was and that I had been forced to abandon the lecture-tour and stay in London, he would have come to see me. As I say, he had shown a genial, worldly charm with Ben Manisi and with Philip. I could have sent him a short note: *how right you were. It did prove dangerous to work alone. I have been very ill. I shall be here for another month and then I'm going to Switzerland. I must again apologise for what you may well consider a spiritual intrusion. I have let all that go.*

It is true that I did have something up my sleeve, that September day. But I did not know what it was.

. . . . .

I had read a great deal and was a student of philosophy and the new psychology. But what I had up my sleeve was no pedantic approach to the verities - and no reproach to Lord Howell. It was the submerged memory of a Greek play. With the intellectual memory, was the even more poignant and more deeply submerged emotional one. As a girl of sixteen, just growing out of childhood, I had been struck with madness. There was the puritan in me that Lord Howell spoke of, at our first meeting. But there was also the Egyptian dancing-girl - or shall we say the Greek dancing-girl with the green hair? The Greek girl circled for perhaps ten minutes, in the arms of one far above her. Or so it must have seemed to her. But it was he, the prince of Athens or Laconia - I don't know where Pylades came from - who had, with singular directness and it may be with a recognition, momentarily at any rate, beyond the mere boundaries of time and space, approached me. It was he who had singled me out. But I had already laid my snares for him. My emotion and my mind had merged, one flame, untrammelled by any conventional restrictions, when the young scholar stepped on the stage. I did not at first recognize Pylades but when we stood in the garden, there was a most apposite superimposition of the present on the past. It was moreover, a superimposition of the past on the eternal. Out of the legend, the history, the myth of all religions, the white-robed perfect image had stepped, clad in contemporary garments, to greet me.

. . . . .

   Gareth said Lord Howell had a blind spot and so had I. I did not call this vague questioning, this refusal to accept as final, any of my later infatuations, a blind spot. I simply realized that as things had gone wrong emotionally, in the past, they were likely to go wrong in the future. I was looking for the perfect image in time, superimposed on a dramatic personification or a character in a book, out of time, or in the world of imagination, poetry or drama. When, after hearing Lord Howell lecture, I began to wonder how it was that he and a handful of RAF pilots had saved, as the phrase was, civilization - then, I realized the possibility of an outstanding contemporary figure acting, as it were, or re-living a story already told. I spoke of this story as an actual historical event; I called it Thermopylae. I had endeavoured to avoid speculation on the reincarnation theory, but it seemed that I had met Lord Howell before.

   Leonidas, to my mind, belonged to the same category as mythical Achilles and Odysseus. In a way, my speculation or my equation was not without foundation. Only this contemporary Odysseus seemed to be denying his great heritage. It was not altogether a question of hero-worship on my part, but true to the outline of the Homeric true tale, Lord Howell, I suspected had listened to the syren-voices. No doubt, they brought him comfort, and his inner conflicts must have been insupportable. But the lotus-land or the summer-land of a somewhat parochial England, was not apparently acceptable to the warriors of the Viking ship. They wanted the true tale, without the intermediary syren-voices of: "*Everything is fine here - just met George and Harry - shot down two more on the way over,"* or *"Can't hear very well - bombers - give love to Alice - nice country but changes all the time,"* or *peace soon - busy on new plans,* or. . . . but why continue? It is the tone of voice, the quality not necessarily the quantity of the words that matter.

This "everything fine" tone of voice was not absent from Lord Howell's own books. But he was trying, I realized, to bring help to others, therefore I reserved my judgment or my criticism.

I do not mean that Lord Howell consciously or unconsciously, was listening to lying spirits or "beings of a lower order," when he wrote his books and lectured on communications from the RAF and other services. I reserved my judgment on Lord Howell and I reserved it on myself.

. . . . .

I finally assessed my findings as authentic, as far as we can judge anything in this controversial and as yet un-established science of psychic-communication. But though I had recalled and re-lived certain past relationships, I had recalled them with my mind and had over-stressed perhaps, my own ability to adjust the delicate balance of cause and effect. What I had up my sleeve that September day, when Lord Howell delivered what I called the *coup de grâce*, was a streak of authentic madness. The Egyptian dancing-girl or the Greek dancing-girl, however, was controlled by another whom Lord Howell called the North American puritan. It was the puritan who watched Lord Howell and did not interrupt his tirade about New York gangsters and Hollywood entities. It was the puritan who took the force of the blow, "and that *Hal -* " It was the puritan who waited, who renewed the battle in a lost cause, who flung out the final challenge which brought the second *coup de grâce*, "these messages are both frivolous and uninspiring." But it was the madness of the Greek dancing-girl that recognized in Lord Howell, a kindred streak of madness. I have at last, traced my own madness to its source, the source of all western poetry, the source of philosophy and mythology, the Greek drama. I can to a certain extent, therefore, assess, recognise and marvel at it. But I have no means of assessing the madness of Lord Howell or tracing it to its source. I can only judge him by my own standards, and his may be very different.

. . . . .

The dove had returned to the Ark. The waters had receded. But ironically, the firmer my foot-hold here in Switzerland, the more England was buffeted by tempests and submerged with the flood-waters. The dove had darted through the crashing rocks, the Scylla and Carybdis of Lord Howell's double repudiation, but somehow, it had shown the way for the ship to follow. The dove had returned when I heard the roll of drums in Westminster Abbey, that September Sunday.

Although this true tale purports to be one of heroic or epic, rather than lyric import, I can not dismiss the madness of a child infatuation.

It was, to be frank about it, a child who offered the hero in a legend, the gift of its own faith. It was a child who listened to other children, endeavouring to communicate in the manner of their elders, with words and letters. It was a group, a circle which had refused to be taken in by grown-up devices and reiteration of "everything fine over here." There was nothing fine anywhere. But at least we could huddle in a corner and whisper, so that our elders and betters should not hear us. There might be one of them to help us. He had carved that wooden boat, do you remember? He had fitted it with mast and yard and tackle, and he had told the more clever of us, the names of these things. He had even run away himself and tested out the balance of the ship. It rode the miniature wavelets, and he showed us how the wind could be predicted. We couldn't spell very well but we could write awkwardly, all helping one another, g-a-l-e, o-a-r. He would like that. Together, we painfully printed out our letter.

. . . . .

They wanted some simple things, things I didn't have but I said I would try to get them. It all seemed very easy. But I didn't understand exactly what they wanted. They said I wouldn't understand. It was something to do with their work, but he would understand.

"Why don't you tell him about it, yourselves, then?"

They whispered together and seemed to shove one another forward. Let Larry tell, let Lad, let Ralph, they seemed to argue. "Why don't you explain this? Do you think I'd tell your secrets?" They didn't even answer. That wasn't what they were afraid of. But while I waited, stubborn and proud and a little hurt (though I didn't think they knew it), Ralph edged forward, "You help," he whispered. They had said that before, but I was no good to them or anybody. They wanted him, it wasn't me they wanted.

"You want him, then why don't you get him?"

"Door shut," they said.

"Surely you can open the door - and if you can't, I can't."

"Write," they said.

So I could get him that way. I could write to him. I confess now, that I was perhaps just a little proud of my own writing. They had done other things, but I could write. I was flattered, perhaps a little overawed that my new-found companions trusted me. I must be careful how I wrote him. I would tell him, carefully spacing the lines and trying not to blot the paper, about my own affairs. I would tell him about stories I had read, even about stories that I had never read but just made up. He seemed to like one of the stories about a ship. Would I tell him more, if there was any more, of the same story? I told more of the story.

They would keep out of the way. I wanted them to come and talk to him, but they said he didn't want them. That seemed impossible.

In my house, there was a Buddha with red and green bits of glass, set in his gilt, carved robe. He stood on gold doll-feet on the wide shelf. Some of the little octagonal bits of glass were missing. He wore a peaked cap and his arms hung down by his sides, under the carved folds of the cloth. The little hands were open, one or two fingers were missing. Lord Howell didn't say anything about the Buddha but he stood, leaning against the shelf, looking at a ball on a stand.

"It's only glass," I said.

"Oh," he said, "I thought it was your working-crystal."

"No," I said. "I only see things in door-handles, reflections in windows or in the bowl of a silver tea-spoon."

"What sort of things?" he asked.

I said, "Always the same - tiny, but very tiny Greek temples. I never see people."

It seemed so easy at that moment, to talk to him. I would show him all my treasures. I knew he did not ask about the Buddha because he felt I loved it so much. There was nothing I couldn't tell him.

Perhaps it was all right, according to his ethic, to talk about crystals and to discuss Aztec and Inca ruins, as we did that last time, when they asked me to repeat without a break, the singular but not too unusual word. They said the word spoken twice, in that way, would prove conclusively, who they were, what they wanted and why they had chosen me to give the messages. As I have said, the word spoken twice with no break in the sentence, or brought in, in two succeeding sentences, with no break in the sequence, brought down a veritable landslide of information on the layers of civilization to be found in ancient Mexico. The not too unusual word, I gathered, was the clue or code-word to the work that possibly they and Lord Howell had already planned, before they left him. But though the arid, but this time scholarly information left me cold and more than ever indifferent to Aztec or any ruins, I was somehow happier. His trying to break across, when I first brought in the word, encouraged me to believe in at least the possibility of its being an already established code-word between them. But Lord Howell left soon after. And on my restatement of the aims and ambitions of the group, Lord Howell sent that last decisive repudiation of myself, the table and the work that we might have done together.

In the light of later events, I see my own shortcomings. He was not ungracious. He accepted my first findings. He could enter into my consciousness, could know and acknowledge my perception. It was perhaps untactful of me to continue writing. It was no question of his not understanding, he understood only too well. I had blundered into a private desolation - the broken rocking-horse, the box of soldiers, the toy-railway with its signal-boxes. I had no understanding of these things, re-assembled, wrapped up and put away.

. . . . .

But if I had blundered into his desolation, I had my own desolation, then closed and secret to me. The desolation once re-established, became a waltz, a circling within the orbit of another time-dimension. The orbit of the dance belonged, by association, to the hieratic circling of Maidens in a Greek play. I was a maiden in a Greek play, therefore in line with the source of inspiration of all later dance and music. Lord Howell's well directed blow, "and that *Hal* - " had by the very force and character of its delivery, awakened the memory of that first shock. But the awakened memory was dormant. This sounds a paradox. Indeed, the memory of Iphigenia, the Ivy Ball, the sudden shattering of an infatuation in contemporary time, that was yet originally inspired by a character in a Greek play, might have remained dormant but for the chance intervention of a dream. Whether the dream had or had not the quality of a so-called psychic materialization, or was projected by the submerged content of the subconscious mind, is beside the point. The dream, neatly and deftly, followed the pattern of my life. It was as if I had been working, my whole adult life, on an elaborate tapestry, but working as they say some weavers do, on the wrong side of the loom. What I mean is, I was spinning a web, the web I had begun to spin in the Academy of Music in Philadelphia, that June day in 1903, when the *Prince Lointain* appeared from Tauris, Argolis or Athens to explain everything. What he explained, in the rôle of messenger, near the end of the play, I had no means of knowing. He was talking Greek.

. . . . .

I worked on the wrong side of the tapestry; the threads reached from Philadelphia to Tauris, from London to Paris, from London to Athens and to Karnak, from London (and for the last time, on the reverse or under-side), to Lausanne. It must have been a not altogether unkindly fate that led me to so deep and compelling an attachment to a young intellectual, the favourite student of the husband of my mother's friend. The goddess who, at the end of the *Iphigenia* speaks, "in the machine," as Allen Flint called it, though armed and bearing the invincible spear and wearing the silver helmet, was yet, we recall with a new shock of wonder, the patron or the patroness of weaving.

Less than three weeks ago, here in this very town, I let go the threads. The years between wars, the years before wars, the years after were no longer profitless and barren. Myself, I had been singularly favoured. Not only had I lived to finish the intricate pattern that seemed, at times, to be too loosely hung upon the loom, but when I stepped forward, to look at last, on the finished picture, I saw not, as I might well have anticipated, a disproportionate space of private desolation and sterile abstraction, but a circle of Greek maidens, all blessed by the gift of Love, and I myself, among them.

Love, they tell us, is the oldest of the Fates. The wrong side or the underside of the tapestry, seemed to stress the usual, mythical rivalry of the three goddesses. But when I stood before the finished picture, I saw Love, crowned with white violets, with the Moon, her most powerful rival, and the goddess of war. They were hardly to be distinguished, in subtlety and beauty. If there were a Paris to award the apple to the most beautiful, it was a Paris giving the apple or the apples to all three, without discrimination. The Moon, it must be remembered, is the guardian of children and it is the Moon whose beneficent light brings dream. The final dream, the Moon's gift, was yet a dream in which Love herself was the theme and inspiration. As to the goddess of the Parthenon whose attributes are justice and victory, this was a victory after her own heart, yet again it was a victory of Love. Love had tempered the arrows of madness and the sword-thrust of the victor, and Love had adjusted the quivering balance till finally it stood level and at rest.

. . . . .

There is no pro or con, no right or wrong any longer, in the matter or the manner of my singular experience that began with Ben Manisi and his "I have a picture for Delia." That happened in London. It must have been 1943 and before Christmas, for on the strength of Manisi's picture, I answered a letter that had caused me to wonder what Lord Howell and I could, after all, possibly have in common. That letter was followed by the first Christmas card, the ordinary ship on the blue water, and the one star.

I was lurking in the wings, as it were, of an enormous theatre, where somewhere there was a curious suspicion of fused wires and smouldering lathes, mixed with the dead fumes of innumerable, burnt-out cigarettes. There was always the ominous shuffle of a restless audience. Why did I stay? My devoted friends urged me to accept the first offer of lecturing in America. "The whole place is bound to go up in smoke, at any moment," they said. I confess that I felt trapped, suffocated and in hourly terror, lest that oddly assorted audience should also perceive the peculiar acrid sting, as of wires fusing behind thin, match-box partitions - and there would be a panic. It is true, I was neither audience nor actor. I was doubly protected and I was doubly vulnerable. But sometimes, I had a curious premonition, some streak or freak of perception, apprehension, even a minor sort of prophecy. Mine was not the wailing of Cassandra nor the drugged utterance of the Sybil, but I felt that I was watching an old play.

I had read this story somewhere. The characters were familiar to me.

It was a passionate devotion to the drama that held me there in London, as well as a curious foretaste of inevitable disaster. But the disaster would come crowned with victory, and the victory would be followed by the solution of some mystery. It was a mystery-play, it would explain everything. Death would appear, in his familiar trappings. Plague, War and Famine would be his Apocryphal companions. There might even be a later falling off of the company of players. I, myself, might be asked to walk on, in a crowd scene. The air became more lurid. There was a stage-clap of thunder. There was a mechanical flight of winged devils. There were other curious devices. Then the curtain dropped and there was a brief interlude. We heard the roll of drums, the blare of silver trumpets. At last, I had a place in the vast pageant and a place that was near the altar.

———————

V

Traces of Direction

I have been in Lugano a week. A letter comes. It is left downstairs, on a small round table in the drawing-room. The ceiling is painted blue. There is an arabesque of fruit, leaves and flowers. The long French windows open out, on a porch or balcony. There are dim medallions painted in the corners of the arabesque, Gandria, Morcote, San Salvatore and nearer at hand, the cathedral San Lorenzo.

I could see the cathedral if I stepped over to the window. It is on a lower slope or shelf, just below the house. There is a great flowering magnolia against its grey walls. I pass San Lorenzo every day, on my way down to the arcaded market. But I do not look out of the window. It is almost dark in the room, I have been asleep upstairs. I suppose it is almost morning. The elderly English lady who leaves the letter, does not speak. She wears an old-fashioned travelling cape, and I am under the impression that she is on her way to the Lugano station, to catch the early-morning train. The letter is from London. She is going back to London. The letter is not in an envelope. She places the two sheets on the table. When I look up again, the lady has gone.

It seems to have grown lighter, for I read the letter: *I can not thank you enough for the help you gave me, the last year of the war. I have work now to do with all the services in London.* There was more but I can not remember it. The writing was the same, a little firmer or else he had used another sort of ink. There was one full page and half of another page.

. . . . .

I look at the room this morning, with new interest. There is the centre table where the lady left the letter. It is heavier than our table at home, but it has the same tripod feet. The surface is inlaid with a geometrical star pattern. The mantlepiece is marble, embossed with vine-leaves and clusters of grapes. An old-fashioned clock stands on the marble shelf. A bronze and gold warrior holds a scroll in one hand, and a trumpet in the other. On the writing-desk, there is a cluster of camellias. Under the mirror, between the two French windows, there is a bowl of lilac. I look at the gilt-framed pictures. There is the usual collection, villages with snowy, familiar, distant peaks or ranges of wooded mountains.

I am suddenly at home here. I have had a letter. Again, as in my Palm Sunday dream, I am enchanted with the subtlety of the dream-creation. It does not matter whether, as in that instance, the dream was a synthesis of my own unconscious mind or a fantasy or wish-fulfillment, or whether this lady is a certain friend of Lord Howell's, about whom he had written. She or her daughter had conveyed messages to Lord Howell that had to do with Glastonbury. These two, I imagine, belong to an earlier phase of Lord Howell's work. The dream in any case, re-stated the possibility of life continuing along normal lines in sleep and so, we may affirm, by the same laws of being, after death.

. . . . .

I carefully counted the points of this star. I thought of my comparison of the Round Table with the sun-cycle, the twelve signs of the zodiac, the twelve hours of the day, the twelve hours of the night. But the star was more intricate than that. Actually when I examined it, I saw that the outer rim enclosed another, and there was a series of star-patterns diminishing toward the centre of the table. I had jumped to the conclusion that there would be twelve points, but counting round, away from the mirror and the bowl of lilac, I became confused. I began again. Carefully counting from the mirror to the mantlepiece to the hall-door, round toward the desk with the cluster of camellias, and back again to the mirror, I find there are sixteen points to this star.

. . . . .

I am the same person that I was in the dream. The room is the same in all particulars, except that the French windows are wide open and the lilac is fresh-gathered from the garden, or brought up before breakfast, from the market. I had pre-visioned no unusual dream adventure, when I first stepped into this room. I had not even noticed that the table was round and had tripod feet, as I had taken a chair across the room, the few minutes that I waited before dinner. Actually, other guests, three English ladies, had confiscated that special table, and laid their books and knitting on it. I can not remember ever seeing the table empty, or without one of them keeping guard over it and the three chairs they had appropriated. The first time I saw the room empty was in a dream, and the second time was when I went in, this morning after breakfast.

I can scarcely believe in the fatality and the felicity that conspired together, to introduce or to produce that simple device of a star-table. But the table is here. It has been here every evening. There is a small square table, drawn up before the couch, and another, the other side of the mantlepiece. There is the usual assortment of newspapers, travel-folders and time-tables and a modest sprinkling of ash-trays. Over the centre table, there is an inverted porcelain lamp-bowl, with a circle of mermaids holding conch-shells. I note now, that below the arabesque on the ceiling, there are mouldings of flat scallop-shells. All these things take on a new meaning, as if actually the sixteen points of the inlaid star had worked some spell. I wonder why there are sixteen, when twelve is the zodiac and the clock number. The four triangles of the zodiac make a twelve-pointed star. But sixteen? I see now. This star is made of squares, not triangles. There are four squares to this star.

There is another fatality or felicity about the number sixteen. I was sixteen years old when I laid the foundation-stone of my life. And laid it, I find at last, four-square. There were four later infatuations or emotional experiences, but until I found the original foundation, they were dispersed and disproportionate. It was only after I had left London that the sequence became clear and with it, the experience with Lord Howell. This third square is related to the first square, four-square in all particulars. The last square is more difficult to define, it is the sort of crown or affirmation of the others.

The sun slants across the carpet. The wall is a deep red. This singular red might be vulgar and clash with the assortment of ornaments, the red-plush arm-chairs, the carpet. But oddly, though it would be easy to criticise the tall grey-green vases, either side of the clock, with their ornate glass-girdle of projecting rose-leaves, or the marble group of Neopolitan fisher-boys, there is some indefinable elegance about the whole, that makes criticism itself seem vulgar. Maybe, it is the sun shining on the carpet, but the luminous southern daylight should by all logic, "show up" the discrepancies of the salon of the *Pensione Ghirlanda*. Perhaps one is still a little surprised, a little wondering how such things still exist and by what miracle, exist whole, without crack or flaw.

Fragrance is difficult to define, almost impossible, but there is a sort of pulse, an intermittent breath, or is it my own breathing that gives a heart-beat or rhythm to this room? It is the forgotten familiar scent of lilac. There is the opening and shutting of doors, the different sounds of steps on the irregular paved walks of the garden. There is the sound of feet overhead. These sounds can be identified, can be described exactly. But the scent of the lilac, under the gold-framed mirror, can only be felt, be sensed, be perceived. It is like that with the fourth square of the star-pattern, its dimension penetrates the senses. It can be felt, this fourth of the four squares. It can be apprehended but perhaps it can not be understood.

It can be received, be perceived, as we recognize a familiar fragrance, long forgotten.

. . . . .

We can relate or compare this fragrance to others. It evokes emotions and we can accept or dismiss the scenes, the places, the rooms, the people that we associate with this flower. So we can relate scenes and emotions to the fourth square, but it is the very essence of the fourth square that it eludes description. But without the "traces of direction" of the other three squares, the fourth would have remained unrealized.

The first square can be placed in time, yet it includes the other or immortal time of fifth-century Athens. The second square was by far the most difficult to recall or recollect. The four sides were like the matchsticks that we learned to count with, to make patterns of, in kindergarten. With the four intermediate friendships, I had made at best, a short, crooked railway that came from nowhere and ran off into nothing. The third square, by its very dynamic content, shaped itself but it was placed on a false or an insecure foundation. The fourth square needed the other three, each separate and complete in itself, yet each equal to and related to the others. We do not need "messages" to assure us of eternity. But without the "messages," the other squares would have remained dispersed, unshaped and unassembled.

It was the third square or the creator of it, who added, as I said, a grain of alien substance to what I called a test-tube, and crystallized out the unresolved emotional content of my adult life. But it was the unrecognized or as yet undefined fourth square that projected the first dream, which opened the door of memory. And it was this same square that followed with the letter. It lay here, on this very table.

. . . . .

The fourth square or the qualities that I attribute to it, can of course, penetrate the others, as the fragrance of the lilac fills this room. We do not need a geometric analysis of our life, in order to appreciate or recognize the fragrance of a flower. But the perfume of a flower can be distilled, adulterated and preserved, though no labelled, crystal bottle can ever contain the spirit or the ghost of the flower. There are certain potent distillations, however, that intoxicate the senses. There are others like the blue poppy, that bring sleep. There are others that create the drug addict's world of illusion. There are others, the heal-all of affliction. So it seems to me, that I can relate my limited yet authentic experience of psychic phenomena to one or the other of these stimulants or narcotics.

The sixteen-pointed sun-pattern, when I come to think of it, is really more familiar than the triangle formation that divides the houses of the zodiac. One sees this pattern on old maps. The first square is placed upright on one of its four points and a cross is marked inside it. The points are N, E, S and W and the second square, with its sides parallel to the four sides of the map, modifies the N, E, S and W with NE, SE, SW and NW. The two other squares take up the story with their variations. It is the obvious pattern of "traces of direction." The dimly outlined four squares are often tinted yellow, so that we are left in no doubt that the sun is ruler of life and fate and of all "traces of direction."

Within this room, I seem to find my final and complete "traces of direction." It is true that the first three squares had been established before I came to Lugano. But I did not think of them as squares; I was still thinking of life in terms of the circles on circles on the sea that Ben Manisi has visualised for me. It will be six years, this coming Christmas, since I met Ben Manisi at Stanford House. I finished the first section of these notes, in Lausanne, before Christmas 1946. I did not expect to go on with them. I had parted conclusively with Lord Howell and with the work. But I had made my testament, I had been witness to the strange truth of a rare adventure. I had finished, though in so sketchy a form, a novel or story that had obsessed my imagination, ever since I climbed the steps of the Acropolis in Athens after the first war, with a certain Peter van Eck. But the form and matter of the story had eluded me and I did, emotionally at least, "throw it away," as Manisi had advised me to do. But the story, as I said, came back. I said it was the same story. But I did not realize the exact truth of that final statement, until my own unconscious mind prompted me, or until I met (as the Eastern mystics say we may meet, out of our bodies, in another dimension), Lord Howell in a dream.

I would probably never have noticed this pattern on the table, if it had not been for the second dream of the letter laid upon it.

. . . . .

The circles on circles on the sea, touching but not merging with one another that Manisi had "given" me, in that first picture, were certainly not static. They may not have merged but they must have moved. Later, I said that the circles seemed concentric and the table like the proverbial pebble, thrown on the surface of a pond. But again, there was movement, though this time, from within, as each circle grew larger, spreading from the small centre out, toward the horizon. But the pattern on this table gives me a sense of completion, of finality. My mind may follow any one of the sixteen "traces of direction," in memory or in retrospect, but I myself remain where I am, unconcerned with the future, reconciled to the past. The first corner of the first square, that is, the one in direct line with the mirror, points east; the second, opposite the fire-place, south; the next, west through the open door; the last, toward the writing desk, north. It is north to Lucerne. I came here, by way of Lucerne, eight days ago.

We must consult our second square. It is north-west to London. To the right of the mirror, through the first French window, the south-east corner of the second square leads to Athens. The next, continued through the vine-leaves of the marble mantle-piece, brings us through the mountains, to the plains of Umbria. The door opens into the hall. Outside there is the wisteria which has changed since yesterday, from purple to pale lavender. Through this door, our north-west takes us to America.

. . . . .

But these places are all here. It is the fourth square or the lilac that has brought them. There are other flowers, it is true, whose fragrance is equally compelling, or the mere sight of which may be enough to establish contact. There was, for instance, a cluster in a shaded corner of the market, that recalled the spring when I saw these calla-lilies in the *mercato vecchio* in Venice. It was Holy Year; it was 1934, if I am not mistaken. I had been in Venice with Geoffrey, as long ago as 1913, but I had forgotten the wisteria festooning the walls, and the moon-bridges, as we called them, until the unresolved solution of my adult emotional life began to simmer. In 1934, I re-visited the *Ca d'oro* and spent many hours in the *Sciavione* and Saint Mark's. These same lilies were placed in sea-green Venetian-glass bowls, either side of the jewelled altar. I remember how I was pushed forward by the crowd, and found myself on Maundy Thursday, wedged against the wall, at the turn of the lion-stairway. I felt that I was cheating or had "stolen grace," as the phrase is, when I was told afterwards, that the fragile, lace-robed figure who blessed the few fortunate, collected below the stairs from which he was descending, was the Patriarch of Venice, Pierre de la Fontaine.

It is odd that I should remember this, and only just remember it. As I say, the sixteen-pointed sun-star seems to have cast a spell upon me.

. . . . .

By some irony of fate, it is the shocks and wounds we have received that we remember best. Perhaps it is a beneficent provision of nature, in the proverbial manner of a burnt child shuns the fire. The more daring among us, however, are apt to revisit the scene of disaster or to relive the conflict that caused our first defeat. We are not satisfied until we prove to ourselves that we can not be defeated, or until we are defeated utterly. The re-assembling of the squares showed me the gaps in the fortification. The third square brought the final testing, but while uncovering the broken four walls of the second square, it revealed the first, built in archaic splendour, upon a rock. It was only when I thought that I was vanquished, that I found refuge in that impregnable, Athenian fortress. The fourth square is not so much a fortress, as a sanctuary.

. . . . .

It does not always need the sight of the flower, as of those calla-lilies, glimpsed through the arcades of the market, to evoke or recall a fragrance. This morning at one of the little café tables in the main square, I was writing to a friend in London. The slopes of Monte San Salvatore have turned gold in the last few days. It is the acacia-wood in blossom. I said in my letter, that I thought the acacia belonged to the locust family. I do not remember the locust-tree in England, but in southern Germany, I saw and identified a tree that in America, we call the honey-locust. The fragrance is poignant and unmistakable. Passing the sheds of the rather extensive main Lugano station, on my way back, I was surprised by an overpowering sweetness - the honey-locust? I thought perhaps there might be a tree on the road, below the high wall that leads to San Lorenzo. I retraced my steps, peering into the gardens, but I found no trace of the white, flowering tree. Was it after all, the acacia from the distant slopes of Monte San Salvatore? Impossible, for the fragrance then, would have followed me, but I lost trace of the honey-flower when I turned off the rather arid stretch of road before the station, nor did I find it again in the garden of the *Ghirlanda*.

. . . . .

I said that the table was like a stone which sent out circle on concentric circle to the horizon. The sun-star of the four superimposed squares on this little table, seems on the other hand, a sort of mesh or net. The inner stars diminish until they reach a circle of about six inches in diameter, in the centre of the table.

In this innermost circle, there is a conventional, geometric pattern. This flower-pattern has eight petals. It is the living heart of the circle, the eight-legged spider at the centre of the web, the Venus fly-trap if you will, pulsing to trap unwary and unpredictable motes of memory.

It is the purely formal, decorative motive that you see painted on Indian pottery. I had not thought that this room and the assorted treasure of the *Ghirlanda* would ever remotely, suggest Aztec and Inca ruins. But I see how this star-circle with its angles and diminishing flat perspective, might decorate the altar of a pyramid-temple in South America, Mexico or Yucatan.

Nearer home, this sun or star-pattern has been endlessly repeated in the insets of Moorish doors and windows. It recalls as well, the filagree marble-screens of the halls of the Alhambra and the palace windows that look out, across the canals and the lagoons of Venice. "All the perfumes of Arabia" are curiously invoked by a pattern that the merest accident uncovered for my consideration. It is dexterously woven on the upper or right side of the tapestry, but it is woven from threads, worked on the underside, so long ago in London.

It is the legitimate reward of my devotion to the "work," the intense, broken sessions when I concentrated so feverishly on the messages from the RAF, or when if you will, I drew on the submerged content of my own subconscious mind and created a group of lovers or of brothers, to compensate for my own loss and disappointment. However it came about, I found the thread and followed it through the labyrinth.

I followed it there in London, to the north with the Viking ship. I followed it west and south, to the "bump-out of land," as Manisi called it, of Central America. I followed it south to Crete, spinning industriously but spinning blindly.

I already held the thread that was finally to lead me through the labyrinth, the year we established what Manisi said "the movement" called a "home circle." I was sitting at the table or the loom with the three others, but I was keeping my own council, observing, criticising, accepting and discarding.

"But this doesn't make sense," Manisi had said when Z spelt out his name and followed it with the word Yucatan. I took the "traces of direction" out of Manisi's hands, when I insisted on following up Z. Although I didn't know it at the time, and although I was working blind on the wrong side of the tapestry, I had begun then to weave that very thread into this symbolic, decorative motive. Now, I stand on the outer or right side of the tapestry and look at the polished surface of the table.

. . . . .

I recall my memories of Crete. There is a fringe of flying-fish and shells. Here in this room, I have noted the mermaids with their conch-shells, and the flat scallop-shells under the arabesque of roses, convolvulus, carnations and blue lilies on the ceiling. It may seem a far cry from the palace of Knossos to the drawing-room of the *Pensione Ghirlanda* in Lugano. But the sea-horses and the crocus-fields of the famous frescoes, find their "traces of direction" here in this room. The heart or centre of the inlaid table, presents a common-place, eight-petalled pattern, such as we learn to make in kindergarten, by folding squares of bright-coloured paper. The red and blue, yellow and green primary colours are repeated, in those miraculously preserved frescoes of pre-Homeric Knossos. So here, we re-assess our Cretan findings. The actual geometric pattern of our inlaid-wood flower appears on the amphora, bowls, ivory ornaments and silver plaques of the treasure of King Minos.

There is as well, the never-to-be forgotten motive of the flat silhouette of lilies. It seems almost as if their shadow were thrown on a sunlit wall and, there and then, filled in with Chinese white. Though so stylized and conventional, these lilies seem to be living, more living than the lovely Victorian flower-plates, so treasured by collectors. The lilies with their stalks and small leaves are as shadows are, profiled and flat. They do not belong to the category of the eight-pointed flower that appears sometimes with sixteen or more petals. I have heard this familiar motive referred to as the daisy-pattern. It is invariably found in any museum case that contains the golden cups, the ivory statuettes and the silver clasps and buckles. But the daisy, the sun-flower or the marigold is still fashioned on a geometric pattern. The special lily that I refer to, is like the living specimens of sea-weed that are found on the slopes of mountains. The lily, like the fossilized sea-weed, is naturalistic and living. It is not the calla-lily nor the heraldic iris. There is no mistaking the texture of the green leaves nor the grain of the white petals. We know the hidden stamens are powdered with pollen, and we know that there are bees somewhere.

I have seldom seen this so-called Annunciation lily so startlingly alive anywhere, except possibly in the background of the Botticelli in the Kaiser Frederick museum in Berlin, or in the jar or vase at the feet of the Carlo Crivelli Madonna in Verona. I remember too, a forgotten early Flemish painter whose single staff in the hands of Gabriel, invoked the fragrance as well as the shape of this flower. But of them all, the pre-Homeric outline remains the most vivid, the most invincible, the most enduring. The labyrinth of the vanished Cretan city makes me think of Venice. But I should never remotely have associated the arid desert of the dead Aztec civilization with the earlier or contemporary kingdom of King Minos or with the sumptuous Venetian republic, if it had not been for the spell cast on me by the sixteen-pointed sun-star, on the surface of the table in the *Ghirlanda* drawing-room.

It is true that Manisi, in my last talk or "sitting" as he called it, had visualized the "bump out of Yucatan," after telling me of another city which he said was not Greek. I already knew that. It was the mother-city whose colonists founded Mycenae and Troy. We can not imagine a frail ghost of Yucatan, called Helen. We can not imagine this lily carved or painted on the altars of the sun-god of Yucatan. But we can easily visualize, we almost expect to see it, this actual white cluster, painted in pale fresco, at Sienna or Assisi.

The Cretan artist saw the lily growing. Although he did not discard the original, primitive flower-motive, the whorl of open petals, he varied the perspective. He drew the profiled lily, or filled in the shadow. We imagine the Cretan, not so much discarding the old hieratic symbols, as informing them with new life. So the Annunciation lily, when we look into the open flower, presents again the same pattern, though I do not know how many points or petals there are to this white star. The most obvious of all the open lilies, is the lotus of the Nile, and it is said that some of the rough-hewn decorative motives, on the borders of the Aztec temples, are supposed to represent the Egyptian lily. But as the Cretan subtlized his original plant-motives, the Aztec hardened and stiffened them into repellent, jagged triangles and stone peaks. There seems to be a threat in his artificial bird-and-beast portrayals. The Cretan dolphins, flying-fish and butterflies, like the Annunciation lily, soothe and console us, not only with the hope, but with the certainty of resurrection. There is no resurrection in the stone motives of Yucatan, yet fundamentally the same patterns are used. The Aztec even carved the lily on the temple gate-ways, in a manner reminiscent of the earlier paintings on the walls of Karnak.

. . . . .

I say earlier paintings, but I do not actually know if the Aztec civilization preceded or followed the dynasties of Egypt. To my mind, the Aztec belongs almost to a cave-man period and his pyramid temples to a savage murder ritual. Historically, I may be quite wrong. There is a freshness about some of the more naturalistic Egyptian wall-paintings, that brings them nearer to Crete, but the fish in the water, the duck in the reed, the papyrus-grass, the incense-trees and the sycamores are outlined by a serious craftsman. The Cretan is as frivolous as the Japanese who spent his hours and years contemplating a single cherry-branch in blossom, and who at the end of his life, was satisfied to have added one inimitable moment to eternity.

These things belong to the world of eternal beauty, the world at variance with self-seeking and self-slaughter. The double-axe was a symbol of sacrifice, but this one Cretan weapon was employed, we are told, only in the ceremony of the bull-ritual. The hordes that descended upon Knossos with their arrows, shields and spear-shafts were destined to impose the rule of war upon western civilization. Troy fell because it had sheltered Helen.

But that frail ghost bequeathed her priceless inheritance not only to the victor but to the vanquished. The rule of war did not preclude the rule of Beauty. The word Aztec, even as I write it, makes me shudder. I am afraid of the word and doubly afraid of its related Yucatan. I was not afraid of it in London, when the table spelt out Z's name. But I am afraid of it now. I am even afraid of Z's name. Who was this Z? Why did he come to me? How could it be possible that these same curious syllables had been "given" to Lord Howell, and I judged from his last book, "given" years before I met him? Why did Manisi, usually receptive to new names or new presences at the table, abruptly endeavour to dismiss Z, with "but this is nonsense"? Why did I, who had up to that moment, followed Manisi's prompting or his "guidance," insist upon the authenticity of the curious syllables? Why did Ada Manisi say: "If you are in doubt, ask K"? Why did K, as against Ben Manisi's judgment, insist that Z was a "good Indian"? Why did Z come back and why did he spell n-e-n-u-f-a-r? Why did he, when Manisi would have again dismissed him, spell carefully, w-a-t-e-r l-i-s? Why did Z spell, on more than one occasion, Y-u-c-a-t-a-n?

There is no answer to these questions, though we may attempt to solve this problem or to read this riddle. Was the Aztec Yucatan of Z contemporary with Crete? Did they originally build their cities on the same pattern? Was the Cretan labyrinth, as some imagine, a map of the stars in their apparent courses? Were the pyramid-temples of Yucatan descended from or contemporary with the great pyramids of Egypt? Did these three civilizations spring from the same source, and was that source Atlantis?

Three mountains or three pyramids or three peaks of civilization emerged from the flood-waters; there was not one Ark, but three.

If the lily of Crete, the lily of Troy can still be seen in the old churches of Italy, if Francis of Assisi and Catherine of Sienna bear this staff as their specific attribute of spiritual power, so the angular decorative motives of the gate-ways and fortifications of Yucatan are repeated endlessly, in our modern weapons of destruction.

You may argue that Yucatan and what it stood for, out-lasted Crete and Egypt. The great empire of Egypt received its first intimation of disruption when a hopeless idealist praised the bird in the egg, the bird in the nest, the fledgling in the river-reeds, the wild bird on the wing rather than the long established, set and stylized winged-disc of the sun-god. The delicate plaques and frescoes that survived the wholesale destruction of Akhnaton's worship or religion of life (rather than of death), have been compared to the creations of early *quatrocento* Florence. Minos of Crete might have been a contemporary of Akhnaton's, but we know nothing of him. So you may argue that the overthrow of Akhnaton by the army, saved Egypt and re-established a prestige that challenged even the later might of Caesar.

Crete went first. Egypt would have followed but for the intervention of its armies. Crete became mythology, Egypt, ancient history but the Aztec kingdom of Central America continued its rites and sacrificial ceremonies, into the days of Ferdinand and Isabella of Spain and Henry VIII of England.

. . . . .

Perhaps Z wanted to remind us that Yucatan had not always been dedicated to blood-sacrifice, when he spelt out *nénufar*. When K said, "good Indian," I thought of the tribes of North America. But Z had insisted on Yucatan so, not unnaturally, I confused the issue. I said I was afraid of the word Aztec, but it must be remembered that certain of the Alonquin tribes, notably the Powatans, have been proved by anthropologists to have descended from the Aztecs. Though hunters like all Indians, their bows and arrows and their spears were employed, for the most part, in procuring venison from the forest or fish from the Potomac. It was they who introduced the cultivation of corn or maize, planted tobacco and tapped the maple-tree for sugar. If I think of Z as a brother or even as a warrior of Powatan, I am no longer afraid. The Powatans who brought the starving colony of Jamestown, berries in their woven baskets and corn-loaves baked on their flat stones, were soon doomed to extinction. Their feather-crowns have been compared to the elaborate head-dresses of the Aztecs, and it was their princess, Pocahantas, who lives in the annals of English history, as the Lady Rebecca Rolfe.

. . . . .

Like a wild animal or a "savage" Indian, I have found my way through the intricate windings, twistings and turnings of the labyrinth. I have sometimes traced and retraced my footsteps, but since parting with Manisi, almost two years ago, and with Lord Howell, over a year ago, I have followed my own "traces of direction." I have said that the last square penetrated or permeated the others, like the fragrance of the lilac under the gold-framed mirror. This is a fragrance, dear and familiar to all American children of my state and generation. But the familiar garden-clusters and the bushes run riot in old farmyards, were introduced by the colonists of middle-Europe and of England. But again, the purple and white plumes with their heart-shaped leaves, are not native to the Continent of Europe nor to England. "All the perfumes of Arabia" must have contained among them, the exquisite, delicate yet poignant scent of this Persian flower.

I remember single trees of the honey-locust, along country lanes and on the edges of the woods of Pennsylvania, but the trees I saw in Germany were planted on the outskirts of the city. This makes me wonder if the locust was introduced into America from Europe. But the water-lily of the grass-fringed, reedy ponds and of the shallow, inland lakes is native to the country and has not yet disappeared, as did the wild white-swan and the "savage" Indian.

So at last, the sun-pattern on the table, with its inner circles of smaller petals, becomes by the alchemy of memory, an actual flower. I would have hesitated, if I had been asked to name the flower that represented or might represent America to me, in the same way that the rose represents and is almost synonymous with England, the fleur-de-lys with France and the violet with Athens. For the hieratic lotus of the Nile has overshadowed the lesser or less sumptuous members of the water-lily family. But the simple white water-lily, so difficult to reproduce in line and colour, is to the blue and rose Nile lily, as the early Cretan Annunciation lily is to the geometric whorls of the original sun-pattern, or to the painted hieroglyphs on the walls of Karnak.

With Yucatan I visualised at best, the crude, barbaric stone-flowers carved on the temple gate-ways. But with the reassembling of the four squares, I find Z's few pronouncements or "traces of direction" lead me, not to the arid platforms of a deserted Aztec city and the jagged angles of a temple pyramid, but to the slopes of a Pennsylvania pasture and to where (behind the sand-dunes of New Jersey), the white nenuphar lies open to the sunlight.

. . . . .

We have proved conclusively at last, that two plus two makes four. Not only has each square its four sides but there are four squares to our final pattern. The last square, although I have said it eludes definition by its very essence, yet relates the material to the spiritual, as the fragrance of the lilac recalls old scenes and events. The scenes and events can be described in minute detail, though the fragrance of the flower eludes description.

Among the various decorations and ornaments of the *Ghirlanda* drawing-room, I find my *Little Mermaid*. She is one of four on the inverted, opalescent lamp-bowl; the spiral-shell I spoke of as a carapax enclosing the soul, is coral-coloured and each of the four mermaids holds one, uplifted in her hands. The gold and bronze warrior under the bell-jar by the clock, holds as well as his scroll, a herald's trumpet. There are more shells painted on the ceiling. These things and others, scarcely less important, would hardly have claimed my attention, and perhaps would have escaped my notice altogether, if it had not been for a letter, laid in a dream, upon the table in the centre of the room. I do not know what law of the working of the subconscious mind or what train of association, projected this dream. But I do know that the dream led me to ponder on the curious coincidence of the letter, not only being laid on a tripod-table, not much larger than the one in London, on which I had received the messages of the RAF and the "traces of direction" from Z, but that this very table had worked upon its surface, a geometric pattern that exactly reproduced the form and possibly the number of the white, luminous petals of the *nénufar*.

. . . . .

Only the child, the artist or the devout have the gift of endowing material objects with life. I find the material objects are assembled here, as if placed for the very purpose of recalling and concentrating, even of consecrating the curious sequence of thoughts and dreams that make up the sum total of the crowning experience of my life, the talks with Ben Manisi, the messages from the table, my meeting with Lord Howell.

I could not have invented nor imagined this room. The French window opens on a wide balcony, unlike, but recalling the porch of Mrs. Atherton's house in Philadelphia. The scene beyond the window was not projected by me, but it recalls the tiny pictures that I, in moments of fatigue and desperation, glimpsed in a tea-spoon, a door-handle or a glass of water. The tiny Greek temples are not there, but the slopes and crags, the bays and indentations of this luminous small lake remind me of Crete and the Ionian Islands. It is a background of mountain, sky and water such as the columns of the Parthenon frame in Athens.

But the Parthenon is now associated with another temple, the temple of Artemis in Tauris. The *deus ex machina* seems to have had a hand, not only in the subtle weaving of my thoughts and dreams, but in the actual materialization of them. But the *deus* or *dea* is not a formalized abstraction, nor does he-she lack a sense of tenderness, pathos and of humour. I myself would never have thought of placing a crusader or a knight of King Arthur, on the mantelpiece, under a bell-jar, nor would I have painted that border of incredible carnations and blue lilies on the ceiling. The mermaids, like the fragrance of the lilac, elude description. They are like china dolls. I have that affection for them. I said, what we all know, life advances in a spiral, but I should never have had the humour nor the wit to remind myself of my somewhat laboured analogy of the soul's progress, by placing glass conch-shells in the hands of china mermaids.

To refer back to Lord Howell's lecture that I attended in London, that October day in 1943, who but a being of what he called the "higher orders" could have had the subtlety, the temerity and the wit to employ a name which was, as it happened, the very one used by Lord Howell's "guide" or guardian spirit? I have of course, no proof whatever, that this Z is in fact, the Z of Lord Howell's circle. I speak with all humility, yet I cannot help wondering, if our own Z was later dismissed by Lord Howell, as a Hollywood impersonator. But the more we think about our own experience, the more reason and logic combine to show how delicately the consolation was rendered and the blessing bestowed, and with what incredible grace and subtlety, the lesson was conveyed.

. . . . .

Whether or not Z was a disembodied spirit, he showed a specific knowledge of things outside my own mind. It is true that in certain instances, he might have drawn on my thoughts, as I suspected Manisi had done. I have said that Mr. van Eck, who was in my mind because of the unfinished novel, had worked with Sir Arthur Evans in Crete. He had drawn for me, plant-forms from Egyptian paintings, Cretan pottery and Aztec and American-Indian designs, giving me even then, as far back as 1920, the idea of comparing these decorative symbols. But though Mr. van Eck had explained the underlying similarity of the motives, I had not thought of them as contemporary. In any case, Egypt, Crete and Yucatan were divided by the waters of the Mediterranean, the Atlantic and the Caribbean. But my recent preoccupation with the sixteen-pointed sun-pattern on the table, has drawn these three together. The points of the sun or star, directed outward, have in fact, like so many magnets, attracted the various memories, scattered in time and space, and drawn them all together.

It has also served as a sort of lode-stone, like the wishing-ring or lamp of Arabian legend. For not only did it assemble or materialize the room and the room's contents, as if on purpose for me, but it drew out of my own submerged self, my most secret desires. The hero or heroine of the legend has a wish, or usually, three wishes. I never remember reading in any of the numerous variations of the familiar story, of the lucky possessor of the wishing-ring hesitating for one moment to express his wish or his three wishes. If in the old tradition, when I ran my fingers over the table, a form clad in Arabian robes had stepped through the window, I cannot say that I would have been unduly surprised. And if again, true to type, he had pronounced some formal greeting and announced that I had run my fingers round the sixteen-pointed star, in a way that created a spell or charm to which he was the obedient and willing slave, and that he was there to grant my wish or my three wishes - even then, his offer would have seemed inevitable. The only awkwardness would have been due to the fact that face to face at last, with the ineradicable child-fantasy, I would not have known what I wanted.

Perhaps, approached in this way, I should have answered, as evidently an answer was expected, "Health, wealth and happiness." One would have to say something. But my answer would have been purely automatic. If I had hesitated a moment, there would have been no answer, for after the long trial in London, I felt stronger here in Switzerland than I had for many years; as to wealth, provided I had enough to continue living as I was now doing (and I had that), money had lost its meaning. As to happiness, I can not remember ever having been so happy, since I was a school-girl. If I had, on the contrary, run my fingers over the octagonal glass-insets of the Buddha in my room in London, and this same question had arisen, I would have known what I wanted. Health, certainly, wealth, if it would bring comfort and security - and happiness. I have said I was unhappy - what thinking person was not, in those Apocryphal years? But my supreme happiness would have been to realize the dream or the ambition, conveyed to me by the little table.

All my faculties would have been dedicated to their dream. There was no political or social problem that held any attraction for me. I had no special desire to travel. The work with the table had concentrated my scattered thoughts and energy and had given me hope. I was not lacking in faith and I loved them very dearly. But in the end, I was working alone. The idea was there. I was asked to deliver certain messages. I had tried to do this. But when the messages were repudiated, I felt that I had no place any longer, in this world.

But if I had stayed in London, given even ideal conditions for experiment in radio-communication, I would by this time, have broken down completely. Famine and constant preoccupation with the problems of sheer, every-day existence, would finally have undermined my constitution. I would have stayed in London. Is it possible that Lord Howell's Z prompted him to dissuade me?

. . . . .

When Ben Manisi said, "There is work, there is America," I confess that I translated his words into terms of New York skyscrapers and Boston intellectuals. I did not see myself nor Lord Howell in that America, although I had made an effort to re-establish myself there, with my notes and lectures. But now I wonder if Manisi referred to the earlier America, at the moment when the first "discoverer," Leif or Eric Ericson landed from Greenland. I have mentioned relics of his visit, helmets and skulls found in Rhode Island. The Algonquin were at one time, the chief tribesmen of New England. Translators of the early legends say that many of them suggest the Nordic saga, not only in the outline of the stories but in the very metres employed.

When Z spelt Yucatan, I thought of arid mountains and dead cities. I did not even know exactly where Yucatan was. Manisi had said Mexico and I believe politically that Yucatan is part of Mexico, though its position on the north-east curve of the jagged isthmus makes it geographically at least, Central America. I have said that the Vikings might have sailed from the North into the Caribbean, but it was not necessary for Ericson to go so far, to meet the Aztecs. Perhaps the ancestors of Powatan had been colonists like the Cretans who founded Mycenae and Troy. Or perhaps, they were descendants of a priestly caste who left the cities to continue the cultivation of the arts of peace in a new country, before the Aztec ritual had degenerated into the later orgies of human sacrifice.

However that may be, the last traces of the early Aztec civilization lived on longest, in America. When I say civilization, I refer to the cultivation of the earth, the cherishing of old songs and legends, the arts of weaving baskets and grass-nets, the elaborate and distinctive patterns of their feather-capes and of their swan-crowns.

I think now of ripe melons and clusters of grapes. It seems to have been by no mere chance, that Eric Ericson called the country, *Vineland*. It was possibly not only the vine that he referred to, but the preoccupation of the people with the grain and fruit. No doubt, the same law of hospitality held in the days of Eric Ericson that pertained later, when the starving colony of Jamestown was saved by the bounty of the friendly Indians. Perhaps Eric Ericson landed at the time of harvest, and perhaps what most impressed the Viking, was the formal presentation of baskets of purple grapes.

. . . . .

I do not know how long they stayed there, but I doubt if they went to the Caribbean or to Crete. I had first visualized the circles on circles on the sea that Ben Manisi spoke of, as representing certain states of being or different places of habitation, as the Nordic fiord or island from which they had set sail, Crete and Yucatan. Or reversing the course of their journey, Crete, Yucatan and the headlands of Rhode Island. But I was reasoning in one dimension, in one unit of time. Then, I said that the ship itself was like or even was the table on which or from which I received the messages, and whose orders I had obeyed.

But whose orders had I obeyed? We have consistently endeavoured to avoid any but the most casual reference to reincarnation, but the Viking ship had risen above the horizon at a time of unparalleled danger. Was this what Lord Howell meant when he said that at this time, "beings of a higher order" could communicate with the "lower circles"? Lord Howell read certain messages that had been "given" him. How were these messages "given" and who gave them?

I have tried to describe accurately the details of the messages "given" to me by a young Eurasian. I have related as well, the short history of our "home circle" and how in the end and under what circumstances, I received the messages from the RAF. I have tried to restrain a romantic or imaginative impulse to carry these impressions further, and reviewing my experiences, as time gave me a clearer outline of the sequence of events that led up to my final conclusions, I have retraced my steps, recalled fresh details and uncovered buried memories and emotions. But though Lord Howell introduced the subject of reincarnation at our first meeting (although he said it didn't matter), I have so far avoided the temptation.

The little table was the property of an artist who was known personally to some of my older friends of the last war period. Lord Howell was not Hal Brith, but as I have so far resisted the temptation of introducing any reference to my own, Gareth's, Ben Manisi's or Lord Howell's "past lives," I must allow myself one exception to my self-imposed rule. Lord Howell was not Hal Brith, but William Morris was. And Hal Brith was Eric Ericson.

Hal, I believe, means sea and possibly Britt or Brith is a simplification of another word or an archaic word, that means chieftain or king. Manisi had said it sounded like Britt but "they pronounce it differently." He had said, "his name is Halbritt" and Gareth had said, "His name is Hal Brith." But I never mentioned Hal Brith again to Gareth and Manisi had said, "You are saying good-bye to them." With them, went the Viking chieftain or sea-king. It was after he had gone away, that his warriors or the RAF came back. But Hal Brith did not sponsor the messages, though I said that the table was like, or was the ship.

The messages were sponsored by Z.

. . . . .

I had written Lord Howell at some length about the "good Indian" who had given me the words, Yucatan and *Nénufar*. But Lord Howell made no comment on Z, and it was only after the appearance of his second book, in which he stated that Z was his personal "guide" or older brother, that he dismissed my later findings with "we also have Z in our circle," as if he had said as he did on the occasion of my first approaching him with the RAF messages, "in any case, if there were messages of any importance, they would come to me in my own circle."

Why did Z manifest at the little table? Why did I insist on his authenticity, when Manisi dismissed the odd syllables of his name as "Nonsense"? Why did Z take over the group, Ralph, John, Lad, Larry and the rest of them? Was Z in time, a contemporary of Eric Ericson and had they conspired together to recall *Vineland*? When Manisi insisted on Lord Howell and myself having work to do together in America, did he translate an archaic place-name, in terms of to-day, and did he mean that Lord Howell and myself were working or would be working with an American, in other words, an Algonquin Indian? I had no opportunity of discussing this matter with Lord Howell. There was no-one else to go to. What did Z mean by his repeated Yucatan and -

Yucatan
A part in plan?

What was or what is this plan?

Perhaps Lord Howell knows the answer. I do not. I can theorize on Z's curious insistence on the word Yucatan. I can argue that the original place or tribal names of the Algonquin Indians have been forgotten or through the centuries changed so, that the later syllables bear little or no relationship to the originals. I can say that the word Yucatan contains the same primitive force and authenticity as the syllables of Z's own ancient Aztec, Mayan or Algonquin name. I can say that Yucatan is still a geographic place-name, while the tribal-names of the North American Indians and the names of their settlements, have become the sole property of the anthropologist and the specialist in folk-lore. I can say that Z took the name of the Mayan district from which his tribe descended. I can say that perhaps, he deliberately chose the name of a place in which I had no interest and which was even repellent to me, so that the impact of the word would rouse my curiosity and perhaps my antagonism. I can hazard a guess that Yucatan was not repellent to Lord Howell and that Z wanted to give, as well as his own strange name, another name or clue that would prove conclusively, that he was Lord Howell's Z.

VI

Chapel Perilous

I do not know why Z wanted to do this, unless there were a "plan" having to do with some authentic, scientific method or means of psychic communication. It is well known that the tribesmen of inner Africa and the Hindus of the Himalayas send messages to the coast, in some secret manner unknown to the white races. Clairvoyants, as a rule, are sensitive but not scientific. The table had not wanted me to join Lord Howell's circle, nor did it send any direct messages to him until after our own home-circle was given up. If Lord Howell was engaged in what the RAF called "wave work" and if he were experimenting in new fields opened up by the comparatively recent discoveries of radiolocation, neither he nor his former pilots would wish to discuss the matter with any but a few specialists, like themselves. Perhaps I over-rated my own power of perception or perhaps, as is more likely, the receiving of the messages drew too strongly on what little reserve of strength I then had, but I knew to the fraction of a second, at what exact moment, the connection was broken. But I refused to believe that Lord Howell who had studied psychic phenomena and had attended many séances, would have deliberately severed a connecting wire of psychic communication, once the messages had begun to come through.

I had said, "Avallon." He had said, "Thank you." The connection was made. But when I began to explain the nature of the messages, Lord Howell abruptly cut the communication. I need not dwell on the effect this sudden *volte face* had upon me. But I could at least, rationalize Lord Howell's repudiation of the messages, by arguing that he was perhaps engaged on "wave work" of a highly specialized nature, and working in secret.

I choose to believe this, although I have weighed the evidence against it. If Manisi whose perceptions I trusted, tried to dismiss Z as "nonsense," although he could have no possible reason for distrusting this "good Indian," is it not possible that Lord Howell dismissed Z - that is, the Z of my own Yucatan - not only as "nonsense" but as a spiritual imposter?

Why did Lord Howell descend from the heights or from the fields of Aval-lon, so abruptly and sink immediately into the bathos of New York gangsters and Hollywood imposters? The transition was too sudden. We might argue, if Lord Howell's reaction was immediate and instinctive and the outcome of a life dedicated to discipline and self-control, that having been as he obviously was, touched by my first words, his immediate reaction would be to try to conceal or to retrieve any trace of emotion that had betrayed him. He had not altogether succeeded in doing this. Therefore, he over-emphasized or over-stressed his ob-jections and his counter-arguments. I have finally come to the conclusion that he was putting up defences, with his suggestion that gangsters and impersonators might be likely to interfere with any psychic communication that we might have established. Against what was Lord Howell defending himself?

He had been trained in offensive and defensive warfare but I was, at his own confession, not "a being of the lower orders." Therefore, he must have thought me controlled or "guided" by some mischievous or malign influence. Why should he think that?

But apparently he did think it or wanted to argue himself into thinking it. If he dismissed me as, not exactly an imposter but as a victim of entities of the lower orders, then his own course, whatever that course was, was clear. I or the messages or Z stood in his way. He must at all costs, defend his own position. If he had been surer of his psychic ground, he would not have turned against me. But the very fact of his violent denunciation, showed the weakness of his own defence.

If I could have discussed the matter with him and he had courteously but conclusively explained his own position - whatever that position was - I think in a short time, I would have given up the table and have realized that the "work" was beyond me and really out of my sphere. I had other work to do. Those were the war-years, I might have said, now everything is different. But the enigma, the problem, the riddle was not lessened by Lord Howell's repudiation. In fact, his sudden *volte face* served to drive in the impressions deeper, to heighten my perception and to act as a sort of flint or whet-stone to sharpen my mind.

. . . . .

Yucatan was "a part in plan." I mentioned Yucatan, in the first part of this nar-rative, but I was only recording a word or a message that the table had given me. Later, I saw the pattern on the table in the *Ghirlanda* drawing-room and realized that it represented a sixteen-pointed lily. This served to concentrate and to relate the word *nénufar* to the present and to my own personal surroundings, as well as to my actual birth-place. The word Yucatan by way of Mexico, New Mexico and the Arizona desert, became synonymous with America. But the America that finally resolved from the vast territories, was the America of the *nénufar* or water-lily. It was the America of Eric Ericson.

I said the Viking ship was the table. Perhaps, we may conclude that the Viking ship was England. England is the inheritor of the tradition of the sea-kings. But all the physical or material horizons have been explored. But other horizons have lately been opened up, by new and terrible weapons of destruction. I have said that the angular motives of the gate-ways and fortifications of Yucatan are repeated endlessly in the weapons of modern warfare. If the motive of slaughter and blood-sacrifice, which I had associated with the pyramid-temples of Yucatan, had or could have any "plan," then the recent unparalleled destruction of the peoples of the world, would by some miracle and only by some miracle, be justified. Then Yucatan, meaning blood-sacrifice, had or might have a "plan" or a "part in plan."

. . . . .

For my own part, I have found the boundaries so far explored by psychic-research workers, cloudy and amorphous. My chief objection to the recorded findings of the spiritualists is that their messages and voices seem to come from a vague and commonplace no-man's-land. The spiritualists themselves confess that "they can't tell time over there." That is their chief excuse for the flood of messages in and around 1940. They explain the familiar "peace soon," as due to the fact that "soon" might mean three weeks, three months or three or more years. If the so-called "disembodied" can enter a room and accurately describe the whereabouts of the lost will or the letter that contains the address of the soldier son who has been missing for some time, in India or in Africa, why can they not, casually in passing, glance at the calendar on the writing-desk or the grandfather-clock, ticking so benignly in the hall?

When the literary resources of the "disembodied" are over-taxed, they seem to have a neat trick of saying, "All this defies description, words can not possibly convey any idea of what is going on over here." This being the case, why does not some robust Robert Browning or some sensitive but competent John Keats step forward and fill in the gap? Recent communications, purporting to come from the poet Shelley, are illiterate to a degree, and the stanzas palmed off as his "disembodied" utterances, are a desecration to his memory.

Why do so-called Indian "guides" talk like Salvation Army Lassies? Red Feather and Prairie Flower do not even give us their names. It should be easy to utter them phonetically, even if the spelling of the syllables did not entirely agree with that of the annotated lists of Indian words that scholars have collected for us. Though I admit that even the most superficial investigation into the authenticity of the original Indian syllables that roughly translated, would mean Red Feather and Prairie Flower, would be difficult. For the North American Indians were a vast race of wandering tribes and their unrecorded speech was not one, but at least thirty languages.

If a message came from Europe, we would immediately think in terms of separate nations, France, Germany, Scandanavia or the Latin countries. The American Indians were as scattered as the nations or tribes of Europe. Frankly, I do not entirely discredit the stories of lost wills and missing sons. A friend tells me of a message she had given her, in German. The gifted medium said, "Perhaps this is not fair, I know a little German, but this message comes from your mother, though I do not think she was a German." My friend was deeply touched as the medium gave her the first stanza of a German lyric that she and her mother had often sung together.

. . . . .

There are two courses open to the psychic-research worker, that of science and that of illumination. But even within my own memory, I have heard people speak of the "miracle" of the telephone. That "miracle" has been extended and amplified. We have had only recently still further manifestation of the "miracle," in radiolocation. New wave-lengths have been recorded and it seems that we are very near the boundary. But when any question arises, as to rational communication with the dead, there seems to be a schism in consciousness. Even the most advanced stop short with "We are not ready," or the spiritually awakened say, "We are tempting Providence."

It may be that thinking in vast abstractions is a rest to the mind. It is not, as a matter of fact, easy to express a generalization in concrete terms. Moreover, not so much new words as an exact understanding of old words is needed. Moreover, if we are communicating with so-called "foreign" peoples, we must know their languages and their dialects. We hear of so-and-so having an Egyptian, a Chinese or a Hindu "guide," or more usually, a Red Feather or a Prairie Flower. But all the recorded messages I have read from these sources, are indistinguishable from one another. It is almost as if their wordy and amorphous manner of expression were a badge of authenticity, suggesting loose ungirdled garments, bare arms, vast and insignificant gestures. It may be that the "instrument," so-called, of Red Feather or Prairie Flower may convey a message which brings consolation and answers a spiritual need. But why is it necessary to introduce these intermediaries, these robed, beneficent, banal and friendly spirits?

It almost seems that it is the hall-mark of respectability to take things on faith and to refuse to let the mind "interfere."

The inventors of the engines of destruction have no inhibitions about using their minds. If "We are not ready" to place psychic communication on a scientific, practical basis now, at this very moment, when will we be? Lord Howell himself said, in a public lecture in 1943, that now was the moment when beings from the higher circles could and did communicate with planes, to which they descended because of the danger that threatened the world. Perhaps these beings have delivered their last messages and have withdrawn again to the higher spheres.

But if we have contacted or believe we have contacted, any being of the higher spheres, even if the messages have now ceased, we have a duty, the duty of recording our experience. I have tried to do that. My spiritual life was enriched and my mind refreshed by my contact, or by my imagined contact, with Z and with the group that he sponsored. Perhaps we are not ready for them but they apparently, were ready for us. Perhaps Lord Howell is continuing his work along specific lines, now closed to me. I have at least, the reward of having at last, seen my way clearly. I owe the unravelling of the tangled threads of what I call the second square (or the second panel of the tapestry), to my contact with Lord Howell. I can not say how it came about, but I owe the discovery or the uncovering of the first square to a chance dream.

"Soon, I will see myself looking at myself, in your eyes."

I have looked at myself or tried to look at myself with the eyes of Lord Howell, who repudiated my findings and who possibly doubted my integrity. When I had assembled the three squares, or seen the pattern of the three panels, their sequence and relationship, I discovered again, by the chance mediation of a dream, the fourth and last square. It was a letter, written absent-mindedly that repeated in substance, a letter written only a few days before, that led me to Lord Howell. There was a letter on the table, in the second dream.

. . . . .

We have had volumes of wordy letters from the dead. I studied the somewhat formidable catalogue of the Stanford House library, and during the years 1942, 1943 and 1944, I did try to give the subject my careful and unbiassed consideration. I found many interesting histories or case-histories of dual personality, projection of the "double," telepathic and other psychic communications, messages received from the living, as well as the familiar last words of soldier sons, posted in distant colonies. The most scientific of these volumes were the accurately recorded data of Camille Flammarion. I avoided the temptation of looking over the shelves, devoted to bound periodicals of various English and American psychic-research societies. I rejected the volumes devoted to spirit photography and found the "spirit" photographs, not only patently faked, but inartistic to a degree and in the worst of taste. I read with interest a diary or notebook of an Austrian lady which so delightfully conjured up the actual surroundings of her group, that I was not even shocked at her introduction of *aports*. It was at this time, that I tried to follow the trail of Red Feather to the west, but he became involved with long descriptions of sunsets, the colours and miasmic transparencies of which eventually defied description. The poetry of Blue Lotus was deplorable. But I found scholarly resumés of various religions and philosophies, cults and rituals. I was able to fill in the gaps of my not altogether clarified ideas of the Grail, the Round Table and King Arthur's *Chapel Perilous*.

Being in daily peril of imminent destruction by the high-explosives, perhaps I found the letters from the dead, too vague and elusive. Our material foundations were being undermined. At such a time, we need a surer certainty of heaven. I do not mean the fact of there being a heaven, but the facts *of* heaven. There were park-like enclosures, there were groups of people, there were old friends. But the groups of strangers and the old friends seemed alike colourless. One lady whose letters from the dead were, I believe at one time widely circulated, confessed that her old school-friends could hardly be distinguished from one another. Time of course, was non-existent. Leafing over the two volumes, one had a feeling of sincerity. They were happy, of course. They wanted other people to be happy. But their spiritual life seemed to be, on the whole, without any apparent "traces of direction." I tried to visualize their paradise but again, though I received an impression of peace and vague beatitude, there was no dynamic impact to be sensed or to be anticipated. Perhaps again, it is not quite respectable to be alive in heaven.

. . . . .

The heaven that so graphically defies description, lacks depth, lacks definition, lacks a sort of sounding-board to concentrate and strengthen the voices that try to convey to us the hope of eternal salvation. One returns even to the familiar ticking of the clock, the sound, of the door-bell, the ringing of the telephone with a sense of at least momentary security. Does one, after all, want to go to heaven? One wants to escape hell, certainly, but the threat of being caught in a burning building, suffocated in the underground, pinned down beneath fallen masonry and girders was the constant preoccupation of all London people at that time. We did not have to read about hell. Perhaps references to the lower regions were more explicit, but the tales of suicides, murderers and drunkards were actually outside the sphere of our work. We are not concerned with the after-life of gangsters and crooks.

There is another point. When we arranged to meet the Manisis regularly, Gareth was most anxious to keep our friends from knowing about our group or our "home-circle." Not only would it have involved tiresome, personal explanations, but I am certain that sooner or later, others would have asked to join us. Manisi's "guide" or the table had emphatically dismissed the idea of enlarging our group. I did not want to talk about this until actually the work with the Manisis was over. Later, I confess, I should have liked to discuss my problems with some outside person. But I went direct to the new work with Z and the RAF, and they discouraged my recalling Ben Manisi or returning to Stanford House. Gareth told me too, that there was an unwritten law or if you will, a superstition that anyone discussing a private circle outside the immediate group, would find himself sooner or later, dropped by his own circle and unable to make other contacts afterwards. This being the case, we are bound to confess that there may be a tradition or superstition that it is even more dangerous to write about these matters. We may have been on the fringe of a highly organized body of secret research workers.

Manisi was explicit in his details of the "picture for Delia" that really started the whole thing. He had said that there were circles on circles on the sea, touching but not merging with one another. Is it possible that this was a sort of picture-writing and that the circles were actually intended to indicate the fact that we were, for that short time at any rate, one of a vast network of secret workers? When our particular circle was broken, I was almost immediately transferred to another. That circle wished to include Lord Howell and eventually, other people.

But I had to abandon my work alone with the table, because of my sudden illness. I say work "alone," but I was never less alone in my whole life. It is true my chief concern was to deliver the messages to Lord Howell and it may appear, from this narrative, that I failed. I may have failed in making the desired contacts but after I left London the why and the wherefore of that failure became questions of such burning interest, that I went back step by step and relived the first talks with Manisi at Stanford House, the various phases of our work in my apartment, the fact that an article in a newspaper by a certain Air Marshal left me curiously indifferent, the fact that Manisi was unexpectedly called to Scotland and asked me to take his ticket for Lord Howell's lecture, October 1943, my writing to Lord Howell, his apparent carelessness in answering the letter twice, the indifferent reply that I had when I brought this fact to his notice and my question put to the table, with the qualification or determinative *wings*, that drew the Viking ship from what perhaps Lord Howell had referred to, in his lecture as the "higher spheres."

I have asked, does one after all, want to go to Heaven? Heaven, a very vivid presentation of courage, vitality and life, came, as it happened, to the little table.

"They are shouting and laughing," said Manisi. There was a flash of wings, there was a hawk perched on the wrist of one of the warriors, there was a suggestion that a problem in runic divination was being presented to someone whom Manisi called the "seer." He had implied that I was this seer. I had denied this. But if there is a riddle to be read, a problem to be solved, an answer to be given, who is there but myself to attempt the solution of the mystery?

If Lord Howell had followed the suggestion of the RAF, and jotted down the numbers and letters that they wanted me to give him, I would have been in a sense, sworn to secrecy. If there had been preliminary experiments dictated by them, I would have been happy to feel that I could contribute something to the forwarding of this work. But the radio-communication would have been left to others, and I would have remained a fortunate and anonymous assistant in some great work. As it was, my messages were at first tolerated but finally dismissed. It may have seemed that I was dismissed with them, but to quote my friend Gareth, on the occasion of her reading Lord Howell's last letter to me, "It's not lost. This will go on somewhere."

"We are going somewhere," Manisi had said. We were certainly going somewhere but at the time, I did not know where. I have said that our circle was broken but I have now come to the conclusion that these circles are never broken. The groups may separate, individual members may find themselves as I did, in a new circle, others give up the work altogether, but the circles remain unbroken. The work that was apparently planned for Lord Howell and myself, may have gone to another circle. These circles touch one another but do not merge. If we were given a glimpse of heaven, no doubt, others have had as strange and as startling illuminations. But if, as Gareth stated, there is an unwritten law about speaking or writing of these things, no doubt, the more important findings of the inner circles of psychic-research workers are not made public. My own findings would have remained a comfort and solace to me, but if I had succeeded in assembling the body of specialists that the RAF indicated were waiting and anxious to communicate with them, I myself would have been absolved from the, at times, painful task of recording these impressions.

It is difficult to explain the presence of Lord Howell on the Viking ship. What I mean is, his presence seemed inevitable but it is difficult to explain why this should be so. We have spoken of Camille Flammarion's collection of authentic instances of various psychic phenomena, among others, of the projection in daylight of the "doubles" of living persons. I should say that the Lord Howell of the Viking ship was the one I recognized on September 3, 1945, as the Sir John Howell of the last war. Lord Howell's attitude to myself, our circle, the "picture for Delia" and my later contact with his pilots, was in retrospect, both baffling and contradictory. I have said that the crashing-rocks, the Scylla and Carybdis of Lord Howell's double repudiation, had parted for a moment, at the word "Avallon." I have said that I held a dove in my hand and if the dove, according to the old Greek legend, could dart through the crashing-rocks, the ship could follow. My key-word was wings, and at the risk of appearing a little banal, I must say that the wings of hope or the wings of aspiration have lifted me above the doubt, depression and discouragement that followed my forced abdication of the little tripod-table of the poet, William Morris.

Ah once again, ah once again,
The black prow plunges through the sea,

Nor yet shall all your dreams be vain
Nor you forgot, O Minyae.

I have said that their dreams shall not be vain, nor they forgot while I am alive to remember them.
May 6, 1947.

BOOK II

Summerdream

We are such stuff as dreams are made on

I

Sempione

Lugano, Paradiso, Campione, Bissone, Melide - that will be far enough. Melide, melissa, melitta - I will get off at Bissone. The snow swirls against the window. My mind is intent on the arcades, the boats with their wooden frames. Some of the boats have awnings; the half-circles of the wooden frames remind me of the hoops we rolled in childhood. Nets are hung between the arches. This is a picture in a picture-book called *Lugano Mendrisiotto*. It is a cold winter.

There is a bridge connecting Bissone and Melide. I will get off at Bissone. I will walk under the arches, look for the church, perhaps push open a door and rest in the darkness. It will be hot outside. Then I will hesitate at the bridge. It is not far to Campione and the *Madonna dei Ghirli*. The sun casts darker shadows from the cypress-trees. But I must get to Melide. But now I have ceased to believe in the bridge-dyke. It seems a contradiction in terms. I manage in French: "Is it possible, sir, to traverse the bridge from Bissone to Melide?" "It is, of course, possible, Madame." "Then, is it that the boat makes the return?" I am aware of a great decision. I could not be more anxious if I were going to Byzantium. I flutter my precious *orario* folder. It is 17.31 at Melide, when the boat returns. I must be sure it will come back; 14.05 Lugano, 14.39 Bissone - that gives me 17.31 minus 14.39 hours of exploration. But the boat may never come back. The bridge-dyke may be a fabulous invention. I unfold the *orario* map. There is a black line across blue, marked *ponte diga*. "This," I say, "here - is it that it takes long on foot?" "A half-hour," he says.

. . . . .

14.25 Campione. The icicles had not begun to drip. They were part of the iron-balcony, they were decoration or they were a fringe of small stalactites strung under the eaves. He had written, "Mountain, go back to Persia," and "Hot-scented Egypt," or "I sense in the heat the fragrance of Egypt," or "Egypt wafts incense in the heat." They had said there was no translation of his poetry. How could there be? He turned a *Zauberring* on his finger and he himself had conjured this up, out of the past. He spoke of *Winterschlaf* and *Sommertraum* and huddled under my bed-quilt, I tried to conjure up from my own not inconsiderable treasure, the word that would fit the word, the word that would reveal the word, the word that would transcribe or translate "*Berge . . . fliege nach Persien.*" Go back to Persia, mountain, you don't belong here.

There was, there had been a vague fantasy. I would translate these poems. It would be easy for the famous poet to discover in me, the long-sought perfect English transcriber of his verses. But it was not so easy for the translator.

He leaned in the night upon the iron-railing of his own balcony. Snow-white, a giant summer-magnolia, pale moon . . . spilled Zitrone-flower-fragrance from its ivory cup. I could not bring myself to change the Z to C and the *Zitrone* to Citron. It was the same with *Zeder* and *Zauberring*.

14.25 Campione. It is not Persia, it is India. I do not really care to see them. He had retired to Kareno, some years ago. I cannot reconcile the Wintersleep and the Summerdream. It would be better to go back to Garry. Her house is austere and a glass-wall looks out on a range of mountains that are as mountains should be. They keep their distance. Even in summer they are edged with snow. They repeat themselves in a dividing stretch of water which is again tempered by a glacial river. Garry has books there. She has written me to come back. *Campione*.

I do not know what it is about their voices. It is the O, especially. It is the stress, the unexpected pause, as if the o-o-o note were held for three beats. The houses are irregular, each one is different yet they form a single row, almost to the edge of the wide river. The houses are white, pastel-blue and pale coral. Some of them have frescoes or borders of painted wreaths and garlands. But this is a lake, it is not a river, it is not the Ganges.

They told me where the house was, but I was afraid they would see me, so I trailed through the daisies and wild-oats and avoided the stony hill path. He might be working in the garden. He wore a straw hat pushed back on his head and he had a spade, half buried in a furrow. I would know him but he would not know me. They were pleased, they wrote, with what I said about him. Philip Manning said that he would like an article for his London paper. I had every excuse to go there. I had the little volume of his last poems, with his name scribbled on the fly-leaf. I had the Nobel Prize notice with the photograph of him in the straw hat. I knew this and this about him. I had said that my star-pattern on the table in the *Ghirlanda* drawing-room was like a magic-ring. I had said that I had my traces of direction. This was one of them.

But magic-ring is *Zauberring*. You see what I mean. The word "magic" for us has lost its meaning. But we, he and I (German and English speaking) are not only affiliated but are one in the word *ring*. It was Z who first indicated to me this sort of divination. He began it with nenufar, but the dictionary spells it nenuphar; in English it is a specialized word, though the French *nénufar* is the name for water-lily. But that was not enough. Z balanced, simplified or coded it, by spelling water-lis. That suggested *fleur-de-lis* and Z, I think, meant us to understand by water-lis that English-French was indicated. One can perhaps become too deeply involved with this sort of decoding, but I don't think so. Z spelt nenufar instead of nenuphar. I looked at the word for a long time. Then I got out Garry's hieroglyphs. There was a little picture of Nenu, the Egyptian sky-god. His name is found in the zodiac. His picture or his name is ⌇⌇⌇ which is the sign of the eleventh house of the Zodiac, Aquarius. And *far* was all right, too - *phar* would have spoiled it. So we had ancient Egypt and the present, and *far* spelt backwards, is RAF.

Well, that was a long time ago. I think, though I am not sure, that I wrote Lord Howell of my findings. I had found Lord Howell but I had not exactly placed him on my chart or my sky-map. I place him now. He is the Winter King, and the poet at the top of the steep mountain-path that you turn into, off the stone steps above Melide, is the Summer King. We have Hal Brith, the Sea King and we have a fourth. This is Z or Nenu, the Sky King. He was near at the little table, but *far* with the warriors of the Viking ship. This lake-boat is called *Sempione*. It is the Italian for Simplon.

. . . . .

When I think of it now - I mean, the little tripod-table - things seem even less complicated than they did when I took the RAF messages for Lord Howell, in London. I said we had our shorthand technique and I said it was the winged word that they wanted. Z had given me the first clue or code. They said that I would "hear" this but that he would understand it. They wanted Lord Howell and myself to work together.

I was thinking of Melide and of how, in Lausanne, last winter, it suggested melissa or melitta, the Greek word for Bee. I said there was a swarm of us, but that we had no king or queen to gather us together. But they had Lord Howell and people said, in the beginning, that they communicated like a flock of birds. Lord Howell was that "lone eagle" that Ben Manisi said, hovered above the table. Manisi had said, "He has a nest somewhere." The nest was the little tripod-table of the poet, William Morris. The full-grown eaglets, hawks or falcons had flown off, but they were still one flock or family. They understood each other without speaking, but they wanted others to understand them, as well.

"You help," they said, when I tried to explain to them how difficult it was for me, to reach Lord Howell. They said it should not be difficult; it would be easy for me to transcribe their messages but it would need Lord Howell to translate them. I was thinking of *Zitrone, Zeder* and *Zauberring* and of the depth of tone that Z gave to the words, when I thought of our Z and of how he had sponsored the messages from the RAF, that last year in London. They were a flock or swarm, and Z was their sponsor there, as Lord Howell was here. They wanted the cloud-swarm or the star-swarm and the bee-swarm to work together.

We and they, they insisted, spoke the same language. But they wanted to establish a means of communication that could be shared by other people. When I thought of *Zitrone, Zeder*, I saw the Z differently, and as I say, I thought of our Z and I saw that the shape of the letter Z was a graph on a map. I realized then, that Z is really a bee-letter or the bee-letter. The bee speaks very clearly. He says - Zzzz-zz.

He whispers or drones. He buzzes or hums. Words are not necessary. They could have dictated a graph on a map. Without words and our sometimes clumsy spelling, they could have zzz-ed a detailed line-drawing. I could easily have transcribed the rhythm, the up-and-down, the pause and beat on ruled music-paper. But they wanted Lord Howell to translate the music - or the weather-chart. What music is more compelling than the zzz-zzz of a great bumble-bee in the summer grass?

Now, it seems almost too easy. They had only to indicate to me the type of ruled, numbered and lettered paper that they wanted. I imagined it blocked off in tiny squares and the size of a not-too-large map that could be conveniently rolled up or pinned on a wall. At first, they would tap out N or S or E or W or NE or SW, or variations of these, as I saw them in the compass sun-pattern on the *Ghirlanda* table. These would indicate directions or simply the side of the sheet of map-paper on which the graph began. There would be numbers, latitude and longitude. There must be a great variety of these marked and numbered papers, with seconds and degrees. They had only to indicate what sort of graph or map-paper they wanted and Howell would find it for them.

"Wave work," they had said. The hieroglyph or graph of Z or Nenu's own name is ⋙, the wave symbol. It is W, twice repeated in one graph, and W, twice repeated below it. It would be a zzz-zzz way of talking. But it might have been too easy. We could find, at last, felicity. I had said that Lord Howell had written somewhat extravagantly at times, of luminous scenes and summer-land felicity. I had said that there was a qualification about summer-land, it might be winter-land.

I confess that I am more at home in winter-land. I am confused and disarmed. I do not know where I am. I wanted to run down the steps from Kareno to Melide. A single cypress cast a shadow on the sun-dial of the stone court before the Cathedral of San Georgio. The painted dragon in the fresco above the cathedral door, was pierced by the sword-thrust of the victor. A damsel out of the *Roman de la Rose*, clasped her hands under a mountain boulder. I sat in the shadow.

The clock struck. There was no-one anywhere. It was a city in a dream, with painted palaces. That same eagle, hawk or falcon swirled in the empty space between the sky and the solid blue beneath. I had watched him, day after day, from the lake-edge. Now, he was level with my eyes. Now, he swerved lower. Now, the swallows pierced the air. There was nothing to hold on to. I tried to visualize the swallow-graph, the dart and flight, so different from the eagle's. Between the houses, along the narrow cobbled street there came a slow ambling bullock. The boy that followed the wooden cart encouraged him with sounds of muffled lowing. I didn't know what to do. Even if I ran for dear life, down the steep mountain-path to the Melide stair-way, I might miss the last boat. I had an hour to wait for the *postauto*. Two ambulating mounds of grass moved toward me. They climbed the narrow steps behind the wall. I wondered how old these old, old women could be.

I wondered why the *Sempione* did not move on. Perhaps, after all, I had better get off at Campione. I worked my way through the crowd in the salon, found the gang-way but they wouldn't let me get off. It appeared we were not the Ganges, we were not even Switzerland, we were Italy. This was the reason for our waiting. They were actually examining passports and papers. I sat down in the cool salon. It was a relief to hear an English voice speaking. It said,

"No - that was 1943 - the doodles hadn't come yet. Don't you remember? That *was* a time, but there was worse to follow."

I kept on wondering about the flight or graph of the eagle or the falcon.

"He has a nest somewhere," Ben Manisi had said. The nest was the little tri-pod-table. If there was a nest, there must have been two eagles, hawks or falcons. He had no rival anywhere. He would know what to say, what to write. He would make it seem inevitable, the final honour; they too could share it. But they couldn't share it. No-one could share the pride he had in them. They couldn't share it, for they couldn't understand it. No woman on earth could share the glory with them.

Ad Astra. They were all his sons.

I read about it in the Battle of Britain article for that year. It was Battle of Britain Sunday. There was his photograph, the staring eyes. I cut out the photograph of Lord Howell and carried it in my hand-bag with my accumulation of - mascots does not seem the word, somehow, but we all carried our assortment of various charms and talisman around with us, in those days. The article said the air-force called him - that funny name they called him - because of his dry, humourless manner. Before sending them out, Howell had growled at them,

"You see - every one of you - you are all my sons."

I tried not to think too much about it. But I had to think about it. I wrote down the "true tale" of Lad, Larry, Ralph and the "others - many." I didn't like to think of them as separate or different or more important than the others, but they gave me those names and - John. John really came first.

Geoffrey had called me Astraea. It was written in the circle round the albatross, on the September 16, 1945 Westminster Abbey folder. It was my name, Ad Astra - per ardua - it wasn't easy. That didn't matter because I loved them. If they wanted him, it didn't matter about me, or what he thought about me. It didn't matter how I felt or how ill I might be. It only mattered if I died, because then the communication would stop. What happened over there, didn't matter. What happened here, didn't matter. Why describe scenery and situations? It wasn't easy, but they wanted the albatross and his "circle" to go on. Per ardua - it was too easy, but then I was beginning to feel happy. He was stronger, of course, and he knew how to deal with people. But I had kept watch over the crag where the nest was.

I wondered if he flared out at them, in order to make them angry - "We'll show him." I wondered, if one of them had an idea and managed shyly, to convey it to him, if he turned those eyes on the offender and struck him with "This thing is utterly impossible." Was it a convention, this repudiation? Was it a way of testing the strength and sincerity of the culprit? What had we done? The baffling thing about it was that until he turned on us, we thought that he was not only in sympathy with us but that he himself had originally suggested the plan of communication that we, in our small way, were ready to take seriously. But something went wrong somewhere. How did we offend Lord Howell? Was his plan of psychic radio-communication only a vague dream? But he wasn't like that, when we first knew him. Had we challenged him? Had we said, you hold forth about beings of a higher order and communications from the higher spheres. . . well, had we intimated that it was time perhaps that we had some direct proof of their concern about our welfare? That is, concern on a practical level, such as he himself had seemed at first to indicate with his own suggestion of psychic-radio communication. What had happened?

They seemed to say: you could get certain stations but you couldn't get others. (They were talking to Lord Howell.) We saw what you were doing and we had no intention of interfering with your private line. But this was different. It was what you yourself had wanted from the beginning. We would start first with ordinary conversation. There were all sorts of problems but this table acted as a sort of sounding-board. It had been Hal's table, we believe she explained that to you. He had not been over here, such a very long time. She knew people who had known him. All these things help. She was living on the edge of time, as you know very well. We on our side, were also living on the edge of time. We met in that no-man's-land - but it was Hal's land, Winterland, she called it. He could reach her because she knew his poetry. She could reach us because she loved us. We could reach you through her.

They did say: you could get certain stations but you couldn't get others. Your ideas were all right, but you were using the wrong station. Hal put us through, and we tapped out messages. Nothing went wrong, anywhere. It was your idea, really. She was carrying out her orders. Strike and strike quickly - you had said that to us. We struck quickly. It was your way of fighting. Other people might have got through to her, but she said this was our special station. She was keeping it for you. She asked us how we knew she was there. "Table lights up," we spelt. It is true the incandescent burner might have cracked, but why did you switch off the light?

. . . . .

They come drifting out of the blue sky; admiral, fox, swallow-tail, king-mantle and mother-of-pearl: the shy dove-tail and the red bear: the mourning-robe and the thistle-butterfly. It was another sort of ecstasy. The light was too strong. He couldn't bear it. It was, as I have said, radium and snow. They had gone away. Ben Manisi had said, "They are going after treasure." I was going after treasure.

No-one can stand this flame-life forever. You can't burn all your lights forever . . . with music from the castle windows and the thousand candles. It was a different sort of burning, but the poet who lived at Kareno, at the top of the Melide stair-case, knew all about it.

. . . . .

There was a crash, a bell ringing. But it was only the *Sempione* jamming against the jetty, and the ship-bell. "I'll never forget that evening," there was a sort of exaltation in the voice, "a whole basket exploded in our square - that was before the candelabra - pretty, they were. Our station was right in the track of the doodles - yes, it was doodlebug alley."

I told them I was just going to look out of the window.

"Better stay here," Garry said.

Howard was going on to Lisbon, the next day. He had rushed in at the last minute, to ask me what I wanted. I said, "Bring me a castle-in-Spain, Howard."

We shut the room doors and sat in the hall. Garry was sitting in the chair where Lord Howell had laid his hat and gloves that first time he came to see us. I said,

"They say there is a new white flare; they call it the candelabra."

"Who calls it?" said Howard.

"Oh - it was Paul's Watch."

"What's that?" said Howard.

"It's the - it's the - "

"Architects," said Garry. "They fight for the privilege of getting bombed in the cathedral."

"It's a friend of ours," I said. "I told you they had those Rossetti letters."

"Oh, those - " said Howard. "For Christ-sake, don't let them get bumped off, before I see the letters."

"I've arranged for you to see them when you get back," said Garry. "They're the people we're always talking about, the Burtons, you remember."

"What's he doing with the architects?" said Howard.

"He has charge of the archives," said Garry.

"I'll go while it's quiet," I said.

"Don't stay too long," said Howard.

But I only saw the black flash. I dropped the curtain. It was not the first time the house had swayed. The hall-door swung open. There was a crooked triangle of light. The chair I had been sitting in had slid forward. Howard's legs were crossed, his shoes stuck out, just as they had done when I almost stumbled over them on the way to my room. There was the rumbling of thunder in a canyon.

"Well," Howard said, "did you see the candelabra?"

. . . . .

"Chief trouble was the kiddies."

"But we cleared ours out, in early forty."

"All right for you - a cushy job at Plymouth."

"I mean the London children."

"Yes, but they brought ours all back - requisitioned their old place, then cleared it again. It was too near the coast. What I mean is, it was no use. We thought best to make them think it was *our* flares. Then, we had the bright idea of passing on the good news. Do you know, I don't think there was more than one out of ten in London, in the end, that knew the truth about them."

The house was swaying. I looked out of the window. There was the usual terrace, pushed into the water. There was palm, cedar, chestnut, Judas-tree, eucalyptus, burning-bush and the creepers, trailing from the walls and balconies, wisteria and - *Lianen*. But I didn't know what *Lianen* was, so I skipped a half-page and saw a white chapel from the *endlosen Walde* - but you couldn't say "endless forest" or "infinite forest," but the white chapel was right and it was haunted and old.

I cut out things that I wanted to remember. But I wanted to forget. It was another shelter. He had begun a story. He was sitting up in a shelter-bed. His head was bandaged and he had his arm in a sling. I read this in the *Standard*. He went on telling them the story.

"Once upon a time, there was a house. Everybody was very happy. There was a dog. He talked. He was a big dog."

The other children sat round. One of them wore a fireman's jacket. The sleeves hung down and a girl in a helmet said, "It will not be long now, Jessie, put on your coat."

"It's not my coat," said Jessie. "It's too big."

"Put your arms in, that's right, Jessie."

"And then the father-wolf came in; he said 'I have a nice house in the woods.' They all got laughing and singing. The dog barked at the wolf."

"That's Red-riding Hood," said Jessie.

"What's Riding-hood?" asked the one in the shawl.

"It's his story, anyhow. Go on Tommie," said the fire-girl.

"They got cherries off trees. They got apples, as many as they wanted."

"You see, I told you it wouldn't be long - it's the all-clear," said the fire-girl.

But it went on, zzz-z in my head. The house stopped swaying. I was looking at a picture. There was too much in it. It was a tangle of mock-orange and wild-roses. I saw the stone-steps to the left of the church and I remembered that I was getting off at Bissone and walking across the bridge to Melide. But this was Melide. But now, I couldn't get up the stone-steps. There were spider-webs with the dew on them, he wrote. There was honeysuckle and oleander. They said the chestnuts were red and gold. But this was June. I didn't know where I was. The English voice went on talking.

I couldn't get off the boat now, so how could I walk up the Melide steps through the woods, to Kareno? The *Sempione* was moving. There were more pictures. They hung, evenly spaced, in a row on a level with my eyes. But one picture after another moved out of its frame, into the next frame and then, there was a whole new row of pictures. They were all out of a picture-book called *Lugano Mendrisiotto*, but the ones I had first looked at in Lausanne last winter, were plain and these were coloured. They were too highly coloured. The blue was too blue, the green that ended at the top of the frames, was too green. There was an attempt however, to modify the green, by washing in silver. The silver was the tassels of the chestnut-trees. I don't mean the pink and white flowering chestnuts. These are the *marron glacé* trees. You see sugared heaps of *marron glacé* in the confectioners' windows. I never passed a window without thinking of them. What could I do about it? It was thinking about the children that had made me so ill in London. But I was well now. I might be able to do something, sometime. I didn't know what. The next station was Brusino. But I wouldn't get off there. It was the one after that, Morcote that was Persia. I would have known that, even if the poet hadn't said "*Berge . . . fliege nach Persien.*"

I had gone to Morcote through the valley, in April, but I wouldn't let myself go back there until I had seen more of the other shrines and villages. They said, taken all in all, there were about a hundred pilgrimages to be taken. It was a climb to the Morcote minaret, I mean the campanile of Santa Maria. A few peach-trees were still flowering on the north terraces. It was all terraces. The fig-trees were already in full leaf but the leaves were almost transparent. They spread their wings to the sun, like butterflies, just out of the cocoon. I had never seen a green butterfly as large as the new fig-leaves - or had I? I didn't know what he meant by "red bear" and "fox," in his butterfly poem. I could get off at Morcote and climb up through the labyrinth. But the camellias were over. I could not think of Morcote without camellias.

He meant red-admiral when he said admiral. We both had swallow-tail but which was the painted-lady? Not mourning-robe - but perhaps widow-butterfly would translate his *trauermantel* better; there was the widow-iris and the black-tulip. Perhaps our painted-lady was his king-mantle or even thistle-butterfly. I could ask him these things. There was no need to talk about the messages. But he had travelled in Ceylon and India. Perhaps he would understand. I would be driven, haunted until I circumscribed the circle, I mean, until I was sure of the circumference. We were to take the messages, they said, Howell and myself and when we had established the connection, there would be others. They even gave me the initials of the members of the first group, that is, the first circumference. The circles would go on. I gathered that the first group or the first circumference was to be made up, chiefly of men in the services.

There were other services. I knew they would understand. It was the poet William Morris (Hal Brith) who had brought them. Garry had said, "It isn't lost. This will go on somewhere." It had already gone on somewhere. I sent the typed manuscript of *Wintersleep* to Randolph Spencer. I had known Randolph in the old days, but I had lost track of him. He was a newspaper correspondent and had been for many years in India. He had recently been transferred to Paris. Paris was not far. I wanted advice and I asked Randolph about the manuscript.

He wrote back, "In its present form the book is publishable but has little chance of a popular success. It will be well reviewed but not sell. Do you remember the hero of William Morris' *The Glittering Plain* is called Hallblithe?"

I did not remember, but I had my next circumference.

Randolph went on about *wings*.

"Since you quote wings and William Morris together but do not refer to his poem *Golden Wings*, I am sending an extract in which the word is frequently repeated."

. . . . .

Now, I am completely at sea. I mean, having clung to a plank in mid-ocean alone, for so long, I am lost and bewildered when I find someone to help me. I can clatter across the rough stones of the market-square in my Ticino sandals, or loiter in the shadow of the arcades, without thinking in two dimensions, all the time. If things still reel a little, I know that is to be expected. People are land-sick sometimes, even after a comparatively calm crossing and our crossing was very stormy. No wonder, I was land-sick. . . . I brushed through the tangle of spiraea, at the last turn of the zig-zag. I broke a branch of wild oleander. I tore off the lower leaves of my oleander-branch. It was white oleander. The leaves were silver-willow. Someone had dropped the awnings. They fell straight from the upper windows, over the porch or portico. It was not really a porch, it was a terrace paved with flat stones. The burnt-umber awnings were like the sails you see in Venice. There was no margin. The garden began where the forest left off. The field with the daisies and the wild-oats was the other side of the house.

Brusino, he says. But I am not getting off here. There will be a church, a shrine. *Dante wrote a century of sonnets* - that was one of Geoffrey's favourites. I began to make a list of the hundred shrines and churches that I wanted to see. I don't know how many I've seen. There is the weathered Madonna in the market-place. I don't know who she is. I mean, only the fine ones have names. There is the *Madonna dei Ghirli* but perhaps I shouldn't count her as I didn't get off at Bissone, after all, as I had intended. I saw more than one shrine at Kareno that day I watched the hawk or falcon. San Georgio was the most important but there were the pictures along the road, the wooden crosses and the saints painted on the houses. Morcote had a St. Antony chapel on the way up to Santa Maria, and there were the stations as well. I don't know how far I have got by this time. I only know that this is the resurrection. I will get off at Morcote, even if the camellias are over, and take the *postauto* back through the valley to Lugano.

. . . . .

Randolph wrote funny satirical verses when I knew him. I didn't really think he would be interested, but he was in touch with publishers, and in any case, I thought his reaction would help me. If he didn't like the book, he wouldn't hesitate to say so and then I would try someone else. I didn't know who I would approach next, but I had to swim ashore somehow and there was still the poet at Kareno. No wonder I was land-sick. I think I was more upset by what Randolph said than I would have been if he had simply torn *Wintersleep* to pieces, with his old satirical detachment. I could trust him anyway.

It was bad enough - his discovery of Hallblithe. That is what they must have been shouting, for Ben Manisi had said, "His name is Halbritt . . . but they say it differently."

Randolph said, "I write frankly as one old comrade to another. The only piece of material to be supplied is Lord Howell's motive - he has saved England once, has the chance to save her a second time; why doesn't he? He is jealous of Delia's priority? There is another woman? Or what?"

I hadn't thought of Delia's priority. Things stopped going round, I mean I didn't feel land-sick any longer. I could live now and think in one dimension. There was someone outside.

Randolph had been in the last war. Perhaps there were other people who had been in the last war, who would feel as he did. Lad, Larry, Ralph and John had given me initials of other people in the services, for the next circumference. But I had thought only of this war. Perhaps the second circumference would, after all, go to the services.

But I didn't remember the initials they had given me. Randolph's may have been among them. I had scribbled down the numbers and the letters, but as they had asked me to tell them, not to write them to Lord Howell, and as he had finally repudiated the whole thing as "uninspiring," I carefully shredded the rough jottings and burnt them. I had typed out the story of the Viking ship for him, and some of my findings about Z and the work, and I had made carbon copies for my own reference. But Lord Howell was to tell the "true tale" and in what I called my post-war spring-cleaning, I destroyed the carbon copies. I had naturally concluded that the initials of the first circumference belonged to men in the air-force. It was their story but apparently since Lord Howell wouldn't or couldn't, someone outside had to tell the "true tale."

It was Hal Brith or Hallblithe, the sea-king who gathered them together. But it was the sky-king, Nenu whom we called Z, who had helped and sponsored them, "Well, try it." We presume that someone had charge of these things. It couldn't happen to ordinary people, in ordinary times. It had happened to them because they wanted to live and had gone on living. It had happened to me because I wanted to die and had gone on living. That first time he came in, when he stood before the fire-place, Lord Howell said, "I have nothing to live for." I remember exactly when he said it. I had heard that part of his house had been destroyed. He lived on the outskirts of London, near the air-fields. I said,

"It's terrible to think of - you of all people."

He said, "Why - of all people? We all have to suffer together."

"But surely now - they've put your house in order?"

I thought of Lord Howell having what Randolph called priority.

"They've boarded up some of the windows," he said.

I didn't know what to say.

"There's so much to look forward to," I said, just to fill in the gap. He said,

"I have nothing to look forward to. I don't want to go on living."

It was just an ordinary statement. It didn't call for sympathy, it didn't need an answer.

I wanted to go on living. That is to say, I wanted to go on living so as to give their message or their messages. I have just said that I wanted to die but actually I didn't want to die after I made the contact with Hallblithe. And in any case, I wanted to die in my own way, not pinned down under red-hot girders. Even at the worst, I had a stubborn will to keep alive until I could die in my own way. I didn't want to find myself struggling to get out of a mangled cocoon, and then wading through ash and rubble. But I didn't want a vague Nirvana - *to sleep, to dream*; that was always the question, *what dreams may come.*

We could dream in this life as well as in the other.

II

Albatross

I copied out the butterflies for Garry. I said, of course his admiral is our red-admiral and swallow-tail is the same, but which do you think is the painted-lady? Kingmantle might be, or thistle-butterfly. Do we have a dove-tail in England?

Garry didn't answer my questions but she sent me a Swiss butterfly-book. I found his *Kaisermantel* on the same page as the mother-of-pearl, but neither of them, I am sure, are the painted-lady. I could only remember cabbage-white, swallow-tail, red-admiral and painted-lady.

Some of the pages of this butterfly-primer have the caterpillars. They are dragons rearing horn or tusk out of the jungle of grass-blades and weeds. The bear drags his hairy length along the sun-baked earth. I see how the bears in this series, derive their pedigrees. These butterflies lay claim to the brown and red bear, by way of their primaeval ancestor, the bear-dragon. They are not only individually related to the bear-dragon, but each has lived or manifested in his image. The frightening image of the caterpillar magnifies itself to my perception and I remember the sun-baked stones of the Kareno court-yard and the San Georgio in the fresco.

Saint George had killed the dragon. He had become in my imagination, a symbol of England. I was not the damsel out of the *Roman de la Rose*, who knelt in faded blue in the Kareno fresco. I was not that painted lady. She belongs to another world, another England. There was a swarm of them - or a flock.

They swayed silver-blue with the sun reflected from their wings. There were red and white markings under their wings. They choose the albatross. In the shadow, they were blue-black but seen in the distance, they were silver. The ice-bird showed them the way. We could not follow. But we could see reflections and catch as in a crystal, the message of their heliograph. They flashed a dot and a pause or a beam and a shadow. There were infinite varieties of flash and pause, of double-flash, half-pause and so on. It only needed the translator to put their dots and dashes into words.

The moth having seen the light never returns to the darkness. They had seen the darkness but they had hurled themselves straight into the light. "Table lights up," they had spelt, but it was a reflection of their own light. It was not ordinary light. Yet the ordinary daylight grew wan and colourless, the nearer I came to the meaning of their message. It would sweep across the darkness like a searchlight. It would burn out folly and lassitude. They were not one person but they were at-one, as a snow-cloud is one cloud and at the same time, a collection of infinite snowflakes. But they were not vaguely "infinite," they had names and they were numbered. It was, as I had said, a star-nebula, they were separate stars yet converging to a centre. I have said that their albatross was the Viking, Hal Brith.

I thought I had the final answer but when Randolph wrote me, I began to wonder again.

"Is this your working-crystal?" Lord Howell had asked me.

It was a little joke between us. I thought I had settled the question of Lord Howell's motive, but Randolph made me feel that *Wintersleep* still left the problem unsolved. In the end, I persuaded myself that Lord Howell refused to listen to me because he knew from experience that only a certain type of person is conditioned to receive psychic communications. As a rule, I have said, clairvoyants are sensitive but not intellectual. He would know, I argued, that I had been under a great strain during the war years in London. He had said,

"And in any case, if there were messages of any importance, they would come to me from my own circle."

He was trying to discourage me, I argued. He knew or thought he knew that anyone as highly strung as I was, would be bound to break. I had said I was going to America, but he knew, he must have known that I would not hesitate to break my lecture contract, if he gave me the least encouragement to go on with the messages. I would have freedom and food in America, and no doubt, congenial occupation. But it needed only a gesture on his part and I would scrap America. Even after I had my papers and my passport, my heart was obviously not in it. He might have temporized. He might have said that the work was difficult now, because of the general unrest everywhere, but later, we might talk things over. We had only to wait. But he did not mean to temporize nor to minimize the force of his intention.

Randolph had asked if he was jealous of Delia's priority or if there was another woman, "or what?" I don't think it was a question of priority or of another woman. I have a feeling that he might have shown himself in another light, if it had been a question of "another woman," myself or any other. But it was not a question of another woman, whether suppliant, as the blue-robed damsel in the Kareno fresco, or as the companion or queen of one of the three kings in the *Roman de la Rose* card that I sent him that second Christmas. I think I have answered two of Randolph's questions to my own satisfaction. There is still the third question, "Or what?"

The ship of state had weathered the storm but by some strange law of cause and effect, it had for no known reason, swerved from its course. It was battered and old but it had never known defeat. It was not defeated by the enemy but by a great tide-wave of unpredictable events. Even the lightning of the equator playing around its masts, had not actually split the oak. But the crew was weakened by starvation and the ship sailed on, into an uncharted ocean.

He saw them die of hunger and thirst. They all died. There were only ghosts left, and two of them, madness and death, threw dice for his soul. He had accepted his martyrdom. The ice closed in about him.

It would go on. It could go on. But he was alone. What use are thirty or more years of discipline if they have not conditioned one to the idea of suffering? He had accepted his fate. There is a gleam of light, dim but distinct from the polar-mist about it. But he had been misled before, by hope, by that far signal. The alba-tross swerved nearer. For a moment, his heart stopped beating. Then he ignored it, but it followed the ship. He refused to scan horizons that showed only peak after peak of black ice, in the outer darkness. The ice opened and the ship drifted on. The bird swayed, circling the dead mast.

It was a phantom, another ghost. It was not an albatross.

. . . . .

There were too many of these messages. There were too many altogether. They had to stop somewhere. It is true, for the most part, they all said the same thing. But this was something different. He didn't wish to discriminate, to show favou-ritism or to neglect familiar inquiries and common memories. But this woman was asking something different and she had no personal claim on him or memory of any one of them. He had to stop somewhere. He was patient enough and he conscientiously answered practically all the letters he received about the Battle of Britain and his public lectures.

If she had been illiterate, he would have let her down more gently. But she could look after herself. He hadn't seen any of her writing, but you aren't asked to lecture in America, these days, unless you have some literary connection of some sort or other. Writing? He could have written himself, he had seen enough in his time. How easy with a little imagination to invent - she had plenty of imagination - then to embellish. You couldn't be too careful. He looked at Delia Alton's last letter again. This one was not like any of the others. She had got rath-er out of her depth, with astrology and the Round Table, at one time. But she had always kept a certain - what shall we say? - discretion or detachment. There were, for instance, those white and red roses, there was that sonnet. She apolo-gised, he remembered, "and this inevitably," she had said and quoted - *watcher of the skies* - something or other - *when a new planet swims within his ken*. And she had written about him, about them. . . . a cloud-nebula. There was too much cloud altogether.

But this phase of familiarity was a new one. Not her familiarity - and yet, it must be. It was Charles, this time, as to John, there couldn't be less than fifty of that name. Of course, she couldn't know that "the few" numbered almost one thousand five hundred. That was their last estimate. There was - but he couldn't name them. But anyone could name them and with them, the five she had named. There must have been; there must have been -

He thought he had sufficiently indicated with his gangsters and crooks, Hollywood impersonators and amateurs led astray by lying messages, what line he intended to take.

The albatross swayed nearer. But this was finally, irrevocably impossible. If she had received these last messages from Charles or any of the others, then they or she were trying some new tricks. It wasn't *them*, of course. She didn't know one of them.

The snow swirled across the deck, the sun had never been. His hands were frozen but he reached . . . he would wait. There might be daylight. The bird, the mist, the sea, the ice - even death and madness had left him. He saw quite clearly.

The clouds parted, *door opens*, she said they said. There was the pale but luminous circle of the moon-disc. Stark skeletons, the girders and blanched walls of the dead city lay before him. There were other dead cities. The sea washed over the ice now, the cities were drowned in it. The moon with wings was settling on the deck-rail. The bird was too near. If he startled it sufficiently, it would take off, rise in the air. The bird swayed slowly upward, as if to circle a new benison. His hand was not quite frozen. He did not mean to temporize nor to minimize the force of his intention. *With my cross-bow I shot the albatross.*

. . . . .

Saul has slain his thousands and David his ten thousands . . . O, Jonathan slain in the midst of battle. Greater than the love of woman . . . "But you can't go on that way," Charles said. This was the first time that Charles spoke to me. It was John, Ralph, Lad and Larry who had come forward, or they had been pushed forward by the "others - many." I don't know whether Charles was pushed forward by them or whether he elbowed his way in. His manner was anything but deferential.

"I don't know what you mean by these funny words," I told him.

"John sends love," he said.

I said, "I know, you all send love, you said it before."

"They said it," he said.

I can't remember how we compromised but I told him in the end, that I would write just one funny word for him, as a clue or code-word. It was a letter this time.

My half-packed bags were lying on the floor. I was sorting out papers when I felt that one of them wanted to talk to me. I had moved the little tripod-table into my room. I had written my last letter to Lord Howell. But someone wanted me to write another. My letter wouldn't reach Lord Howell until after I had gone, it lay with a few others on the top of my desk.

I confess now, that I wondered afterwards if the little note that I took from Charles' dictation, seemed cheeky. It was not like their other messages, but I enclosed it in the envelope with my original letter. I decided to send it at once. I was afraid I might change my mind, so I rushed out to the pillar-box on the corner. I remembered how I had dropped my Christmas letters and cards in there, and the years and years. I didn't keep a copy of Charles' letter.

There was a letter from Lord Howell in the early morning post. I thought then, that Charles was right after all, to be informal and chatty. Perhaps we had been too formal altogether. Charles with his boyish slang and familiarity had succeeded where the others with their beautiful formality, had failed. I opened Lord Howell's letter.

"No. I can not be expected to receive messages of this sort. They are both frivolous and uninspiring." Charles' letter fell out. I stooped down and picked it up from the floor. I saw my own hand-writing - "John sends love."

There wasn't any question of inspiration. The little note was friendly, familiar, if you will; it was quite different from anything else I sent Lord Howell. I looked at the letter from the dead. It had been a letter from the living when I sent it. It was now only a question of finishing my packing. I would get off somehow. I put the letter with my passport and my travelling-papers. I didn't tell Garry that I had sent Lord Howell a letter from the dead, but I showed her his letter to me. It was then that Garry said, "It isn't lost. This will go on somewhere."

I tied up Lord Howell's letters and the Battle of Britain cuttings I had saved and the one he sent me, and flung them in the drawer of my desk. I had already put the September Abbey folder in my travelling-case with my lecture-notes. I had the Abbey folder and I had the last message from Charles. Then Garry came back with that cold and temperature. Miss Wardour had meningitis but Garry did get off, and I was so ill.

I had heard their voices in an early broadcast. It seemed an impromptu occasion. I don't know how many of them there were. The young voices were uneven and the song rose and faded, as if they were wandering about the air-field, waiting to take off.

No-one wants to see us round,
Walking on the ground.

Lad and Larry might have been among them, Ralph might have been there. They did not stay round long, walking on the ground. I re-read the little letter from the dead. I tried to puzzle it out. Why was Lord Howell angry? It was not meant to be inspiring, so that jibe fell wide of the mark. Frivolous? Perhaps it was, perhaps we were too friendly altogether.

. . . . .

Had he killed the albatross? Or had he only killed my hope of being of some use to them? He almost did that but he could not finally succeed while I was still, inconsiderately, living.

I said in *Wintersleep*, that Lord Howell added a grain of alien substance to a solution in a test-tube, and crystallized out Geoffrey and the others.

But until I saw Lord Howell alone on the ship, I had not really crystallized *him* out. I was not, in my heart of hearts, completely satisfied with my explanation of his attitude to myself and the RAF messages, until I saw him as part of that world of poetry. I had seen the young Sir John Howell of the last war, on the Viking ship; I saw the later Lord Howell on that ship of state when the ice closed in about him. The picture answered Randolph Spencer's question about Lord Howell's motive. The answer satisfied me. But my satisfaction was of something not so much dead, as frozen, final, static and irrevocable.

Now however, the scene changes and I open a new book.

———————

III

Acropolis

I was not the painted lady in the Kareno fresco, above the door of the Cathedral of San Georgio. I was another painted lady. My position however, had been unassailable. But in any case, by this time, there was no one left to challenge my ascent to the Acropolis.

He wanted me to leave Athens - but I had still one friend here, my dear - but I will not name him. I had told him that I would leave Athens when the Parthenon was finished, and if Athens fell, I would fall with it. His last command was autocratic and irrefutable. But I did not always obey his commands. There were a few others like me. One of them was hiding, perhaps among the last marble blocks they had shipped us from Miletus. Some of the islands had already broken away.

It was dark. The wind was howling from the Sunium head-lands. Under my cloak, I hugged the precious brown loaf and the flagon of wine. It happened to be one of his favourites - that is, Pericles' favourites - no-one had touched them before. But "Hound out that great bear," he had commanded and "lock the inner portals of the citadel." He still called it the citadel. No-one but free-born Athenians were to touch a stone, no other artisan however adroit, was to chip a single fragment of the rock. The rock was to stand forever, polished Pentelicus.

There were to be no vermilion key-patterns painted under the pediments, what metal of harness or spear-shaft there was, was to be pure gold. Pericles! Everyone could remember the charred ruins. But nothing was impossible.

"Trust to the wooden walls," said the oracle at Delphi. We had done that before. But the wooden walls were threatened.

The Bear must be getting hungry.

He insisted on working like a blacksmith. Pericles had caught him at it. That was why he called him the Bear - his shaggy mantle was girded about his loins, his arms were burnt with the sun and with the scorching fires of the smelting-pots.

But his snow-carved Victories stepped out of the rock, their elegant draperies fluttering in the wind. That is how he said I helped him.

"Stand there against Hymettus," he would command, and his was a command that I had never yet disobeyed. We were such friends.

He would be surprised to see me.

He was a giant but his marble butterflies were as delicate as the verses of the Ionian poets.

The enemy was almost at the threshold but there was perhaps a greater, already within the gates.

He would wrap me in his old cloak.

Soon the trumpet would sound the advance, we would hear the stamping of the horses and then the clatter of galloping hooves would no longer echo from the Isthmian highway.

My friend would cover me with his shaggy bear-skin. If the plague had already touched us, we would die together.

. . . . .

Pericles was inconsistent. But there was no use pointing that out to him. If the goldsmiths from the outer islands had been dismissed and the stone-carvers from Thessaly, who - but no-one dared put the question to him - was to finish the work? If the great blocks of unhewn marble were too unwieldy for the Athenian craftsmen, who was to heave and shove and invent new pulleys and levers to drag them into place? If, in fact, the very material was to be "free-born," what of that last questionable shipment of gold-leaf from Smyrna? The gold-leaf could go. Then who was to decide which Athenian lady's armlets were worthy to be dedicated to the sandals of Hermes or the bridles of the Dioskouri?

There were these and many other questions. Pericles' decree was absolute. But who was to decide the weight and merit of the offering? Who was to heave the great blocks? Who was to kindle the fires and smelt down the ore? This was no task for a master-craftsman. The Bear could do it.

"You disobeyed his orders," he growled at me.

"It is not the first time," I said, "though it may be the last. I lied to his steward when he came to shut down the house. I lied with delicacy and with my usual discretion. That was five days ago. It must have been about then, that you too, left Athens. The steward had his orders - but he let me keep the house-key. You must tell me later, where you have been hiding. But first, I must ask you for my bracelets."

I had really come to get them. I had left Pericles' other gifts with the steward.

"Do you really want your bracelets?" he said.

I said, "No. I only want you to take them back to Pericles - "

"They are dedicated," he said, "to Pericles."

"Like all of Athens?" I did not know what I said. I did not care what I said. I must get the bracelets.

I said, "Did you hear that hateful trumpet?" He did not answer. "Well - now that I am here, now that they have gone - do you hear them gallop? . . . And now they really have gone."

But he was not listening to me.

"I say they have gone," I shouted. "Can't we get out of this wind? Can't you hide me somewhere while you dig my bracelets out of your buried treasure? I am cold. I am too cold. I ran all the way here. I have only now to run back. Once I have the bracelets - "

"I thought," he said, "that you wanted me to take the bracelets to Pericles."

"I do want you to take the bracelets to Pericles." My teeth were chattering.

"Then why," he said, "do you want me to dig them out of what you call my buried treasure?"

"Dear friend," I said, "is this a time for quibbling?" I had intended to give him the house-key. I had intended to tell him to take the house-key and the bracelets back to Pericles. But that was a long time ago, the rehearsal of that intention. I had come a long way in the dark, creeping against walls, lest some possible malign influence should strike out at me. I thought of "influences," of "emanations," not of people. The people had left Athens.

There were only two people left in Athens.

The other said, "If you will wait here, I will get my precious brazier. It is hidden in my cella or my cellar."

"Why should I not wait?" I said.

"Why should you?" he said.

"I am still surprised," I said, "after all these years in Athens, at the way you answer a question."

"What do you mean by the way we answer a question?"

"I mean just that," I said. "You ask another question - and another question - you never answer anything."

"But you," he said, "are always most consistent."

"That is another thing," I said. "This irony - but stop. I mean, my very dear, stop me - stop me from saying something silly. Get that brazier if there is one. Let me look at the bracelets - I was afraid - I was afraid they might be - stolen."

"You wanted to see your bracelets. You wanted to remember. But you will never see them."

But he went away before I had time to ask him what he meant. I was still hugging the brown loaf and the precious flagon under my cloak. It was well that I had cat-eyes, as they called them. I could have found my way, blindfold but I was glad to be able to distinguish the old familiar properties. There was the great block of unhewn stone to my left as I stood there. I had crept round the back of the almost finished Parthenon. I did not know where he was, but I knew the most likely place to find him would be here, just where I was standing. There was a cluster of un-roofed pillars and he made a tent sometimes, with his old sack-cloth and worked here.

He could not have heard me coming but he might have sensed my presence, just as at a given moment, as I hesitated in the Propylaea, I knew that he had crept out of whatever burrow or cave he had found or made for himself. Pericles valued him. He wanted to see the temple finished. He had ordered him out of Athens.

I had come, the long way round, back of the Parthenon.

I laid the loaf and the flagon on the pavement beside the great stone.

This time, I saw him coming. His cloak was wrapped round the brazier.

"It is a deep bowl," he said, "and there is still light in it." He placed the tripod out of the wind. I crept round the stone and knelt, warming my hands under the bowl. "I will get your gold now," he said.

When he came back, he flung down a roll of sheep-skins.

"You'd better sit here," he said, "and we will discuss the bracelets."

"You said there were no bracelets." I could rest here on the sheep-skins, for a moment.

"I did not say there were no bracelets," he said. "I said, if I remember, 'but you will never see them.' It was not exactly what I meant. But judge for yourself."

I could see those powerful fingers in the glow of the red coals, his were the hands of some giant but frustrated with too trivial a business.

"Give me your pouch," I said. He laid the leather bag on my lap. But I did not unfasten the tightly-knotted drawstring. "So these are my bracelets," I said.

I laid the leather bag with its great lump of gold on the floor at my feet.

"I do not want to see this - treasure," I said. "You have melted them down. But even Pericles himself can not sanctify this gift. By his last decree, you remember, only free-born Athenians were to present their offerings."

But my friend did not answer.

I said, "And you have cheated again," for he placed two silver goblets on the flat stone. The cluster of pillars made a temple of our shelter. "The bread is there beside you," I said, "and there is the wine."

But "There is time for all that," he said, "and the silver goblets can be melted later. I had plenty of silver with the old coins - the tortoise, the ear-of-wheat, the owl, the ship, the tettinx and the rest of them went to the helmet of the goddess. I wonder he didn't take our ivory. Ivory is not Greek."

"What is Greek?" I asked him, and I answered, "Pericles, you will tell me. There will come a day," I went on, "when even you will be forgotten. They will give Pericles the credit for all this."

"Pericles and Athens are inseparable," he answered. "When Athens is forgotten and not before, Pericles will be."

I wanted him to break the brown loaf but he would not. There was something we must do first, he said. We would wait for a moment and then he would tell me of it.

"But while we are waiting," I said, "must we discuss Pericles?" He did not remind me that it was I myself, who had started this discussion. "Let us rather," I said, "declaim the deathless stanzas of Aeschylus or of Sophocles. They are Athens."

"Without Pericles, Athens would have fallen."

"*Would* have? You have been skulking here too long. There is no Athens." I wanted to make him angry. "And Pericles has gone off, taking with him his choice bodyguard, as usual. There is no-one in the city.

"You might at least, have buried this gold," I went on. "Men are so impractical. And he might have let you finish the Parthenon before he started on his latest little foray."

"The Parthenon?" said the Bear, as if he had heard of our famous temple for the first time.

"You heard what I said - ah, I see - *Parthenos* - you invoke the goddess. I thought you were asking a question again. Who built it? Who designed it? Who squared the circle, or whatever you call it, by tapering the columns in this modern manner, and - Ictinus or Praxitiles, was it? Or do you take the credit for the famous straight line of the curved steps? It is all a contradiction. But do not, I beseech you, pour out that wine as a libation to your Parthenos, Virgin Thrice-crowned. Stir up the fire - are these all the embers there are left of this once smouldering Persian ruin? Let us have no Parthenos libation. Let us drink the wine, rather. I'm cold. This silver cup is icier than the heart of that same goddess," I said, as I took the goblet from his hand.

Why did I want to make him angry?

"We need no snow from Hymettus to cool our beverage," I went on, "but if we have the plague, let us at least, die rejoicing. Let us think of gay things - not Pericles, not Parthenos. I would have warm words with this cold wine.

"And when you said there was time for melting down these silver goblets," I continued, "just what did you mean? But before you answer that question, tell me, what are you doing with my bracelets?"

"I have saved them for the spear-shaft," he said.

The wine had frozen the goblet or the goblet had drawn warmth from my hands. My hands were colder than the silver. He must have seen how nearly im-possible it was for me to lift the goblet, for he placed back his cup untasted and knelt to detach one of the sheep-skins and wrap it round my knees. "I think we better have our tent, as you used to call it," he said, and he began unroping the lengths of sail-cloth that he kept for covering his marble. "I hid all this too," he said, "my precious tools and tackle."

I knew this tent-making from long experience. I had rested here before, out of the wind, and I had rested at noon, summer and autumn, after the workmen had left. I would wait till he finished with that rope-end and stepped back off the canvas to weigh down the hem of the sail or wall, with the flat stones he kept there for the purpose.

I would slip away, back of the Parthenon again, and step off - I knew each crag and stone. I knew the out-jutting shelf that I must avoid. I had crept down there last year for winter-poppies. Pheidias had told me that daisies, camomile, bluets, rue and speedwell had sprung up literally overnight, in the charred foundations. I had counted butterflies with him between the unroofed pillars of our shelter, before the workmen had finally tramped down the patches of thyme and melilot growing between the paving-stones. As I say, winter or summer, I knew each slope and shelf of our hill. I would first locate what I called the winter-poppy shelf. There was the sheer drop as you turned sideways, facing Sunium. The wind would help me.

Pheidias had his sail-cloth, his old cloak, his brazier, his flagon of wine and - the Parthenon. He might think I had just slipped away. He had his memories, the owl, the tettinx; he had Athens. This mountain would be forever sacred to him. The rumour of the still unplaced marble plaques that he had designed for Prax-itiles, had long since reached Macedonia and beyond the Bosphorous. I knew where they were standing, those unparalleled horsemen. Perhaps I was jealous of them. They were the bodyguard of Pericles.

They were Athens, they were victory.

Pheidias spoke of the Parthenon frieze as if the marble horsemen were already placed beneath the gables.

I was standing, waiting to dive out. I had slipped off my cloak in order to run the better, and as the wind tore at it, I bent down to place a stone on it. In this wind, Pheidias would not hear the scrape of the unhewn block on the cracked paving of the old floor. To steady myself, before taking my plunge, I placed my hand on the fluted surface of the pillar. The wind had whipped the brazier to a fresh flame.

But Pheidias had stepped round the sail-cloth.

"Has the wind taken your cloak?" he asked me.

"Not yet, I'm standing on it," I said.

"There are three winged Victories and there is the wingless Victory," he said. "She shall stand there. Never in time, never out of time, shall men forget her. She is an attribute of Parthenos. I have wondered. I no longer wonder. I did not see her hand upon a pillar but bearing a silver olive-branch."

I saw that he had trapped me.

"There are plenty of - favourites to stand for you."

"Where are they?" he asked.

"Where would they be?" I answered. "The scum of the Piraeus will soon be on the move, with Pericles out of Athens. They will rise like a foul miasma from the very pavements. I came here to get a breath of fresh air and, as I have already told you, to ask you for my bracelets."

"They shall be redeemed," he said.

He finished tightening the sail-cloth round the inner pillars, before he picked up my cloak.

"Why did you weight it with the stone?" he asked me, "and why when you had weighted it, did you say you were standing on it?"

"My teeth are chattering - how you Athenians chatter - "

"*You* Athenians," he said.

"Athenians then, the least speck or mote in the air is more important to you than the celestial aether."

"The mote may be the bird of Zeus about to descend with the divine decree." He lifted my hand from the pillar. I seemed to have frozen, to have become one with it. He straightened my arm, as a child straightens the wooden limbs of a jointed doll. "You may lie with delicacy but it is not discreet of you, at this hour, to go below."

My flippancy sustained me. "Can you not escort me?"

"No," he said, "I have made provision. For weeks I have been collecting firewood for this moment."

"Everyone knows there has been no fire-wood within a half day's walk of Athens, since the panic."

"Some weeks ago, I discovered the under-vault of the old serpent-temple. It was filled with archaic images - olive-wood, seasoned by time, burns well."

"But Pericles had the ground levelled before you began to lay the Parthenon foundation."

"That's what I mean, the cella was earthed over. It would have remained so for centuries but for the chance glancing of my spade. I told no-one - not even you - of my discovery. We will burn the images. They will send out a blaze as of high-festival. It will be High Festival. The country people in the near-by farms will believe that Pericles has already announced his victory. They will send out their own signals till Corinth and Arcadia rally to his little company. The thieves and brigands waiting on Lycabettus, will vanish in the valleys."

"I do not believe in your olive-images," I said, "and in any case, I do not want to stay here."

He pushed me gently back on the pile of sheep-skins and wrapped my cloak about me.

"Your plan is excellent," I said, "but Pericles will think the vandals are already in possession."

"Pericles knows that there is no wood for burning. The growing olive, provided we or they, the vandals lopped off the branches in their descent through the orchards, would, provided it burnt at all, send out a cloud of black smoke."

"You think of everything."

"I think I will not rope you to a pillar like Andromeda, waiting for the dragon. I am going to fetch some fire-wood. You are wondering why I am lying to you. You must admit, however, that the lie has both delicacy and discretion. It has, in addition, originality. You are curious to know if I am speaking the truth. Your curiosity will hold you here for the short time it takes me to cross the courtyard again and return from the old temple. We Athenians are like that."

I was not alone long.

Pheidias said, "I would rather shrine this image in the new Parthenon than set up the chryselephantine Pallas that I dream of. This is nearer to reality." He placed the wooden doll in my arms.

I did not look at the doll.

"There is another thing," I said, "the vandals, as you call them, being vandals, can easily break up household furniture, on the way here. There is plenty of seasoned fire-wood, left in Athens."

"There are two arguments against that, more maybe. One - only the very poor in the outer district would leave their chattels lying about and their doors unbolted. Provided the poor which is unlikely, had by this time, any chattels to leave about. And even if they themselves had not already burnt their lighter furniture, the vandals would hardly linger in the quarter where the plague, if plague there were, would be most likely to attack them. Two - well - did you leave your own door unlocked? I will answer for you. You did not. I have not the eyes or the eye of the three crones which Perseus stole from them, and returned only when he had received the answer that he demanded. But you need not answer - now where did you hide the house-key? Even the anticipation of death by plague or - other, did not reconcile you. You did not want the vandals or even one almost-near to you to cross the atrium. You were waiting. The rose and pale-rose oleanders, the rose-laurel swept against the leaf-gold walls of the room you sat in. That is, to be exact, they were outside, within the second wall. And - do not interrupt me - I feel the cold as you do - it is summer. Do you remember how you asked Pericles to send a painter to you? That was an odd request he made me. A villa, he explained - well, he did not explain anything. He told me where it was and that told me all that I needed to know. She will not be too young, I pondered over it, for she has held him for some time. It is the same house, so she can not be a mere dancing-girl. She may have danced in her time, but he was zealous for her. I knew when every house in Athens was built. But he had not built this for her. Yet, in just that - relation, she had not had a predecessor. By that relation, I mean the friendship that Pericles has made fashionable. There was no word then for this inspiration, this companion. She had, I knew, a feeling for tint and colour, the old wash was not too bad but I saw what she meant. I looked over the place - over the wall - it was the oleanders. Oh yes - the oleanders. The terracotta of the house-wall was too red for the rose blossoms."

I said, "I go on saying, you see everything." I could taste the bitter words. "But you have not told me where I hid the house-key."

"I have a great deal to tell you before we get to the point in the story where the lady lifts a square stone - it is a little heavy for her - but that comes later. She had to get a loaf, wine - Pericles' favourite? She knew by that time, what mine was. But it was Pericles' Chian that she brought me."

The sail-cloth pulled and strained at the taut ropes.

"When do we begin our festival?" I asked him. The berries of the deadly night-shade would have tasted sweet beside the bitterness of my *festival*.

"We have already begun," he said, "the evening is half over. But I confess that my heart is broken. I delay the final ceremony. I count on your strength."

Was he laughing at me? "I knew that you had a sense of the ultimate - of Beauty, I mean, when Pericles asked me to look in at the villa. It would not worry him, the fact, I mean, that the terracotta was a shade too red for the deep rose oleanders. She will be like that."

"Well - was she?" I looked up at him. But it was a new face that I saw in the light of the glowing embers. He had been speaking evenly, perhaps too evenly. He had caught his underlip in his teeth, as if he would retract the words he had just spoken - or as if he would gnaw them to pieces, dismember and destroy them. Perhaps, I still had strength enough - at any rate, to reach over my shoulder, as if I had turned my head to adjust my cloak-hood. I laid the doll down on the pavement beside the square block of stone. I needed both hands - but for what? I clutched the folds of my cloak, though the wind, it seemed to me, was falling. I knew that he was going to plea for Pericles - when or if he came back. But I didn't care any more. There were other dancing-girls about the city.

I don't know if he realized that I had stared straight into the face of the ultimate - well, Agony. I would never know that. Beside his desolation, mine was a personal, you might say - vanity. What did he mean by my strength and what did he want with it?

"The wind is falling," I said, "what do you want with my strength, as you call it?" I remembered how I first saw Pheidias. The house-boy told me that he had asked the painter to wait in the court-yard, as it was a question of the outer walls.

"Your brazier wants replenishing. You are host here. I can hardly, according to the old law, stir your hearth-fire. Are these the kindlings that you boast of? Are they all here? Is this the lot, tied up in that old sack, your brown cloak? In any case, you'd better put on your coat. Open the bundle. I'll help you sort the faggots. Is that all? You are keeping something from me, cheating as you did with my bracelets and the silver goblets. I'm sure you've left something in the famous cella that you spoke of. Best bring the whole lot. You needn't rope me to a pillar. I am cold enough and here is promise of a fine blaze. No, don't wait while I go over them. We need much more than this lot. So they stacked them in the cellar - in the cella as you call it? But tell me, how did these escape the burning of the old wooden temple? Or is the whole thing a dream - was there ever any temple, painted like a child's toy-house, sea-blue and vermilion? You have only hearsay for it. Or did you see it? I can not keep track of these wars - was it you or Sophocles who fought at Marathon? But you are not as old as Sophocles - or are you? Why do you let me go on talking this way? I do not think there ever was a serpent-temple to Athené. Are we dreaming the same dream? Will I wake up and find myself - well, never mind where. You are right about Pericles. He never notices."

I didn't know if Pheidias were listening or if he had gone again.

"Hurry," I said, "or this sooty flame will die out."

I bent down. I picked up a rough, uneven half-ball. But it was not, as I had first thought, a discarded broken plaything. It was a wooden tortoise.

Aegina. Yes, Aegina had been loyal, perhaps still was. But we must begin with lighter kindlings. I felt round in the dark. Pheidias had come back.

"The cella was protected by the stone-floor of the temple," he said, as if our conversation had not been interrupted.

"But this is not all," I said, as he placed two more baskets on the stone floor. "Bring everything." He had said that he wanted my strength. Well, he would have it. I was almost happy again, scolding him. "You can't deceive me - cheating, as I've already told you. You have cheated enough with gold and silver - but this wood is worthless." Did he hear me? I felt that he had gone again, according to my orders - but I had found something.

The shape was familiar but the texture was wrong. It was frail and brittle and quite dry. I could break this wooden scallop-shell if he wouldn't. So this is why he wanted my strength. There were boxes and shallow trays and baskets piled with plunder from the sea-shore. There were sea-horses, hollowed-out conch-shells, handfuls of mussel-shells and more painted, fragile scallops. There were thin, carved whorls, I think of sea-weed.

My heart turned sick within me.

I had a heart now. I thought it had been trampled (this time irretrievably) underfoot, by the flinty hooves of his Thessalian chargers. His horses, his horsemen at any rate, meant more to him than any woman.

But there was something flinty in me, too. Perhaps that is what Pheidias had meant when he said that he counted on my strength. But what strength I had summoned a moment ago, to order him off for more faggots, as I called them, was gone. We couldn't burn these things. Let Athens go, rather. Even the vandals would respect this treasure, they could trade with them as the Egyptians do with the plunder from their old tombs. But I had never seen anything from Egypt like the carved and painted wood-shell that I held in my hands. It didn't matter who had these things or where they might go. They would carry with them what Pheidias called the ultimate - Beauty.

"The vandals know the value of these things. They have learned that from our sailors. Let the vandals sack the city. There is nothing in our houses worth the taking, compared with these treasures." Pheidias had come back. "We won't burn anything," I went on. "If you have left a trap-door open or a slab loose over the entrance to your sanctum, don't put it back. That is the last and the best thing that you can do. We have time to sort these over. But tell me, where did they come from? They are not Greek. Did Achilles bring them from Troy?"

"I count on your strength," was the only answer he gave.

"I am not strong enough to burn these. Let the fire die out."

Now it was very quiet. The wind had gone down. I bent back my head. Soon, there might be a few stars.

"The wind has died down," he said.

"It is what I was thinking," I said. Soon, the fire would go out. I wondered if he still had a handful of this smelting soot or if he had saved a last square of precious dried moss. "Have you any more fuel?" I asked.

He said, "Yes" and laid one of the baskets on my lap. I reached out and touched the brazier. The outer rim was almost cold now, but there was a heap of ash still glowing in the deep bowl. I put my hand in the basket.

"I must see this, in what light we have left," I said. "I think it is a sea-urchin or a sea-horse." I held the precious bit of carved wood over the fire-bowl. "It is a sea-horse," I said and dropped it. For a moment, I stopped breathing. I heard the sharp in-take of his breath. He actually was breathing. There was a faint hiss as of a few dried pine-needles. The little horse had answered. I closed my eyes. I felt the surface of the basket for the small, lighter objects. I don't know what I found there. I had only to reach forward. They were small things. Some were rough and felt like brittle pine-cones. I think they were the sea-urchins.

But I went on talking.

"I don't think this is olive-wood," I told him. "Olive has a different sort of crackle."

"You see everything," he mocked, but his voice was low and tender.

"I don't see anything," I said. "My eyes are tight shut - like that guessing-game - do you remember? But perhaps you Athenian children had better games than we had. They filled a basket with assorted treasure, pebbles, a green apple or a crab-apple, a pine-cone of course was always necessary, perhaps one of the great-ones donated something from her workbasket, maybe a broken distaff. The chosen child was blindfold. I am blindfold. Now I must guess what these are. Here is one of the smaller scallops, you know that from the fluted edge. Here is a - a fish actually, but it's humped its back. I thought it was a flying-fish at first, but it must be a leaping dolphin. Are they painted? But don't tell me.

"No - don't tell me. I will tell you. There are - yes, more than one but they are tangled together and they have twisted themselves into different shapes, but even with your eyes shut, you can see these star-fish. But here is something different, and considerably larger. It's tangled with the others. It has fins or feelers - ah - eight." I shook the octopus free of the star-fish. I opened my eyes. He was painted bright vermilion. His many eyes were marked in black.

I was staring like a witch-woman, or like the drugged Pythia, at something that wasn't there.

The flame was mounting higher, we did not need the wind-screen.

"Unfurl the sails," I told him, "or rather furl them. Take down the sail-cloth. We have reached our island. This light must shine even further than Aegina, where the fishing-boats wait the signal."

. . . . .

While Pheidias unknotted the rope-ends, I watched the varnish crackle and peel off.

I went on burning single objects, trying not to look at them. But when he finally had the sails down, I waited a moment, holding the last treasure in my hand. It was a painted conch-shell. I wondered why there had not been more of them, but perhaps there were more in the other baskets. Or had I, blindfold, already placed some of these tinted spiral-shells in the brazier?

"This is no Greek pigment," I said, "it is more like the Egyptian - fadeless. Nevertheless, tell me how it was that the scorched paving-stones of the old floor spared this colour."

"Actually," he said, "it was not the first floor. The foundation of the old serpent-temple had been levelled, but there was a still earlier temple underneath it. The earliest temple was built perhaps, at the time of the Cyclopean wall."

"I see," I said, "I see everything. You hid there, bear-fashion, hibernating. Did you sleep well?"

"I slept little. My one problem was to keep the brazier going. I still had a sack of fuel, when I went in. I closed the first pavement-door behind me. It wasn't difficult to prop it up, from inside. I had the first foundation with its walled partitions, to store the things in. I dragged them up from the old vault - it was like what they tell of Egypt. I had the dim light of the brazier. I lost count of time. I came out, at last, when everything was quiet. They had stopped looking for me."

I wondered if he had had food and water, but I did not ask him.

It no longer mattered. It had never happened. In delirium, one dreams of tombs, of lairs under the ground, such as hare or fox tunnel. In delirium, a roof of heavy stone or metal may crack and fall and bury one. In delirium, a house folds inward to trap one and it may be the walls are flaming. In delirium, one is caught, buried alive or burnt to death. His story of the temple under the temple was part of the delirium. In delirium, I asked him, "Where have we seen these things? For we have seen them."

It no longer mattered. I poured the contents of the half-empty basket on the flames. I did not even trouble to select the separate dolphins, star-fish, sea-urchins, flying-fish and conch-shells. I flung them all in. The flame crackled and leapt higher and I could discern the outline of Hymettus. The night was dark but it glowed now like a black crystal.

I turned and looked at the row of precious images. They were standing upright, staring at me with their slanting, great eyes.

"Where are we, Pheidias?"

I said, "It is almost too hot, my friend. What is this aromatic scent - is it cedar? I said it was not olive." I buried my face in my arms. "Let me rest. I will trust you to lay the painted dolls on the brazier." But I did not trust him. "Go away, Pheidias. I will wait here. I have known from the beginning, that you would be sure to hide something. Take my cloak this time."

But he did not wait for me to slip off my mantle ... He turned away ... I lifted a robed figure. "Little king," I said, "we have met somewhere."

He did not answer me. He actually said nothing. In my madness, I expected him to speak like the olive-wood statue of Athené that the Argo carried. Had that same Argo brought these to the goddess? Would Achilles have cared enough to have saved them from the burning city? Did Helen persuade Menelaus at the end, that it would be a fitting and pious gesture to lay these treasures at the feet of Pallas? Why were there no jewels and ornaments among them? But I knew the answer to that question. Gold could be melted down for sword-hilts or fresh coinage, jewels were portable and more convenient than the early ring and seal-coins. There was no value in these things.

The flame grew steadier, mounted higher to a point above the king's crown, as he stood there in the brazier. I think Pheidias came back while the first king was burning. I don't remember. There was a double row of them, but they burnt quickly.

We were enclosed in a black crystal. We were in a crystal. We were not any-where in this world. Someone outside, was staring in a crystal. Someone outside, saw a light flare beyond Lycabettus - Parnes answered, then Pentelicus. Someone in a crystal saw an answering mountain-fire from Salamis. The whole Aegean answered, Milos, Samos, even the southern islands. It flashed beyond Thessaly and across to Asia Minor.

"I see the Parthenon," said Pheidias, "I see the chryselephantine Pallas, as I dreamed her. Your bracelets were - are waiting for the gold point of her silver spear. I see the light reflected from the gold spear and the silver helmet, so that mariners, rounding the cape at Sunium, are guided as by a lighthouse. I see the Parthenon," said Pheidias, "and I see before it and long after."

. . . . .

"But," I said, "I see other things - this fire is too hot." The last king was burning. "We have committed a sacrilege. We have sacrificed Beauty - and to what? You will tell me to the spear-shaft of the goddess. You will tell me that the past will live after us, or this present. But these inviolate images belonged to the Eternal. I do not need to turn my head to know that Lycabettus has already answered. Pheidias, they have answered. We must keep these last things."

"If the fire dies down now," he said, "they will think the enemy has scaled the walls, has retaken the Acropolis."

"But we have burnt everything."

"Not everything," he said.

I knew we had not burnt everything. I knew that he had hidden the things he loved most. There was also my first doll. If I sacrificed her, perhaps he would save the others. I groped in my blindness and found her where I had laid her, beside the flat rock that we called the table. I could not see anything.

"My eyes are smarting with this flame," I told him. "This is the slant-eyed doll that you said you would rather see shrined in the new Parthenon - how did you say it? You said, 'I would rather shrine this image in the new Parthenon than set up the chryselephantine image that I dream of.' But already, you have forgotten. I have nothing more to give the goddess, and if you have saved anything, the destruction of more kings and flying-fish and leaping dolphins would be desecration. Must there be desecration? All the treasures of the sea have been sacrificed. It is time to stop now. I do not need to turn my head to see the fire answering from Pentelicus." I dried my eyes on my sleeve.

I saw a crocus-field. There was a whorl of petals in the centre of one tray, like a sun-flower. There was a spray of lilies. There were other flowers. There was the butterfly tray....

I did not need to look long at them. He handed them to me, one by one. The wooden panels burnt quickly like the others. But the sun was rising. I mean, it was still dark outside, but the sun was rising in my heart.

———————

IV

The Road to Daphne

I know what Pheidias saw before the Parthenon. He saw the palace of Knossos. In Crete, he had counselled the king. He directed the court-pageants and the great spring-festival. The walls were blue. He superintended the new decorations, the hall of the cup-bearer, the familiar boy standing in the crocus-field and the lily-panels of the queen's bed-chamber. He said, "Stand against the blue wall" and she stood there. Her dress, you might say, was copied from Botticelli's *Primavera*, but Botticelli and that *quatrocento* came more than three thousand years later, so perhaps we are mistaken. I see the familiar scene. I have the same delirium. Balls of fire are flung by catapults from strange ships. They are not like our ships. I could see further but I am now, my own arbiter. If Pheidias once counted on my strength, he can not count on it now.

But perhaps we fled. Perhaps, in our light-hearted manner, we made a picnic of it. Perhaps our frivolity stood us in good stead - I mean, there was Ida, the birthplace of Zeus and it was the Cretan dolphins who had led the priests to Delphi. Perhaps some of us followed the dolphins. I refuse to look on the new-old scene of devastation. It was - well, shall we say Achilles who sacked Knossos?

Afterwards, they called it Troy, for it reflected little credit on their valiant ancestors that the Greeks had descended from their head-lands, master of a new war-weapon and a new technique, and attacked a defenceless people without warning. They plundered and wantonly destroyed perhaps the most beautiful city, outside legend and mythology, the world has ever known.

It became legend, it became mythology. A whole hierarchy of heroes was invented, only a shade less heroic than the Greeks, for what credit is it to the warrior caste to have gained a victory over an unarmed, defenceless nation? It was better to forget Crete. It was better to forget Knossos. It might be awkward when our grand-children asked us of our exploits.

The poet has his uses. But even the legendary Homer did not give the real facts. A city, a civilization had been destroyed. It was not Greek but it was allied to Greece - or rather, it had colonized the mainland before the so-called Greeks arrived there. There was Delphi, for instance. The sun-god fought for the Trojans, you remember. But lest some latter-day father of lies put in an appearance, let us be downright and efficient. There was a war. But only ourselves who made it, saw it. What was the attraction? The Greeks went back, drawn like the proverbial murderer, to the scene of the crime. They had actually rebuilt the city.

We were, as I say, frivolous. We had learned nothing from the warriors of the new iron-age, the new war-age. We might at least, have hammered our plough-shares - but I forget. We have only wooden harrows - we have only gold and silver. The double-axe was one of our sacred symbols, strange symbol for a warless people. Perhaps not so strange. Why Helen?

The enemy (the Trojan) had originally stolen Helen.

The Greeks took back Helen, but lest again, the grandchild prove a problem, they destroyed the city. In the very end, perhaps it was an earthquake that buried the crocus-field and the lily-panels for the last time.

But Achilles was right. Even though the poet immortalize his heroic stature, he can not be trusted.

Pheidias pointed that out to her. He told her that the vine never flowered and bore fruit, at the same time, anywhere in Greece. There were the green-grapes too, in Homer's famous passage and green-grapes are rarely mentioned in Greek poetry. Pheidias saw what he remembered or he remembered what he had seen, the terraced vineyards rising from the level, into other seasons, on Mount Ida.

There was no mountain in Greece that would support three seasons, the vine in flower, the green-grape and the red, at one and the same time. Perhaps, too the Cretan mountain was volcanic. As we say, we would like to feel it was the mountain and not Achilles, who buried the lilies and the crocus-field for the last time.

We left Pheidias and the painted-lady on the Acropolis. Athené was, if ever goddess was, pure Greek. But was she? Pheidias remembered her elsewhere, as guardian of the labyrinth. We must go further than Botticelli to find the fashion-able elegance of the Cretan serpent-goddess. Yet she remained on the Acropolis long after the sack of Knossos. The Persians burnt the old wooden temple, her second. But her original frivolity was to be immortalized, in the still later ceremo-nial of the offering of the flowered garment to the stern guardian of the citadel.

We had not far to go to Crete. Crete flowered in the mysteries of Eleusis and Delphi was, as every Greek knew, the centre of the world. Neither Dionysus, the younger Zeus, nor Helios were warriors. Nor was Zeus. There was a split in consciousness. The Greeks made war. Shall we, like the legendary Trojans be defeated? We must make our preparations.

We can not dismiss the serpent-goddess from the citadel. She has been there too long. It was not only the Delphian (the dolphin) Apollo who came from the cradle of Zeus, his sister came with him. Athens like Troy, Mycenae and Delphi was a Cretan colony. But shall our goddess be swept to oblivion? We will arm her and we will arm the youth of our city.

All this happened a long time ago. Once upon a time, Pheidias - we called him master-of-festival in Crete - gathered us together. Rumour of strange activities had been reported by the Cretan sailors. Our master-of-festival may have consulted the priests, for if Delphi was a colony of Crete, Knossos must have had its oracle. The master-of-festival in the king's household, may have suggested a pageant or a pilgrimage. We would march up through the terraced vineyards, to the shrine of Zeus on the summit of Mount Ida. Once upon a time . . . I like to see it that way.

Once upon a time. . . it was Pheidias who helped me to remember what became of the painted-lady.

. . . . .

She had long talks with him. She remembered how he had told her, when they burnt the images, that the country people in the near-by farms would be heartened and repeat the signal. It was indeed High Festival, as he had promised. Before they had finished their brown loaf and while they were lingering over the last cup of wine, there was the distant sound of cart-wheels.

"Some of my people are sure to be among them," said Pheidias, "I told them when the time came, I would send word to them. I did not tell them the manner of the sending, for I did not myself know."

"You know now," I said.

"Know what?" he said.

"We have come back to Athens," I answered, "this is the old Athenian way of talking. Do not say 'What is the old Athenian way of talking' for with this wine of gladness, I may tell you. Asking a question to gain time, looking for the second question before the first is answered; but I am adept now, Athenian. I think this gold, this white wine is more inspiring than any other. What a night, and now what a day is coming. How long will it take your ox-carts to get here? I suppose they started when we started really, and Daphne is a good road. I want to stay here now, forever. But if you insist, I will come back with you - for I have the answer to so many questions. I will never have to ask one, you can do all the asking. And how we will laugh together. Tell me - " but I remember how my head fell forward and how, soon after, I was gently led in the first dawn, through the pillars of the Propylaea, down the wide steps and into the waiting ox-cart.

We had long talks together in the budding vineyards and in the shadow of the porch, when it was too hot. But that came later. We had long talks together before the oak-logs, where wrapped in those same sheep-skins, I began to get well. I said, I would not ask him questions but that was before I began to see the pictures.

. . . . .

A moth or a night-butterfly bashed its furred body and its stupid, horned head against the window-ledge, rebounded and fell off on the floor. But this is not Daphne, this is a picture from the golden house in Athens. The house-boy holds a napkin uplifted in his hand. I will go mad. He is bare-foot. I do not think he will step on the butterfly. It has a swollen, furred and mottled body. He will have to clean up, if he tramples on it. He will lash it with his napkin and sweep it off the pavement. I do not like this picture, but I see it. I do not have to look at it but it holds some clue. I want to know what became of the painted-lady, I want to know why she left him, if she left him. But this happened before she left Athens. I have only these clues to work on. The boy does not hit the butterfly.

But it is not Pericles who forbids it. Maybe, he didn't see it. There were things that he did not see. Pheidias was with them that evening, he was one of their few guests. Their few guests, I say, for Pericles had his family, his duties, his military and political banquets and other social ties and obligations. She was a relaxation and the household managed by one of his own stewards, was run to perfection. But that doesn't tell this story, *Summerdream* I call it.

Pheidias rescued the moth. He moved toward the window. He reached out in the darkness.

"I have left it on the oleander," he said.

She said, "It will come back."

It came back. Pericles could not miss two unparalleled campaigns, beside that, these were different. She was not always with him. She waited for the supreme and last, she hoped, demonstration. I don't know how many times he came back, nor how many times she came back. The point was, to get them both together at the turn of the tide - I mean, the turn-about or turn-over of one civilization or one era to another. He was right when he said, it doesn't matter what you are or what you have been. All that mattered, was to get them both together. When the message came she would receive it, he would carry it out.

"All that matters," Pheidias told her, "is to remember." He had that villa and the farm-lands on the road to Daphne. The villa was called Daphne, it lay beyond the town, nearer the sea. I can smell the pine-trees. There are red-currants and before that, the slightly acrid clusters of currant-blossoms. I see the fruit, the first year, rather than the flower of that unparalleled, miraculous spring. I had expected to die there under his brown cloak. But that was the first winter. Pericles, he told me, was still out of Athens. But I could not see Pericles. That is, I could not see him, when I saw the first spray of wild-plum that Pheidias put in my hands.

"Come," he said, "this butterfly must make an effort."

"Do butterflies make efforts?" I asked him.

"We have been long enough in this cocoon," he said, and he disentangled me from the sheep-skins. But I crawled back.

"I have been so happy, Pheidias, let me stay here a little longer. I began to see the pictures that night, on the Acropolis. I was huddled on these same sheep-skins and I dreamed of this old cloak all along the road in the dark. It was your old coat that saved me."

He said he'd let me rest a little longer.

I followed the labyrinth. The pictures took me to Crete, but they blurred sometimes, then Pheidias would tell me what I had left out. Those were the first pictures. That was why I was happy at the end, even though I had begged him to save the last painted wooden trays or panels. When I saw the whorl of the daisy-petals and the double stalk of the white lily, I knew that the pictures would never leave me. Indeed, they had never left me, but it was only after I was (as I then thought) dismissed from the golden house, that I began to see them clearly, that is, to see them as pictures, things actual, tangible and eternal. There is that hair-line between imagination and vision - and that night, on the Acropolis, I crossed it.

The going back would not be possible, Pheidias had told me, if one remem-bered, that is, if one remembered everything. For the supreme moment, one had to be prepared to make the sacrifice, to sacrifice in fact, everything but the message. But the word "sacrifice" does not really convey what I mean. It was no sacrifice to sacrifice anything but the supreme moment. She had sacrificed the supreme moment - or shall we say, she had been its sacrifice?

But sacrifice by this time, had lost its meaning. There were others who were more important. The whole thing would lose its poignancy, it would be spoiled somehow, if we were warned beforehand. Her whole life had been a preparation, though she did not know it.

None of them had the absolute choice of the place and the time of their re-turning. Pheidias explained that. But the laws of being, the laws of vibration, of aptitude, of concentration, of former desire and experience would decide that. They would be swept back together and "if the sea lies between us," Pheidias told her, "I will send out a signal. You will remember the doll I put into your arms. You will remember this first spray of the wild-plum blossom. You will breathe in the scent of pine-trees mingled with the balsam-cedar and you will remember Daphne. You will always remember Daphne, though you will not see the pictures until we meet again in the darkness. And do not think that you escaped Pericles, on the road to Daphne. He will not change much."

. . . . .

I had gone on. It was Pheidias who had saved me. It was Pheidias who taught me to remember. "I count on your strength," he had said, when we burnt the images. There was burning. There were ashes. I remembered Knossos.

I remembered the fire-balls that fell on the painted houses, and how we ran down to the sea and were driven back into the fire.

He had promised us High Festival? Was this the festival?

We had put on our flowered garments in honour of the earth-mother. We were going out to gather flowers for the altar. We were chosen by the matrons. I had waited, it seemed a long time for this day. Other comrades of our household were chosen before I was, though now I felt that I was almost too tall to walk in the spring-chosen procession. I was taller than the others. It was a secret they were always whispering. But now I knew their secret.

We had gone out early into the fields. But they had summoned us back. We said he had told us to go out, we were to meet him on the mountain. They said that was not the ceremony, it wouldn't work - whatever it was - if we, that year's spring-chosen did not walk in the procession with the goddess. We said the master-of-festival had explained everything. It was High Festival. He told us (the Mother told him to tell us) to go along the labyrinth, through the old vineyards. He said, she said it was for the vineyards.

We started along the cliff-path. It was too narrow for the oxen or even for the donkeys.

"We are sent to fetch you," our old nurses jabbered. But we were free, we had outgrown the nurses. "He-commands-it," they said. It was one word. I did not hear the word as they spoke it, but it was a word that was seldom spoken and I knew it was one word and I knew they said it. They would not say it if it were not true, for their tongues would shrivel up and drop out. We could not disobey, "He-commands-it."

They said we must leave the baskets. I was older. I was taller. I had special privileges that year, I was head of the spring-chosen.

"We will come back," I said, "we will come back."

We came back.

We were pushed forward. But I don't remember. They had been told to bring us to the palace. Then we were running from the falling stones. We were running to the sea.

"Not that way," I called, "you remember we must get the baskets."

I knew every turn of the labyrinth. The master-of-festival had taken me with him and shown me how to find my way, down the narrow stairs. Some of the flat roofs were part of the pavement, the city was built in terraces like the vineyards. They looked alike, but every corner, every turn, every stone-step, every stone actually, had a meaning. If you had the key, as he called it, you could go anywhere. I was not afraid, really.

The others didn't know the labyrinth. There was the roof, the steep ladder-steps, two flat-roofs, a turn left, two right - this was that roof.

It looked like the others and it looked like the pavement, but there was a small cross marked on that one stone, in the right-hand corner. There were other crosses, but here, I knew my way without them. We were back of the palace now. We had only to find the cliff-path or the goat-path, as the old nurses called it.

We found our baskets.

I did not drop mine as the others did, and run back along the goat-path.

. . . . .

I was the tallest. I was head of the spring-chosen. I shouted, "He-commands-it," though I knew it was a word that was never spoken except by the king's orders. My tongue would shrivel up and drop out, if I spoke it without the king's order. It must have been the king's order, for you can not speak if your tongue shrivels and drops out.

They were running back to the burning city.

Their violets lay on the goat-path where they had fallen from the spring-chosen baskets.

"He-commands-it," I said and then I shouted, "He-commands-it," but they did not turn back.

I kept on saying, "He-commands-it," to the man who stood before me on the goat-path.

He spoke as sailors speak, not as we do. That is, he spoke our language though his words were not our words. Though the words were not our words, I understood him.

"I-command," he said.

He sent the others away. There were other sailors. He said if I would wait, he would come back, but I followed him.

I followed him till the path grew wider and the wall began. I counted the stones, for this time, I might miss the opening to the labyrinth.

There were three openings before you came to the one with the little cross, marked on the right-hand corner of the flat stone. The openings all looked alike, but the first stone-step of the vineyard-labyrinth was hidden behind the vines, beyond the fourth opening.

I looked behind me once more. The cliff hid the city but the smoke was rising. They had told us of the volcano but there was no stream of fire flowing from the mountain.

I did not know how the sailors had managed to find their way. The steps the nurses used, when they went to their fisher-people, were further on, but the steps were only for the nurses. The fisher-people didn't come up that way.

The goat-path and the vineyard were part of the labyrinth.

I went in, at the fourth opening.

I brushed past the vines. I found the step. There was the platform just beyond, with the flat stone in the right-hand corner, marked with a cross.

I waited on the platform.

Perhaps some of them had gone early to Mount Ida. I would go there, any-way. They never said the earthquake spit fire, but they did say that strange ships sometimes put in or were washed ashore by the tide-wave. This is what must have happened.

But I would go on.

He - our dear master-of-festival - had told us to meet him on the mountain.

But I did not meet our master-of-festival on the mountain.

I still held my basket of flowers.

He had followed me through the vineyard.

V

And Five Others

"I-command," but that was later and he said it differently. He always said it, it was a sort of joke we had together. Even after the third went to the ship-yard, he still said, "I-command," and we were young again. It would have been impossible to keep them. He laughed at me, every time one of them went off on the coast-patrol, "Of course he won't come back. Why should he?" I had said good-bye so often. I had said it to him - and to them, over and over again. I would never say it again.

There was I-command and five others.

"What would you do with them if you kept them?" he said.

It was hard to go back. I waded through ash and fire to get there.

"They could build - build - build - " I shouted.

"They are building," he said.

"Something else," I said, "something different."

"They are different," he said, but I did not want to hear about the new ones, their strength, their give, their balance. They even had to make up new Greek words for these things. If they went to the mountains, it was only to fell trees. Why should I want to keep the last one?

I still had one thing left that was my own and different. I had my mountain-madness, as they called it.

I would be rid of them forever.

I followed the goat-path round the cliff-edge. If I had jumped that day of the spring-festival, none of this would have happened. There would be five less Greek sailors in this world. Where did they come from? Why did they come to me? Who sent them? Why did they come here? I had already asked these questions.

Why hadn't I jumped that day? I wanted to tell the man on the goat-path what I thought of him - that was the reason. I wanted to tell him just what I thought of him. I thought the strange sailors had been washed ashore by a tide-wave, but that was no excuse for breaking into the labyrinth. The ambassadors approached our mountain reverently and in princely garments. No-one had the key to the labyrinth but the palace and the household. None of us would betray the pathway through the vineyard. I had shown him the way.

I even told him later about the guardian-mother and the little crosses. Who was he with his "I-command?" It was I with "He-commands-it." We were going to the festival. We were going to the mountain. Earthquake? Now I knew all about it. But even after I knew about it, it didn't make any difference. That is what drew me, raging to the mountain.

I had betrayed them, I had betrayed the mountain. But then, after my brief absence, I would go back. Why did I go back? I had goat-milk, berries and spring-water. I talked to our dear master-of-festival. I sang songs with the old words. I wove garlands of wood-violets, and placed them on a flat stone for an altar. I was alone who was never less alone. I slid over the crevice to the other side, where I could not see the ocean that had brought him.

I went back.

I always went back.

This time, I would not go back.

I always asked the same question. There were different ways of getting answers. If you ask a question and wait long enough for an answer, you will get it. Sometimes it is a leaf, drifting down, if it falls straight, the answer is yes; if it turns and drifts and spins in the air, the answer is, turn your question round and round, turn it over and over, before you make up your mind. I would ask, "Is this another sailor?" I was on the other side of the mountain, out of sight of the sea. I waited for the answer.

It was the same answer that I had had the first time. The same eagle swam out of the blue sky. I would avoid the crag the next time, if there was a next time.

There was a next time. With my eyes shut, I scraped up a handful of fallen leaves. I selected one leaf. I opened my eyes. It was an oak-leaf. I had thought there were no oak-trees this side of the mountain. I had carefully avoided the slopes where they were cutting the trees. Oak meant ships, it did not mean the procession to the sacred-grove and the pronouncements of the oracle. Or did it? Would we establish the oracle here in our - in their forest? That was the third time.

I began to hope again, I mean to hope when I was hopeless. For I knew that I would go back. He had betrayed me. I loved him.

. . . . .

When the time came for the third to make up his mind, I went out and selected an oak-leaf. Perhaps this answer would be different from the others. I laid the oak-leaf on the table. It was a beautiful table; I had come to love this simple furniture and the plain strips of cloth that the women wove for us. I waited for them to come in. I would have the third answer. Their father had been talking, as he always talked now, of the ship-yard. The third carved beautifully. He had turned me some new bowls recently. I put away the platters and set out the bowls in their place.

I remembered how our old nurses sometimes got their answers. The first words spoken by the first person you met in the market-place, would give the answer. The first one that came in would give the answer.

None of them came in. I waited and waited. I was always waiting. For what?

He came in - that is, the third one. I thought, it will be all right this time, this one will be different.

I wondered if he would see the oak-leaf. He noticed more things than the others. He saw the oak-leaf. It would be all right.

I said, "I have just come back, the leaves are already turning. The oak-wood was so beautiful."

He said, "Yes, but I like the pine-trees, they are better for masts."

I wouldn't ask any more questions.

I couldn't keep the little ones from their brothers. It was impossible. The first one followed his father, that was all right, but the second one followed the first one. Perhaps that was all right, too, but it had to stop somewhere. It had stopped somewhere. They had all gone.

. . . . .

Even his father said, after that harsh winter, that the fourth one could do other things. There were other things. There was the pressing and dyeing of the loom-cloth, for instance. Except for the smaller pieces, that was man and boy work. I was happy again. We talked about colours, about the roots and berries for the dye-vats, we even went out together to collect them and we tried new mixtures of yellow and blue for that special green I wanted.

We talked about the different shades of green and I told him about the paintings in the palace. He was never tired of listening. He grew stronger and his eyes did not inevitably turn to the sky, as theirs did, but sometimes to earth, the shape of stone, the curve of branch, the colour of flower. He was always asking me about Knossos. He thought I would be happy when he told me. It was a merchant-vessel from the islands.

I would never talk about painting again. I would never describe beautiful things. He had gone off to look for them. But as I say, it is a hopeless struggle.

The little one clutched the edge of the table. He glared and stared at what the fourth was doing. He stamped off and dragged up a stool and climbed up on it. He laid his elbows on the table, propped his chin on his hands and his owl-eyes followed each stroke of his brother's charcoal stick or paint-brush. But when his brother went away, I hid the paints and brushes.

But he had friends round and about the dye-vats. He had friends everywhere. He was keeping it for a surprise.

"Where did you get this?" I asked him.

I was angry with him. I didn't want to be reminded of the fourth one. But at least, he was out of all this. How could any of them imagine that I was so stupid? No-one could get away now from the hammers, the forge-fires glowed all night. I was not to be told about it, but I seldom saw any of them now, anyway. The Greek women were proud of their sons. I could understand them. But there had been rumours before, hammerings and forge-fires. Sometimes, the forge-fires were for other people. It didn't mean that we - that they - "*this is a sort of decoration*," the fifth was saying. "*It comes along the side in a curve, then the other side. It's blue. Then, the men with the oars are in the middle. There are oars both sides.*"

I had heard this before. I was to hear it again. I knew what he would say before he said it. I had seen the picture before. I would see it again. I would always see it, unless I got away into the mountains and found our master-of-festival. He would know what to do about it. He would have enchanting games and contests. The sea wasn't everything. They would take part in processions, there were the contests of the boy musicians. They scaled the mountains and made new path-ways. There were marvellous treasure-hunts around the labyrinth and all the intricate secrets of the labyrinth to come later. There were the contests of the painters. I thought this was the panel that his brother had painted, when I told him about the contests.

But someone else had done this.

"Who painted this?" I said. I was staring at the picture. I don't know if he answered me, but "*What were very blue?*" I said, *although I knew perfectly well what he meant.*

"*I have just told you,*" he said, "*they curved over, they weren't decoration exactly. I mean, they were part of the boat.*"

"*What were part of the boat?*" I asked him again, knowing perfectly well what he meant.

"*The blue wings,*" he said.

. . . . .

He had betrayed me. I loved them.

Of course, I knew that sooner or later, they would all go. I only wanted time to catch up, to prepare, to be ready for the supreme moment. This was the supreme moment but I was not ready for it. It was a great joke, my mountain-madness. Even the little one, but he was - he was - was he this tall boy standing here beside me?

"Why did you paint this picture," I said, "if you did paint it, and why did you hide it from me, the painting, I mean?"

"I wanted to surprise you. And anyway, you hid the brushes. You didn't want me to be a painter."

"I did want you - I did want you - " I almost shouted at him, "but look at your brother - " Then somehow, I saw it clearly. "You paint better than your brother did at your age, or at any age. You think he'll find you a place near him in the islands?"

He said, "Yes."

"I suppose this was arranged before he left us?"

He said, "Yes."

"But they have better painters than we - than you have, in the islands."

"Not for ship pictures," he said.

"But you can't spend your life painting pictures of ships, can you?"

"I could," he said, "but there are other things to do in the new ship-yard."

"The new ship-yard?"

"I mean - "

"You mean that your brother went away to work just the same, to hammer, to grind, to beat out shields and spear-shafts - "

"No, no," he said, "we are the master-craftsmen."

"We - "

"Well, I only lately," he said.

"He said - your father said that your brother was going with the merchants."

"He did go with the merchants."

I told him not to say it, I would say it.

"To buy sail-cloth for the new ships," I said.

It must have been a great joke they had together, about the new ship-yard - almost as funny as my mountain-madness.

. . . . .

So I was not like the Greek women. It was their strength that bore strong sons. But my sons were stronger than any of their sons, even the fourth, though he almost died that winter. There was no mother here who would have been lied to, propitiated with half-lies - the merchants! I had dreamed of our dragon-bowls, the green for which there was no word here, that I tried to mix for the fourth. It was my stories that had saved him. He had not wanted to stay. Although of course, even before they could walk, their father stole them and took them out with him in the boats, he did not take the fourth. I often wondered even then, how they thought it possible to deceive me.

The Maiden loved them, if it could be possible, as much as I did, she would I knew, fight for them like a lioness. But I didn't know the sea-charms. She would take them to her grand-mother and sit helping with the nets, long afternoons, and the two big ones would go with her. I was waiting for the third then. No doubt, the Maiden thought I would be apprehensive for I didn't know the sea-charms.

But I knew other charms. Can you break a child's heart by making him feel different? Yes. "They came on the ships," I said, "they came to us. We did not go to them. For we had everything they wanted.

"They came from Lybia; even your father has never been to Lybia. They were great chiefs and their ships were much larger than our ships. When they went away, the maidens walked in the procession down to the sea. The master-of-festival - "

"What festival?" he interrupted. I realised then that I had never spoken about the festival and the spring-chosen, to any of them.

"Oh - the master-of-festival? He chose the best boys to mix the colours for him. He only gave the best boys brushes. He went down to the sea and the best boys headed the procession. The master would only trust the boys with the dragon-bowls. Not even the girls were allowed to touch them.

"There were two dragons painted on the bowls. He explained them to us. One flew or swam in one direction, the other went the other way round the bowl-rim. One dragon was red, the other was blue. The chieftains brought their artists to learn how to make the - but we have no Greek word for what we called the wet-leaf-finish of the glazed - well, there is no word for that either, because the pottery we have here, the bowls and amphora are dull and only painted with black pictures. But there were special furnaces under the cliffs for the dragon-bowls. I wish I had asked the master-of-festival more about it. That green I tried to show you was dragon-green, as we called it. There were goblets too, like green and blue-green water. You could see right through them. The master-of-ceremonies himself selected the sand for those furnaces."

"You can't see through sand," the fourth said.

"We could. That is why the chieftains brought their artists."

"We had everything we wanted, at least we thought we had, until they brought us more things." I was thinking of the cheetahs.

"One of them was larger than the largest cat anyone could imagine. But it was the smallest one they brought us, it was a baby-cheetah. The master-of-festival let us keep it in the household, until it was too big. We begged and begged him to let us keep the baby-cheetah, but he said, 'It isn't a baby any longer. When you grow up, we have processions for you. We will have a procession for this grown-up cheetah.'"

The fourth was so excited that he did not even ask me what a cheetah was. I saw him catch fire. I saw the light come back.

. . . . .

"The master-of-festival found me. I was hiding. He said, 'What are you doing?' I said I wasn't doing anything, there wasn't anything to do. He said, 'But you always go with them to the mountains to find the roots and berries for me.' He let us get the berries for his colours. 'I thought you liked the colours.' 'I don't like anything,' I said. 'This is the first time,' he said, 'that you didn't go with them. I sent them all off. I wondered what had happened to you. I looked everywhere.' It seemed strange that the master-of-festival who knew everything, didn't know."

"What didn't he know?" the fourth asked.

"Well, guess," I said.

"What is a cheetah?" the fourth said.

I said, "I would rather not talk about it. I told you it was a cat, bigger than the biggest cat anyone could imagine. But it was a kitten. It began to purr. It was a very loud purr. If you put your hand on its throat, you could feel the purr right through you. It was almost white when they brought it, but now it was striped with brown. The master-of-festival said, 'This is the first time you have ever been rude to me.' I said, 'You were rude to us.' He said, 'I told you the cheetah was grown up.' 'I shall always keep it,' I said, 'I will never go up on the mountains again. It will remind me of your - procession.' 'It was a very beautiful procession,' he answered, 'almost as beautiful as the procession of the spring-chosen. Soon, you will walk up to Mount Ida, through the vineyards with the spring-chosen.' 'I won't walk with anyone,' I said. 'Come, come - I'll tell you something dreadful.' I looked at the master-of-festival. I wouldn't even look at him, at first. 'I disobeyed the Household Keeper,' he said, 'and you know what he's like.' 'But you can disobey everybody,' I said. 'Not everybody,' he said.

"'But I'll tell you how it happened. The Household Keeper said, you can't bring it in here. We never had a cheetah in the household. Then, I said, there is no rule about bringing it in, is there? He said, there are rules and rules - you know what he is like. It's too big anyway, he went on. We have rules about indoor and outdoor peacocks, hounds and falcons. But, I said, this animal is not a peacock nor a hound nor yet a falcon. You have heard what I said, said the Household Keeper, I wouldn't have my children touch it. My children are different, I told him. It's your risk, he said. I said, I'll risk it.'

"The master-of-festival said 'Your hands are cold.' He had taken my hands in his.

"'And then I got another scolding. That's better,' he said, for to think of the master-of-festival being scolded made me laugh. He said, 'I said, but it wasn't her fault, it was the cheetah. The robe-keeper - you know what she's like - said it had been her opinion from the first, that the creature was not suitable. She had actually sent a messenger to invite me to the robe-room. I thought it was to discuss this evening's ceremony. Well, in a way, it was. This can't happen again, she said, but she said it more politely. She had sent she said, to ask my advice. It was beyond the skill even of the chief-embroideress to reclaim the blue-hyacinth border. Well, you know those hyacinths. It's your Great Occasion costume.'

"He waited for me to say something but I was crying. I wasn't crying because of the hyacinth-border nor even because of the cheetah.

"'You needn't cry,' he said. 'I told her you were getting too tall for the robe, anyway.' But he knew I wasn't crying about that. 'I selected a new robe. It's very pretty. It isn't just a border. It has little flowers worked all over it. It's a field of spring-flowers. We must keep it, the robe-mistress said, until she is spring-chosen. But I said, you must wear it to-night. Yes, you are right, I can disobey everyone but - '

"I looked and looked at the master-of-festival. 'You don't mean - ' 'Yes,' he said, 'it was He-commands-it.'"

VI

Athens

I had seen the end. Now I saw the beginning. It was Pheidias who helped me to remember.

There was a great deal in between. The scenes shifted and changed and I cried for the children I had lost and for the children I would never have. But Pheidias had shown me the way through the labyrinth and I still had the key to the golden house and the oleander garden.

Of course, Pheidias had known all the time that the key was strung on the silk cord that I wore under my dress. It was true that I had come back to reclaim the bracelets, that was quite true. But I had not thought of leaving the key with him when I was about to dive out into the darkness. I still had the key though Pheidias had melted down the bracelets.

I had said to Pheidias, on the Acropolis, that I had lied with delicacy and discretion to the steward when he came to close the golden house. But actually, I told no lies and the delicacy and discretion were the steward's.

"I'll keep the wine-cups, miss, with our other household silver."

I might have been a daughter of the house, the way he said it.

"Never did hold with melting down old silver - "

"Here is the key to that chest," I said, "and this is the smaller box - "

"Rather awkward, this chest - should have sacked that house-boy long ago, but it was one of those things - his mother, my niece, and her expecting again, that is my sister's youngest - begging your pardon. I do recall telling that - well - that boy to oil all these here fittings. There - that does it - but as I was saying, miss - "

"There are two keys," I said. He took the small key,

"Um - you've already locked it - too big to carry with you?"

He weighed the small case with both hands.

"Should think you could manage. It's usually customary when ladies closes up their houses, to take their personal-like belongings."

I waited for him to go but there was the last thing, the house-key.

"I still have my bracelets, they won't fit in this box. I'll send them later with the house-key."

He was pretending to fasten the indoor shutters. He knew I wasn't going. The heavy curtains had already been taken down.

"Worse than a barracks this place - not that I hold with this new-fangled communal soldiering. Why we was glad enough to sleep at all, let alone sleeping in barracks as they call them. Stuff such as you don't get these days, our coats was. They was blanket, bed and houses. Something personal-like about it. You rolled it up and everything in it, on your back. Off they goes - smart as paint, I'll grant you - but horses? What would you have done on the old track, I ask you, with a charger? The springs, I mean - Thermopylae. And who was our allies then? You wouldn't be old enough to remember, but I'll tell you, just in case you don't know. The Spartans was our allies in the last war - no word was good enough then, for our noble allies. A bit confusing-like, I call it. Fight? Well, *he* - if you get my meaning - has some new tricks. Of course, we all know it's them or us, this time. But massed attack! You can't attack in masses, you got to fight single. Then this clearing out the city. No-one left Athens in the last war."

I had heard another story but I did not contradict him. I waited for him to take the small box and go.

"Marathon - we was the few, they called us."

I did not want to hear him talk of Marathon.

"They take anybody in this war - not that his personal ain't something special. But for following up, for cleaning up, they calls it, they just take along the rabble. There weren't anything to clean up after Marathon, if you get my meaning. We done all that. Want me to leave an extra blanket? It's turned colder." He went out; he came back with a wicker-tray of fresh wood. "Quite like old times, burning sticks in a brazier. These oil-lamps with the built-round hood are more trouble than they're worth, I'm always saying. They don't give rightly a real character to a room. Pretty in the summer, miss, with all those oleanders.

"Talk, talk, talk. And all this legislation. Athens was Athens in the old days, there was nothing free-born about us. Chariots is pretty to look at. My youngest got the olive in the games. Pretty in the procession, but it's only foreigners who fight with chariots. Horses is no good on mountains, but we had to fight them in the open. Whoever heard of fighting in the open? But we done it - for the last time, they said. There's never going to be a last time. It was killing the horses that got me, had to kill the horses to kill them. But I don't like killing horses - inhuman, I call it.

"Something like them boats. Chain a man to a bench - they even took down the sails. What was the idea? Since you ask me, miss, I'll tell you. There was no hope for them, anyway - but have you ever tried not breathing? If you half-drown and come up - but I wasn't drowning. It was something I couldn't imagine - drowning. I tried to imagine, in fact, I dreamed about it. Anything is better than drowning, I thought. Every sailor knows that, but they don't stop to think about it. I was no sailor or I'd have stopped thinking about it. It was them or us, all right. Trust to the wooden walls, they told us and my father said, as long as the walls wood, trust them. What do you mean, we asked - him and my two brothers was all sailors. Mark my words, my father said, the minute you begin to edge a decent prow with metal, the wall's not wood.

"Now here they was, you couldn't see the water for the flash of their oars. All along the sides it came, almost as if the oars was gold and silver. Some of them was painted. Some had spears set like the oars in a gallery above them. Murder-machines, they was. They took two scythe-blades or something like them, only bigger and set them in the prow. It might have been all right - for them, I mean. We got the idea but trust to the wooden walls was the oracle. There was time to fix up something, but the master - my father's - was an old man and he said he wouldn't have it. The younger ones, some of them, was inclined to laugh at what they called the superstition. We hadn't a hope.

"My father said, the master said, 'Remember you lads, you can fight for it, you can swim. They've chained their galleys.'

"The straits was narrow. There was nothing to stop them."

I said, "But I told you there were two keys."

"When I said, we hadn't a hope, I meant them. I was only at Marathon. But things you see, like that old master telling them, is more real than places you was. Well, I heard it from my own father, that's true, but I heard it from the old master when he was telling the youngest they would be more use alongshore. He said he was reconnoitering-like. He would come back and fetch them.

"I was only at Marathon. I don't like drowning.

"It wasn't just the things they picked up afterwards. They was lined in sort of ladder-steps on platforms. The sun caught the helmets, it was steel walls or towers, we were fighting. We had our leather helmets. Our first arrows glanced off. Trust to the wooden walls, but what good are wood walls against steel ones? If it was just us - but they'd chain the lads to the benches."

I said, "I'd like to stay here five days."

He said, "Some of our people are still waiting for the ox-carts. From what *he* says, they'll not get past the Isthmus - I mean, *them*. There's the stations all along the road to Delphi. I can arrange for you to go with the last ox-carts. Perhaps you're right. You won't need these at Delphi." He tucked the case under his arm.

I said again, "I'll send the house-key later, with the bracelets."

"When the war's over," he said, "I'll know where to find you.

"What I was saying was, we don't think enough about them. Now and again, there's a celebration. But we don't really think about them. I tried for a time, regular each morning and at sun-set, to recall my agony. I mean, about drowning. Then even the dreams left me. I didn't dream about them struggling in the water and I didn't dream that worse dream of them chained that couldn't struggle. I didn't hear the old master; that is, I heard him when I listened but I didn't hear him other times. I could see the steel wall when I thought about it, but it didn't rise up when I was talking casual in the market and it didn't ram down on me under the apple-trees. I stopped breathing, as much as I could stand it and a little longer, for memory and to remember how good the air was and how good the land was and to feel my whole body full of apple-blossoms with the in-take, or full of ripe apples or apples rotting in the long grass. It was to remember. There was the vine-remembering, the blossom and the ripe grape. I tasted the fragrance for them who couldn't taste, nor see, nor feel - for our sakes. I listened special to the sound of hard snow and of soft snow, to make out the different feeling in their falling - for their sake. It might be they was around somewhere.

"It's true they'll get there quicker with the horses. I didn't even dream about the horses, any more. I went off into the mountains but the trees was full of them. I was under the water with them. If we'd all stopped to remember, this never would have happened."

He put the case back on the table. He tilted the wood blocks out on the floor. When he came back, he had a flagon of wine, cheese and brown bread on a plat-ter. He must have brought them with him; I had been out there before he took the first boxes and there was nothing in the larder. Now, there was only the silver-chest and the small case. He wouldn't come back. He shook out the bundle of keys and opened the chest. He put a goblet on the table.

"Don't close it," I said. I put the second goblet on the table. "You're tired," I said. "Sit down." I filled his goblet.

. . . . .

"You see what I mean. We hadn't a hope but he had, the old master. Ship after ship went down and them struggling in the water. More moved up. It was the last wall now."

He said, "I left another flagon of his special."

"For my remembrance?" I said, the words burned in my throat. I felt that I had shouted but I knew that I had spoken softly, perhaps he hadn't heard me. He tilted the flagon over my cup.

"For your remembrance," he said.

"For remembrance when you see the trees in blossom, for remembrance of what tree blossomed. It was the oak-tree mostly. It was the last wall. He hadn't any more to move up."

I knew the story or I thought I knew the story.

"When the wind came, it was something special. Or maybe it was just what the old master had expected. I couldn't see any more, for the tangle of oars and ladders. They wasn't balanced proper. They tilted and fell and when they listed, they went over like lead. There was no swimming for them, I mean, the invulnerables upon the platforms. They was weighed down with all that polished metal. They rammed one another and you could hear the oars snap off. There was spars and masts and my - brothers floating in the water. You can't mix wood and metal. There's something in the wood that's different. They talk in the wood beyond Delphi, at Dodona. You can't talk in metal."

"There are silver trumpets," I said.

. . . . .

I had heard the trumpets when I was at Delphi with the temple-players. The elders, the arcons, the prefects, the visiting delegates had all taken their places. We were waiting as usual, behind the screens that were set between the pillars. Hermes was about to go on but the stage-manager grumbled, "they ought to take lessons in etiquette or something - keeping us waiting." Hermes said, mouthing it in a whisper,

"*Eternal crags, haunt of the bird of Zeus* - ye gods, if I say it again, I'll forget it. I've said it too often. Why didn't they put on a new play for his lordship of - *the golden sands untrodden by the hordes* of - whatever it is, that's Dionysus, not me. Where is the old fellow, Scrag, I mean, anyway? Scrag, I said, not crag - he used to be in this play. If I don't see him before I go on, will you tell him that he'll find me *where clear Castalia and Phaedriades* - I'm going for a swim; it's rather warm and my invisible cloak isn't working this afternoon. If 'twere, lord of god-a-mighty Thebes, would I not be quit of this Athenian invasion? Why do they come up, anyway? What are you doing to-day? I said to-day, I mean you-Day. I didn't say Ray or *golden herald waiting to proclaim* - whatever it is he is proclaiming or not proclaiming, or have the Persians sacked Athens again? *The armèd hosts approach the citadel* - that's them. Let me look, it's my cue to go on - my, my, what an array of the good and the beautiful. Don't look anybody, this is my show. Dear, dear! Precedence, procedure - but god-a-mighty, asking us to wait for that lot."

I pushed him away from our favourite peep-hole. There seemed to be a special hush - you know what I mean. There was always some sort of shuffling or fluttering in the audience, just before the Prologue went on, but this time, they sat as one, frozen.

"What's the matter?" I said.

"Here, let me look them over," said the stage-manager, "there may be something up. The third herald may want to give a signal."

Ray spun on his heels. He leaned down and whispered to the stage-manager - "Any orders - special, I mean?"

"Not yet - not what you mean, no impromptu lines, as far as I know, nor funny business - nor anything - "

"Not even, nor anything?"

"Haven't had any directions - any hint, I should say."

"Any hint *not* - I mean, funny business?"

"Haven't heard a word about it - must have took 'em by storm. Taking his time about it, too; I'm just waiting for herald three to wave his trumpet or not wave it - or just look casual."

"Is herald three looking casual?"

"Not him - anything but. But he hasn't done a thing that you could interpret otherwise."

"They're leaving it to us, you mean?"

"I wouldn't go so far, my lad, as to mean anything."

"You mean, I might make a mistake or something?"

"You kids are too well-trained, and they all know it, to make a mistake in this diplomatic business."

"Oh, la-la, I won't make a mistake, then."

Ray had spun round and was on the stage before we knew it.

"Phew! That's done it," said the manager. "I hoped he'd take things into his own hands."

The line of what Ray called the good and beautiful was still standing. That blocked the stage from the first rows of the audience but that wasn't so important. That was what the prologue was for, just to indicate that the actual play would soon be starting. The first lines of Ray's speech didn't matter, it was only when the audience had finally settled, that Ray lifted his Hermes staff, as if to command attention. But we never officially began until all the delegates were seated. The good and the beautiful couldn't sit down until he did. I looked at him. He didn't sit down. Ray lifted his staff, but this time, although he had not even begun speaking, he banged it down on the stage-floor.

It was very quiet.

Ray could speak now, for Pericles - they called him - sat down.

. . . . .

"He made his declaration," said Ray, "this diplomatic business - no mistake about that." He was unstrapping his winged sandals. "I just asked you - well, some time back, before the war started, what are you doing, you-Day?" Everything out front seemed to be going on as usual. It had to be more as usual, than usual because of the declaration. "I mean, Day-darling, bright Day-star, what are you going to do *now* to-day?"

"You mean, now that the war's started?" I asked him.

"Precisely. I'm off."

"But you never go off when there's to be a reception. Aren't you even going to stay to - quip them?"

"I've done my quip, might really get into trouble, not that he wants to see *me*, in the usual formal, informal, most diplomatic, undiplomatic business of our little back-stage reception after the show. But we just thought - no names mentioned - in fact, *we* didn't even think of it. We left it to other people who left it to other people - it's as important as all that. Now my idea is - not *my* idea, I wouldn't even think it. We don't think at Delphi. We're inspirational. We don't fight either, we let other people do the fighting for us. Did you see them beauties? Ye gods, and to think of those Spartan louts last year."

"Why didn't they turn up this year? Or were they lost on the way?" I asked him.

"Alas no, I fear they are not lost yet - it will take some time. I don't mean anything. But last year - did you notice? But of course we never notice - there was a good bit of - well, as-you-might-say on their part and as-you-might-say on our part - not that we're not always polite to visitors."

"You mean the oracle told the archon - "

"Not him, not them, not the oracle exactly. It didn't need the Voice to explain what they were up to. But the Spartans didn't come this year, and he did. You can't have two Supremacies."

"But we never take sides."

"Don't make me laugh, Day-star. But to get down to business, stage-business after the show. I'm off. I've orders to get out of here, and all the other principals but Scrag, must follow. Now you're not a principal and you're not one of the many, not so many Maenads, Trojan women or sacred dancers of Aulis, Dodona, Argolis or what-not. They all go in a bunch, anyway. Just help get everyone off the premises. But you, stick round."

"You want me to *do* something?"

"Not exactly *do* something - he'll make it all right, the third herald - I mean, someone has summoned us for rehearsal at the Sacred College. We are all very sorry - our dear children were heart-broken not to be able to rub shoulders, on this auspicious, official, non-official, most undiplomatic occasion with their own youth and beauty. But someone's got to stay and see how *he* takes it."

"He won't even notice," I said.

"Well, Scrag has the speaking part. You just stay round - casual."

. . . . .

They all seemed to clear out very quickly, even the manager, dressers and extras. They left things lying around, as if on purpose. Scrag said,

"I've got to keep on these trappings till he comes. Then I do a quick strip. I'm late as it is - but I'm supposed to be late, I gather. I get the idea - the others were hanging around, note props - in the hope, what a hope, of presentation. Summons - Sacred College calls for the last rehearsal of the new chorus. The show was late beginning. That was his fault and he knows what Sacred College stands for. You can't get around that."

I was getting a little tired of all this. I said,

"I liked Ray making him sit down like that."

"Making him sit down, my dear child; were you born yesterday?"

"What do you mean, was I born yesterday?"

"What do you think he was standing up for? But don't answer; if you're as dense as all that, you'll never see through a brick wall. What do you think he was standing up for? He was standing up to show he'd come to help us."

I knew Scrag was excited, he always was after the *Maenads*, it was a big part, and Myra had just told me, while I was helping her, that she had had to prompt him in his last long speech. I envied him and I envied Myra and Ray. I wasn't even in the chorus. They were always promising to give me a small part, not just "propping up a pillar," as Scrag called it. I was always standing at the top of the steps, I was even people - or gods rather - on the roof - but they never let me say anything. Sometimes I was afraid that I would wake up one morning and find I'd lost my voice altogether. I was a temple-child. I was the only temple-child among the players. Scrag always said he wished he were and I think, in a way, they envied me, but they all went home to their families in the winter. I was a temple-child and I was always "propping up a pillar," but it had all been too exciting. I didn't like Scrag turning on me, but he was jumpy, you could see that, and Myra had said he was very exalté in that last scene.

"Scrag," I said, "it will be all right, whatever it is. But Ray told me to stay and to stand around - casual. And I haven't the least idea what I'm to be casual about."

"Never mind," he said, "I'll tell you afterwards. Try to say something funny," he said, "Day-star. Try to make me look rather - inefficient, careless, temperamental."

"You always look that, I mean temperamental. And beautiful."

"You mean my ivy - just tidy it a bit, will you?"

"Sit down, I'm almost as tall as you are but not quite. But no, they'll catch us at it; they'll think we stayed on purpose."

"Good, good girl," he said, "I didn't mean that about the brick wall. But they're to catch us - loitering; we've got to look a little guilty. We're late, we've got to begin changing - that is - " But the door opened.

We jumped apart. We couldn't have done it better. He had taken my hand when he said good, good girl. His wreath was a little crooked and he put up his hand and pulled off the ivy.

The third herald said, "What's all this? What's going on in here?" The others came in. There were two tall boys. They didn't snigger nor look down or look away as the Spartan boys had done last year. He seemed interested. "Rehearsal?" he said.

"No, no," the herald said, "the children must be heartbroken, the others, I mean. At least, I suppose that is what has become of them. We thought the Sacred College - just this time - would understand. You know what things are. But if the college messenger did rout you all out," he turned on Scrag, "what are you two doing?"

Scrag was pretending to re-arrange his leopard-skin.

"Sorry, sir," he said, "it's my fault. She - "

"I wasn't speaking of her," said the herald. "You all have your orders."

The general stepped forward. "When do you think we will see you play in Athens?" he asked Scrag. He should have asked the herald, but by that time I didn't in the least know who should or shouldn't ask who - what. I still wore my blue priestess-robe. The general said, "Is this Ariadne?" He waved the boys forward and the herald stepped back.

Scrag looked at the boys, "I - I'm afraid I do look a fool," he said, "it's this damned - I beg your pardon, sir - panther." Scrag gave that throaty laugh; everyone loved Scrag.

"But I asked you about Ariadne," said the general. Scrag turned and looked at me; he wasn't jumpy any more and his eyes said good, good girl. He looked back at the general.

"This isn't Ariadne," he said, "it's only Day-star."

. . . . .

I saw it all now. I went over and over it. I saw everything. Nobody could officially rebuke the Athenian general - nor even that last Spartan. But the Spartans had not attended the festival that year, and if we openly applauded the Athenian gesture, we were confessed partisans. There would be more trouble. Some of us - of them would be sent home. We had to keep the balance. Ray delivered an unofficial rebuke to Athens - that balanced it.

I went over it and over it, the five days I waited there in Athens after the steward had left me. It was all keeping the balance. It would be like that, they told us, when we went to Athens that next autumn, at his special invitation.

If things could be balanced, war might be averted. But I don't think they really thought, by that time, that things could be balanced. It was all simple, friendly and what Ray called casual. We went to Athens for the Dionysia; we had a new play and as usual, I "propped up a pillar." There were meetings and informal re-ceptions. He always made a point of looking for me. There was the second festi-val at Delphi, a second play in Athens - and that time I stayed in Athens. There was the winter between the first play in Athens and the second Delphic festival. The college had special work that winter and I was training some of the younger children for the preliminary stage-trials. That was "official," but unofficially, there were other matters. There was come and go of various legations. I don't yet quite know or see the sequence. But no doubt I will see it later.

I didn't expect things to happen so quickly. There was so much that I still wanted to do at Delphi. But they told Ray to give the message; it seemed they wanted me to stay in Athens. It was only, in the end, the Voice that mattered.

. . . . .

I scarcely knew him the last time I saw him. I placed the goblets on the table, but he waved them aside.

"I have a matter of some importance," he said, and sat down. I knew that he was busy, harassed and worried, they all were. "It's this D for - Delphi," he said and he spread the parchment on the table. "I presume you had instructions your end," he went on. "We have not been ungenerous. You are to leave Athens. The stations have a full description of you and your past activities. I presume you - or they, before you left them - made arrangements. Alternative arrangements, that is. May I ask, as a mere matter of curiosity, where you planned going?"

I said, "I had no plans and no plans were made for me. I will stay in Athens."

"It would be unsuitable for you to stay here."

"Most unsuitable," I answered, though I did not know what he meant.

"I learned from our friend, Pheidias - " but I stopped him:

"Leave Pheidias out of this. What is all this nonsense?"

"No-one stays officially at the College who has not official business."

"I was training the younger children."

"For what? Even children can be useful - "

"Stop," I said, "this is desecration - I will be sorry for you presently. Have you gone mad?"

"Come - come - this is no sacred tragedy; no stage-scenes, I entreat you. This is, may I point out, Athens. You were sent here."

"I came here with the players at the request, the invitation of your - of you, sir."

"Yes. I wanted to find out what the Sacred College taught you. You seemed the most likely - subject to examine. The examination has been thorough. We knew, of course, from the beginning, that the College sent you."

"The College did not send me," I said.

"You just came? They had groomed you to perfection. You stood around. You supported pillars, you remember your - joke. But this is no joking matter. We have our own college. Even in Delphi we have our - voices."

"I am glad I do not have to listen to them."

"You had friends there - special friends, but you never saw them. You must have communicated somehow - but that is of small importance at this moment. You loitered in the market, you had many friends among the market-women and the flower-girls. Did it ever strike you as strange that the dark - Viola, for instance, disappeared one morning? When you went to get your violets, she was not there. But you passed on to Iris - such pretty names you girls have. You do not need *parchments* for messages - " he brought his fist down on the table. I felt, suddenly, he must be joking. He couldn't, no-one could be as inartistic as all that. He turned the parchment over, "Ah, here after - Delphi, Iris. There is no margin. Shall I read it to you?"

"Pray do," I said, "I never saw you in the Forum, but I have heard that you speak beautifully."

It wasn't true. None of it was true. I had got a speaking part at last, but it was in the wrong play.

. . . . .

He was very busy, they all were. I understood his not coming; I had hardly seen him for six months. That was why I went so often to the Acropolis to talk to Pheidias. I had heard the story of the young sculptor from the islands. I tried to avoid reference to other incidents, as Pheidias called them. I even stopped asking him when the frieze would be set up. He would say, "You can't look at them from the ground," though I told him they looked beautiful from any angle. We didn't joke any more about the wingless Victory. That joke started because his winged Victories were still standing on the floor, in a corner of the Parthenon.

"I'll do the next one without wings. They have no use for their wings," he said.

The Parthenon was almost finished and we talked endlessly of the festival to celebrate the dedication, the Panathenea, they were going to call it. It's true I had my place here. They were right to tell me to stay in Athens. My life began to form and move around the Parthenon. I did not forget Pericles for a moment. It was his Athens.

That last sculptor Pheidias lost had come from Cyprus. He had strolled up to the Parthenon with the sailors.

"Pan-Athené sent him," said Pheidias. "I knew she'd help me with that last un-carved block - the altar. Ye gods - he stepped out of the sea, like his own Aphrogenia." He was a tall youth. He would stay in Athens. He did not stay in Athens.

I was standing. But I was not standing by the altar, as I had been when he first saw me in the sacred drama, at Delphi. Or was I?

There was something I must say, and I must say it quickly. Pericles still appeared to be studying the parchment. He did not look up.

"My stage-training must not be forgotten," I said. "I am grateful to you for reminding me of it. I did not have much to say at Delphi, but I have a great deal to say in Athens. I will stay in Athens - whatever you do, I will stay in Athens. There are few ghosts, few - emanations. That is why I love it. It is all spirit. Pericles stepped forward. He was out of one of our dramas. He had - he would save Athens. I grant you, there were those at Delphi who discussed the matter. After that first festival, there was much heated discussion about Pericles. Some said his gesture was theatrical, some said he had gone out of his way to insult the priesthood. I am as sick as you or anybody with the necromancy that went on outside the precinct. But the Sacred College did not harbour witch-doctors, fortune-tellers and magicians. Your informers do not need to inform you of that. My only criticism of the College is that, if anything, it was over-scrupulous. They were always sorting things over, sorting things out, assessing and balancing. If they stood in judgment on a cause or a case, a new play or an old one, on the suitability or the unsuitability of receiving tribute from this island or royal gifts from that potentate, they did it thoroughly. They had - parchments. They had records. Did you consult their records before you finished your - "

"Dossier," he prompted.

"Thank you," I said.

"Have you ever spent a winter on Parnassus?" I continued.

He began rolling up the parchment.

"You shall not leave until you hear this. It was cold. It was so cold that it was warm. Unless you know the spring-warmth of being frozen to death, you do not know what I mean. The gables and the roof were carved of snow but the columns were honey-coloured. It almost seems that the snow melted on the columns, although of course that wind from the Twin-lights swirled the snow upward or piled it high in drifts, in the inner porch and in the courtyard. It is - it was the most beautiful temple in the whole world, and always and always there was a handful, a few from the inner precinct, to drive necromancy down to the valley.

"Lying and cheating is a form of necromancy. Somebody has bewitched you."

He laid down the parchment.

"One of my friends or all of them may have the same distinction as I have, and attained the honour of a - dossier. But I am thinking at the moment of the one we called Ray. He may be entered under Rhodes, though that is not his island. He spent the winter with his archers. I saw him last in Athens, that second festival. He was not returning to the theatre. It was his idea - his joke, really. I will never forget that moment. I saw them first, with his eyes, though I saw them afterwards as the world will always see them. You had exceeded that last fraction of a moment that the College allows its delegates for untoward incident. Your punctuality, I learned afterwards, was proverbial. That meant, heart-beat by heart-beat, that the audience and the world was being threatened. But I was not aware of the actual imminence of danger; Ray was. He would know what I did not know, what, no doubt, the Spartan did know. Athens was not ready. Even the third herald, the most important in the theatre, did not know what to do about it. Your gesture was beautiful and well-timed, but made things perhaps just a little - awkward for us. We dared not applaud your coming openly, I mean your coming as you did with your personal bodyguard to Delphi. They stood in a semi-circle, facing the stage.

"The over-wrought stage-manager was waiting for a signal from the third herald. The third herald did not give it. Ray, out of bravoura or a kind of inspiration, did. The theatre, as you know, is under the direction of the Sacred College. Had the staff of Hermes anything to do with your curious insinuations? I mean, you spoke of the Sacred College in a manner that was not only unseemly but unjust.

"It was Ray's joke, but afterwards we always called them - I mean, Ray was waiting for his cue, his eye on the third herald, when you entered. I will never forget how Ray said, 'At last *the arméd hosts approach the citadel*.' And then - but laughing, it was only a joke, remember, 'What an array of the good and the beautiful.'

"That is how we felt about them - about you. But perhaps you have entered Ray under his own name, the name of his own family and another island - Samothrace."

I had finished, though I would never finish. I had not been trained at the theatre for nothing, he was right about that. Even the prologue or the divine messenger (the god-on-the-roof, we called him) came to the end of the longest speech, sometime. The speech summed up a nation, a spiritual crisis, a warring of emotional intensities. But it was spoken without interruption and by one person. I had only begun to talk but I turned and took up my cloak. I do not know if I did or did not fling it round me, in one of those gestures I had practiced at the theatre.

At last I had a speaking part, and a part in the right play.

I walked to the door.

. . . . .

It was the same cloak I sat in, huddled over the brazier, those last days in the golden house. I must get my bracelets. I must take the house-key to Pheidias. It lay there on the table, where Pericles had spread his dossier. It was a new word. I don't know what we called the records and the lists at Delphi, perhaps they called them dossiers. I don't know. But there was something about the word, as he pronounced it, that was degrading. "Such pretty names you girls have." I would know sometime what dossier meant and what had happened. I did not know now. It had to do, I reasoned, with my trips to the Acropolis. I had to think of some reason for his *volte face*.

I went at odd hours to talk to Pheidias. Sometimes I carried scarves or an extra cloak over my arm. Even though Pericles came so rarely, I was happy. The war was coming and the war would be over and we would have the opening festival. I hung my scarves over the Victory Plaques. I bound my hair higher on my head or in a braid or a knot as Pheidias wanted it. He was still making charcoal sketches for the wingless Victory. He selected this or that scarf, and he would ask me to stand alternately in the sun and shadow, and in the wind when the wind was blowing. I am glad to think how carelessly I did this. It was no new game to me; I had been standing about among the marble pillars ever since I could remember. But Pericles was right, I could only see it that way. Delphi was not Athens and Athens was not Delphi.

It seemed stupid that I had not seen it sooner. I suppose I was the only woman in Athens who trailed up to the Acropolis at all hours of the day and night. Certainly, I was the only woman who chatted with the workmen, openly that is - the others - "Such pretty names you girls have."

The fourth day in the golden house, I was laughing. I had used up all the firewood. I was keeping the last loaf and the flagon of wine for Pheidias. I was lightheaded. But I had to wait till the footsteps stopped altogether. It was very quiet. Perhaps they had all gone. Perhaps I could go now, but there might yet be the Watch. But I could not get out of my chair. Perhaps I could not go to-morrow. I did not hear the Watch pass. I had been waiting for days now, for this moment.

I would sleep to-night and go to-morrow. If I could sleep to-night. I was too tired to sleep now. But I went on talking. I talked and talked. I said all the things that I had said to Pericles over again, with variations, and I made fresh speeches. The more I said, the more and more luminous ideas came crowding in upon me. I was telling them about the festival.

I don't know if I managed finally to stand up, or if in some way I projected my body from me. Something happened. I, in my light-headed ecstasy, was describing what Pheidias and I had planned together. I was standing by the table, where I had stood that last day when I made my farewell speech to Pericles.

I said: "Pheidias sent me to the markets. It wasn't only the proctors, the lictors, the archons, the High Priests, the generals that we invited to walk in the great Pan-Athené procession, after the Victory. It was Pericles' victory, it was our procession, but our procession was his victory."

The words sounded astonishing, they re-echoed from Parnassus. I was standing on the roof, declaiming to a vast assembly.

"We chose the very market-baskets they would carry. Do you think we would forget the goat-herd on Hymettus? He would walk in the procession with his goats, and I argued with the flower-girls about garlands. Do you think we would forget the least flower-girl in the market? They would come with their wicker-trays of violets, and the shepherds from Eleusis would come after. O men of Athens, we have met to celebrate the final victory of the good and the beautiful.

"O men of Athens," I said, "here is the man of Athens."

"But I asked you about Ariadne," he said.

"This isn't Ariadne," Scrag said, "it's only Day-star."

I said, "Here is the key to that chest and this is the smaller box - " The key was lying on the table. I tilted the flagon over his cup. I shouted to Parnassus, "One greater than Aeschylus will tell you of Salamis."

He said, "My father said, the master said, remember you lads, you can breathe, you can fight for it, you can swim. They've chained their galleys."

I said, "But I told you there were two keys."

He said, "What good are wood walls against steel ones? If it was just us - but they'd chain the lads to the benches."

He said, "I left another flagon of his special."

"For my remembrance?" I said.

He said, "For your remembrance."

It was morning.

I waited until evening. Under my cloak, I hugged the precious brown-loaf and the flagon of wine.

———————

VII

The Queen

The war ended? Pericles came back? I had imagined they might meet at the long-deferred Panathenea, but they didn't. Or if they did, it was a matter of small importance, dim, lifeless beside the flaming torch-fire of their last recriminations. Perhaps she went back to Delphi, I don't know. In any case, the Parthenon was finished.

But the flame of their recriminations, accusations and intensities shows palaces, arches, arcades. I myself said, I will watch them into and out of Athens. It would be impossible to deal with the entire sequence, we would limit it to Knossos, Athens, London. I had said that he came back, that she came back, but I didn't know how often. I didn't especially want to know. It was difficult enough to follow the threads, disentangle and re-work them for those three panels, scenes or pictures.

But even before the painted-lady recovered from her fever or her frenzy, that last night in the golden house in Athens, there is another golden house. It is called the golden house, or the *Ca d'Oro*. It is not shut behind walls in a correct, yet shall we say, slightly indiscreet quarter of the city, but it stands for all the world to wonder at, on the Grand Canal in Venice. And as I strive to dismiss this scene, one of my friends from Delphi sweeps his ridiculous hat to the floor and with no words but with that grace for which we loved him, finishes the gesture, with the plume falling over his shoulder in the direction of the throne-room.

It would be bad enough if my friend from Delphi were in the second golden house. But the ridiculous puffed-hat is out of another period and another story.

I did not ask them here, my friends from Delphi. I did not ask them to dress up and parade around the world in other than our first and dearest properties. Yet fearing the worst and saying that the painted-lady found her place in Athens, in fact, arguing that she never lost it - I will see what happens. The *Ca d'Oro* holds another clue. I will go to Venice. But I must first go back to Delphi.

"Someone else has got to put away my props." Myra flung off her vine-leaves, but they were not the usual property leaves; I had helped her gather them this morning when we went out for fresh ivy for Scrag. "Ray told me that we were to throw our things down, anyhow. I don't know what it's all about."

"Just kick off your sandals," I said, "I'll take your thyrsus - the pine-cone's getting shaky - "

"What pine-cone wouldn't, after that show?" She sank down on the prop chest and leaned her head against a pillar. The last chorus of tymbrals and flutes had started. The property-girl picked up the sandals.

"Just leave them," I said, "leave everything. I was told to tell all of you not to wait after the play." But she waited, she wanted to know why she was being sent off, she didn't want to miss anything. But fortunately the dresser rushed in. "The dresser wants you," I said. "Myra, pull off your ceremonials, and be quick about it. Ray told me to stay around and help get you all off - and then to stay around, casual."

"Casual? Is it as important as all that? But don't tell me if you don't want to. But I gather I needn't stay round."

"No - no-one but me and Scrag."

"Scrag? There's nothing left of him to stay round."

"That's why they want him, I suppose. I don't really know myself, what it's all about. Ray went at once; he was afraid he'd get into trouble, he said."

"The trouble he'll get into is as nothing to my trouble."

"Sit down," I said. I pushed her back on the chest. "I'll get the snakes out of your hair." I ran a comb through her dark hair and smoothed it back over her ears.

"Don't ask me," she said, "and don't say I didn't warn you. Never ask for a speaking part again or you may get it. They'll either give me the laurel for my fine performance or they'll hoof me off the premises. Don't ask me," she said again, although I hadn't asked her. "I spoke my lines - Oh, that intensity, I mean out front. Everyone was watching us to see what we'd do next, after Ray's little side-show. They weren't just watching - casual. It seemed that anything might be interpreted to mean something else, after Ray gave us the lead. I think they thought we were going to work up something at the end. Well, we didn't disappoint them." I went on braiding her hair.

"Can't we be natural sometimes? Well, Scrag was. And that was worse than Ray, though thanks to me I don't think any but the High Priests and the proctors noticed. It was that speech to the people before the temple at Thebes. Well, we've all heard it often enough. Go on propping up a pillar. I spoke my last five lines twice, seeing the state Scrag was in, caught away, I ask you, ecstasy, the divine fire. Well, he's supposed to talk about it, to act it if you will, but not to *be* it, not to that extent to be it. Unless it was just a superlative performance. It was that. But what about the rest of us? The third herald gave the second trumpet signal and you know what that means. But nobody took the hint or the command and rushed in to fill the breach. I had to. *I* was caught away, I said my lines again, like an incantation. That was the third time. I improvised a bit with quite unrelated gestures, but as I say only the censors knew that. That gave me the opportunity of prodding him with my thyrsus. I whispered, 'Snap out of it, quick.' Either I get the laurel or I'm kicked out."

"You won't be kicked out, Myra," I said.

"What's up," I said to my friend from Delphi, that is the one with the odd, new property-hat. We seemed to be going on from where we had left off - somewhere, sometime. Our costumes were more elaborate, the setting was less formal but we were out of the same play.

There was something going on out front, or we were in the wings and the throne-room was the stage. The throne-room was the stage, certainly. "I'm not supposed to go on," I said, "I'm off-duty."

"You can't miss this," Scrag said, "he's come back."

"Who's come back?" I asked him.

"Why him - who else - "

"Do you mean Devereux?"

"Who else would I mean?"

"Did she expect him?"

"She didn't - not official. But he could hardly walk in, over their dead bodies, unless she had - commanded."

"But, Scrag," I said, "I'm frankly - not so interested."

"Well, I am," he said, "and I've got to talk it over - and over and over with someone or I'll bust. If you miss seeing him, I'll have no-one. You know I can't discuss him with the others."

"They aren't all against him," I said.

"No, pretty sweeting, but you know very well I can't talk to them like I do to you, without somebody suspecting something. And anyway, she likes to see us whispering in corners - heaven knows why - and they say she's an old - well, you know."

"I'm not going, Scrag," I said, but he begged me.

"For the love of God, don't leave me. It isn't just fun. The old-oaks are a solid block against him and she'll never let down her ancients - the Armadas, I mean."

I knew what he meant.

I said, "It hasn't got to that point, has it? Then, there's no hope for him. She'd walk to the block herself, if the old-oaks sent her. Isn't there anything else?"

"That's what I'm trying to find out."

But I wasn't looking at him, I mean at Devereux.

Scrag had the key to the musician's gallery and we crouched there, behind the railings. I was looking at the Queen. I don't know how I knew it, but I knew how much she loved him. Her face hadn't a chance of expression, it was a mask, what was left of it and to my mind, there was more left than ever had been there - I mean, in the days of the early Holbeins.

But then, I didn't know her in those days. I only knew her when she sat rigid, her eyes staring.

Her chin, her throat, her brow cut through the water, like the figure-head of a ship. She seemed to cut through something that was going on down there in the throne-room. She was pointing the way. Though the storm-waves were rising, she went on right through them. Scrag was trying to hear what was going on beneath the gallery; I didn't hear anything but the thunder and crash of the breakers that she heard.

I stared and stared at Queen Elizabeth. Essex hadn't moved either. The court-iers were carrying on a desultory sort of conversation, but I knew that they were all thinking about Essex. He wore a leather jerkin and his short hair was brushed back. He stood at ease, you might say, if you didn't know that he had been brought back (for he must have been brought back) by the old-oaks. I imagined him dark with the Spanish sun or the sun of Virginia. Where had he been, I wondered. I was glad now that Scrag had insisted on my coming. He had told me all about it, the insurrection, the plot. But there were contradictory rumours. Scrag said that only one person could have got Essex out of it, and got him out of it by sending him away. He had come back - but the old-oaks must have brought him.

She wasn't there. She was a painted figure-head. She was somewhere else. I had only been here a year. They said she wouldn't have young women to attend her, but we were not young women - the new lot - we were all girls. She had sent the others away before any of us came. Scrag wanted me to find out what the others thought, but they were like me, they had just come, and anyway I knew more than any of them, because of Scrag.

She would creep out at night, in a dark cloak, with the hood over her head and he would put his arms around her, in the orchard. He wouldn't see what we saw, but we loved what we saw: the gaunt face, the hollow cheeks, the fine wisps of white hair that we brushed before tieing on the lace cap.

She was like - she wasn't like anything, she was simply a mask, what was there. It was a mask that would fit Clytemnestra or Hecuba or one of those queens from the stories in the play-books that Scrag borrowed from the players. I clutched the banisters of the musicians' gallery. It was I who was facing breakers. Essex had turned round.

It was as if having bowed to Queen Elizabeth, he had received permission. Per-mission for what? He would, if this were a play, make a speech now, like Henry or like Gaunt. He had something to say but he didn't say it. Nobody talked now. The musicians' gallery swayed and I swayed with it but Scrag was there and the worst I could do was to faint - or rather, the worst I could do was to scream. I don't know what I wanted to scream about, but she loved him.

I saw what he hoped would happen, what didn't, what couldn't happen. His eyes were half-closed as if he were scanning the horizon and he turned his head from right to left, like a shipwrecked mariner looking for a sail. He turned his head slowly as if there were plenty of time, because it was the last time. What couldn't happen, was a sail on the horizon. He didn't wait. He turned round again and bowed to Queen Elizabeth. There was no sound of anything, only the sound of the voice saying, "Your Majesty dismisses me?"

She didn't say anything. He waited. The Queen said,

"We dismiss you."

He bowed again and walked to the door. No-one followed him. The guard was waiting outside.

I had seen him only once, just that one time. I had heard him speak four words. His face was dark as I had thought it would be. Scrag dragged me from the gallery. I don't mean that I had fainted.

It was something else. We were in the green-room. Scrag fastened the door. I saw a dais and a throne, but that was for the players. There were velvet curtains flung down with some drums and trumpets. I looked round the room slowly, turning my head as he did. There was no sail on the horizon.

. . . . .

There was a sail on the horizon but he did not see it. It was part of the old-oaks, it was part of England.

Geoffrey, I mean Scrag, had another name. It is not necessary to record it here. It has already been recorded among the lesser stars of that vast constellation that revolved around William Shakespeare. Geoffrey's "pretty sweeting" may or may not have recognized a familiar presence in the person of Robert Devereux, Earl of Essex. However that may be, Essex was there, the Queen was there, Geoffrey and I were crouching in the musicians' gallery.

The blow that ended three years later, in the Queen's death, had been delivered before I met Geoffrey. But the Queen really died when she said, "We dismiss you." Someone was tapping on the green-room door, calling softly - but we will not confuse things, let us say that he called, "Geoffrey."

Geoffrey was standing by the dais. I was sitting in one of the armchairs. Geoffrey said, "That can only mean one thing. Vere always knows where to find me. Do you mind if I let Vere in?" He unfastened the door. Geoffrey said, "Is there any hurry?"

Vere looked at me, he looked at Geoffrey. "Perhaps we can manage," he said.

"What happened to the old girl?" said Geoffrey.

"She turned to Gascoigne," said Vere. "She said, 'We are waiting - did we not command consultation on the new play?' I didn't know there was a new play, not one, at any rate, that needed commands and consultations."

"I'm coming," said Geoffrey.

. . . . .

I could not think of Robert Devereux as a traitor. Geoffrey and his "pretty sweeting" could not know what we know, nor see what we see. But she saw that Essex in his leather jerkin and his cropped head was out of the picture. To us, he is more than out of the picture, he is out of the period.

We had tried to imagine the reason for his plot, his insurrection. At first, we thought it might have something to do with the still-seething bitterness about Mary Tudor. But Essex as he stood there, seemed to have no affinity with the old Catholic party. He was cast for another part, in another play. His plot was immature. It was only later that this round-head joined forces with Oliver Cromwell.

The trumpet-call of the leader of the Commonwealth had roused a dying nation. This time, an older Essex was there with "the few" to answer it.

But there is still the Queen. He has killed her. She will go on living three more years. Geoffrey and the painted-lady will leave the court soon after her death. We do not see Geoffrey and the painted-lady in their beautiful Warwickshire surroundings. Perhaps happiness is best forgotten. It is the moments of agony that must be resolved, or the riddles of misunderstanding and cruelty that must be solved. Why did Essex strike at the Queen? He had in some way under-estimated her intelligence. It is true she loved him, but she received her death-blow when she realized that he thought she did not see through him. He had swept aside her arguments with his rebellion. That was easily put down, but she had found a rare antagonist and she spared him. The old-oaks did not, however, spare her. For that, she was rewarded.

. . . . .

The painted-lady wondered about the Queen. Well, first there would be the matter of unfastening the hoops, the ruffs, re-sorting the jewels, ear-rings and brooches before her waiting-women left her. Perhaps the lace-cap is already tied under her chin. Her worn velvet gown falls to the floor. She is not over-tall but tall, and her delicate hands are folded on her breast. In the dim glow of the night-light, the eagle, the golden hawk has vanished.

It is an old gown. She smoothes the worn velvet lovingly, as if it were the breast of a bird. She walks to the door and takes down the garden-cloak that is always hanging there. She does not fling it about her as the painted-lady did when she had that last scene with Pericles. She carefully adjusts the folds of the dark cloak and draws the hood over the cobweb of frail lace. Her hands fondle this rough texture as lovingly as they had the velvet. She is a girl again, who never had a girl-hood, a tall girl, overgrown, awkward but with singular distinction.

Of course, he couldn't send anyone to tell her that he wasn't coming. It would be too dangerous. He would make his excuses later, there would be a note in the morning brought her, as usual, by her oldest tiring-woman. He might have been killed - he might have killed someone - for me, for me, for England. He might have been forced to flee England. She was afraid to move. The guard was always waiting somewhere, or patrolling the long walls. She breathed the scent of apple-blossom - for remembrance of the girl who never had a girlhood. The mist rose from the orchard grasses.

It couldn't go on this way. There was no-one she could go to.

He had under-estimated two things, her love and her intelligence.

. . . . .

Shrewdly the gold hawk plotted, not to trap Robert Devereux but so to lay the nets that an appearance of fine skill might be presented. She was shrewd, no-one can get the better of the Queen, the oaks assented, nodding, remembering. They were about to take him - but he got away. She took it very well. She did not blame the old-oaks, nor did she blame them when the Earl of Essex stood before her.

. . . . .

We left the painted-lady alone in the green-room. But she was not alone long.

"Not that this is my place, miss, and I must beg your pardon for intruding. But I heard there was talk of a new play." He stooped and picked up a length of velvet. "Now, lying about this way - things they don't half know the value of. Fine length - and I shouldn't wonder if but what one of the gentlemen brought it back from Italy. 'Better let robes look over the velvets,' says ceremonies, but she says, like what she's always been saying, 'The best goes to the players. Robes can have the leavings.' No wonder robes and ceremonies gets put out. A pretty frock it would make - nice colour - now, what would you call it, miss? Not green like we have here. I'd say it's from one of them cities you get in the plays, Venice or Verona-like. You know more than I do about these things - stuffs, damasks. What would you hazard as a guess, miss, supposing we was to guess and our lives -

"But what really makes me ask is - " he was folding up the velvet " - these drums. Do you think - we're always asking downstairs, would they use the same drums in, say, Mr. Jonson's Athens as in his. There was plenty of argument about that in the kitchen. Cook says, 'One lot of drums for the lot of them; it's only the play-actors and I wouldn't know antique-like Athens if I saw it, and he was only using Mr. Jonson's idea, anyway, what with all that talk.'

"'Mr. Jonson couldn't not have done it,' spoke up second-footman, that is, he happened by at that moment with upstairs orders. 'What he does,' says second, 'is to mix them up on purpose.' Well, miss, that got us all to thinking. What do you think, miss, is it right, as you might say, to have downstairs people mix in? Like what I mean is, the weaver -

"'Started with mixing,' said cook. 'It was none of my affairs,' says I, 'it was the upstairs boys,' - I mean, miss, the young gentlemen what started it. 'What happened wasn't none of my fault, it was ceremonies,' says I. 'What happened?' says our boys. 'Well, let it be a lesson to you,' says I, 'ceremonies gave it to them good and proper.' Cook says, 'A little more ceremonies downstairs wouldn't hurt no-one. Mixing is the trouble.' 'I was only trying to help the young gentlemen put the chairs back,' says I. 'What was the chairs out for?' says our boys. 'It was them asking the Lord High Admiral's players if thus or so was the position,' says I. 'The players is the players,' says cook, 'how would the players be expected to learn from him, the Lord High, I'm meaning, what was them there tac-ticks.' The kitchen boys said, 'Did the Lord High tell them anything what you ain't already told us?' Well, it was that way, miss, how the argument started.

"Argue, argue, argue, they does. Second can't half wait to tell us what they're arguing before he's off upstairs to hear more argument. Some say *him*, for example, cut, like you might say, a length off this velvet, patched it to a bit of - well, the proper hanging curtain, making a seam in the wrong place, showing up the Italian cloth for what it's worth, sleezy - though if you ask me, miss, this will wear as well as our best home-wove. Just run your hand over it - now, the Queen, she's always doing that, have you noticed? Oh, not that others would notice, but she knows fine velvets - so I say - well, I was saying about *him*.

"Some say it was patch-work out of other pieces, what with weaver, joiner and his other pals - weaver's other pals, I mean - working up in their tool-shop a sort of Christmas revel, as you might say, for the Lord High and his lady in Athens. It was no use explaining to pantry, that it didn't make no difference, if or if not they did or didn't have Christmas in Athens, and anyway, it wasn't specified that the revel was for Christmas, it was a sort of celebration for the Lord High and his lady - you remember?

"'And why bring in such argument?' says I to pantry, 'it don't mean a thing.' Pantry says, 'It means a good deal.' 'How do you mean?' says I to pantry. 'It's the way they carried on,' says pantry; 'they called it Midsummer but things only get out-of-hand like, that way, at Christmas. It was a Christmas revel,' says pantry, 'done at Midsummer.'

"Argument? That sort of argument. But does it signify anything? I mean, you know what I mean - it's *Summerdream*, I speak of."

. . . . .

I saw a portrait of her when I was with Geoffrey in Venice. I think it was in the *Ca d'Oro* but in any case the golden house comes back. The portrait was in one of the side rooms, the canvas was dark and cracked. We had been leaning out of the window watching the gondolas and a bell was ringing. There was always a bell ringing. When we turned to go, Geoffrey said,

"Wonder who did that portrait of the old girl - not very good - "

I turned and looked at the picture. My eyes were blinded by the sun and the reflection on the water. The face was familiar, it seemed slightly phosphorescent on that dark canvas.

"Pity it's so cracked," said Geoffrey. "Holbein's paint didn't peel off, but it's not Holbein. We had to get a foreigner. It's true we had the miniatures, but no decent oils of our own at that time. This must have been early - but no - shocking I calls it, sending such a second-rate, third-rate portrait of Her Majesty to the Great Republic."

"It's not her," I said.

"I beg to differ," said Geoffrey. "Does all my midnight oil go for nothing? I'd know her anywhere. Wait till I get out my book. But rotten as this is, it's interesting. It has a place somewhere and I don't think they've got a copy even at the Bodleian."

"Don't be silly, Geoffrey, it's not her."

"There's got to be a curator, or something, somewhere, though they leave you decently alone here, to absorb the atmosphere. What a lad - old Franchetti - giving his life and fortune to restore this place. It's living, it's alive. I'm going to find out about the old girl." He had a way of getting light-headed when it came to a question of a new find for his ambitious Elizabethan compilation. "Coming?" he said.

"I'll wait till you come back," I said. I didn't wait long.

"Damn - " he said. "You know I'll have to put your name on the cover. I wanted to keep you out of it. A woman's place is in the home. Right again - you, I mean - it's only a blinking Medici."

I had felt the story tugging me toward Venice but I had said to myself, one mustn't just imagine things, one must see them. I hadn't actually seen him in Venice when I said the flame of their recriminations shows palaces, arches, arcades. Now I saw, or I began to see. But I have seen so many other things. How assess them? They crowd on one another; inartistically, they push in, out of time, out of sequence and sometimes they are superimposed on one another, like the portrait of Queen Elizabeth that was only a "blinking Medici."

No. Why should they crowd so? They are the people of the play but we should finish one play before we begin another. Caesar Svorzia steps forward. Who are we to stop him?

We will wed the sea, as usual. The Adriatic will look after us. We have been worn down with the eternal come and go of armies, crusaders for the most part.

Saint George stands on a porphyry pillar in the Piazetta to welcome them, and the body of the blessed Saint Mark lies embalmed in the Basilica.

It is a somewhat over-ornate assembly this year, his company, I mean. His delegates, pages and attendants outnumber ours, but our neighbours stand beside us, Verona and the northern provinces, though Milan is conspicuously absent. Who are we to question the Pope's authority and his ambassador?

His Holiness has sent Caesar Svorzia to Venice. His Holiness but not ours, our Republic has its own Patriarch. But these are troubled times. I cling to the stone-ledge of the balcony. We are in the Ducal Palace. The Doge says, "The Patriarch will bless the ships as usual."

The Patriarch is a frail, old man, and he is wearing a worn habit, not the usual embroidered Wedding Garments.

"His Holiness," said Caesar Svorzia, "sends special representative of his own sacred person." But the Doge did not hear him.

Caesar Svorzia's right-hand is still resting on his sword-hilt. The blow may have come from Milan. We did not see who delivered it. But my uncle stepped forward.

I am afraid to look at Bianca. I am afraid to look at the scene before me. I am standing beside Bianca's mother, in the place of honour. I had told Bianca that I could not stand with them on the centre balcony of the Doge's palace because I had - bitter confession for a child of sixteen - nothing to wear. Bianca laughed at me. "You wear Venice," she said. "Pappa said we ought to have come sooner but you know how they talk. The Duke of Padua was with us, and this year mamma has brought chests of linen and her old dowery banners."

Some of the banners were hanging from the balcony we stood on. "I'm half Venetian, anyway," said Bianca, and she dragged me to her mother's apartment in the *Ca d'Oro*. "Mamma," she said, "Bianca - " (we were both Bianca) " - is too proud to stand with us to-morrow."

My dear, dear Aunt Julietta saw that I was crying.

"All that never happened," she said, "it was a bad dream." She meant last winter and the famine and our hospitals being overcrowded, and how at the end *Santa Maria dei Miracoli* finally stopped the plague.

"We had our candles burning for you, night and day," said Aunt Julietta, "and your uncle was only waiting." Bianca made me wear her ceremonial costume and stand next to her mother on the balcony. I didn't know what had happened. Bianca's father had been standing in the background. He was no longer in the background. The friars had placed the Doge on a litter. The crowd opened up before them. The Duke of Verona said,

"We regret there may be a slight delay in the usual procedure. The new Doge must be elected before we wed the Adriatic." The Duke of Verona's company had moved forward. The Duke continued, "The assembly is only waiting until the Doge is placed before the altar in the Basilica. There will be a delay of possibly two hours. My personal bodyguard is waiting at Ravenna. They will escort you through the city. Pisa, Genoa and Padua will attend you further, if need be. But I think you will find the way still open from Ravenna."

We had lost our banners but there was a Lion fluttering on the spear-shaft of the Duke's standard-bearer. It was our Lion. Perhaps it was one of dear Aunt Julietta's dowry banners. They had only just unfurled it. I looked for more Lions, some had been left by the crusaders and a prince called Lion-heart, on the way to the Holy Land. Another banner fluttered, it was as if Saint George had sent the wind from the Adriatic to unfurl it. I had not seen this one before. It was another Lion, but it was a Lion with Lilies.

———————

VIII

Belle Dame

I was not the painted lady on the Kareno fresco above the door of the Cathedral of San Georgio.

But we found St. George again in Venice.

We did not get off the *Sempione* that June day and pay our respects to the poet, whose poems and *Märchen* had previsioned *Lugano Mendrisiotto* to us last winter. We have given up the idea of translating his *Märchen* for we have our own poems and fairy-tales to transcribe.

But it was his butterfly-poem that inspired us. We would find the painted-lady.

That last year in London, we had fantasies and nightmares of underground fortresses and tunnels. But the nightmare tunnels materialized as the *Sempione* (or the Simplon) and the St. Gothard that brought off through, under and around the mountains. We will pay our respects to the poet and ask him about his butterflies when our fairy-tale is finished.

I have found the painted-lady in a second copy of the primer that Garry sent me. The first was called *Schmetterlinge und Nachfalter*, the new book is *Papillons de la Suisse*.

They are the same butterflies but their names are different.

I was right in thinking his thistle-butterfly might be the painted-lady. It is *Vanesse des Chardons* or *La Belle Dame*, in French.

We did not get off the *Sempione* at Melide, that June day. We were recalled to London by another fairy-tale. Moreover, we had just received the letter from Randolph Spencer; we had found another poet to whom we could entrust the first circumference of the little tripod-table that brought the messages from Hallblithe and the young warriors of the Viking ship.

If Lord Howell had abruptly and perhaps ruthlessly dismissed us, it was so that we should be free.

But we are no longer alone. And though we did not get off at Melide - melissa, melitta - we found the beehive and the Queen.

There were other voices on the *Sempione* that brought us back to England. "We thought it best to make 'em think it was our flares. Then we had the bright idea of passing on the good news. Do you know, I don't think there was one out of ten in London in the end that knew the truth about them."

. . . . .

We followed the Z or the bee-line in its zig-zag track or path across time. Time was conveniently pleated and the pleats lay flat under the chart or map that took us from London to Lausanne, to Lugano, to Knossos, to Athens, to Delphi . . . back to London, to Venice. . . . There are to-and-fro journeys and return flights, but this briefly is our path or our zig-zag in space. Time is another matter. But this bee-line or Z-line has this advantage over time, time is neatly folded; the pleats are disproportionate, it is true, but under the Z-map, no-one will notice. It is very easy to understand this, if you like fairy-tales or *Märchen*.

If you do not like fairy-tales, it is not easy to understand. Once upon a time

. . .

There was another voice from London, "Once upon a time, there was a house. Everybody was happy."

We follow our fairy-tale away from and back to London. It was the Viking ship that showed us the way - that is, it was Hallblithe's early Saxon skiff that he built from the oak-trees felled in:

THE GLITTERING PLAIN, WHICH HAS BEEN ALSO CALLED THE LAND OF LIVING MEN OR THE ACRE OF THE UNDYING.

IX

Delphi

"Pretty in the summer, miss, with all those oleanders."

The steward in Athens was reminding the painted-lady that there had been a summer. I had visualised the pilgrimage or so-called path as winding up a mountain, spiral fashion, as I explained in speaking of that sea-shell earlier. But it seems to me that the steward, talking endlessly - she couldn't interrupt him - was recalling (and with his apple-blossoms) another path, or if I may return to my own idea about the messages from the RAF, another graph on a map.

The spiritual map would contain various layers of experience, different lives, if you will or manifestations of the same life. But as I have said, it was accordion-pleated - it was pleated anyway, yet laid flat.

It had gone on in other countries, in other periods of history. It was like those sliced-animals of our childhood. You might get the wings of an eagle, the head of a lion and the claws of a dragon. But that is heraldry. So our pictures sometimes seem to be made up of unrelated segments, yet they spell something. They are the clue to the final answer. They are, among the million paving-stones of the labyrinth, the ones with the little cross marked on them.

The cross is the plus sign, Knossos plus Athens plus London, or Athens plus Venice plus London again. There is negation, despair, disillusion running through it. But we have had enough of negation and discouragement, of horror, fear, sickness and wasted cities.

Our spiritual map is pleated but it is spread out flat on the table. Pericles thumps the table:

"You do not need *parchment* for messages," he says.

The painted-lady in Athens tried to interrupt the meanderings of the old steward. But she couldn't stop him. He just went on talking. Ray said it was only in the end the voice that mattered, but the voice may manifest in various fashions. It was the pronouncements of the Elizabethan old-oak that led me to Verona and to Venice. It answered the question that I didn't dare ask, as I sat there in the green-room, after Geoffrey left me. Where is Essex? Will they wait? Will they take him to the tower? Has it already happened?

But Essex walked out of the palace into Saint Mark's Square. The map was pieced or seamed there, with the Italian velvet and what the steward called "the proper hanging curtain." But the map was folded over and the years were the flat pleats under it. We hear about a bee-line, but a bee, though he may fly straight, makes a zig-zag or a Z line, from flower to flower.

. . . . .

"You do not need *parchment* for messages." Why did she interrupt him?

"It's this D for Delphi," he said. He had the itinerary mapped out, details, separate directions for each station. He thought she'd better take the passport with her. He said, "The stations have a full description of you and your past activities." He was overwrought, he knew, he spoke quickly. "It would be unsuitable for you to remain in Athens. I learned from our friend Pheidias - " He was about to tell her that with all his care there had been fresh infiltration - they called it Medizing in the old days. He wanted to warn her. He supposed he should have brought up the matter sooner. He had mentioned the College because of her work there, her life might be in danger.

"Even children can be useful," he had said. He did not want to speak of these last degrading revelations, but the same thing might happen in Delphi. He had said that he wanted to find out what the Sacred College taught her - in order to check up, if possible at this late date, and to ask her if she would warn the prefects. He said he had known the College sent her, he took for granted that she knew what he meant.

The young Samothracian had made a full report to the council. She was not technically an agent. He thought she knew, they knew that.

But suddenly she stared at him and said, "The College did not send me," as if he had made an accusation. Perhaps they had put her through some frightening oath of secrecy. He turned it off with their time-worn joke about holding up a pillar, lest she imagine that she had given away instructions or the fact that she had had instructions.

"Even in Delphi, we have our - voices," he had said. He meant that the warden of the Athenian treasure-house had spoken well of her. He had spoken of her friends, perhaps abruptly. He thought she would be happy to see - Myra, he thought they called her. Perhaps he had been short-sighted, she should have had some of her old friends near her here in Athens. But he had wanted to break her with her past association with the Oracle.

He spoke of her violets - those violets she placed before the little statue of Athené that he had given her. It stood on the shelf, there. He did not like to remember the little stories she had told him, she must have been lonely sometimes. Viola, Iris - he said, "Such pretty names you girls have." She had stopped talking about Viola some time ago, but his steward had found out where the girl had gone and he had wanted to tell her of it. He had entered Iris on the same passport. He had thought she should have someone with her. He was about to explain. But now he didn't know her. He wanted to tell her that his steward had arranged for Iris to go with her. She should have had a maid or a companion, here in the golden house, but she seemed to prefer being alone.

He spread the passport on the table. "Shall I read it to you?" he said, but she answered with mock courtesy:

"You speak beautifully."

He was going to explain the passport or the dossier, but she said she would not leave Athens.

He supposed the Sacred College had frightened her, for she went on about Athens, "There are few ghosts - few emanations." He had thought from the beginning - she was so strange - that even as a child they had used her as a mouthpiece for the oracle.

But he had not referred to that when he spoke of children: "Even children can be useful." It was then that she broke across with her talk of desecration and "Have you gone mad?" It was she who had gone mad at the mere thought of what the priests had done to her. He was sure that she had begun earlier than the age reported to him by the warden of the treasure-house. The warden had had the assurance of the High Priest that the girl was independent and could choose for herself. But his friend, the warden had expressed his own opinion; she had been one of the "voices" of the Oracle.

The treasurer was, like himself, an orthodox believer and upholder of the State religion. But the treasurer's wife had told him that the girl wanted to take part in the sacred drama but they would not let her - that is, she stood about - "They had groomed you to perfection," he had said, he didn't know why he said it.

He knew the priests were afraid they would lose her; if she had her own way, she would become too deeply interested in the drama and lose - touch - lose - He should have had this out with her, in the beginning, but he had wanted to spare her, he had wanted her to be happy - he believed she had been. There would no longer be any danger on that score, from the Oracle. But there were other dangers. What had happened to her there? He had often wondered.

Those winters - but he sat back in his chair and let her go on talking about the snow.

She spoke of ghosts, of there being no ghosts in Athens.

She spoke of necromancy and said, "Somebody has bewitched you."

She was still singularly naive about some matters.

But she wanted to stay in Athens.

She went on about that first meeting. He had not forgotten. He had wondered what her name was. When he first saw her, she was standing by the altar. She held the golden bowl, till the priest took it from her. He had waited for her to speak but she had said nothing on the stage.

She had just said, "I did not have much to say in Delphi." He had heard a different story from the treasurer. She had had a great deal to say, but it was behind locked doors.

The warden of the treasure-house, before obtaining access to the Voice, had given the usual pledge of secrecy. But he violated no law of human decency when he confided to Pericles the history of the girl who gave the message to him. Pericles remembered how she stood afterwards, in the dressing-room. She didn't speak then, either. It was the young wine-god who said,

"This is Day-star."

He had been curious to know what went on behind the locked doors of the greater arcana. There were the lesser oracles; like everyone else, he had made his pilgrimages and been given the usual cryptic messages. But it was left to the warden of the Athenian treasure-house at Delphi to put the questions to the Inner Voice, that is, the state-questions that had to do with ceremonial or new undertakings. It would have been considered a breach of etiquette if the warden had not officially, at least, received sanction from the Oracle and the blessing that went with it.

We had trusted the wooden walls and we went on trusting them - with reservations.

"What is the fate of the treasure-house of Athens?" the warden had put the first courteously official question.

"The treasure-house of Athens - is the world worthy?" the girl or the Voice had answered.

She may have been prompted by the priests. But he had curbed his curiosity. He had had occasion enough to question her and he was by nature curious, especially as to what went on in the inner sanctum.

But she was railing at him, explaining the obvious gesture of the young Samothracian when he first appeared as Prologue. And why the tirade about witch-doctors, fortune-tellers and magicians?

No doubt she had been attached to the young Samothracian, but he had official duties in the islands. And while she was still held in reserve by the priests for the utterances of the Voice, they would see to it that she remained - unattached. She was no longer unattached, so he knew that she had lost her old prestige as seer or prophetess.

Theoretically, he knew the Sacred College. But they must have frightened her. She seemed to be putting up a sort of defence, going on about a gesture that the herald had not made.

"We dared not applaud your coming openly," she said. It was not only the priests that she was afraid of. "She is afraid," he thought, "of Pericles."

She walked to the door.

. . . . .

We had wondered about Delphi. But it was not our question, it was Pericles' question, "What had happened to her there?" that gave the answer to us.

. . . . .

They called her Ida and she had told me that Ida was a mountain, but of course I knew that.

The mountain sent the dolphins. The dolphins brought them from Crete. The dolphins danced round the ship. We had our dolphin-dance. We were the dolphins. The ship was set up on the altar. I said,

"Ida, you will never finish." It was a big picture. It was blue. It was the same ship.

The dolphins were dancing in the water. We did not dance like those dolphins, we just went round the altar in a circle.

I said, "Ida, why do you spin the picture? Take me to the mountain."

"It's too hot," said Ida.

"Look," I said, "you haven't got the things right."

"What things?" said Ida.

I said, "*It comes along the side in a curve, then the other side. It's blue.*"

"It does come round," said Ida, "it is blue." I looked and looked at the picture.

"Maybe it's all right," I said, "I'll help you finish."

"Come," she said, "kittens only tangle the threads."

"What shall I do, Ida? Come to the mountain."

"I tell you, it's too hot."

"It's not hot," I said, "you don't know anything."

"Well, tell me," she said.

"It's cold, the snow is falling."

But I didn't like her spinning at the picture.

"Why must you spin the picture?"

"I'm not spinning," said Ida.

I told them about the mountain. I was older. There were marks on the stones.

I told them about the snow, but I was older.

I told them there was gold that you could see through, there were bowls made of sunlight.

They asked me about the sunlight.

I couldn't explain it, but I saw it.

The clear ice didn't melt though you held it in your hands and it was smooth and hard like ice, but it wasn't cold. It didn't melt when you held it in your hands and they poured wine into the ice-chalices and they emptied the bowls or cups or chalices. And the ice didn't melt.

The first time I stood by the altar they asked me about Athens.

"The honey-comb is full - why are the people hungry?" was the answer. You made up the answer by asking another question.

They would keep me for the altar.

I didn't always answer properly, at least it didn't always sound right. But I answered.

"When the wave breaks the wall - will the sea vanish?" But the sea couldn't vanish, but that was one of the questions that gave the answer that they asked for.

If you think too much about the answer, you cannot ask the question - the question, that is, that answers their question.

One could only give the question. They had to answer or to work out the question-answer themselves.

"Two eagles claim Parnassus - whose nest is empty?"

"Two ships become one ship - which mariner has lost his?"

"A flight of bees, a swarm of gulls - is flight swarm?"

That was all very simple. I felt that anyone could do it. But Ida, who was much older, said they couldn't. I must not talk about it, except to Ida.

Ida had taken me to see them. I had been living with the children but they asked me if I would like to move to the temple-precinct and live in the House with Ida. I didn't say anything, I just looked at Ida.

Then I said, "If Ida wants me." She knelt down and put her arms around me. She was crying.

Ida talked too, but I didn't hear her talk about those things. She talked to different people. She asked me to help with the ship-picture. It was almost finished.

. . . . .

They told me not to tell them any more about it, but I knew they wanted to know what had happened, so that it need never happen again.

"There was a wall of fire. I didn't run back into the fire. I should have stayed with them. I stayed with them. It was an earthquake. It cracked the temples. The temples and the palaces fell down. I ran away. I had my spring-chosen basket. I did not run away."

They said it must have happened two times. I told them more and more about it, then they said,

"Don't look at any more pictures," but I knew they wanted to know about it, so that it could never happen again.

I said, "But there were more earthquakes."

They said, "It is better to talk about the snow-flowers."

"They were small flowers," I said, "sometimes you can see them here, if a single snow-flake falls on a black stone. But they put the ice together. I don't understand. If you look through thin ice, you will see what I mean." But they had tried looking through thin ice and no matter how clear it was they said they couldn't see the things that I told them we saw, how different flakes of snow made different flowers and stars, behind the two or three layers of thin ice, placed over one another on a narrow wood-frame.

"They told us that the snow-flakes were the same but different, so we were all the same but different. That is why we went up on the mountain, it was to celebrate our sameness and our difference. It was the mountain of Zeus, of God," but they knew that.

"You melted, you went back to the mountain. The Cloud took you and the others and you were God. The snow fell, you danced on the mountain. We danced on the mountain in the snow and were God.

"There were no children any more," I did not know how to say it, "they walked but they walked with sticks." I tried to show them.

They said, "Stop - you must not think about it," but I could not forget. Perhaps if I thought about it long enough, the children would change to snow and go back to the mountain.

I didn't expect them to believe me. I didn't believe it myself but I saw the pictures.

They told me that I would die if I thought any more about the pictures. I must do something else and come back later, to the altar. Ida was still with them. She begged me not to think any more about the pictures.

Ida said, "They want you to forget the pictures. There is a golden house. There is a flowering olive - this means, that they want you to help with the Sacred Office and the Drama."

She brought Myra in to see me.

"You must get well," said Myra.

They wouldn't let me talk, they were afraid it would make me too tired. But they wanted me to stay - or *play*, as they said, with Myra and the others.

I didn't feel that I was doing anything. I wanted to help more.

I loved Myra, I loved the funny boy they called Scrag. I loved the tall boy from the islands, they called Ray.

I was older.

I almost forgot the pictures.

. . . . .

I forgot the pictures.

"It's not Ariadne," said Scrag, "it's only Day-star."

_____

X

Rome

Rome - I can hardly bring myself to write it. Why must I think about it? It is foreign and unfamiliar. The new streets cut undeviating, straight lines like his famous roads. The marble for the new buildings is hewn and polished, it reflects the light, it does not absorb it like the old temple above the villa. My temple, as I called it, is too far away to disturb anybody, it is too unimportant to destroy.

I had recently asked the wood-cutters up there, to clear the tangle of bush and trees about it, and I started up through the woods yesterday, to see what they were doing.

It was my dream - the temple as it must originally have been, as Verus wanted it to be. But I will never go there again.

It hurts my eyes to think of Rome, that glare from the new-hewn marble - or it hurts something in the back of my head. He gave up expecting me to be interested in his maps and plans and drawings. Rome had drained the resources of the country, taken our farmers from the fields, uprooted the old tradition. I am no patriot but I love the fields - our vineyards. But there was better wine to be imported. My grandfather always said that the best wine could not be imported. I could have wished to be alone. I was happy. But it was March. I must see him again.

I do not mean that I was happy as I had been, but I was happy in another way. And you must not think I was given to these fancies. It is something that had happened only three times in my whole life - that is, counting this time. It happened before Verus was killed. I did not blame Julius for that. It was as always, a brilliant strategical campaign that led them into what he afterwards called Helvetia. That was the first time.

The second time was the same - I mean, there were the same white lilies, along the path of paved stone. I did not see the lilies but I knew they were there because of the mist over my eyes and the sudden fragrance. I ran back to the villa.

They had been clearing the moss from these paving stones the last time I saw Verus and Ver together.

Perhaps going up there yesterday, simply reminded me of the two other times - but there was no mistaking the summer-scent of lilies.

It had been the same with the second Verus - I mean, Julius had taken him too.

Of course, Julius loved Verus. He did not talk about him but when he came to the villa, it seemed as if Verus were there with us. I thought if I lost Julius, I would lose Verus again. This was the third time - I mean, yesterday, the stab of pain in the back of my head, the mist or film over my eyes, and the unmistakable summer-scent of lilies.

The sudden storm unnerved me. I was almost glad he wasn't coming. But he did come.

"What have you been doing, Stella?" he said, as if we had parted yesterday.

I said, "I have been waiting for you."

He said, "You sent for me."

I said, "I wanted to talk to you, but really talk to you. I want you to stay here three days."

"But you never talk," he said; "in the whole time I have known you, your talking, taken all in all, wouldn't fill three days."

"I am making up for lost time. I have so much to tell you, to ask you - you can talk, too."

"You don't like the things I talk about," he said.

"I don't like these rumours. I'm so out of touch. I want to hear what you are doing. I never go to Rome now, there's so much to do, here in the villa."

"You have your - "

"Nina is getting very old - she is full of gossip. She still goes to the market, and you know Rome is really not far when it comes to rumours. I can't stop her talking. There should be some sort of - faith for these people."

"They have their festivals, our priests have seen to that. The Capital arranges special feast-days for them."

"I don't mean Capitoline Jupiter," I said.

"The Saturnalia?" he questioned with that thin smile that had finally estranged us. "But forgive me," he went on, "you wanted to ask (I gathered from your letter) a special favour of me."

I had loved Julius. He need not have come. I knew that recently there had been riots in the Forum.

"Did they see to your Vulcan, that famous charger? Is it the same one?" He did not answer. "Nina is getting your wine. Are you cold? Are you wet? Are you tired? Are you hungry?" What questions to ask Julius Caesar.

But I had to go on talking. "The place is haunted," I said, "but I love it. It would be all right if they didn't interpret everything, in that morbid way they have. An oak-limb snaps off - death and destruction - and, of course, in these days, someone of importance is sure to die sooner or later. Then the orgy of delight, the 'I told you, Madame, when that toad croaked, out of season.' We have no toads here but no logic will appease them. The worst is, this is my house, my home. 'No-one stays in the country in the winter,' they say. They want to get me out of the place, to sprawl on the divans, to build up the fires, to revel in the larder - not that there's much there to revel in." Why was I saying these things? "You find me harsh, Julius."

I knew he was wondering why I had sent for him.

"May I ask you a question, Julius? Why did you come?"

"You sent for me," he said.

"I am no dictator," I said bitterly, "you did not have to come when I sent for you. Why did you come, Julius?"

Nina had set the tray on the table and had gone out again. She had thrown fresh logs on the fire.

"This is like old times," said Julius.

"No - later - " I pushed away the wine-cup, "but fill yours - you haven't answered."

He drew up his chair. He poured wine from the flagon.

"Drink that," he said, "and I will tell you."

I emptied the goblet slowly. I put it back on the table.

"Tell me," I said.

"We were frank at one time, in the old days," said Julius.

"Too frank," I said.

"I will tell you why I came; you are no cat-and-mouse woman or no mouse-and-cat woman - do you see what I mean?"

"Only too well, Julius."

"Well, virtue - you know what I think of virtue?"

"We have different definitions for the same words. Need we define virtue all over again?"

"Well, there are virtues and virtues - and there is virtue. Is that any nearer?"

"It's near enough," I said. "Is there such a thing as a cat-and-mouse man? There is, Julius."

"But if a cat-and-mouse man meets a mouse-and-cat woman - "

"Stop, Julius - "

"Ah - I feel better. There is still the old flint and stone - still the old spark between us. So my journey has not been in vain - and I needed some fresh air and so did Calliope. Vulcan joined the chargers of Hector and Diomedes - well - time flies - don't let us think of Vulcan and the years that have passed since our last little quarrel."

"I am glad our Trevi still provokes your eloquence," I snapped at him. "I presume you left your young men at the tavern. Why didn't you bring them with you? But don't answer, Julius. Why did you make me angry? I wanted to tell you something."

"Well, tell me," he said, "what is it you want to tell me?"

"It's these old farms, these almost forsaken villas - " but that wasn't really what I had meant to say. It had suddenly occurred to me when - if Julius left - well, I would really be alone then.

"You will be leaving Rome again?"

"Not just yet," he said.

"Well, I was just thinking, the eagles cannot really be defeated." He looked at me with that wry smile. "I think - I'm not sure - that I mean it, this time," I said. That was one of our old arguments; it was, as he had said, like old times to talk about the eagles.

"I'm serious this time. Suppose you do go away on one of your little - forays, as you used to call them. Suppose - it seems odd and you will forgive my saying it."

I stood up. "For luck, Julius, as we used to say, I will bow, as grandfather used to do, to our old household Penates." I crossed the room and returned with one of the images. "It can't happen if I hold old Faunus, as Verus used to call this one. I don't know who he is, he is so old, and Ver thought when he was tiny, that this was his own great-grandpappa. Perhaps he is - the house was my grandfather's, but you know that. But I will put Faunus back on the shelf, he will look after us. I can say it now, Julius. Suppose you go away and do not come back."

"There are other - to use your own word - dictators," he answered.

It was as he had said, like old times. There was no hurry. Vulcan would be waiting in the morning.

"Perhaps," I said, "I wanted to be a dictator myself. Perhaps I really wanted to dictate to you when I told you, that last time, *my* ideas of how the Capitol should be run. Perhaps these people may evolve slowly. I don't know. You remember you had just cleared out the worst quarter of the city. Trevi - our lovely Trevi changed overnight. They had to go somewhere - but why Trevi? But we had quarrelled and I saw these people. I tried to help. I took some of them in the garden and the villa, and after I had worked for years to reclaim grandpappa's beloved Trevi, there was a new - foray. The boys I had trained went in a body to Rome, and the girls - well, Julius, I have had a long time to think about it. Perhaps the sun and the vineyards - we still had the old vineyards - worked some of the old Faunus magic on them. Perhaps they were happy, as they never had been happy. But my lovely Trevi is still a sort of country-slum. So you see, my talk about *my* plans for the people came to nothing. I mean, you were right to clear out that evil quarter. But when I saw them - "

"You must let me send - "

"No, no, no - you cannot send them away now. I do not want a park, a sort of relic, a family monument to be made of Trevi. Julius, it is too late. There are too many people. Something has to be done with all these people. And I was younger and I loved you and those roads and charts and maps took you away from me. *Vae Victis.* I thought of the conquered peoples, but there were so many of them and after you left I began to imagine horrible, horrible things, primitive, unutterable - I had mad fantasies. Oh, Julius, I am not the goddess of Justice, I am not Astraea who holds the balance. I may have thought I was, once. But I had time to review my whole life, after you left. And now I want to know more, to learn more. Only stay this once, and tell me what I can best do to help - Rome."

I went on, "You may say that Rome does not need my help. But it needs your help, Julius. There is so much to be done."

. . . . .

"Listen - must you be going?" He sat down again. He refilled his cup. The room was growing darker. "I have said the house is haunted but I love it. I did not really ask you here, however, to talk about Trevi and the villa. Villa Trevi is full of ghosts but this isn't a matter of the knockings and rappings that I heard last winter. I had perhaps foolishly tried to help them in the village. Well, you know how last winter's fever took people. I wanted to die then. If you go, there is no one to stand between me and the new exodus from the city.

"I blamed you at first, with your aqueducts, your new Forum and your fountains. Not that I don't love fountains - what am I saying?

"I am humiliated. I am afraid of all these people. I thought I loved them, but I don't love them. I am afraid of them. And yesterday I started up through the oak-wood at the back of the house. You remember how you used to laugh at Ver and his 'paved way' as you called it. But he would drag you out of the garden and make you help him with the paving-stones. Was it only Ver who held you? You came often, then you took Ver. That is why I asked you to come back. It was winter, the first time, and oh, the woods were lovely. Verus and Ver had cleared the brush and undergrowth from along the 'paved way.' The square stones were covered with snow. I was so happy. I thought of you safe, resting during the winter months. But not Caesar. When I reached the last turn of the path, there was a stab at the back of my head, *in* my head. I thought at first an icicle might have broken off or a dead branch. I drew back my hand, I expected to see blood. Then I went blind. There was the summer-scent of lilies and I staggered and slipped down through the snow, back to Villa Trevi. That was the first time.

"Just before Ver went, it happened again. That was the second time.

"Yesterday, I went up through the woods. The stones had almost disappeared again under the dead leaves. I never went there after - the second time. But I had asked the wood-cutters to clear the copse around the temple. I wanted to begin all over again. Ver - I had not forgotten Verus - but Ver - my spring had been taken from me.

"I stooped to brush the wet leaves from one of the stones, but I stood up quickly.

"I was afraid I would faint.

"It was the same sudden stab at the back of my head, the same mist and darkness - the same summer-scent of lilies.

"That was the third time."

. . . . .

"You are restless, what are you thinking?" I said. He had been pacing up and down before the hearth, but now he turned and began walking the length of the room. I turned in my chair, I waited for him to come back.

He said, "There are agitators in the city. There always have been, it is true, but these are different. They have hired an old ruffian to wait on street-corners, where they know I am likely to be passing. The sort of person you wouldn't notice, difficult to identify, and anyway - this is a new one."

He seemed to be unaware that if he turned, I could not hear him. But he stopped talking. He came back.

"A new what?" I asked him.

He said, "A new slogan - you know what I mean."

I didn't know what he meant.

"What is this - slogan, as you call it?"

Julius said, "Beware the Ides of March."

"I don't understand, Julius."

"But it is what you have just said. You asked me to wait here three days, that is two more days. That, if the old calendar does not lie as usual, means that you ask me to treat Villa Trevi as a sort of funk-hole or hide-away.

"In two more days, the Ides will be over - by the old calendar. But we must have a new one. I have been working at it now, so many years. It was begun long before Vulcan joined the horses of Diomedes.

"The Ides are already over, by our new computation. So if the soothsayers and their stars have anything to do with it, they are wrong as usual. But there are other stars and there is the comet, as they call it. They say its course is egg-shaped, not a circle like the planets. The Greeks - by way of the Egyptians, I suppose - have already reckoned backward as well as forward. The comet has been here before, it will come again, they say." He stood now before the fireplace.

"I don't understand, Julius."

"The astronomers, I do not mean the soothsayers, have mapped a chart of this star, as I have told you. They say it predicts - calamity."

"You mean last summer - the winged Centaur?"

"Who calls it the winged Centaur?"

"I don't remember, Julius. But it had wings, didn't it? I watched it from the garden. You should have been with me to explain it. Sometimes it looked like a great swarm of bees above the summer-lilies."

"So you watched the comet?" said Julius. He sat down.

Now I was restless. I rearranged the things on the table.

"There is always bread and cheese," I said, "and I'll get Nina to fetch you some more Trevi. About your young men? Shall I tell Nina to send one of the boys to tell them that you are, or that you are not coming? Did they take Vulcan with them?" Julius didn't answer. He was looking into the fire. I took up the riding-cloak he had flung down when he came in. It was heavy. "Perhaps Nina better dry this in the kitchen - but - " I wondered suddenly. "But wasn't it - well - dangerous with all this trouble - your coming here this way, I mean? Surely Nina recognized you?" Still he sat there, looking at the fire, he didn't answer. I felt along the collar of the heavy cloak, then dragged it to the fire.

"It doesn't need drying," he said. But I was thinking now of something else. "What is the matter with my old campaigner?" he asked. "Has the moth found it, at last? It's been too tough even for moths, so far - and it still has occasional out-ings. I take it with Calliope for fresh air - well, of late, it's true, I haven't been out so often." I sat down on the low stool where Ver used to sit and roast chestnuts.

I had seen Julius fairly often, at one time, but I had never seen him without the eagles. We had quarrelled about the eagles, but it was the first time - the fire blurred - that I had ever seen him wearing no insignia of office. "Where are the eagles, Julius?" I said.

"What do you mean - eagles?"

"I mean, you always wore them - there were always the spread wings some-where."

"You asked me three - no, four direct questions and one, at least, indirect one. Yes, I would like some bread and cheese and some more wine, is the answer to the indirect question. About my young men, as you call them, I presume they are in Rome somewhere. I am not coming or I am not going, for the moment - but to the young men, that can be of small moment; they are not in the village tavern, making free of your excellent vino Trevi, as you seem to have imagined. You asked me why I did not bring them to the villa. I did not bring them because they were not there to bring. But that is the answer to another question. To return to the four in question. This is your third: did they take Vulcan with them?"

I looked at Julius.

"But to leave Vulcan. As to the fourth question, Nina of course knew me. But Nina, though she may be getting old and tiresome, is still Nina. I knew her in the old days. Have I answered all your questions?"

I did not answer Julius.

. . . . .

"Now may I ask you a question?" he said. "Would you have me skulk here for two days, while the gangsters take the Capitol? The Ides of March - they have worked it all out. The people are ready and waiting for a demonstration. I would like to stay here to-night. I will go early in the morning and I will come back toward evening. I will need some fresh air, by that time. I am very hungry. No - don't move. I'll just look in on Nina and say good-night to Calliope." He went out.

Nina came in soon after.

"I'll leave your room-fleeces on the couch here, as usual," she said, "Madame. It's nice his coming in that way, friendly in the kitchen. I won't be a minute." She had brought in a covered bowl and platters. She pushed the small round table to one side and drew up the larger square one. "Looks like the sky's clearing," she said, "and what with him in the kitchen, I could see Master Ver like what it was yesterday. 'Nina, Nina, what are you doing, Nina?' 'Peaches,' I said. 'Oh, peaches,' says Master Ver. 'Nina,' he looks so solemn-like, like he did look, 'would you say a peach now or a abri-cote was the better?' 'Depend on how you look at it,' I says. 'Now, would you say, Master Ver, a honey-plum or a red-pear was the better?' 'The honey-plum,' he says. So I says, 'I'll take the red-pear.' Games like guessing how many peases in a pea-pod and me having to for-fit of course, for it was like what you might call cupboard-love and lads has no cupboards, I'd say. 'Now suppose,' I'd say, 'just for once I was to guess right, or as you might say, righter than your guess, what, Master Ver, could I claim, as it was, for for-fit?' 'I could get you some grapes,' he says. 'They ain't fit yet for the hornets and what hornets pass by ain't, by my grandmother's reckoning, fit yet for proper eating - for conserve, it is, of course, different - now take quinces - ' So as I was saying to Master Ver, 'If I guess righter than your guess, you have nothing to give me what I couldn't get for myself in the garden.' But, of course, he had the answer. I expect he tried the same trick on you, more times than you care to remember, Madame. 'What would you give, Master Ver, as for-fit,' I said, 'supposing I guessed the better?' Well, he was solemn when he says it. 'I would give,' he says, 'Nina, myself.'"

He had given himself. I left Nina spreading Julius' cape out, before the fire. She had left the door of my room open. She must have come in from the garden, for the candle-flames blew sideways in the draught. I opened the garden-door and shut it again. The old wood was warped. These things had been neglected. Ver knew every crack, every knot in the old boards, every tile on the roof, every flag-stone in the garden. I bolted the door so that it fitted into the frame, but there was still an eddy of wind round my feet. I crossed the room again and shut the inner door. The candles straightened.

There was rattling and banging but it was clear-sky wind, as Ver used to call it. Yes, those tappings and knockings that had obsessed me last winter were caused by the shrinkage in the boards, the warp and woof, as Nina called it - or by loose tiles slipping. And the billowing of the curtains - I had seen or felt the ghosts behind the curtains. Even in the old days, there had been draughts everywhere, but last winter, the wind was different, everything was different. It took people that way, Nina said, last winter's fever. But it was I, not they who were different. It was one of my first long walks yesterday, the summer-scent of lilies was a matter of association with that wood-path. There was even the same drift of wet leaves on the 'paved way' that there had been. It was association with the second time (and the first time) and I had been ill and I felt faint - then, when the faintness blinded me, I thought of Ver and of the last time that I had taken that path through the oak-wood. The first time, there was snow on the ground, the second time, the leaves were sodden with February. I should have talked of Ver to Nina. Julius had brought Ver back.

Julius had taken Ver - that was our last quarrel.

Was that the reason that Julius wore no wings? The usual eagles on his tunic would have been hidden in any case, under his old campaigner, as he called the rough cape, and Nina, as he said, of course knew him. The eagles? "I hope never to see you again," I had shouted that last time, I was beside myself with agony, "with those hateful eagles." Ver belonged to Trevi and Trevi belonged to Ver. There was no use arguing with Julius. No-one could run Trevi, but Ver.

There was a host dependent on us. Ver was up at dawn, visiting neighbouring farmers, exchanging stock, comparing corn and barley, working with the harvesters, walking miles and miles between the vine-poles, so that he could get to know each one of the gatherers. 'Ah, you were with us last year,' or 'Don't forget Trevi, next September.' It wasn't just a descent of gypsies on the Villa Trevi. Ver wanted to know all of them.

When I remonstrated and said that we expected Lydia or Marius or one of our neighbours for the afternoon, he would say, "They will know where to find me."

And when I said, "Ver, this is ridiculous, you must not forget your manners," he would say, "You never told me, madre-mia, that great-grandpappa had bad manners." He was sixteen then. It was his last September.

But the eagles! I remembered how Julius had explained to Ver that he always wore an eagle on his tunic.

Verus had said, "Your uncle Julius' other name, in case you don't know it,

Verus, is pomp-and-circumstance. But he really is, although you might not guess it, human. If our uncle Julius should ever appear without an eagle - well - but that couldn't happen."

It had happened.

. . . . .

"What would happen if Uncle Julius came without an eagle?" said Ver.

"Well," Verus said, "I don't know. It's one of those contingencies that could not possibly arise, it's one of those questions for which there is no answer. You might say that Uncle Julius was Achilles, and as long as he wears an eagle, he has no heel." Poor Ver. He came to me, as he always did when Verus teased him.

"Mia," he said, "you tell me."

"It's this way, Ver," I said, "at least, I think it's this way. We have old Faunus standing in the corner, and great-grandpappa used to bow to him - for luck, he said. It was partly serious, partly a joke - "

"Like Faunus," said Ver.

"Yes," I said, "exactly like Faunus, he is always smiling but he seems a serious old person with that beard."

"But ours is our Faunus and Aunt Lydia has a different person in the garden. But there are lots of the same eagle."

"If you ask your uncle Julius nicely, Ver, perhaps he will tell you. I don't know the whole story but at the Rubicon - well, ask him."

"You tell me, Mia."

Poor Ver, he evidently thought that he couldn't tackle both of them single-handed.

"I don't know, darling. I should think it was this way. I should think myself, that it's one special eagle that perhaps uncle Julius wears under his coat, that is his - "

"Mascot," said Julius.

"Thank you, Julius."

"What's mascot?" said Ver.

"I told you," said Verus, "it's what Achilles - "

"Don't tease," I said.

"Uncle Julius," said Ver, "do you wear your special eagle under your coat?"

"No, Verus," said Julius, "that would break the charm. It's this one."

Ver left me. "But that eagle is not like the other."

"I told you," said Verus, "Uncle Julius is but human. That old eagle is by far the least impressive of his decorations - but it is the first one - but don't ask him. It's a long story. But uncle Julius crossed the Rubicon. I came, I saw, I conquered, said uncle Julius. Well, have we answered your question, Verus?"

Yes, Julius had brought back Ver. He had brought back Verus.

I looked for my house-coat, but Nina had spread out one of my old dresses on the bed.

. . . . .

She had left the chest open. I had been too busy with the garden-door to notice. It was one of my dower-chests. I hadn't opened it for years, it usually stood against the wall with the fleeces piled on it. Nina had pulled the box out a few feet and now I saw what had happened to the room, I mean, I realised that there was a new pulse or atmosphere - it was, of course, the fragrance of pressed rosemary. I had thought that the key to that chest was lost, but Nina must have had it. I lifted the dress from the bed and shook out the folds, a few leaves fluttered to the floor, but they were dried leaves, not mere dust and powder. Nina must have renewed the rosemary, fairly recently. She must have gone over my things, from time to time. How often?

I pressed the folds against my heart but I could not wear - this.

Did she even remember the last time I wore it?

I was glad I had closed the door. Julius had come back. He and Nina were no doubt discussing - what would they not be discussing? The voices went on while I stared at myself between the candles, in the silver mirror.

It was all a mistake. The room was full of fragrance. This was the summer-scent of lilies. I had thought that Nina and the others wanted the place to themselves, but they must have felt that I was lonely when they urged me to leave the villa in the winter. I might have stayed with Lydia. I might have opened the town-house again. I remembered friends I had forgotten. I had neglected all my old friends. It was all my own fault.

We had been happy, too, those winters. This mirror was from my room there. There had been music, candles; but I had, to use Julius' word, skulked at the Villa Trevi.

I would ask Lydia to come over. We would plan getting things in order again, and Marius would help me - they would all help me.

Next winter, I would go back to Rome. I would wear things like this and silver sandals. It was all a mistake. I folded the dress. I buried my face in it. I laid it back in the dower-chest. I was shivering. Nina would understand. It was too cold to wear it.

. . . . .

"Nina wanted me to dress for the occasion," I said, "but it's cold, so I just got into my house-coat. I see Nina has taken your cape. I heard you talking in here. I suppose, Nina had a lot to tell you. Poor Nina - I was rather a beast about her. I should really have wintered in Rome, and they were very patient with me, when I was so ill. I think I was delirious - and I hadn't been out much. I mean, yesterday in the oak-wood. Nina had spread out some of my old things on the bed and she left the chest open, and just now while I was changing, I realized the fragrance from my clothes-chest could have been translated into lily-fragrance. I mean, my room was full of fragrance but it was easy enough to explain - the summer-scent of lilies is something like bay and orris. Or even the cedar-lining of the chest might have been responsible, or those three together, and perhaps association. Anyhow, I was reminded of the garden - lilies - well, it might have been the cedar and the orris, the summer-scent of lilies. Please - please begin, Julius. Please begin without me. Well, I'll sit down - I'm light-headed, Julius. I don't think I can stand any more of the Trevi. But, Julius, I'm so happy. You see, last winter was worse than other winters."

"Nina told me," said Julius.

He filled my goblet. He seemed to be enjoying Nina's lamb-stew or whatever it was she had brought in. I was glad that he left me to crumble the brown bread and to sip my Trevi slowly. I waited for him to finish.

"What was it Nina told you?" I said.

Julius said, "Among other things, that the house is draughty. I hope you don't mind, but I have an old house-steward. He's retired on a small pension, but he's the devil of a nuisance. He won't stay retired. He plagues me to take him back into the household. He looks after my - private stable. I tell him that's sufficient and he isn't decrepit, by any manner of means. But he just won't stay retired, as I've already told you. I thought Nina might help me. She said the fruit-trees weren't bearing so well last summer, and he could see to these doors. Nina said that she could keep him busy. I'll send him in the morning early, before Nina has time to change her mind. It's late for pruning but he can cut back those fruit-boughs by the stable, and Nina asked me to look into the kitchen-garden. 'It's run a bit wild,' she said, 'it's a pity what with all the work that Master Ver put on it.'"

He refilled my goblet.

"You mustn't, Julius. I'm already full of - "

"Dreams and visions?" asked Julius. "Wasn't it you who said to me - and only two hours ago - 'I am glad our Trevi still provokes your eloquence.'"

"Don't go back, Julius, not even two hours," I said. "There's all of forever and to-morrow. Finish the Trevi. Did you take a look into your old room on the way to say good-night to - Clyte, did you say her name was? A winged horse, wasn't it, or a swarm of bees? And Clyte was a sun-flower. And did Nina put your cape there, in your old room and has she built you a fire? No-one has been in since - "

But I heard Nina at the door. "It's the Trevi - I'll rest here under the fleeces, while Nina clears the table. I am so happy, Julius."

. . . . .

Nina was talking to someone in the hall. "The Madame will be delighted; how thoughtful-like to save all them flower-prunings. Only yesterday I was reminded of these same almond and abri-cote by our talking of Master Ver and uncle Julius, as we calls him in the kitchen, not to be familiar, but in memory-like, like it might be Master Ver his-self was hiding behind the door and would boo out at him and he pretending to be that fearful - it was a rare treat, to see him act fearful, and Master Ver so proud of his uncle Julius. She's sleeping late, the Madame. I'll take these here in, and tidy the room, then I'll come out and fetch you, like at your convenience, to say good-morning to the Madame."

I did not know where I was.

The voices stopped and stolid footsteps passed my window. It must be - I remembered - Julius had said he was sending his old house-steward and sending him early, before Nina had time to change her mind.

I must have fallen asleep after dinner. I never said good-bye to Julius but I remembered saying, "There's all of forever and to-morrow." This was to-morrow.

I heard Nina at the door. I let her place what I supposed was one of our old water-jars on the floor, before Ver's Faunus, before I threw off the fleeces.

I had forgotten how we always had blossoms for Ver's Faunus.

Nina fastened the door back with the low stool.

The sun streamed in from the hall and the paved-court outside.

I was still in my house-coat. I remembered everything.

"I never undressed last night," I said, "why didn't you wake me, Nina."

"He said, meaning Master Ver's uncle Julius, that you seemed to have been wor-it about something. Best let her sleep on, he said." Her arms were full of almond-blossoms. "His steward what he sent here said the peach and abri-cotes wanted clipping. He saved you these here blossoms, he says to greet you with his respects-like, and for the festival."

I said, "I don't remember - March? What festival?"

Nina said, "We always had the blossom, don't you recall, Madame? It's the Ides, I'm meaning."

———————

XI

Distant Island

The steward did not come that morning. Nina took down the indoor shutters and let in the sunlight.

"It's fresher in your room, if I may suggest, Madame. Suppose you finishes that bowl of broth and I'll help you to undress. It's all been a shock like, him coming and our remembering. You can just rest quiet while I do out this room. I want to get the house right, before the steward comes back. He asked to see you, Madame, but he thought best afterwards to go while it was still early, to fetch some more things back. He wasn't dressed, what you might say proper, for the garden."

Nina was right. I could hardly walk across the room. I didn't sleep but I was very happy. I would rest until Julius came back.

I wasn't really sorry when Nina said that Julius wasn't coming that evening. It had tired me to dress and I had taken a long time about it. It was the dress that Nina had laid out last night on the bed. If I had thought about it, I would have said that I was too old to wear it, but I remembered how Julius had looked at me in the firelight, though I was angry and thought that I saw a suspicion of what I had once called his thin smile, and I remembered how I had hated him.

But I didn't hate Julius now.

I looked at myself in the silver mirror. Then I got out my white cloak and folded myself in it. I would sit in the cloak until Julius came. I went out and sat by the fire. The room was fresh with Nina's polishing and smelt of bees-wax. The blossoms glowed in the corner, before Ver's Faunus.

It was then that Nina told me that Julius wasn't coming, but that the steward had brought a message for me.

The steward stood by the round table where Julius had sat when he talked of cat-and-mouse and said that there was the old steel and stone that had once struck the spark between us.

I thanked the steward for the almond-blossom. He said,

"I never have decided, Madame, whether the branch looks prettier indoors or out. They look pretty in the corner."

I thought he looked tired. Nina told me that he had taken two trips to Rome, since morning. I asked him to sit down.

"Well, since you ask me, Madame, I only wanted to say what you no doubt knows already. It was kept strictly private, as you might say, but I expect he hinted like, about what his plans was. I must say, everything went perfect. But he told you?" I said he hadn't told me anything, Nina had heard something, but I didn't know what. Nina, I said, exaggerated, I was ill last winter and they had a lot to say to one another. I told the steward that I thought they had decided that I might worry.

"Well, worry is natural, in some ways," said the steward, "and he would have put it off, he said I was to tell you special. He thought it was better to tell, rather than write; even up to the last there was plenty of snoopers about, but I said I would explain it. The ships was ready and waiting at Ostia. He said I was to say special that he was sick of politics and he'd been planning for a long time to go over to that place he's marked on his new maps.

"There was a lot to do there, he said, things you couldn't make arrangements for, those first times. But he said I was to tell you special, it wasn't war this time, nor even politics. He said it was legislation, as you might say, that took him to Britannia.

"There was many things he used to talk to me of - private, in what he called the stables. Well, they was stables, in the manner of speaking, but he kept a few odd things there, old coats and rugs to sleep in. We had, it is true, three horses and he asked special if they could stay here. Fact is, in the manner of speaking, they was my horses but the place was his, for all he made it over to me, when he wouldn't take me to Helvetia. He said, diplomatic-like, that I would be more use in Rome. He knew what I felt, him leaving me behind for the first time. I was, as you might say, retired, but he said I could get about private, where the household would be spotted - or where official police somehow shows something somewhere; they can't natural take things easy, like you, he would say, and they don't grumble natural, he would say. Oh, the times, oh the customs, it was one of our little jokes - him, I mean, you remember that time what with Catiline? Do your times-and-customs, he would say, grumble natural, like you does and say the household let you down, and you having been one of his personal, having to hire out horses. There was the way through the garden along the wall - well, you know him, cat-like he was and enjoying his-self and that makes all the difference if you want to make a getaway. And me enjoying myself. Special household rule about gossip outside, but I was once household though gone down in the world something pitiful, and grumble, he says, natural like you does and find out who's likely or likely not to poison the artichokes. Took it all as a joke, but you know what things was. As I said, worry is natural, in some ways.

"Well, I'm glad, I must say, to hear the last of Ostia, for the time being. Maps and charts and plans spread out on the table, and tucked away, after, under the horse-feed. Not that I didn't enjoy myself - and him - 'Look,' he says, 'we'll leave this to them Nordics for the moment. Fight,' he says, 'I wouldn't like to meet them - not me - but later, maybe. Wish we knew more about them. They paint their ships. They make dragons of them, with blue wings. But,' he says, 'the wall first.' You could almost see that wall, it cut the peninsula or the island in half. He had it all ready, the plan he's been planning since Helvetia - but only the building. Oh, don't worry, Madame, he isn't going to fight them - 'Not me,' he says, 'not Caesar. We'll build the wall first.'

"Some day, Madame, when you have a few minutes to spare, you might like to look over some of the old maps with me. He took the fresh draft with him, but we can make out his intention from the rough copy. I told him I'd be look- ing forward to his book on Britain. The new place was called Britain. It was almost like being there and him talking terse, like he did campaigning - I mean, the Gaul War. I told him, Helvetia across the mountains - it was all mountains, he said - and that Gaul ought to be enough, even for him. But he said, 'There's always ultimate to look forward to.' What he meant was *ultimus Brittanus*, like someone called it or them, islands or peninsulas, I don't know which.

"Shouldn't wonder but what he stopped off to say good-bye to old Eloquence on the way - did you ever see his new place and the theatre? Not far from Ostia - I mean, Cicero. Well, Eloquence is all right but his Catilines was a bit long- winded, that is, beside the Gaul War.

"But he's off on his holiday and good luck to him."

"I hope Nina will make you comfortable," I said. "I wonder, as you have his old maps, if it wouldn't be - home-like for them and for you - to take - well, to make use of his room." It would be a comfort to have Julius' steward in the villa and Nina had moved to this side of the house, to look after me, last winter. "I hope you won't find it dull here after the Capitol."

"I'll be glad of a rest," he said, "and I want to take my time about the garden. He said some of the gentlemen were already settled in their villas, over in Britain, and they want home-like gardens before sending for their families. He wanted me to take special note of what I thought would grow there. Oh, they have a sort of wild-apple, the gentlemen call it a crab for sourness. But there's always graft- ing. He wanted me to try this and that. Have you wild-plum perhaps, up past the oak-wood, for instance? If I may make free about the place, I'll try grafting sweet- apple on the wild and honey-plum on the wild-plum and see how they take, for sending cuttings later. The housekeeper tells me you was beginning to clear the woods but before they cut out the tangle, might I have permission to select a few trees? The housekeeper said she used to go up there with Master Ver, for berries.

"Well, what I mean is, Madame - but fancy me planning for you. It's his plans really, and yours, in the manner of speaking. What I thought was, we might leave those berries; the wild ones, the housekeeper tells me, is better for her conserve. We might even do our grafting up there. I have an idea from what she tells me, that the hill-slope there and the other side, might have been the original of this place. She says there's some more pavings beyond the tangle, and what might have been a lady's garden. There was lilies, she said, smaller and run wild-like, but the same as your garden lilies. She must have told you. It was Master Ver's play-house, she told me, those walls and ruins. We might make what she said Master Ver planned for it, a wild garden.

"But ladies know more about these matters. I'm thinking of those ladies in Britain. I'm thinking what they'd most miss, what they'd most want in their gardens. First, I take it they want rue, marjoram, bay-leaf, wax-berry and of course *ros maris*, that rosemary, like the housekeeper calls it. It can't be equalled for the cupboards and for the oak and cedar chests; though you don't rightly need *ros maris* when you have cedar, there's still its leaf for sweetness. There's other things for chests - iris or orris, as they call the ground-root. There must be orris-lilies for the ground-root and other lilies, just for themselves.

"But I must not keep you, Madame. I must have tired you with my talking. If I might suggest, would it be suitable for me to make my report to-morrow, about this time, after the garden-work is over?"

. . . . .

I had spent the day going over my old things. I was surprised to find how pretty some of the frocks were. I tried some of them on, before the mirror and altered a sleeve or a hem or a fold on the shoulder. I selected the blue gown. I remembered how I had last worn it.

I felt a little shy and strange and the evenings were still cold, so I sat in my cloak, but it was the dark one this time. I remembered how I had flung Julius' old campaigner, as he called it, down here before the fire, only last night - I mean, only night before last. I felt almost as if Julius were coming, as I waited. But Julius was coming, I mean, the steward brought Julius with him.

I don't think, even in the old days with Julius, I was happier than I was now.

I had been thinking of the questions the steward had asked and I wondered if he were indirectly hinting at something that Julius may have touched on. He spoke of the gentlemen sending for their families. He said, he wondered what the ladies would most want in their gardens as if - almost as if - well, he said, I remembered how he said it, "But it's his plans really, and yours, in the manner of speaking."

The steward said that Julius had asked him to make notes of what he thought would best grow in Britain; "What," he asked, "would ladies most miss?" He was trying to tell me that Julius perhaps, wouldn't come back, but that he wanted me to join him.

I told the steward to sit down again, when he came in. Perhaps I was a little too abrupt. I said,

"When do you think we can send out our first roots and cuttings?" And then I said, "Do you think the next ships will soon be sailing?"

He answered me, I thought, a little harshly,

"Madame," he said, "it would be worth my life, even now, to discuss ship-plans and movements."

"I didn't mean to pry into official secrets," I said. I felt the old bitterness creep into my voice. But I looked at the steward. His head was bent forward, his hands were clasped on his knees. I said, "You look tired, you should rest for a few days or explore the country. I would like you to look in, too, on some of my neighbours - we always used to plan things together. They would be interested in our garden and the experiments with grafting. Are the horses happy in the old stalls? I hope Nina put you - in his room."

The steward said, "I must ask you to forgive me, Madame, that I spoke sharp. You see, it's this way - I miss him.

"But as to the ships, Madame, I understand you perfectly. From the beginning, I begged - well, not begged exactly - but I made it clear without too much appearing to seem to push my way in, that I wanted to go with him. Let us put it this way. I am frank with you, like sometimes it was difficult to be with him. I mean, I was to be sure, retired and my status was non-official, for that reason requiring the more exact, you might say, convention. Put it this way: I put my all and glad to have something to take my mind off, into this place. The time comes, he sends. We plan the roots and cuttings, the moss-lined baskets for the root-plants, the special earth for the bulbs, the jars of seeds - why, Madame, it occurs, we might take bees over. Do you think it possible? There's sure to be wild-honey, of course, but it's rare to find and hard, as a rule, to get at, when found. But putting aside the bee-question, you could say, confidential, that you took to me, that you wouldn't trust no-one else with your precious bulbs and baskets. This maybe, is putting myself forward, but somebody has got to look after those plants. Well, I know how these things are done. You speaking to the captain - if I hadn't been in office and non-official (which makes it twice worse), I'd have had my way and I'd soon now be sighting the island. Malta, they calls it - Melitta on the old maps. Perhaps, though, they put in first for a day in Sicily. I didn't like to ask him, but I don't know - but it occurs, it might be better, Madame, to pick up the bees in Malta, in Melitta which translated, if I'm not mistaken means great-bee. It might be romantic or symbolic-like to take the bees from Malta. But who am I, Madame, to be talking of bees on ship-board? You must think me fair daft."

. . . . .

I did not think him daft, I thought he was worn out and unhappy at the thought of the long parting.

I did care. I wonder how it happened but even then, I realized that I was happier, dreaming of a distant island, with my Roman hyacinths growing along the wood-paths than I had been, even in my most felicitous days with Julius.

Julius was there, it was his island, but I came to care more for the rosemary-hedge and the cypress-walk (though the steward doubted, he said, if cypress would do well there) than I cared for Julius. Then, Julius was not there, he had gone north, I would argue, to see about the Great Wall. I set out a border of heliotrope that summer, I mean that summer in the island. There were several summers, though Julius had only been gone three months.

The steward spread out his old maps, there were marginal notes in Julius' cramped writing. Sometimes, the steward read the notes out to me, and the dates.

"Sometimes these dates is double," he said, "but I expect he explained it to you, and his new calendar."

"He did say something, the last time I saw him" I said. "He said they were wrong, for instance, about March."

"*March*," said the steward and he began rolling up the map.

"The Ides of March," I said. He stopped rolling up the map.

"I can't remember," he said. "Oh - *that*. That was a fair joke between us - you mean the old ruffian, as he called him, what we called Beware-the-Ides?"

I said, "I remember his telling me about someone standing on street corners. That was how we happened to talk about the calendar. I had been foolish and imagined things - well, I asked him to wait three days."

"You mean because of the Ides?" asked the steward.

"No, it was something different."

"Was you worried like Nina was about the star-cloud last summer - what they called the comet? Some said it was predicting the end of the world - I ask you."

"No, it wasn't the star-cloud," I said, and then I knew everything.

He went on rolling up the map. I had been happy for three months, happier even than I had been with Julius. I had stored up happiness. I had stored up enough happiness to live on for the rest of my life - to live on and perhaps, to help others to live on.

———————

XII

Normandy

I had no intention, no desire to return to the Normandy beaches. That D-day is yesterday. But there are other D-days, and Stella remembered having said, "There is all of forever and to-morrow." I could not think of him there, nor of myself there, but though I was happy when I thought of Athens, I did not want to think of Rome. Yet Rome led to "all of forever and to-morrow," and to-morrow, Lambert, Oliver, Guienne, Geffray, Dennis, Bordeaux, Guesclin and Guilbert are coming with us to say good-bye to the Sieur Guillaume.

We are Margaret, Alice, Constance, Jehane, Yoland, Louise, Isabeau and Stella. They are sailing early in the morning.

I note our names in their order, with one exception. Stella follows Constance.

. . . . .

We have been practising our order of precedence and our procession. It is part of the *courtezia* of the Lady Duchess that we know each other's names in full and the rank and titles of the nobility that surround her. The Duchess said that she did not like the slippery sea-stairs and she had said good-bye to the Duke so often, she would kiss him in the garden and go back to the castle, and when the Duke reached his ship, we would go to him and give him her love and her last good-bye messages.

There was a great deal of argument about how we would get out and would they let us climb the rope-ladders, and if we, Margaret, Alice, Constance and the rest of us wore our grown-up dresses, could we climb the ropes - and there was much laughter among the ladies and some of them pretended to be angry with the Lady Duchess because she was sending us and not them.

"If they can climb the cliff," said the Duchess, "and they are always scrambling up and down, they can climb anything."

But Louise said she didn't like the sea-stairs and Jehane, her friend said they were sure to tread on a crab or a frog and slip down and break their necks. The

Duchess said, "Well, Louise, well, Jehane, perhaps you prefer to stay with me here," that annoyed them but they pretended to be flattered.

"But - do you really want us?"

The Duchess said, "Of course, nothing would give me greater pleasure," but she was teasing them because they had made me unhappy. It was about precedence.

I had upset the whole procession - that is, the last time they had a procession, I was still in the convent.

Louise said, in front of all the others, "I'm moving up, I'm third from last and Jehane, you're near the top - you are four now."

But one of the ladies who was arranging us in the long hall, pulled me forward. I was walking last with Guilbert, but the Lady Beauvais said, "Stella - this is your place. Will you walk with Stella, Geffray?"

Geffray had been very kind when I tried to hide behind the curtains, yesterday. Louise had said,

"But why should she walk in the Normandy procession at all? She isn't anybody, since they lost their castle."

I pretended not to hear, but I couldn't get out of the long hall. It was our first practice.

This was our second. It was only a matter of keeping one's place in the procession and remembering the Lady Duchess' few words of greeting to the Duke. The Duchess had rehearsed the greetings yesterday. The Lady Beauvais explained that we must not expect the procession itself, to be exactly like the rehearsals. Unexpected things always happened. The Duke, for instance, might speak to us out of turn, but Lady Beauvais said, she knew she could trust Lambert and Margaret to fill in the gaps, and Oliver and Alice to improvise if anyone should stutter or become tongue-tied - and it happened even to older people, only the Duke didn't frighten young people, "as most of you know," she said.

Then she added, "Guienne and Constance will look after late arrivals, if there are any. That is one, two and three of the Lady Duchess' company - now four - " it was then that the real trouble began. Jehane was standing with Geffray. Louise said,

"I thought we talked that out yesterday."

Lady Beauvais said, "Yes, I heard the Duchess say that she would be happy to have you stay with her, on Normandy Day. But of course," she turned to another lady, "in that case, the last four damozels must be rearranged. Tell me, Ellayne, do you think Provence and Ursula are old enough to take the places of Louise and Jehane?"

. . . . .

I had wanted to stay with Mother Beata and Sister Rose-Mary and the other sisters. It had happened last summer, but they did not tell me about it until afterwards. Mother let me help with the painted pictures. I was working on a Nativity in the Book of Hours when she told me. She said that I could put in the angels and the star, because my name was Stella. I had almost forgotten that my name was Stella. I think it was the first time that the Lady Abbess had ever reminded me. I said,

"Mother, why do you call me Stella?"

She said, "Because it is your name, Blanchfleur."

I said, "There is something wrong - what has happened? The girls in the convent said last summer, that something terrible would happen because of that star."

"I told them about the star," said Mother Beata, "and you Blanchfleur, I thought I could have trusted you, of all people, not to let evil superstition sway you. Girls always chatter - but Sister Rose-Mary said that you were different. That is why she let you help her with the manuscripts and Latin."

"The Latin is not difficult, Mother, but - "

"There is one star, Blanchfleur, in our faith, the star of our Lord's Nativity."

"Mother - something terrible has happened?"

"Yes - but we have a beautiful plan for you, Blanchfleur."

"What has happened, Mother Beata?"

"It happened long ago, you must think of it that way. We wanted you to be happy, especially happy this winter."

"I have been - so very happy," I said, "only don't tell me that I must leave you?"

"Your father would have wished it."

"Would have wished it?"

"You have your faith, Stella, the light of our faith tells us - "

"You mean my father is - he did not send the usual Christmas messages. You said he had gone with the blessing of the Church to our Lord's Sepulchre. Mother, do you mean- "

"He has gone with the blessing of the Church. He was a gallant gentleman."

"But then, I must go back to the castle at Montjoie?"

"There is no castle, Stella."

That is what had made them so kind. They were always kind but that is why Sister Rose-Mary let me fill in the margins, the thing I loved best, with the little pansies. She let me do all but the larger animals for the Ark, and we were working on the Ship that took St. Paul to Malta. I remembered how she had told me that Malta in the old text, is Melitta and melitta or melissa is the Greek for Bee. I thought we should work some bee-hives into the opening letter, but Sister said she didn't know - we must ask the Lady Abbess. Mother Beata said, yes, there was Our Lord after the resurrection and the honeycomb and there was the proverb about wisdom from the old dispensation as well, "sweeter also than honey in the honeycomb."

"But if the castle has gone," I said, "and - Miles and Robert - then, my father would like me to stay with you."

I couldn't think of him and Miles and Robert as dead. I said to myself, "I am the resurrection," and Mother Beata had said he had gone to the Holy Sepulchre.

"Did Miles and Robert go with my father?" I said.

· · · · ·

There was no question of slippery sea-stairs. We started early, soon after the herald's trumpet sounded the departure of the Duke of Normandy from the castle. There had been early mass in the Duchess' private chapel, and after the Duke's company had gone, the friars formed a line. The priests followed and, then Lady Beauvais called us.

"You are to come back before the formal blessing of the ships," she said. "I wish I could come with you."

She looked different. Her dark blue mantle was wrapped round her and with her veil over her head, she might have been dear Sister Rose-Mary. Her name was Rose, Geffray had told me, and hearing the beautiful *nunc dimittis* sung by the friars, I was suddenly aware that this really was home. I had wanted to stay in the cloister but last night, after the great cathedral service with the candles, and seeing the Lady Duchess and her company in their long capes and veils, I might have been back in the *Mater boni consuli*, as our convent was called.

I had thought at first, after my long winter talks with Mother Beata and Sister Rose (as I sometimes called her) that these ladies, though they were very gracious, seemed not to - not to care as we did for the *Pater Nosters* and the *Aves*. But they did care. Lady Rose Beauvais, in her long cloak, looked taller, as she stood there in the courtyard. Her face was very white and her hands were cold when she stopped beside me and Geffray. She tilted up my face and she kissed me. Perhaps she had kissed Margaret and Alice and Constance but I had not noticed. Her cheek was colder than her hands, as it brushed mine. She whispered, "Add that to your message from the Lady Duchess."

I did not know what she meant. The Lady Duchess said she would kiss him good-bye in the garden. Was this that kiss?

I couldn't look round to see if she kissed the others. Jehane followed me, she was taller than I was. I suppose that is why Louise thought that Jehane should follow Constance. Constance had been so kind. She said, I must go with her the next time she went home, if the Lady Duchess would permit it.

There was no question of sea-stairs, as we went the long way round, below the cliff. There was no question of boats taking us out, or climbing ropes in our grown-up dresses, though our dresses were grown-up, that is, we were dressed like the Duchess' ladies, in out-door capes and long veils.

They had arranged a sort of bridge of boats and the friars went ahead chanting, the priests followed with the Host and censers. We still walked two-and-two, across the broad planks. There was a mist, I couldn't see the other ships, they were outside, Geffray had told me. The Duke's ship was only waiting for the blessing.

There was no question of rope-ladders. They had slanted the wide boards from the last boat, up to the lower deck. We followed the friars and priests. We hadn't time to see much but Geffray whispered, "Look - he's brought Fleet and Goldwings."

I asked, "Who are Fleet and Goldwings?"

"There they are," said Geffray, "I wonder if he brought any of the others."

The lower deck was dark, it was a large room, more like our great barn at home. It did not seem strange to see the falcons, hunched on their perches in the corner.

When we rehearsed the procession, it was all very different. Lady Beauvais was right about that. There hadn't been many ladies at Montjoie since my mother died, and though we were serious at *Boni Consuli*, it was really very gay there. Now it was both gay and serious here, too, and I knew that Mother Beata was right to send me. She had said, "Your mother, my own dearest Alys, wanted to stay with me. We were the same age and the Lady Duchess was our friend. That is why the Duchess wants you - and for other reasons - in Normandy. If your mother had stayed at *Boni Consuli* with me, you would never have been born." Mother Beata went on, "It is the divine rule of heaven - Our Lord, you remember said, Suffer little children to come unto Me."

. . . . .

The friars and priests had gone up the narrow stairs and one of the sailors said to Lambert,

"You'd better hurry them along, sir, they'll be setting up the Host and we was informed you young gentlemen and ladies was returning before the blessing."

We pushed up the steps together and when we got to the top, Lambert said, "Come along, Alice - and the rest of you follow." We worked our way through the friars, over the ropes and tackle. There was a heap of cross-bows and bundles of arrows.

Lambert had asked the soldiers to make way for us. He found the Duke. He made his speech and the Duke said, "Next time, perhaps, Lambert, you will be coming with us — And this is Margaret? Well, Margaret, we will be back soon. Oliver, my dear fellow, don't forget the chord - you remember, we were a bit slack on the line, last time. I've left some of the old fellows, and Peter has had special orders to see that you don't forget what I taught you, on our little outings. Alice? How like your lovely mother you are growing."

They hardly had a chance to get in their speeches, but they managed somehow and I remembered how Lady Beauvais had said that he might talk to us.

"Thank the Duchess, Constance, for her thought of us - and of course, you Margaret and Alice, take our love back. Guienne, my dear boy. No - we'll be back soon, and I expect you and Oliver will be coming along with Lambert, next time. Geffray - I'm sorry, Geffray, I'm taking your Goldwings with me. You did have a way with her - but I'll bring her back. And - ?"

"This is Stella," said Geffray. "You remember - "

"Ah - Montjoie," said the Duke. "Now your father knew one hawk from another."

I said my greeting and then added, "There was another message."

The Duke's gentlemen were chatting with the others. I don't know why I felt that I must whisper, but the Lady Beauvais had whispered to me.

"The Lady Beauvais," I said, "wanted me - " I could not think what she wanted me to say, but the Duke had turned to Dennis.

Constance said, "Margaret says we must hurry."

Guienne said to Geffray, "We can't look at the sails and ropes now - Oliver says, hurry."

We went down the stairs and followed two of the sailors over the boat-bridge.

. . . . .

The others were hurrying along the cliff-path. I wondered if they were thinking as I was, of the bowl of broth and the brown bread that Lady Beauvais said would be waiting for us. It was cold.

"I'm hungry," I said, "Geffray."

But Geffray wouldn't hurry. The old sailor said,

"Better run along, Master Geffray, we've got to get these boats in."

The boys had already gone out to the first boat and the men on the shore, were dragging in the boards.

"Got to get this gangway shipshape," said the sailor, "and I reckon our lads are, like the young lady says, hungry. All very well, these Hosts and blessings - God keep Normandy - and him as set in his ways, as always, could a' done with a few extra hands, I told him, but he as ever, left me behind. Got to have someone capable, along shore, he says, as if I was along-shore already. But God bless him, as I already said, though I had a snack before I come out, what with the Missus in a stew, fearful to the last, I might make a getaway, in spite of everything. Better run along, Master Geffray."

The second and third boats were rowing back. "They'll take a spill there, number four, if they ain't careful. Awkward, these gang-boards. Why are you waiting, Master Geffray - can't you see the young lady looks cold and peaked-like? I don't think now, miss, I've seen you with the young folks?"

"It's Montjoie," said Geffray.

"Bless my soul," said the old sailor, "would have knowed you, miss, anywhere - and then, I didn't know you. But the young people is always happy with the Duchess - now there's a lady for you. Now you run on, Master Geffray - he wouldn't like you loitering."

"But he likes me to talk," said Geffray.

"Times is different, this is hard times - and what would we have to talk about, anyway, now he's gone?"

"We can talk about him," said Geffray.

"What would we say about him - and anyway, this is serious - won't do to discuss ships and ship-movements, you ought to know that, Master Geffray, open-like on the beaches."

"I wasn't talking ship-movements," said Geffray, "I only wanted to talk about Cousin Guill."

But Geffray seemed annoyed with the old sailor and started to run after the others.

"Manners," said the sailor, "but I reckon he'll wait for you; head-strong is our young master at times, but not so bad - though that ain't my province - Peter tells me, with the hawkers."

"What is the matter?" I said, when I caught up.

"Nothing's the matter," said Geffray, "but why did he take Goldwings?"

. . . . .

There were two things that I didn't understand, one was, why when the Sieur Guillaume had the sheds full of beautiful birds, he should have taken Geffray's own Goldwings; the other was, why he had turned away without thanking me for my message. He had thanked Margaret and Alice and Constance. I didn't think he was angry with me. I felt he was angry with the Lady Beauvais and that made it much worse.

I told the Lady Duchess that the Duke thanked her and sent her his love, but he hadn't. Then afterwards I thought that I had better give Lady Beauvais a message as well, though he had turned away. I was helping Lady Beauvais in the library, as Mother Beata had told the Duchess that I knew Latin and had helped with the painted pictures. This was the first time that I had been alone with Lady Beauvais. The Duchess wanted us to sort out some books to send to her daughter in Burgundy. And she wanted us to find her own first Book of Hours and bring it to her, and there were the song-books.

The manuscripts were rather untidy and I felt happy about that, for there would be a lot to do here and the Duchess had said that Mother Beata had told her how I used to help them mend and bind the parchments. It made me happy to feel that I could come here, for I enjoyed the painted pictures and I did not like embroidery. But I didn't think Lady Beauvais looked very happy.

"We did this at the convent," I said, "but I must get my old smock or Mother Beata will be angry."

"We are not in the convent," said Lady Beauvais, "no-one will be angry with you here, and we have plenty of time for this work, now that they've gone."

That reminded me of the message she had asked me to give. We had all told the Duchess separately, that he said he would be back soon or that he sent his love, or something of that sort, so I thought that perhaps Lady Beauvais expected a message from him, too.

It was Lady Beauvais who had started talking about the song-books and then the Duchess remembered that her daughter had been asking for them. I felt somehow, that Lady Beauvais didn't want me to give the message - though there was no message - in front of the others. I went to one of the tables and started trying to sort out the folios. But Lady Beauvais didn't seem interested, she just sat there.

"The folios are dusty," I said, "I'll get my smock and ask for paste and brushes and come back."

Lady Beauvais said, "You will go away and you will never come back." Her eyes were staring and she frowned at someone who wasn't there.

"I forgot to tell you," I said, "Lady Beauvais, what the Duke said when I gave him your message."

"There was no message," she said. "Well, it wasn't exactly a message to tell," I said, "it was like your message."

"What do you mean?" she got up, she stood by the table, I saw that she was trembling.

I pushed her back in the chair. She looked so odd. It was as if I had never seen her, and I remembered how I had first seen her - laughing.

"It wasn't exactly a message," I said, "but I told him you had kissed me good-bye." I didn't know what to say now. I said, "The Duke said, 'Tell Lady Beauvais that I send you' - "

What would he send me to do? Lady Beauvais looked at me. She waited.

"The Duke said," I repeated, "'Tell Lady Beauvais that I send you' - he meant that he sent me."

"Of course," said Lady Beauvais.

I said, "The Duke said, 'Tell Lady Beauvais that I send you to look after my - Rose.'"

. . . . .

That had happened a long time ago. Well, it seems a long time ago because I was a child then, but I am a woman now.

It wasn't only children that Mother Beata meant when she said the Duke wanted me. The Duke wanted Montjoie and it seems that he could claim it, if I married Geffray.

The Lady Duchess said that I was too young to marry, but the Duke said that things couldn't be postponed much longer.

Lady Beauvais or Rose, as I now called her, had asked me to help her select the songs. I helped now with the younger children. They sang and I read aloud (I had often read aloud at the Convent) from a new folio called *The Romance of the Rose*.

Geffray helped with the jongleurs and we were very happy.

I loved Geffray so much, he was like my younger brother, it almost seemed sometimes, he must be Robert come back. I don't think the Duke liked Geffray to be so friendly with the jongleurs, and Constance told me that I was the only girl who had ever read aloud to music, in the long hall. I can not tell you how happy I was to read to music.

Rose had said that she would help me with the songs but she knew that I had already chosen them, so I thought she wanted to talk to me alone. We went into the library.

Rose said, "Don't let him spoil things for you."

I said, "How can he spoil anything? I love Geffray."

Rose said, "It always starts that way. It started that way with me. Now, you are happy with Geffray. You have helped them to understand."

She sat down in the same chair she had sat in, that first day we were alone together.

"What have I helped them to understand?" I pulled up the stool beside her.

"You have helped them to understand that a girl - that a woman may have, may one day have a complete life of her own."

"But my life would be nothing," I said, "without you and Geffray."

"That isn't what I mean. That isn't how it is, at all. I was happy with Giles. I was your age when I married him. We might have gone on being happy, really happy and together - but somehow - how can I say it? They called you Blanchfleur at the convent, well, it was like that. Our love though complete - and we might have had children later - was *blanchfleur*. Then there was the same question, my lost islands. I was happy. I had almost forgotten the islands. It is true, I could remember, like remembering a dream or trying to remember a dream. Giles, they said, must get back the islands. It was the same story. Giles was a distant cousin of the Duke of Brittany. That was the Duke's claim to the islands. He got the islands but I lost Giles."

She had never spoken to me of her husband, though I knew of course, that Rose Beauvais had been married.

"This is the same story, Blanchfleur. I hear them talking of it. Once you marry Geffray, you are, as I was in Brittany, our dear cousin. And our dear cousin's lands must be reclaimed and there is a jingle of harness and a blare of trumpets and red roses - Oh, my dear, red roses."

I did not understand. I got up and bolted the door. It was growing dark. I was frightened. I remembered Montjoie and the snowy winters and the howling of the wolves, beyond the castle in the forest. It was the way she said red roses. I was frightened.

But Geffray and I had talked and talked - we had thought that Rose Beauvais loved the Sieur Guillaume.

"How I would have laughed, if there had been anyone to share the joke with me - at you, my dear, that first time we talked alone together."

"I don't remember, Rose Beauvais," I said. I knelt on the floor beside her. "You have such cold, cold hands, Rose. I remember too, how it felt, your cheek as it brushed mine, that first time you kissed me. But why would you laugh, Rose Beauvais?" I said.

"I would laugh," she said, "at a conundrum or a riddle."

"Do people laugh at riddles? But what riddle?" I said.

"The riddle in the riddle - the heart of the rose." She went on, "Rose? You said, 'The Duke said, tell Lady Beauvais that I send you to look after my - Rose.'"

"I remember," I said.

"I have the answer to the riddle," said Rose Beauvais, "but it is hard to find the words with which to ask it. It was like this. Normandy would never have said such a thing. But the quaint lie of Mother Beata's best beloved had charmed me. Oh, how we had listened to dear Beata when she came to us that winter, after Christmas. There never had been and there never would be another such a Blanchfleur. Of course, we must not spoil her. But God in his grace and wisdom, had wanted a bride for the Duke's child-cousin, Geffray de Froissart. 'The very thing,' says the Lady Duchess, 'She shall be as our own daughter, if you, Beata will part with her.'

"There was much talk of Montjoie, its strategic position and if the Duke didn't protect the neighbouring provinces, there were others to the east, who were well equipped to do so. We did not want other peoples' protectors, so to speak, on our door-step. 'But another glass, Beata, I must tell you about Britain.'

"I do not want you to lose faith in your Beata and you won't do that. Even I can not take Beata from you. Am I jealous of Beata? And all those animals your next beloved, Sister Rose-Mary let you paint for the day of judgment or the last trump or whatever it was? Am I jealous of Sister Rose-Mary? Am I jealous of the bee-hives and the honeycomb and the angels? Did your Ark animals do for the Nativity or did you have to invent new ones? Did your Ark do for the Nativity stall and did you and Sister Rose-Mary mix fresh blue for the blue robe of Our Lady? Were you happy, Blanchfleur, with Rose-Mary and the Ark and the bee-hives and the gold letters and the borders of little pansies?"

"I was very happy, Rose Beauvais," I said.

"But there is something that is happiness - but different. It isn't tragic. It's funny. It's this way - but a joke should stand on its own feet - the minute you try to explain a joke, it falls down. But let me make a statement and explain the joke afterwards. Normandy would never in this world have said, 'I send you to look after my - Rose.' It was Brittany who said it.

"There were so many jokes, and so far, there has been no-one to share them with me. But now, I have you, Blanchfleur. That is another joke, a legend, a story. Iseult's name was Blanchfleur - one of the Iseults. There were two of them, you remember. The other one - well, it was the same one. It was the same story: Iseult of Brittany and Iseult of the West were one. And now that our cousin Guill has taken Britain, what will happen to Brittany? I mean, it was a joke about Blanch-fleur, because dear Beata was so sententious about it. Like the lecture you told me about."

"What lecture?" I said. But before she could answer, I said, "Rose Beauvais, could Geffray come and talk with us - here, I mean, alone?"

"That's what I want, I mean you and Geffray and myself alone - together. But you remember Goldwings?"

"But it was all right," I said, "the Duke brought back Goldwings."

"There are some things that even our Normandy could not bring back. He could take Blanchfleur - "

"No, no," I said, "Rose Beauvais, not with you here to - "

"You are not really frightened. You once told me that the howling of the wolves in the forest around Montjoie frightened you, but you clutched your blankets and crouched down in your bed and shivered with an ecstasy of apprehension. You are curious. You are not really frightened. You might love Normandy."

"I do love the Duke," I said, but I wondered. "Has he made you unhappy, Rose Beauvais?"

"He has made me very happy - but there is more than that to this story of Britain and Brittany - or should I say now, Normandy and Brittany?" she said.

"But we will call it Britain," she concluded, "because of the old stories."

She said, "It will always be Britain, even though our cousin Guill has conquered it. The old stories will be stronger, even than Normandy."

. . . . .

"But we must go," I said, "they will be waiting for us." I was a little surprised when Rose said,

"We are not poor relations."

"But is it quite polite," I said, "to stay here?"

"It would be very rude of you to leave me, dearest. I started to tell you the story of Britain and Brittany. But I can't go on now, let us go back to Iseult Blanchfleur. The other was Blanchmain. They were, as I have said, the same person. But the waves rose and the rains fell - it is of your Ark that I am speaking - and Britain and Brittany were parted.

"Some say, at one time, you could have walked across, well, perhaps not all the way, but with islands for stepping-stones. There are still a few scattered islands left but the causeway or the bridge was broken.

"But this is fantasy or dream - it must be - only Brittany said he and I and others had once lived in that dream. I am trying to remember the dream - about that, perhaps I do know something. I have asked Geffray (or rather I have asked the Duchess to ask Geffray) to help us with the books here. We may find something more about the stories that came from the dream people - Tristran and the Grail. You and I never got very far with the books, after Friar Paulus gave you the parchment, and you began filling in the lost pages of the Duchess' old Book of Hours. Just to sit here with you, helped me to see the pictures.

"You were painting pictures or making copies for Friar Paulus. I too - but the only Tristran or *tristesse* in this Iseult story is that I cannot keep my pictures.

"If I try to keep one, remember it too exactly, there is no time for the next one. I am in the pictures but I am watching them too. And I am very happy.

"If I forget everything as I did in Brittany with the Duke, the pictures fade or I have to think about them. If I think too much about them, other peoples' pictures get in the way, or I see tiresome or unhappy things - things that I actually have seen or heard about or even worse things, dreadful things that I imagine.

"If I am - and I trust that I am - polite as you call it, it fills the hours, when I cannot open my own Book of Hours.

"It is a sort of devotion and no matter how devout we are, unless we are professed nuns or friars, our devotion grows dead or stale or at least half-hearted, unless we have the background of our worldly life and interests.

"I may have seemed to speak harshly of Mother Beata and the Duchess. It was only that I envied them, two friends together. But I don't envy them now. Will you be my friend, Blanchfleur?"

"And that was another thing - about Beata calling you Blanchfleur. She meant that you were like the proverbial field-lily. And I was - I was not polite about it. I was wondering if Beata had ever heard the story of Iseult Blanchmain and Iseult Blanchfleur and Tristran - if she knew how those two ladies - well, she could not have imagined or countenanced comparison. The only Tristran in this story is my *tristesse* that I cannot share my story."

"I want to hear the story," I said. "But why do you ask if I will be your friend, when you know how much I love you?"

"I mean," said Rose Beauvais, "I want you to be my friend, after I have told you about Brittany."

It was all rather confusing with the two Iseults and my name being Blanch-fleur.

. . . . .

She told me the story.

She did not tell it to me all at once, and she did not tell it, straight through, from the beginning to the end. She told me different parts of the story at differ-ent times. The story itself, the story about Brittany was mostly about the dream.

I could not see why she should suggest that I might love "our cousin Guill" as she called him, but she said these things were always unexpected. It was only her way, she said, of trying to make me understand or to see her story. It was a story that one had to see, somehow, and even if she could write it, she said it would be impossible to write it properly. Geffray wasn't with us when she told the story; when he was with us, she asked him to read from the old romances. Geffray read tales of knights and ladies to us, and stories of Gawain and Persival and the other knights of the roundtable, the *San Graal*, the quest and how Tristran slew the dragon.

But the real story began when Rose Beauvais and I were alone together.

XIII

The Story

Rose said:

It was not anything that needed to be explained. It had happened long ago. The pledge we made then was the pledge we made now. It wasn't a matter of words, it was religion.

He didn't have to explain much. There was no discourtesy to his Duchess or to other people.

The only real wrong or sin would be, he said, discourtesy or to hurt other people.

We could hurt people in various ways, other ladies, for instance, might wonder why the Duke had singled me out. It might start a precedence - the wrong people might come together, I mean men - and women too - might break across simple love, the *blanchfleur* love, the love I had had with Giles. Giles was dead. I had no time to think about it. The Duke was standing in my room. He said, he hoped he hadn't startled me. He saw a candle burning, it seemed to be wavering against the curtain. The flame seemed too near the curtain. It was very late. He presumed I had dismissed my women. He thought that I had not undressed because the candle was set on the window-ledge. He said, he thought that I might have fallen asleep in my chair and the candle might set fire to the curtain. He had come in through the garden-door. He wondered why my women had left the door unbolted. He thought, if I did not mind, he would place my waiting-women in the other wing. He felt that they had grown careless. He would send one of his own young attendants to look after me. The boy could bring my meals in. He had not seen me in the long hall, but he knew that I had been worried about the islands. He would come again, another night, at about the same time, and tell me about the islands.

The next morning when I woke, the boy was standing by my bed. The boy said, "The Duke said, tell Lady Beauvais that I send you to look after my - Rose."

The message you gave me from the Duke of Normandy wasn't a lie, really. I can't even say that you made it up, Blanchfleur. It came to you somehow, the way these things come to people sometimes. It was as if the Duke of Brittany had sent you, just as he sent the boy - Florian, his name was. We had not written. But he said, at the end, if there were any message, I would receive it. I had thought in the beginning, that, in some way, the Duke of Normandy, our cousin Guill, was part of this religion. I don't know quite how to put it - it is written, but written in a sort of secret way in the Story of the Round Table. That is why I got Geffray to read to us. I did not ask Geffray questions, but from time to time he made some remark or re-read a passage in a way that made me feel sure he knew what was underneath it. Geffray did not himself know that he knew this. But I thought that the Duke of Normandy actually did know the secret.

But although I loved the children, I was beginning to feel a little cold, a little lost, as in a tangled wood - when I thought about Normandy. I knew that he was helping. What did I know about the necessities of battle? But I wanted to be reassured somehow. I said to myself, I will kiss Blanchfleur and she will give me the answer, if there is an answer. The question was, "Is Normandy part of the Round Table?" The answer was, "The Duke said, tell Lady Beauvais that I send you to look after my - Rose."

But I knew the Duke of Normandy had not said that to you. The answer had come from outside. Therefore, the answer was more important than if the Duke of Normandy had himself given you a message for me.

You ask me, Blanchfleur, why if I believe the Duke of Normandy to be one of the Round Table that I have set my will against his. Or you may ask me again, if I really do believe that he is one of the knights. Well - I had the message; I believe in the message, that is what I hold on to. I believe in you, you would not have been chosen to deliver the message, my Blanchfleur, if you yourself were not one of those - oh, my dear, *at Ladies' Gard*. I knew Geffray the moment I saw him. I have met no-one else here or anywhere, but you two, and *Ladies' Gard must meet the war*. Here is our knight par excellence, Normandy, but when the trial came or when I thought the trial was over and that he was one of us, he turned and flared out at me - well, I will come to that part of the story later. I told you that I had quarrelled with him about you and Geffray.

I might say now, before we go on with the story, that whatever I say later does not change my first impression of Normandy. He is a keen huntsman, it may be that he was loosening his bird, giving the full length of the cord - you have watched him with the falcons - so as to try the strength, the courage, the assurance, the inevitability of the new wings. But you cannot really tame a falcon.

If he could tame this new intruder, Beauvais (whom Brittany had sent to stay with the Lady Duchess) then Beauvais could take her place, and welcome, among the Normandy ladies and the other visitors.

But if Beauvais could not be tamed, then Beauvais had a place among the wings.

But get Beauvais among the wings, there are still problems.

I do not know what the problems are, Blanchfleur, I only know that the Duke of Brittany had asked me to stay here.

Then if Normandy did not want me or appeared to want to get rid of me, I must say that this apparent or real repudiation of Beauvais was part of the plan. I must argue that this was a further test of the quality and strength of Beauvais. If *Ladies Gard must meet the war*, then *Ladies' Gard* must be tested and tried, and all weakness uncovered. My weakness was my strength. My weakness was and is my love for you and Geffray.

But, Blanchfleur, you are waiting for the story.

. . . . .

Florian slipped in and out, very quietly. Every few hours he would appear with a fresh tray, a few peaches in a leaf-lined basket or a goblet of wine.

He said that the Duke had explained to the physician and the physician sent these things.

Sometimes there was a cordial that tasted of quinces.

I sat in my chair. I walked around the room and down the corridor to the garden-door. The door was left open. The boy was always within calling-distance, but I seldom called him.

One day he brought a tray with a slice of melon.

"Have you noticed," he said, "that the melon-flower is the same colour as the melon-fruit - the inside-fruit, I mean?" He did not wait for me to answer. "And apples, the red is darker than the blossom, but the blossom is also the same colour."

I looked at this boy Florian. "But pears," I said, "have a white flower and quinces, which are green - well, quince-yellow - have flowers like the apple-blossom, only they grow singly and are larger."

The boy said, "I will tell the Duke that you are better."

. . . . .

The Duke said, "The star-cloud is growing fainter."

I said, "Do the ladies still watch it, above the summer-lilies?"

He said, "I think we will come back together when the star-cloud comes back."

You remember, Blanchfleur, that was the chief objection to what your dear Beata called the superstition about the star-cloud - the idea that it had any meaning. At best, it just happened they said, though the more learned among the Fathers had explained the matter to us, the periodic return of the star-cloud, that is, as a possibility, not as a mere superstition. There had been, they told us, just some such apparition at the time of the death of Julius Caesar in Rome. And Caesar's death was followed by the birth of our Lord. It was not, as some tried to argue, the Nativity star but a preliminary sign - oh, I know Beata's argument about forbidden signs and portents. I asked you about the lecture that she gave you, for I was diligent, as the Duke of Brittany put it, in curiosity.

They had been together certainly, the Duke of Brittany and Rose de Beauvais, or whatever her name happened to be in other phases of the circle of the star.

The star brought change, at any rate; everyone seemed to be unanimous on that point.

"But for us," the Duke said, "what changes there are, will be for the better."

I think, Blanchfleur, we should think of it that way, though for you the time of the star-manifestation coincided with your loss of Montjoie and for me, although Brittany had reclaimed the islands, I lost Giles. There were other losses, readjustments and new problems. The star-nebula or the star-cloud or the star-swarm as we called it when it hung above the lilies, predicted some way the fall - or the rise - of Britain.

The Duke of Brittany said, "Giles is safe somewhere. Our problem is settled, our Britain-Brittany is one sea-kingdom. But I do not know what is in the stars for Normandy. His problem, as regards the other part of Britain is quite different from ours. We welcome and were welcomed by our own people. King Arthur kept the west country and he as well as Brittany were, in a sense, independent of Rome. Normandy's Britain had been abandoned by Rome, and it was in the first instance, conquered by Rome. But the small empire of the *San Graal* was never affiliated with Rome, and never conquered by it.

"I do not think disaster is written in the stars for Normandy. But he inherits Caesar's Britain and he has consolidated our position, as you might say that the legions of Caesar consolidated Arthur's kingdom. That is, the later legions. For the knights of the *San Graal* were scattered and in danger of being absorbed into the more successful and domineering Church of Rome. It is always a temptation to become part of a great successful body - particularly if that body-spiritual offers rewards worth the striving and competition of its servitors. But even there, there was a small body within the safety, aye too, within the sanctity of Rome that still held itself secretly apart. Within the great Cathedrals as well as in the snowy forest of the *Chapel Perilous* there was always a handful of the few."

The Duke had a way of breaking off abruptly, in the midst of some fascinating revelation; I think he was afraid that he would tire me.

"Does Florian disturb you?" he asked.

"Disturb me?" I said. "He appears like a child-magician, out of the air, with a goblet of that cordial, your physician ordered for me. Except to ask me if I want anything, we only began this morning to talk together."

"What did you talk about?" the Duke asked.

I said, "We compared fruit and blossom and he said that the blossom of the melon, for instance, and the fruit or the inside-fruit, as he called it, were the same colour. I reminded him that the yellow-quince and the single five-petalled wild-rose quince-blossom are different."

"But there are peaches," said the Duke, "and the pomegranate. The pome-granate-flower is red, the same wine-red as the juice of the ripe fruit. But per-haps you are right - in any case, it leads to wonder - and I wonder about the fig-tree blossom? I ought to know, but I confess that my interest in the southern-wall begins when the fruit ripens. But I am certain that the blossom cannot com-pare to the fruit for fragrance and distinction; it should be (but I am sure it is not) a purple flower. And grapes - well, there I do know the tiny gold-green feather of the almost invisible grape-blossom that later miracle transforms into the heavy, hanging clusters. And flowers without fruit, the subject takes us fur-ther - you were asking about the star-bees above the summer-lilies. But fruit? Ah, now I see it - the fruit of the lily is that nectar that the bees gather. But Florian and you, I perceive, have much in common - but I must tell you more about the star-bees.

"We were saying that the star or the comet brings change, and signs and por-tents, I have heard, never come singly. We speak of signs and portents, I do not believe I have ever heard reference to *a* sign and *a* portent. However that may be, the bells of Lyoness have begun their deep-sea tolling. That is what brought me, in the first instance, to this side of the castle. I had to convince myself that it was not the wind blowing alarm from one of our distant strongholds. We have no bells to equal Lyoness in depth and resonance, but I argued, distance may have muffled or amplified the sound, so that there was this sort of double-ringing deep-sea echo. This is a strange confession - the bells deafened me. I had heard, of course, of Lyoness and sometimes out at sea had fancied I heard a dim etherial music. But this deep resonance was not dim, it was deafening.

"I lingered near the guard and after I said good-night, I went back again. He had heard nothing. He said, 'Singular quiet, do you notice, sir, you can hear the wave on the shingle though so far below and it being only ebb-tide.'

"You were right to call the star-cloud a bee-swarm above the summer-lilies.

"The bells hummed or buzzed - do you remember my name in Lyoness?

"Does it matter that the sea covers the islands? They are safe there.

"We are safe here. Are you glad the sea covers the islands? How could we en-dure it - I mean, some earlier Caesar. But Normandy will consolidate the broken cities and rebuild the roads. Let us leave that to Normandy. In the islands we talked of nothing but the great-bees.

. . . . .

"I walked far along the cliff-edge, but the bells neither diminished nor increased. The sound came obviously from the sea, yet it was within my head when I reached the great forest. Perhaps it was a form of madness. I turned back.

"I saw an unexpected light. It was very late, as you remember. I pushed open a door, stumbling as toward sanctuary. It was sanctuary. I had not even remembered, until I drew aside the curtain, that this was your room.

"It did not seem strange to see you.

"I realised, of course, that you had been ill. I was prompted, as by some outside voice or presence. I think my words reached you and reached you in a rational manner. I mean, I do not think you saw what I saw.

"My eyes had turned to the sea and I paused from time to time, as I hurried along the rock. As I say, walking or even running seemed to make no change in the bells' resonance - nor did standing still, intently listening. But there was always a chance that some ship out at sea might be sending out a signal. In the moonlight the sea-surface was as always, but I was made dizzy and light-struck at last, with the GLITTERING PLAIN.

"I saw the burning candle and the burnt-out row on your window-sill. The folds of blue hung as a screen, upon which was projected, at first, the run and ripple of the silver moonlight, gleaming on the waters over Lyoness.

"I went on talking and the bells grew fainter.

"I saw written on your blue curtain as on an altar-cloth, in silver letters, "THE STORY OF THE GLITTERING PLAIN. WHICH HAS BEEN ALSO CALLED THE LAND OF LIVING MEN OR THE ACRE OF THE UNDYING."

. . . . .

Rose said:

Normandy and Brittany had already signed the treaty - that is the treaty of alliance under the banner of St. George. The Fathers at Rome did not want them to go to the Holy Land with the crusaders. They wanted them to stay and strengthen the church in Europe.

I saw the Duke of Brittany for the last time. His standard-bearers bore the cross of St. George and the lion-banner of Normandy. There was as well as Our Lady and the Lilies, the ship-banner. The ship-banner was the oldest. We had worked in new thread last winter, where the sails were worn and the blue-wave faded. That is how I saw the Duke of Brittany for the last time.

. . . . .

That is only the brief outline of the story that Rose Beauvais told me. I did not like to ask too many questions, but it was like the pictures she had told me about; as soon as one question was answered, there was another - and another -

"Tell me," I said, "Rose Beauvais - but perhaps I ask too many questions?"

She said: "You could not ask half as many questions as I do. I will answer any question if I have the answer. And oh, the joy it is to have someone who cares - who cares almost as much as I do for the story. What do you want to know, Blanchfleur?"

"I was thinking," I said, "of that day when the Duke sailed for Britain. You have already told me about the message. But I do not really understand how the Duke of Brittany could give me a message. It seems to me it was just something I made up. I mean, the Duke of Normandy did not give me a message for the Duchess either, but I heard what the others said when they came back and I just said the same thing. But there was no other message for you or for the other ladies from him. And anyway, if you loved the Duke of Brittany and you say he loved you, why did you kiss me and say 'Add that to your message from the Lady Duchess'?"

"Dear Blanchfleur, you ask the same question again - but I am like that. I go over it and over it, trying to find a flaw or a weakness somewhere. Brittany and Normandy were allies. They were fighting the same battle - oh - what shall I say? It almost seems when you get to Lyoness, as if we were all one - one but separate as that swarm or cloud that might have been many bees or a snow-cloud. And I was free and Normandy loved the Duchess. There again - I thought that they two would make some sort of formal announcement to me, that they would say, or one of them would say, 'We too have our *Gard* here' and I dreamed of some heavenly inner-service in the great cathedral, where we would gather secretly. Perhaps there is some such inner-circle, here in Normandy. Perhaps the Duke was himself trying to test my strength before he invited me to join it. There are so many explanations.

"For the present, I accept my status, that of unwelcome guest here."

I did not know what Rose Beauvais meant, everyone seemed to love her and the Duchess had her almost constantly of her company. In fact, I sometimes resented this, but Rose said it was what the Duke of Brittany would have wanted for her.

It was, she said again, ordained that *Ladies' Gard must meet the war* and even if there were no inner-circle here in Normandy, there might be one elsewhere. There was, in any case, and perhaps that was the whole reason for her visit, the matter of the children.

Rose Beauvais said, "I was looking through the chests here in the library one day to find some new songs for the children or to see if they had any of our old tales for the jongleurs. The Duke came in. It was the first time that I had seen him alone. He said, 'I listened to you talking to the children last night.' I closed the chest and came over to the table. The Duke drew up that low stool of yours and waited for me to take this chair. We were sitting as you and I are sitting here, now. There was nothing but talk in the long hall, about the sailings - who was going, when were they going and so on. I did not want to think of the ships and the ship-sailings. But the Duke said, 'You told our children about a ship last night, an enchanted ship - is there more of that story?' He was being courteous, as their way was. I said, 'Well, yes - I mean, I heard the bells ringing last night.' He said, 'There were no bells ringing in the story, as you told it.' I said, 'There is never a story from Brittany without the bells of Lyoness.'

"He was the first person I had talked to, really talked to, since leaving Brittany.

"'I thought,' the Duke of Normandy said, 'that the bells of Lyoness were tolling for the dead and the lost islands.' I said, 'No, not as the - as the Duke of Brittany reads it. He says they are ringing or humming for the living, or for a new manifestation or a new circle of life. I am glad to talk to you of the bells of Lyoness.'

"He said, 'You said the Duke of Brittany reads, as you say - these stories.' 'Well,' I said, 'I really mean he sees them. There are people like that in Brittany.'

"'And may I ask,' he said, 'if the Lady Beauvais reads or *sees* the stories that she tells the children?'

"'Some of them are my stories,' I said, 'but they are old stories. There is a new story, however, about a ship sailing over Lyoness. The ships in Lyoness, under the water, carry the same standards - '

"The Duke started suddenly. I knew what he was thinking. 'Forgive me,' I said. 'I felt for a moment, that I was talking to - to Brittany. We read or interpret this, not as you seem to imagine. The bells are ringing for your victory. The ships of Lyoness and the kings of Avalon are only waiting for your signal, before they return. It is difficult to put this into words,' I said, 'but that is how Brittany reads or sees the story of Normandy. There is only one thing. I do not quite understand,' I said, 'why there are wings on your boat?'

"He sat down again. He said, 'There are wings on the other boats?'

"I said, 'No - but this is your own ship, you are leading them. It may be simply a sign of - of leadership. I don't really know why there are wings.'

"He said, 'Can you - read more about the wings?'

"I said, 'No - only there are two sets of wings, but not - not like a reflection seen in water. I confess that I don't understand it. The Duke of Brittany would know. Perhaps one wing or *wings* has to do with Avalon. But the names are different. I do not know what the names are. Perhaps you can tell me the names of something to do with - with wings,' I said.

"The Duke of Normandy said, 'This is a charming game. No wonder our children love you. I will run over my wings - will you stop me if I name the right one.'

"The Duke said, 'Fleet - '

"I said, 'That is one right one.'

"The Duke said, 'Griffin, Pennant, Eaglet, Owl, Feather, Woodgard, Blason, Forest, Whitecap, Eerie, Rockhaunt - and there are at least fifty others.'

"I said, 'I do not know about these others that you speak of, but the second wing or *wings* is not among those you have named. But Fleet was right the first time.'

"The Duke said, 'Roland, Clisson, Vanguard, Romany, Martel, Aquillus, Thorn, Rover, Return, Flight, Caesar, Poictou, Curzon, Arthur, Lance, Arrow, Beauregard, Regal, Royal, Beaupoint - and again a thousand others.'

"I said, 'I think I have a clue.'

"He waited. I felt that it was almost as enchanting or as exciting for him as it was for me.

"'Eaglet is not right,' I said, 'but Eaglet gives us a clue - the second wings has something to do with another set or perhaps another generation - '

"'Ah,' said the Duke of Normandy, 'will Goldwings - '

"I said, 'Goldwings - that is the answer.'"

. . . . .

I wanted to talk to Rose about Montjoie. The Duke said they couldn't take Montjoie until Geffray and I were married. But Rose said, "We won't talk about that. Geffray understands. We three are as strong as the Duke of Normandy."

I said, "I remember asking you, after Normandy Day, if the Duke had made you unhappy. You were unhappy about something. You were staring at someone who wasn't there. I thought you were talking to the Duke of Normandy when you said, 'You will go away and you will never come back.'"

"I remember," said Rose Beauvais, "but I shouldn't have talked out loud. I was talking to the Duke of Brittany. I was saying good-bye."

"Then you weren't angry with the Duke of Normandy?"

"Not then," she said. "I told you, I think, one day when we were talking about the wolves, that the Duke of Normandy had made me very happy. It was only afterwards that he made me unhappy. And I have already explained that to you. I mean, I told you that I had accepted the message, or the answer to the question that I had asked when I kissed you on Normandy day. His repudiation of our first talks together, may have been by way of a test, as I have already said, of the quality and strength of Beauvais.

"The Duke had asked me about the pictures and followed me in here - not very often but often enough to establish the dream. That is why I was so happy.

But I am even happier now that he has repudiated the dream or appeared to repudiate it. For either the dream was a challenge to him or else he himself wished to strengthen, as I say, the defence of *Ladies Gard*.

"I had just told him that the Duke of Brittany wanted me to interest the children, so that Normandy and Brittany could work and dream together.

"Suddenly the Duke of Normandy said, 'There is too much dream, altogether. Geffray is getting too familiar with the jongleurs. He is neglecting his duties. There are too many plays and readings.' It was the unexpectedness of this that frightened me. I seemed to turn to stone. I didn't say anything. He seemed to be waiting for me to answer him, but his is a quick and polished wit, and I did not wish to expose my story to - to treachery, as I thought of it then. But as I say now, Normandy may have been trying to show me my own weakness so that *Ladies Gard* should be prepared, for *Ladies Gard must meet the war*.

"So that when I say treachery, I speak only of my immediate feeling, for at the time that he turned on me, I felt that he had crept into our secret sanctuary, disguised - well, I felt that the first Duke of Normandy had disappeared and a complete stranger had taken his place. For the Duke had not in the first instance disregarded us, nor had he as it were stormed the walls from without. He had talked about the children. He had asked for more of the story - the first story of the ship and Fleet and Goldwings. He had taken Fleet and Goldwings with him, and that was part of the story. I knew that he had been lately informed of new troubles across the river, to the east, but 'Montjoie is not in the story,' I said.

"'I am not asking for dreams,' the Duke said, 'and hallucinations. The Duke of Brittany was right, it was a clever move on his part - sending you here. You have influence with young people. Now I, on my part, am asking you to use that influence with our cousin, Geffray de Froissart.'

"I said, 'What influence I have with the young Sieur de Froissart, shall be exerted on behalf of the dream.'

"'May I ask you,' said the Duke - he had been walking up and down but he came now and stood before the table - 'was this a planned campaign on the part of Brittany?'

"'It was planned,' I said, 'by Avalon.'

"'I do not want evasions,' said the Duke of Normandy. 'Your attitude to this affair is unnatural. Your friendship with the young Montjoie is unwholesome. Far be it from me to suggest alternative measures, but had you arranged with Brittany to stay here forever?'

"I said, 'Yes.'

"'This is no time for mockery,' he said, 'what *is* your plan?'

"'I have already told you,' I said.

"'Do not let us talk in riddles. Fairy-tales are all right for a winter evening.'

"I said, 'All the same, you took Fleet and Goldwings with you. You came back victorious. They call you now the Conqueror.'

"'I am sorry,' said the Duke of Normandy, 'this is Brittany's - affair, not mine.'

"I did not like the way he said affair.

"'Of course,' he continued, 'it is none of my business. But you are still - a pretty woman - '

"'Thank you,' I said.

"'You have, I presume - well, suitable alliances could be arranged for you?'

"I said, 'Many alliances, and most suitable.'

"'I believe you are now a very wealthy woman.'

"'I am the richest woman in the world.'

"'At one time, I believe it was not so. The Duke of Brittany - was it the present Duke? - arranged a marriage for you.'

"I said, 'Yes - the present Duke arranged the marriage. I was married to his cousin, Giles de Beauvais.'

"'Did the Duke send you here to arrange another marriage?'

"I said, 'No, Sire.'

"'You return then to Brittany?'

"I said, 'I have already told you that I stay here.'

"I said, I do not know why I said it, 'Am I on trial for witchcraft?'"

. . . . .

I did not know what to say to Rose Beauvais. I was sick with apprehension. But Rose Beauvais was laughing.

"I don't think that was a very funny story," I said.

"You are young, my sweet, and I am not as old as I hope to be one day. I have a long time to wait. I will not be able to appreciate this joke for many years. I am an ill-informed and ignorant woman. That is ill-informed, as all women are, in these days. I mean, women will be allowed one day . . . but I do not care about that. What am I saying to you? I do not want to rule, nor to rule rulers. I want to creep softly into the circle of the *Gard*. I do not want to flaunt the dream. I only want to share it. And it is the dream that is so - curious. I told you in the beginning when we first began to talk together here in the library, that a joke must stand on its own feet." I remembered the time she had said it. She had told me so much since; but still I could not see why Rose was happy if she thought the Sieur Guillaume wanted her to leave Normandy. She had said that she was not a poor relation and she did not mean merely that she had possession of the islands. I was, I suppose, a poor relation or I would be till I married Geffray. But I would wait. If Rose de Beauvais was an unwelcome guest, I would be unwelcome with her, though I do not think that I would have been strong enough, if the Sieur Guillaume had approached me, to refuse to do his bidding.

"The joke stands on its own feet," said my dear Rose, "even if you do not see it. That is what I like about Geffray," she said, "he knows a joke when he sees one."

"But this is no laughing matter," I said. I felt stiff and too grown-up when I said it.

She took my cold hands. "Now, don't you turn to stone," she said. "I felt that day that I was a witch, a fury. Perhaps I am a witch, a fury. Perhaps I frightened the Duke of Normandy."

"You frighten me," I said.

"But I don't frighten Geffray," Rose Beauvais said.

I was afraid they would quarrel in the long hall. He had told Geffray that he wouldn't have the new play and the jongleurs.

But Geffray said, "My cousin Guill, these jongleurs are not villeins," and we went on with the play.

————————

XIV

Goldwings

We went on with the play.

We followed it to Elizabethan England and we went back to London.

We did not have time to record the more than fifty, and the more than one thousand.

But we found five of them.

They are enrolled among the 1,495 names of "the few," inscribed on the sheets of vellum of The Battle of Britain book that rests in the centre of the Memorial Chapel in Westminster Abbey.

July 17, 1947

Works Cited

Augustine, Jane. Introduction to *The Gift by H.D.*, edited and annotated by Jane Augustine, 1–28. Gainesville: University Press of Florida, 1998.

———. "Preliminary Comments on the Meaning of H.D.'s *The Sword Went Out to Sea.*" *Sagetrieb* 15, nos. 1–2 (Spring and Fall 1996): 121–32.

Chisholm, Diane. *H.D.'s Freudian Poetics: Psychoanalysis in Translation.* Ithaca, N.Y.: Cornell University Press, 1992.

Collier, Basil. *Leader of the Few: The Authorised Biography of Air Chief Marshall, the Lord Dowding of Bentley Priory.* London: Jarrolds, 1957.

Connor, Rachel. *H.D. and the Image.* Manchester, England, and New York: Manchester University Press, 2004.

Doolittle, Hilda. *Asphodel.* Edited with an introduction by Robert Spoo. Durham, N.C.: Duke University Press, 1992.

———. "H.D. by *Delia Alton.*" Edited by Adalaide Morris. In *Iowa Review* 16, no. 3 (1986): 174–221.

———. *Paint It Today.* Edited with an introduction by Cassandra Laity. New York: New York University Press, 1992.

———. *The Gift by H.D.* Edited and annotated by Jane Augustine. Gainesville: University Press of Florida, 1998.

Edmunds, Susan. *Out of Line: Psychoanalysis and Montage in H.D. Long Poems.* Stanford, Calif.: Stanford University Press, 1994.

Friedman, Susan Stanford. *Mappings: Feminism and the Cultural Geographies of Encounter.* Princeton, N.J.: Princeton University Press, 1998.

———. *Penelope's Web: Gender, Modernity, H.D.'s Fiction.* Cambridge and New York: Cambridge University Press, 1990.

———. *Psyche Reborn: The Emergence of H.D.* Bloomington: Indiana University Press, 1981.

Friedman, Susan Stanford, and Rachel Blau DuPlessis, eds. *Signets: Reading H.D.* Madison: University of Wisconsin Press, 1990.

Gregory, Eileen. *H.D. and Hellenism: Classic Lines.* Cambridge and New York: Cambridge University Press, 1997.

Guest, Barbara. *Herself Defined: The Poet H.D. and Her World.* New York: Doubleday, 1984.

Hollenberg, Donna, ed. *Between History and Poetry: The Letters of H.D. and Norman Holmes Pearson.* Iowa City: University of Iowa Press, 1997.

Laity, Cassandra. *H.D. and the Victorian Fin de Siècle: Gender, Modernism, Decadence.* Cambridge, England, and New York: Cambridge University Press, 1996.

Morris, Adalaide. *How to Live/What to Do: H.D.'s Cultural Poetics.* Urbana: University of Illinois Press, 2004.

Morris, William. *The Defence of Guenevere, and Other Poems.* London: Bell and Daldy, 1858.

———. *The Story of the Glittering Plain which has been also called the Land of the Living Men or the Acre of the Undying.* Hammersmith, England: Kelmscott Press, 1894.

Ogilvie, D. Bruce. "H.D. and Hugh Dowding," *HD Newsletter* 1, no. 2 (Winter 1987): 9–17.

Owen, Alex. *The Place of Enchantment: British Occultism and the Culture of the Modern.* Chicago: University of Chicago Press, 2004.

Ray, John. *The Battle of Britain: New Perspectives Behind the Scenes of the Great Air War*. London: Arms and Armour, 1994.

Sword, Helen. *Ghostwriting Modernism*. Ithaca, N.Y.: Cornell University Press, 2002.

———. "H.D.'s *Majic Ring*." *Tulsa Studies in Women's Literature* 14, no. 2 (Autumn 1995): 347–62.

Tryphonopoulos, Demetres P. Introduction to *Literary Modernism and the Occult Tradition*, edited by Leon Surette and Demetres P. Tryphonopoulos, 19–49. Orono, Maine: National Poetry Foundation, 1996.

Weston, Jessie L. *From Ritual to Romance*. Cambridge, England: Cambridge University Press, 1920.

Winks, Robin W. *Cloak and Gown: Scholars in The Secret War, 1939–1961*. New York: Morrow, 1987.

Woodman, Leonora. "H.D. and the Poetics of Initiation." In *Literary Modernism and the Occult Tradition*, edited by Leon Surette and Demetres P. Tryphonopoulos, 137–46. Orono, Maine: National Poetry Foundation, 1996.

Zilboorg, Caroline, ed. *Richard Aldington and H.D.: The Later Years in Letters*. Manchester, England, and New York: Manchester University Press, 1995.

Index

Cynthia Hogue has published five collections of poetry, including *Flux* (2002) and *The Incognito Body* (2006). She also is the author of *Scheming Women: Poetry, Privilege, and the Politics of Subjectivity* (1995) and the coeditor of *We Who Love to be Astonished: Experimental Women's Writing and Performance Poetics* (2001) and *Innovative Women Poets: An Anthology of Contemporary Poetry and Interviews* (2006). For her work, she has received NEA, NEH (summer seminar), and Fulbright fellowships, and with the coeditor of this volume, Julie Vandivere, the H.D. Fellowship in American Literature at the Beinecke Rare Book and Manuscript Library at Yale University in 2005. She is the Maxine and Jonathan Marshall Chair in Modern and Contemporary Poetry at Arizona State University.

Julie Vandivere is an associate professor of English and director of gender studies at Bloomsburg University. She has published on numerous modernist women writers, including Virginia Woolf, Emily Coleman, Antonia White, Rosa Chacel, and H.D. She is currently at work on a critical study of motherhood in modernism, entitled *Schisms, Mysticism, Madness: Motherhood and Modernism from Mina Loy to Kay Boyle*. She was the 2005 recipient, along with Cynthia Hogue, of the H.D. Fellowship at the Beinecke Rare Book and Manuscript Library at Yale University.